Volume 18

Secrets
Satisfy your desire for more.

Lone Wolf Three by Rae Monet

Planetary politics and squabbling over wolf occupied territory drain former rebel leader Taban Zias. When Taban's second-in-charge sends him a mediator to help negotiate the Elnar land treaty, he's pissed. But his anger quickly turns to desire when he meets, Lakota Blackson. Focused, calm and honorable, the female Wolf Warrior is Taban's perfect mate—now if he can just convince her.

Flesh to Fantasy by Larissa Ione

Kelsa Bradshaw is an intense loner whose job keeps her happily immersed in a fanciful world of virtual reality. Desperate to protect her existence, she wants nothing to do with Trent Jordan, a laid-back paramedic who experiences the harsh realities of life up close and personal. But when their vastly different worlds collide in an erotic eruption of fantasy sex and real-life emotions, can Trent convince Kelsa to turn the fantasy into something real?

Heart Full of Stars by Linda Gayle

Freed at last from alien bondage, singer Fanta Rae finds herself stranded on a lonely Mars outpost with the first human male she's seen in nine years. Ex-Marine Alex Decker lost his family in the Aggressions and guilt drives him into isolation, but Fanta's passion turns his world upside down. When alien assassins come to enslave her, he and Fanta must fight for their lives and a future that holds no guarantees.

The Wolf's Mate by Cynthia Eden

When Michael Morlet finds Katherine "Kat" Hardy fighting for her life in a dark alley, he instantly recognizes her as the mate he's been seeking all of his life. He knows that he will do whatever it takes to claim her, body and soul. But someone's trying to kill Kat, and the attack in the alley is just the first in a series of close calls for her. With danger stalking them at every turn, will Kat trust him enough to become The Wolf's Mate?

Rae Monet

Larissa Ione

Linda Gayle

Cynthia Eden

Volume 18

Secrets

Satisfy your desire for more.

SECRETS Volume 18
This is an original publication of Red Sage Publishing and each individual story herein has never before appeared in print. These stories are a collection of fiction and any similarity to actual persons or events is purely coincidental.

Red Sage Publishing, Inc.
P.O. Box 4844
Seminole, FL 33775
727-391-3847
www.redsagepub.com

SECRETS Volume 18
A Red Sage Publishing book
All Rights Reserved/December 2006
Copyright © 2006 by Red Sage Publishing, Inc.

ISBN: 0-9754516-8-5 / ISBN 13: 978-0-9754516-8-7

Published by arrangement with the authors and copyright holders of the individual works as follows:

LONE WOLF THREE
Copyright © 2006 by Rae Monet

FLESH TO FANTASY
Copyright © 2006 by Larissa Ione

HEART FULL OF STARS
Copyright © 2006 by Linda Gayle

THE WOLF'S MATE
Copyright © 2006 by Cynthia Eden

Photographs:
Cover © 2006 by Tara Kearney; www.tarakearney.com
Cover Model: Aneta Wisniewska and Allen Berube
Setback cover © 2000 by Greg P. Willis; GgnYbr@aol.com

Printed in the U.S.A.

Book typesetting by:

Quill & Mouse Studios, Inc.
www.quillandmouse.com

Contents

Lone Wolf Three

by Rae Monet

To My Reader:

Lone Wolf Three is a continuation of *The Solarian Wolf Warrior Series* and weaves the eradication of the wolves into the story—as do all my *Wolf Warrior* books. Each *Wolf Warrior* book stands on its own, so if you want to further explore this world please come visit me at RaeMonet.com. *Lone Wolf Three* is the fifth book in the series and will introduce you to Wolf Warrior First Class and United Galactic Federation Mediator, Lakota Blackson, along with Elnar Planetary Leader and former rebel, Taban Zias. They will take you into a futuristic world riddled with politics and infighting over the land rights the wolves now occupy. I hope you enjoy Taban and Lakota's story; I know I loved writing it for you. Of course, always close to my heart are the wolves; please visit where my adopted wolf Wana lives, at WolfMountain.com. And I love to hear reader feedback at Rae@RaeMonet.com.

Prologue

"I need you to travel to Elnar and meet the planetary leader, Taban Zias. The ship, Lone Wolf Three, will be at your disposal. You will lead this one," Kabe ordered.

"Sir, yes, sir," the soldier responded with a rigid stance and smart salute.

"At ease, soldier." Kabe glanced up at the female Wolf Warrior before him. She was one of their best; strong, serious, honorable, and always in control. She would serve the Solarians well on this mission. It was her first chance at leading a space team, and Kabe was confident Lakota Blackson would thrive. It was time for her to spread her wings and fly.

Her job would be to establish a rapport and ultimately mediate for Taban Zias. Taban was a stubborn son of a bitch… but a dammed good leader and passionate about the cause. He held so strong to the rebellion principles, they were near another civil war on the planet.

Kabe shook his head, Taban was too young and more than a little brash… Kabe should know, he practically raised the boy into a man. That's why the request from Taban's second in command, to send an emissary who will assist in negotiations with the Elnar council, wasn't such a surprise.

Easing back in his chair, Kabe flashed to his previous life. The rebel edict had said if Kabe should ever fall out of power, then Taban would be assigned to take over as leader. Well, he had fallen, in a big way, to his death. Now, he had to assist Taban in finding his balance, even if it was from the grave. Kabe needed to send someone steady, calm, to help talk some sense into Taban.

Searching for the transfer order, Kabe shifted the paper on his desk from one pile to another. He sorely wished *he* were the Solarian Warrior traveling to Elnar. He missed the friends he left there five years earlier, but he had a much higher purpose now and the fact he was alive, could never be discovered by the Elnarians.

"Kabe, did you sign that transfer paperwork?" Lenora floated into the office, six months pregnant and glowing. His mate's stride didn't break when she interrupted his meeting. As she leaned forward to kiss him on the cheek, he tried not to smile, giving a pointed, subtle inclination of his head toward Lakota. Lenora froze and turned.

"Lakota. How are you, my friend?" Lenora slid around the desk and took his best soldier into her arms. The hardened warrior expression Lakota frequently wore melted. She broke into a grin, her arms settling around his wife. It was funny, in all the years assigned to training Lakota, since she was twenty and ready to move into the space program, Kabe had never seen this unabashed happiness layer her expression. His wife had a way of doing that to people; a warrior herself, heavy with pregnancy, she was irresistible.

He gave up the pretense of shuffling papers to watch the two women before him. Lakota came from a Native American background; she had long, straight, jet-black hair and a golden complexion, with light ice green eyes to make her overall appearance stunning. Her parents had been killed when she was a child during the interplanetary wars; the Solarians had rescued her and given her a chance to live. Now she dedicated her life to their purpose, to protect the wolves.

"I am well, Lenora. Thank you." They broke apart. Lenora nodded toward Lakota's wolf.

"And Striker?" Lenora dipped down her hand to stroke the head of the animal.

Lakota dropped her eyes to her companion. A huge black wolf sat quietly by her side, awaiting her command. Even to him, the wolf intimidated with a telling concentration for his job most lupus lacked. The telepathic connection with his master seemed so strong it was almost as if they were one. Kabe's wolf, Raime, bounced around Striker, obviously vying for his attention to play. Raime lacked discipline; he hadn't grown up on Solaria. He had come with Kabe from

Elnar, but Kabe still loved him, so Raime was indulged. Kabe rolled his eyes. It seemed he lost control of his own meeting.

Striker completely ignored his young gray wolf, his yellow gaze straight ahead, disciplined, beyond the ability to distract. A lot like his master.

The Wolf didn't move a muscle except to stare from Lenora to Lakota. Lakota gave a nod. Responding, the wolf reached out and licked Lenora's hand. Then he turned his head and gave a single wolf snap toward Raime, who promptly whined and retreated behind Lenora's legs. Lenora signaled to Wana, her white wolf, who moved forward to shepherd Raime from the room.

"Striker is well. Always working hard. Please excuse him, he has little tolerance for games."

Kabe wanted to snort and say something to the effect of *wonder who taught him that?* But he refrained.

"Why are you here?" Lenora asked. Lakota was usually assigned as sentry at the Solarian Valley entrance, an honored position amongst Solarian Wolf Warriors, the guard against intruders. The waterfall was the doorway to their hidden home.

"Lenora, Lakota will be leading her first space flight, to Elnar."

A shadow crossed his wife's face. "Is that safe, Kabe?"

He stood, in tune to his mate like no other.

"It will be fine." He moved next to her and folded her body into arms for a gentle hug.

"Don't worry, you know Elnar has been at peace for nearly five years, since you rescued me. I will brief her completely so my hand in this won't be known. We are members of the Intergalactic Mediation Committee. Lakota is fully certified and trained. The Elnarians have no idea, they just sent the standard UG request. It won't be out of the ordinary to send her. There's just some…" he paused, trying to pick the correct words.

In-fighting.

His mate never missed a beat. Although she said the words in his head, he understood her concern. Elnarians had nearly taken his life five years earlier. His rebel team and Taban had done exactly what they were supposed to once their leader had been captured and killed: they rebelled, and they won.

"No," he lowered his voice and glanced at Lakota. He didn't want to seem weak in front of her, but his wife and her piece of mind was his first priority.

"They aren't fighting, they just need a diplomat, an objective third party if you will, to help facilitate some squabbles over land rights and the wolves. Lakota is the ideal choice."

Lenora's knowing gaze strayed to Lakota, who stared at them with an expression of clear curiosity, her head tilted to the side in silent reflection.

"Yes, ideal," Lenora said.

He nodded and walked with her to the door, his hand traveling to the small of her back in a reassuring caress.

"You are not meant to be working. Let me worry about our defenses. You need to be resting, Warrior First Class Folker. You're on pregnancy leave, enjoy it, and fret about Wolf Warrior business later." He ran his hand over her belly. She gave a quiet laugh and laid her head against his shoulder. He kissed the top.

"You're right, I'm sorry. I was just going to do some paperwork—"

"Uh, uh." He cut her off with a finger to her lips. "Go home, Babe."

"Okay, Fly Boy, I'll leave space and our inter-galactic defenses up to you and Lakota."

He chuckled, dipped his knees down and softly kissed her.

"Will you be home for lunch?" she asked.

"I'll definitely be home for lunch."

"I'll see you then."

Straightening, he schooled his features and went back around the desk to sit. "Mission brief in one hour, conference room two. Your flight team will be there. I'm counting on you on this one, Lakota."

"Sir, yes, sir."

"Good, dismissed."

Lakota snapped to attention, sent a smart salute up to her brow and waited. Kabe gave her a single salute back. She did an about face and marched from the room, her wolf trailing behind her.

He buried his face back into the paper on his desk. Yes, she was going to be perfect.

Chapter One

"I absolutely will not compromise on this." Taban threw the Elnar council's request for an amendment of the occupation treaty onto the floor.

"You're being unreasonable," Reack said as he leaned down and retrieved the paper.

Taban pinched the bridge of his nose.

"Unreasonable?" He began pacing. Reack was his most trusted friend and second in command, but he was wrong this time. "They want to kill wolves, Reack."

His assistant slumped into one of the five chairs lining the wall of Taban's personal quarters. Taban strode to the window and took in the view of the city of Elnar. Tall skyscrapers greeted him, rebuilt from the war that ended five years ago, along with mile after mile of new suburban solar housing units sprawled across the land.

"They don't want to kill anything," Reack said. "They simply want a controlled capture and re-assignment... Taban, the wolves are making their way into Class A suburbs. If they end up there, private citizens will kill them, no matter what the law says. You know this."

Taban ran his hand around the back of his neck. "God, I'm tired. I've had five years of this squabbling. I'm not a damn politician, I'm a warrior."

"Someone's got to do it," Reack sat forward in his chair. "The people trust you. You led them to freedom. You and Kabe."

He stood. "Can we not talk about this right now?"

"The Solarian fleet ship, Lone Wolf Three, will be arriving within the hour. The Mediator we requested—"

"You mean the Mediator *you* requested." Huffing out a snarl, Taban reached inside his desk and retrieved the key to his hover cycle. "I'm going out."

"But, the land treaty negotiation meeting—"

"It's not like you can't find me." He pointed to the bracelet with the concealed tracker. Another precaution Reack had insisted on—-he was crazy about Taban's safety.

"Fine, go out then, don't take any of your guards, get kidnapped, get killed," Reack yelled.

Taban's eyes jumped up as he fought the inkling to yell back. *How can I feel resentment toward my best friend?* It was probably a good idea for him to get away, get some exercise. Reack and he had been through a lot together, the war, the devastation and endless hours of re-building. Reack still carried a deep facial scar from saving Taban.

Placing a hand on his friend's shoulder, he softened his voice and said, "I'll be back, don't worry, I can take care of myself."

Striding for the door, Taban made his way to the garage. Pulling on the Mav helmet, he mounted his hover cycle and pushed the ignition button. The high pitch hum of the Zazzer engine lit up the space. Hitting the hover key, Taban touched the accelerator pad, and the bike shot out of its parking space.

Letting out a *whoop*, he gave into the freedom the machine always gifted from the pressure of command. The speed, the wind against his body, the relief was invigorating. A need welled up in him to spend time with the wolves, and he mapped a path to the mountains. With any luck, the mediator would be gone by the time he returned.

If he returned.

Chapter Two

Lakota trekked over the rocky embankment. Her wolf Striker, at her side, scanned for threats. Watching her footing, she stepped over a loose rock. What kind of man simply left his command with no communication whatsoever of his position?

This was her first mediation assignment, and she wasn't going to fly home in defeat. If the planetary leader wouldn't come to her, she'd go to him.

Topping the hill rise, the green of endless trees blanketing the tall mountain range greeted her. A cool, fresh breeze caressed her face. Elnar reminded her of home, Solaria, the cloaked valley, and her position of entrance guard.

This mission was important to Kabe. Per her orders, she would find Taban Zias. Giving up was not an option. She held up the laser-tracking device Reack had given her. It flashed, indicating she was within a quarter click of her primary target. *Good, after a full day of walking, success has to be close.*

Lakota shrugged her shoulders attempting to alleviate the soreness from her pack and mopped the dampness from her forehead. She frowned. She couldn't give into her anger now, she thought, she needed to stay composed, and remember her purpose on this planet; promote peace and solidarity. *Wolf Warrior Mediator... finally, I made my goal, to serve my people, to repay my debt.*

The noise of the flashing tracker broke into her musing. It was lit up like a Solarian stunner. She pushed a set of tree limbs aside and peered down the small incline. Striker stopped and growled low in his throat. In tune with her wolf, Lakota froze.

The picture before her sent her heart skipping.

A man, wearing only a small loincloth, seemed to be fighting a pack of wolves. His muscles flexed as he handled a sparring long-stick, slowly circling the pack. His body consisted of pure sinew, grace, and hard planes, not an ounce of fat on him. Long, dark hair spilled over his shoulders down his back in a cascade of black.

The magnificence of the picture gripped her so hard, Lakota wondered if she was having a daylight dream vision.

A flame sparked inside her, a heat she had never experienced before in the presence of a man. *What is this strange emotion I'm feeling?* A serious mission, like the one she was on, spared no time for fanciful musings, but she seemed frozen in place watching him.

He swirled the stick over his head in a set of intricate moves. His actions flawless, the staff swirled and dipped with the corresponding bend of his body.

The twirling stopped. He brought the staff in front of him, and with his other hand he beckoned the biggest wolf forward. The huge gray animal growled and launched himself at the man, who sidestepped and rapped the wolf's hind leg.

The wolf yelped. At the same instant, another wolf jumped him. He spun, ducked, and struck that wolf in the chest. The wolf barked, bearing his fangs.

Finally, breaking free of her trance, Lakota shed her backpack and rushed forward, drawing her traditional Wolf Warrior sword. She gave Striker a mental command to stay. She didn't want her own wolf involved in what was going on until she could gather more data. Rounding the corner into the man's line of sight, she skidded to a stop.

He paused, made eye contact with her, brows furrowed, and the black wolf leapt at him. He went down with a grunt while letting out a yell.

Lakota signaled Striker, indicating he move to the side. He ran around the back of the pack, flanking them. Hair standing on end, he growled and showed every one of his pointed teeth. Lakota remained motionless. The black wolf was still on top of the man, but so far the man wasn't bitten. If she moved, the others might attack him, and she didn't want to jeopardize him further. She needed to keep the situation under control.

Two wolves turned toward her, while two pivoted and faced Striker, each posturing for a confrontation.

"Sir, may I be of assistance?"

She placed her sword in front of her, ready to rush forward.

"No, no. Hold on." The man's murmured protest came from under the black wolf.

He pushed the wolf off him and sat up. "You only won this time because I was distracted."

The wolf barked and shook its head, then gave the man a huge, sloppy lick to the face. The man laughed.

Seeing the affectionate display, Lakota realized the wolves and the man were playing. She sheathed her sword and signaled to Striker, who stood down and returned to her side.

"My apologies, sir. I assumed you were in trouble."

"You assumed incorrectly." He stood and brushed himself off. Up close, exceptionally attractive didn't begin to describe him; with bright blue eyes and contrasting midnight hair, strong lined features rough—yet forming ruggedly handsome lines—with full and sensual lips. A small scar above his eye only added to his appeal. He made a sweeping motion with his hands, and the wolves silently fled.

"Yes, I see that. I'm sincerely sorry."

"Who are you, pretty lady?" The man picked up his staff from the ground and leaned against it, a smile lurked at the corner of his mouth and a mischievous glint shined in his eyes; being so close to him wove a surprising warm haze around her. As her eyes wandered over his hard body, taking in his skin glowing with a healthy wet gleam from his exertions, she felt an answering heat rise on her face. *Could I be feeling desire?* Shock danced through her. She steadied herself.

"Lakota Blackson, sir. Solarian Wolf Warrior and UG Mediator."

His smile dropped. He turned and made his way to the river, his expression closed. "Who told you I was here?" He dropped his staff in a primitive campsite: a homemade fire pit, and a shiny new hover cycle sitting next to a modern tent.

"It was your aide, sir. Taban Zias, I assume?"

Not answering her, he leaned forward and splashed his face. Water cascaded down his arms and chest. Lakota tried to not watch the drops roll down his bronzed muscles, but couldn't stop wanting to lick the same path as that water. She was close enough she could smell him; man mixed with sweat, spicy, a heady combination that went straight to her heart, sending it pounding.

She pressed a finger to her temple. *What am I doing, fantasizing about this man? He is my assignment.*

"Now that you found me, you can go back to the city and await my return."

Lakota bristled.

"I'm afraid, sir, where you go, I go. I am here to assist you, and I can not do this when not in your presence."

He tipped his head up then, his vivid blue eyes crinkled at the corner as he chuckled.

"So, if I tell you I'm not leaving these woods for a least two weeks, you will, in fact, stay here with me?" He grabbed a towel. Watching her, he eased the cloth over his face and chest.

"That is correct, sir. I have much to teach you that I think will assist with the upcoming treaty negotiations."

He threw the towel into the tent and stood, scowling. He towered over her, and stepping forward, he crowded in.

She raised her chin and braced her feet. She had dealt with men before who tried to scare her off with caveman techniques. Her mediator training, as well as the teaching of her Blackfoot ancestors, allowed her to remain calm. She held her ground.

"Do you have much to teach me, Lakota?" Her name was a slow drawl on his lips. He took another pace closer, stopping only a few inches away. The heat of his nearly unclothed body reached out and touched her. Lakota gulped. She wore her typical warrior traveling gear: suede breeches and soft leather halter-top covered with a hand-made vest. Crafted for Solarian Warriors and fashioned after the leather armor of old, the outfit allowed her to move freely. His gaze raked over her, and her nipples pushed against the soft leather. Leaning toward her, his face came closer. Tilting his head, he aligned their lips.

Surely, he's not going to kiss me?

"I'm here, Lakota, for only one reason, pleasure. Pure, unadulterated, pleasure. If you feel you can help me with this, then by all means, stay."

Lakota opened her mouth to address him... but before she could finish, his lips captured hers. She gasped, which only seemed to encourage him further. His tongue delved into her open mouth.

Soft... his lips were so soft. She tried to protest, her hands lifting to his shoulders to push him away. But the kiss deepened, and her will to push disappeared. All she could think of was this man, the smooth yet rough feel of his shoulders under her fingers, the alluring, sweet taste of him, and his clean, outdoor scent sneaking into her senses.

Without understanding what she was doing, she kissed him back, her lips moving under his, her hands crawling into his hair, sifting through the silk of it. His arms came around her, crushing her body against his. The hardness of his erection touched her belly. Heat spiked ever inch of her as sweat beaded her brow. He ran his hands into her hair and held her head tight.

Just when it felt as if she were going to explode, his lips released hers, and she inhaled a shaky breath. He laughed softly, then his mouth meandered down her throat to the sensitive skin where the slope of her shoulder dipped. Nudging her neck, he moved her head to the side and attacked the area, his tongue lapping. Then he latched on and sucked.

Head falling back, she heard herself groan, her body arched against his, her breasts pearling in arousal. His hands dropped to her halter, pushing the strings to the side. The gruff glide of worn leather on her skin forced awareness back into her brain.

What am I doing?

"Mr. Zias, stop!"

He lifted his mouth from her neck, his blue eyes smoky, his lips glistening wet from their kiss.

He raised his hands from her halter and smiled.

"Feel free to leave anytime. I assume you have a ride back to the city." He turned and began picking up pieces of wood, throwing them into the fire pit.

"I'm not leaving." She lowered herself onto a large, smooth-topped rock.

He pivoted, his eyes widened, then squinted.

"What do you mean?" He stood in front of her and crossed his arms, mouth curved down in a definitive frown. His manner reeked defiance.

This place was clearly his retreat. Some action had driven him here. She wanted to find out what it was and help him find balance.

"My job is to assist you. I have pledged my services as your mediator." She squared her shoulders. "I will not fail."

Taban sank down onto a rock across from her. He studied her closely and as if making a decision, he stuck out his hand. "Taban Zias. Pleased to meet you."

She joined her hand to his, trying not to let her relief show in her expression. "Thank you."

"I hope you won't regret this, Wolf Warrior Blackson. Taming me might not be so easy." He stroked her wrist with his thumb. Awareness zinged through Lakota. "And, we just locked lips in one of the most heated kisses I've had the pleasure of experiencing in a long time. I think you can call me Taban."

He was right. Not only was it silly to stand on ceremony, it was clear he didn't respond well to formality. Her job necessitated learning what made him comfortable and capitalizing on it.

Her hand fell from his grip. "Taban, then."

His eyes flared at her use of his first name. "Welcome to my world, Lakota, the world of the wolf. I'll enjoy sharing it with you."

"And I'll enjoy learning it." She ran her hand along her thigh, thinking she could wipe the fire from his touch away. It didn't work, her hand still burned.

His eyes followed her movements.

She looked forward to learning his ways, but the question was, would she be able to teach him hers?

Chapter Three

"Take in a deep breath and slowly expel it. Allow your mind to fly free. See yourself in a peaceful place and release your stress. Let the natural sound of the water help guide you to that special location." Her voice was serene, tranquil… designed, he was sure, to settle him, but all he could hear was the sexy drawl of the woman who had been testing the edges of his control like no other.

Taban tried to draw a slow breath, but every time he did, he took in Lakota's distinctive flowery aroma. They both sat cross-legged by the stream. The flood of water over the rocks was supposed to act as a soothing agent, but he couldn't hear it over the images his brain projected into his consciousness. *Lakota, naked, easing back against the soft fabric of the blanket in his tent, her nipples taunt with desire, eyes half-closed in her arousal, legs spread, inviting him to taste.* He shook his head.

"Your focus has slipped."

Popping his eyes open, he stared at the object of his frustration. For three days, her encouraging instructions had been driving him *crazy.* He placated her by allowing her to teach him. Simply put, he enjoyed spending time with her and if *this* was what he had to do to be with her, well then he'd do it.

"I'm not made to meditate."

"Everyone is made to acquire this skill. It's a matter of discipline."

"I don't have it."

Dakota lowered her hands from her assumed prayer pose and laid her forearms on her crossed legs.

"You do have it, Taban. You simply choose not to allow the skill into your consciousness."

"Oh something is filtering into my consciousness, alright," he grumbled. Erotic snap-shots of Lakota snuck into every brain wave he formed.

"I'm sorry?" Lakota cocked her head to the side and regarded him with her striking ice-green gaze, her expression blank. There were times he wondered if this woman was a robot. She had such obedience to her teachings.

"Never mind."

"Shall we end this exercise?" She pushed the strands of her black hair behind her ear. He longed to bury his hands into the dark mass while he devoured her mouth.

"No. Okay." He set his forearms on his thighs and opened his hands, pointing his palms up as she had taught and closed his eyes. "Let's try this again."

"Very well. Let's begin. Breathe. Relax. Find your calming place, use the elements of the running water to take you there."

There it was, that voice again, reminding him she sat less than two feet away: exquisite and within touching distance.

He rotated his neck from side to side and tried to release the pressure he felt from the knotting muscles there.

"Seek a place deep down inside where peace and tranquility lie."

Taban gritted his teeth and puffed out an aggravated breath. He opened his eyes and studied Lakota. She seemed at such peace, her eyes closed, her light-chocolate brown skin sparkled with a healthy glow from the sun pounding down on them. She was, by far, the most alluring woman he had ever met, and she didn't even know it. There was an appealing innocence beneath the wise warrior that drew him closer and closer with each passing day.

Her eyes slid opened. The corner of her mouth tilted up. "You are finished with this exercise?" She dropped her hands to her legs.

"I think perhaps I am."

"You went longer than yesterday." She inclined her head as if to applaud his success.

He laughed. "Well, if you call meditating beyond thirty seconds a success, then, yes I did better."

"I call any steps you take toward the path to enlightenment… better."

He laid his elbow in his leg and cradled his chin as he regarded her. "What is your heritage, Lakota?"

"I am of the Blackfoot Nation. What we would call on Earth, Native American."

"That's where your light brown skin comes from then?"

"Yes."

"Gorgeous shade of nutmeg, as beautiful as the woman the color adorns," he said has he continued to stare at her.

She tensed and inhaled a sharp breath. "Those types of comments unnerve me."

"I know." Taban smiled and winked at her. "I have offered for you to leave… at any time."

"I am not leaving."

"Then you will deal with my unnerving comments."

"I guess I will," she said.

"Come." He rose and extended his hand. "Let's go see to dinner."

"Kabon again?" She allowed him to pull her up. He tilted her body against his until she found footing enough to slide away. There would be a time when he wouldn't let Wolf Warrior Lakota Blackson out of his arms. He found her stoic bearing quite a challenge. She wasn't completely immune to him; of this he was confident. Every once in a while, he caught a dreamy facade pass by her face, followed by that lovely cherry blush.

"More than likely. Do you tire of our little furry creature?"

"No, not at all, they're quite tasty."

"Good, watch your step, the path is rocky." He linked their fingers and trailed her behind him as he took the path toward his traps. He didn't need to assist her, but he definitely enjoyed the feel of her hand in his. Greedy, that's what he was, purely selfish with her.

"Maybe we should try fishing tomorrow," he suggested.

"I would enjoy that."

"I'm sure you have an enlightening technique to teach me."

"I do indeed." Her soft laugh made him grin. He should throw her off his mountain, and instead he found himself enjoying every second they spent together.

"I look forward to it. Tomorrow, we will fish."

❧❀❧

"Is there anything you don't do with perfection?" Taban rested on his elbows against the sandy riverbank as he watched Lakota extract yet another fish from the river. Outfitted in her warrior garb and halter, her body wet and shining, he didn't think he'd ever seen anything so beautiful.

"Striving for perfection as you maintain oneness with your being is critical."

Taban shook his head. She was so disciplined. She maintained a balance he would never achieve.

"That should be sufficient." She eased down next to him and brushed off her hands. "My people are taught to worship the sun and the land. The fish swimming in this river live in harmony with their elements. I simply asked them if they would be willing to sacrifice their life for our need... to which they agreed."

"You ask the fish if they would give up their lives for ours?" He leaned over and soothed the silk of her hair back, bearing her rosy face to him.

She dipped her head in a nod. "I did."

"You're amazing." He slid his hand along her cheek, the softness of her skin brushed against his fingertips. "I've never known a woman like you."

"Well... I'm..." She actually blushed at his comment. He was intrigued by her reaction. He fingered the flush, followed it down her throat to the top of her breast where he stroked the flesh with his thumb. Her nipples peaked against the soft leather of her halter-top. The sight of her body's reaction to his touch excited him. He wanted to finger that flush all the way down past the top of her halter and lower, into her wet, heat.

"Well…" he whispered as he leaned in and took her lips with his. Her response was immediate, her fingers delved into his hair, holding his head as he tilted to the side for a better angle. There was nothing he wanted more than to take this woman to his bed.

Nothing.

He dipped his tongue out and danced with hers, chasing until he caught.

He couldn't get enough of her.

He rolled her down against the smooth sand and covered her body with his, never disconnecting their lips. Tangling their legs, Taban lifted his head and ran his tongue along her jaw. She gasped, causing him to grin and celebrate her reaction. Then she tensed, slid a hand to his shoulder and pressed. He recognized the plea for him to halt. He groaned and panted against her neck.

"I caught the fish, therefore you clean them," she said, her voice uneven.

"Ahhhh." He caressed her cheek. Despite the fact she had stopped him, the desire he saw reflected in her eyes pleased him. "So, this agreement you made with the fish does not include cleaning them?"

"That is correct." Then she smiled, a gentle tipping of her lips, which resulted in the instantaneous hardening of his body and made his heart go *thump, thump* against the confines of his chest. She was beautiful, his Lakota, but when she softened under his touch, she was even more irresistible.

He grinned. "Well, then, I think I can teach you something for a change." He ran his thumb along her bottom lip. He could take her now, while under him, malleable, her sleepy gaze hot with her desire. But he didn't want it to be this way between them. When he finally made her his, when they made love, she would have her eyes wide opened and be an eager participant. *Make her mine.* When had he decided this? He eased to his feet, holding his hand out to her.

"I think you can. I would be honored to learn from you."

She accepted his grip. "Well, this isn't really the most enjoyable part of fishing," he tugged her off the ground.

"I imagine it isn't."

They spent the remaining of the afternoon cleaning fish and preparing the evening meal. By the time night rolled around, Taban was full of fish, absolutely infatuated with Lakota, and ready to burst with the need to have her.

"I love it here." Lakota raised her face to the sky as she leaned her back against the log Taban had provided as their seat. He followed her gaze and glanced up.

Stars littered the darkness, a smattering of blinking, distant city lights. The air smelled clean and fresh in the mountains, not like the polluted scent of expelled fuel of the city. The rising dual moons were at their fullest, casting a soft white glow bright enough for Taban to see Lakota's expression of happiness.

Throwing his napkin into the fire, he sat next to her. Pushing his legs out, he crossed them, grabbed his fire stick, and eased his back against the wood.

"This is my favorite place." He dropped his head back. "During the war, that same sky was lit with the tails of Elnar rockets. It's nice to have it peaceful again."

"Yes, I'm sure it is. If you enjoy the peace so much, why are you so determined to avoid this treaty meeting?"

He stiffened. They hadn't reached a point where they had talked about why he had shed his responsibilities and run to the mountains. He hadn't wanted to discuss it. He sighed and ran a hand through his hair.

"I am tired of the political infighting. I'm tired of all of it. I'm a warrior, not a mediator. Do you understand?" He dropped the stick he had been playing with into the fire and stared at the flashing lights of the sky.

"I understand. I also understand you are revered by your people and are a strong leader. They rely on you to guide them. This responsibility can not be taken lightly." She encased his hand in hers and squeezed. He shifted his gaze and studied their married palms. He ran his thumb along her forefinger. Her shoulder touched his and she shivered.

Easing out a long breath he responded, "I know." He brought their hands to his mouth and kissed her knuckles.

"Have you ever wanted to set aside your responsibilities and just be you, not Wolf Warrior, Lakota Blackson?"

Lakota tilted her head. "No. As a Realm guard, I can never take my responsibilities lightly."

"You've never, just for one minute, wanted to run free? Shed all your tasks and dance naked by the light of the fire?" He raised his eyebrows up and down and nodded his head toward the flames.

She laughed. "No."

"Pity. Have you ever danced in the moonlight to the sound of the night Karins?"

"No. I don't think I've ever danced," a wistful note invaded her voice.

"What? Never danced? Let me teach you." He drew her off the ground and walked her into the clearing.

"Close your eyes." Taban released her hand and ran his fingers into her hair, gently combing through it. "Listen to the night Karins."

"Crickets. On earth we have crickets. They sound like this. Very soothing."

He let his hands fall behind her as he drew her body close to his. "Good, now open your eyes and look up. See how bright the moons are, how they light the way for us."

She eased her head back and took in the view. Her body relaxed into his. She sighed and met his stare. "We only have one moon on earth. Strange to see two in the sky like that."

He tucked her hand into his and pressed their combined fingers against his chest. He slid his other hand to her hip. Then he swayed their bodies together.

"This isn't hard. You simply move to the music, relax and enjoy." He laid his chin on the top of her head and led her in a slow circle.

"Ahh, let me give us some serenading." He turned his head to the side and howled. The wolf pack began howling back.

She stopped moving. "That's amazing."

"They like to howl as a pack. Once the leader howls, they will follow."

Striker lingered on the edge of the clearing, howling as loud as the rest of the wolves.

"I don't think I've ever heard Striker join in a group howl before."

"See." He let his hand stray from her hip to settle on her buttock. "Everyone needs to play once in a while."

"You are a compelling man, Taban Zias. I see why your people, and your wolves, consider you such a strong leader."

"And you, Lakota, need to take time to dance and stop working." He twirled her in a circle, then dipped her in a deep arch. She gasped, and when he slid her back into his arms, she let out a hearty giggle. The sound of her laugh invigorated him. He liked it when she loosened up.

"Working is what I do. I take my job seriously and right now, my job is to get you back home," she said, all pretense of fun gone.

He froze and jerked out of her arms. Why couldn't she stop hounding him about his responsibilities? "See, that's where your problem lies, because as far as I'm concerned, I *am* home."

She stepped toward him. He held his ground. "Tell me why you are so troubled."

Taban pressed his fingers against his temples. He hated this. He hated her ruining the moment. "I'm…" He held up his hands.

She reached up and placed her palms against his. The warmth of her touch penetrated his frustration and eased his anger. The strength he admired so much seeped into his veins like a drug.

"Tell me," she whispered.

He studied her, so stoically beautiful, so balanced and disciplined, lately he couldn't seem to get any of that steadiness in his own life. It was as if he was on the edge of a cliff, waiting to be pushed off. "I'm worried."

"Worried about what?" She let him draw her closer, their palms clasped together.

"I don't…" He gnashed his teeth.

She released his palm and rubbed her thumb gently over his temple. He could read the concern in her eyes.

"You don't what?"

He let the feel of her closeness soothe, let her balance reach out and calm him. He rested his forehead against hers. "I don't want to let my people down. This unrest we've had… I haven't been able to control it. What if it reaches the point of another war?"

"Fear of the unknown can cripple even your fiercest enemy. Free your concern and the answer will come."

"You make it sound so easy. But it's not."

"It is easy, Taban, if you let it be."

He wrenched from her embrace. He didn't want to let go of his fear. Fear was what kept him sharp, and during the war—alive.

"I told you I'm not returning. This conversation is over. I'm going to bed. Enjoy the night." He gave her a curt nod. Ignoring her frown, he strode away.

Chapter Four

Lakota had lost ground with Taban. Everything had been going so well, then she applied a small amount of pressure, and he retreated into his usual, closed-off shell. She understood well the fear that came with the huge responsibility of command. She'd experienced it herself when the Solarians adopted her, made her one of their Wolf Warriors, and placed her in charge of the highest position they had to offer. But she had long ago let the doubts of her abilities slide away.

"Taban." She caught up with him as he grabbed the tent flap. Laying her hand on his arm, she kept him from entering. "You made a promise to me."

He pivoted, knocking her hand off. Crossing his arms, he gave her a most unfriendly scowl, brows furrowed. The same expression she recognized from her first day with him. He wanted to be left alone, this was clear, and Lakota was just as determined to break him to her will and return him to his people.

"You promised to teach me how to dance, in the moonlight, to the sounds of nature. I would be most disappointed to lose this opportunity."

Slowly, uncrossing his arms, he took a short step closer.

"If you stop trying to drive me back home, I'll teach you."

She raised her hands in surrender. "I promise. Cross my heart." She made an X on her chest.

His eyes tracked her movement, the sternness in his face shifted to amusement. Now she had her Taban back. *Her Taban*. What was she thinking?

"Why should I trust you?" He gently gathered her into his arms.

"I am here by your rules, remember? Therefore, I will abide by your rules."

"Yes, that's true. Actually, I think what I said was you were here for my pleasure." He settled her into his arms, pressing his muscled body against hers.

So warm, he was always so warm. He smelled like that combination of the outdoors and man, his own spicy scent… She liked it and she liked him. Most of all, she wanted to help him. If she felt any more than responsibility to her mission, she wouldn't admit it to herself.

"Well," she grinned, "I'm not sure we settled on that point."

"Yes, I'm sure we did."

She followed his movements as he walked her through the easy steps of the dance he created. His hand sat at the base of her spine, their entwined fingers rested on his chest. Lakota couldn't seem to concentrate on anything but Taban.

"You are so stubborn," he said in a low voice. He rubbed his cheek against her hair.

"Yes, on that I will agree." His snort rumbled against her head. "My stubbornness has gotten me through many a difficult situation."

He soothed his hand up and down her back. "I'm sure it has." He fell silent. The only noise was the serenade of the surrounding nature; the soft sounds of the wildlife talking to each other, the wind gently whistling through the trees, and her body swaying with his. The feelings he evoked in her were beyond professional, they bordered on carnal. She needed to break the spell he weaved.

"Why do people do this, dance I mean?" She tipped her head back.

"See, dancing isn't about the music, it's about the closeness. Moving in symmetry, touching, feeling the heat of each other's bodies and letting your fantasies run wild. When you're in a room full of people, dancing isn't about those who surround you, it's only about the two of you."

"Have you done this a lot? You seem very accomplished." She felt out of her element as her control tripped with every rock of their pressed bodies.

He swirled Lakota out, then twirled her in, positioning her back to his chest. He wrapped his arms around her, his hands rested on her hips. He dipped his knees and bowed her body with his. "I didn't dance before I became the planetary leader. Unfortunately, political banquets required me to learn."

"You don't enjoy dancing?"

"Normally, no. I never really found a partner I could mesh with. But right now, I can see the allure." He nuzzled her neck.

She trembled in his arms. He had this power to make her forget all about propriety, her position, and anything else but the feel of his body seeping into hers and the passion he promised to teach her.

"Yes, it does have a certain allure," she said as he pressed his hardness against her back. He was aroused, probably as much as she, she thought, as his touch sent a shockwave tripping down her spine to her stomach, then lower.

"Do you feel it, Lakota? Do you feel how enjoyable it can be to think only about your partner, take in the heat of your combined bodies, live for his touch?" He ran his hands up her sides, over her ribs and settled them under her breasts where he paused, his body still moving with hers. He inserted his leg between hers and pressed, riding her thighs with his.

"I certainly feel the pull." Lakota barely recognized her own wispy rasp.

"Then you understand, now, what I was talking about," he said, his voice thick, his mouth soft against her neck. He slid his hands up the side of her breast.

Her heart lurched and she pulled in a quick breath. "Yes… yes." Desire laced through her.

"Now you know why people enjoy dancing."

"I do… Ahhh, maybe we should call it a night." She needed to stop this before she did something she would regret.

He disengaged his body from hers. She turned and faced him.

"There will be a time," he ran his thumb along the pounding pulse in her neck, "when you can no longer deny the passion that passes between us."

She inclined her head, preferring silence to answer for her.

"Bank the fire when you choose to retire." The double meaning in his statement wasn't lost to her.

"I will, and thank you for showing me…" She waved her hand, her thoughts scattered with the flip of her fingers. Did he need to be so attractive, so compelling to be around, so male? He made her want things she couldn't have.

He nodded and turned toward his tent. Lakota's smaller tent was pitched on the other side of camp, so there was no threat of them bumping into each other in the middle of the night. Lakota had made sure of that.

She sank down to the ground and stared into the orange, crackling flames of the fire. Striker positioned himself next to her. She flung an arm around him.

"I might be in over my head with this one," she told Striker. He led out a *ruff.*

She quickly dismissed any notion she had to give up on this assignment. She could handle Taban Zias. She straightened her spine; she was a Wolf Warrior of the highest caliber with a mission to return the planetary leader of Elnar to his rightful place. She could take whatever he had to deal out.

She hoped.

Chapter Five

Two weeks was too short, Lakota thought as she sparred with Taban. They used the wooden practice staffs, each strike echoing off the nearby trees.

She forced herself to concentrate, ignoring the way he filled his close-fitting exercise pants, his hair loose and flowing around his shoulders, his tight shirt showing off his sculpted muscles. He fought with a wildness, in contrast to her smooth, flowing movements. But with his brashness came mistakes. He needed to control his impulses, he needed serenity, he needed *her*.

They had formed a bond in the last two weeks, a strong friendship—and much, much, more. Lakota was ready to detonate in a sensual haze of sexual awareness. Every time they were together, whether eating or simply talking, his persona, his smell, the touch of his shoulders to hers, made her want to give up all pretense of being a teacher and turn into a student.

Day by day, moment-by-moment, her control frayed, until only a few strings were left. Changing their relationship could be dangerous to her mission. But he wasn't making her forbearance easy. He touched her often, taunting her with his masculinity, as seductive as heat on a cold day.

Two weeks wasn't enough, Taban thought as he blocked a blow from Lakota's staff. He had to think of a reason to buy more time.

The next instant, she shifted and ran her staff behind his knee, then tumbled him onto his back. Bending over him, she lodged her stick beneath his Adam's apple.

"You're losing your concentration. Had that been a laser sword, you'd be dead."

No kidding.

Lakota, half naked, was enough to send any man over the edge of sanity. He had learned much from her in the last two-weeks, and the hardest lesson was how to restrain his desire.

With a grin, he pushed her staff away, reached up and toppled her. She landed on him heavily, her eyes wide, her mouth shaped in an O. Not giving her a chance to say a word, he ran his hands down her back… and lower, caressing the smoothness of her skin. She wore her body hugging breeches and skimpy halter-top, only leather straps crossing her back. Her skin glistened from their sparring session and her scent drifted over him, a feminine flowery fragrance, with an underlying uniqueness he was coming to hunger for.

"This is not part of the exercise," she said, but her hands fluttered on his shoulders instead of flattening to push away.

He rolled her, finding a comfortable place between her legs to settle, his hardness thrusting forward, seeking the position it most wanted. Although her head shook, her expression sparkled—and she still didn't stop him.

"I like this exercise better," he said.

Planning her seduction the way he'd deliberated battles, he'd moved their relationship to this point for the entire two-weeks, chipping away at her resistance, a stroke here, a kiss there. He burned for her and her answering fire couldn't be mistaken. It was time.

He tipped his head and kissed her lightly. Her lips softened, and excitement flashed inside him, begging for release. There was a passion in her, one he'd only scratched the surface of, one he craved to explore every inch of, with his lips, his tongue, his hands. He desired her so bad he hurt.

A low growl stopped him. Her wolf stood at his shoulder blade, his mouth curled, his fangs white against his pure black coat.

"It's okay," Lakota said. "Striker, stand down. Go, guard the pack."

The wolf's eyes glowed yellow, but he gave a single bark and loped off.

"He needs to relax." He turned his attention back to her, and stroked her jaw with his thumb.

Fervor flickered in her eyes. "He is serious about his position." Her voice was husky, ragged.

"Yes, like someone else I know." His fingers cruised from her jaw to her neck. He touched her pulse, feeling the thumping of her heart.

"We are linked, telepathically," she said. "All Solarians have a wolf protector. They claim us from a young age, usually before we begin our warrior training. Striker, always a lone wolf, claimed me as soon as I was brought to the Realm."

"How old were you?"

"I was ten." Her eyes shadowed. "I was a product of war, bloodshed, found by the Solarians near death on the spoils of the battlefield," she said.

Her hurt made him want to heal her. He wasn't the only soul in need of saving. He leaned over and ran his lips along her collarbone. She moaned. The low sound reverberated through his body, straight to his cock. God, he wanted her.

"Is that when you were tattooed?" He kissed her right shoulder. She had a design there on her back, two interlinking circles curled around a sword and a wolf.

"I was marked with the Wolf Warrior tattoo as soon as I was accepted into training. I must have been eleven by then."

He lifted his head from her shoulder "I was also a product of war. I know the horrors you must have faced. You're a fine warrior and you've helped me tremendously." His voice deepened. "Now let me help you, let me show you what pleasure can be."

He kissed her. Joining his mouth with hers, he took deeply from her. He thought she would protest, but she buried her hands into his hair, her mouth opening for him. Using his tongue, he delved in and sipped, tasting her, wanting, needing.

"God," he groaned as he came up for air. He cruised his lips along her shoulder, nudging the leather of her halter down her arm.

He bared her breast. She was perfect, a lovely shade of brown, her nipple pink and pearled.

Not giving her time to protest, he rounded her areola then tongued her nipple. She arched under him and sighed. When her body surged up into his, his heart started a rhythm so hard he was surprised his chest didn't explode.

"Taban, we can't," she moaned as he pushed off the other strap and took her second breast.

"We can. Just feel, *Charma*, feel and enjoy. Let yourself go, see how good it will be between us." He had never called anyone by the Elnarian name for love before, but with this woman it felt right. He leaned forward and sucked, taking her nipple into his mouth, teasing it with his tongue.

"Gods, I want to." The sentence came out on the end of a whimper. He lightly bit on her nipples, not enough to hurt, but enough to arouse, rid her of her inhibitions.

"Yessss." She clutched his head with both hands.

He released her and touched his gaze to hers. Her eyes were at half-mast, dreamy, just like he had imagined. She was ready, now was the time.

Moving swiftly, he stood, reached down, and lifted her into his arms. As he carried her into his tent, she anchored her hand behind his neck and played with his hair. A shiver walked down his spine, his skin pearled with sweat. He ached to bury himself inside of her, make them one. He lowered her feet to the ground, then pulled his shirt off, baring himself to her. He placed her hands on his chest.

"Touch all you want."

Lakota opened her fingers against the warm flesh of Taban's neck, then dropped down to caress his broad shoulders, and finally his chest. His heart pounded beneath her palm. Her hand trembled as she trailed her fingers down his abdomen to his erection.

He growled and pushed into her touch. She had never given herself fully to a man before. These intense feelings were so new. But it felt right with Taban; he was the one.

When she stroked him through the cloth of his pants, his eyes hooded with want. Her body took on a mind of its own, dampness pooling between her legs, her heat pulsating, her nipples hardening. She rubbed the peaks of her breasts against his chest. His face tensed and his eyes blazed with the look of a wolf about to pounce. Her breath hitched. He was wild and untamed; everything she ever dreamed her lover would be.

His mouth traveled along her face to her jaw, then his tongue trailed to her neck. He nipped her throat, his teeth scraping against her jugular. She moaned and jumped with a slight jerk of pain.

As his mouth left a wet trail down her body, the new sensations amazed her. He was incredibly strong, yet his lips were gentle.

How astonishing.

How wonderful.

Sexual awareness wrapped around her.

He leaned closer to her ear. "I want you." His voice came out guttural.

Her body tensed. She wanted him as much as he wanted her. Her breath quickened. Blood raced through her veins, throbbing in her head. Nothing mattered but the need for this man to have her. She shivered with anticipation.

"I want to take you, *Charma*. Show you what it can be like, between us. Make you mine."

His low, seductive words drove her senses wild. A primitive yearning sent her over the edge of sanity. His hands caressed her bare skin until he reached the waistband of her leather pants. He stopped. His fingers clenched and unclenched.

She plunged her hand into his hair, pulling his head down for another drugging kiss. Her lips followed the same exploration his had. Kissing his jaw line, she answered, "Yes. Make me yours, Taban."

His breath rushed out, fanning her hair.

"Touch me." She needed his hands on her so bad she could taste it.

His eyes snapped up and met hers. His hands swept up and cupped her bare breasts, kneading them, his thumbs caressing. Her nipples peaked against his palms. When she moaned and writhed, he replaced his fingers with his mouth. Her legs almost collapsed under her.

As his lips and tongue worshipped her breasts, she bit her lip to keep from screaming. She arched against him, her hands pulling his head, her body straining toward his sucking mouth, groans pouring from her throat.

His touch filled her. Her body quivered down to her toes, her breath hummed as his cock brushed against her stomach and his leg rubbed against her thigh. With each brush of his lips, she tensed with anticipation.

What would he do next?

His hands skimmed across her rib cage, then slipped lower to find the fasteners of her pants. He dropped to his knees and pressed his lips to the flat planes of her stomach.

"You're so beautiful," he whispered, "everywhere." He untied her halter-top, dropping it to the tent floor.

Never had she experienced such heady emotions before, she'd only dreamed them and the feelings were almost painful in reality, so intense, searing, the overload to her Wolf Warrior senses made her light-headed. She wanted him to kiss her all over. His mouth was wet and soft, his tongue cool and coarse. The mass of his frame poised below her, contrasting with her smaller one. He made her feel small, and fragile, in a world where her toughness was expected.

She ached to succumb to the sensations of his hands and mouth. When his lips stopped at the junction of her leather pants, she moaned. Unhooking her buttons, he worked his way down, pulling them one at a time through the holes. Her breath came faster, her body pulsating.

Peeling her pants down, he tossed them aside and slowly lowered her to his blankets. His mouth followed his hands until she tingled from his simple touch, yearning for something more than his kisses.

She was naked now, bared to him. Her hips moved, straining against his mouth. She needed him to move lower, to soothe the throbbing ache. His tongue slid out to touch her heat.

Oh Gods. He devoured her dripping wetness. She rotated her hips into his mouth. *Oh Gods, this is sooo good.*

"Ohhhh, Taban."

His tongue delved deeper, lapping at her. She couldn't stand it anymore. She had to touch him, to see him. She had never been with a man in this way so wasn't sure where this sense of urgency came from, but it was there.

She'd thought in her first joining she would be shy, maybe unsure, that was not the case. The need sizzling through her was making her aggressive, as though she could do anything with Taban without consequences. She trusted him completely with her body.

She moved her hands to his chest, pushing him back, craving to touch him, she sat up. "I want to see you naked."

Tugging off his boots, he rose to his knees in front of her, allowing her hands to stroke his bareness, to appease her curiosity. His body was hot and alive with hard curves of muscle. He flexed beneath her touch.

She trailed her hands over his chest, lower to his ribs, his sculptured stomach, and stopped at his pants. He panted, his chest rising and falling. Her hand looked so small next to his body.

Amazing. Arousing.

There were things she desired to try on his body. She wanted to give pleasure. She wanted to take pleasure.

He closed his eyes in response to her touch. His hips thrust against her hand. She stroked him. He grabbed her wrist, staying her movement.

"Tell me what to do," she asked.

"Unzip me," he commanded, his voice was hoarse.

She hesitated. Slowly she laid her hands on the front of him, then she did as he asked.

Following his instructions she completely loosened Taban's pants. He helped her push them down, freeing his hard, veined cock into her hands.

She gasped at the sight of his largeness nestled against a dark stain of curls. It strained upward to his navel. Forcing her hands away, he slid his pants off until he was fully naked.

Her breath came out in pants. "Take me, Taban."

She touched her lips to his chest, running her hands down his back to rest on his tight ass. He opened his mouth against her neck, then trailed lower, to her breasts. He ravaged her with his rough hands, the pace savage in its intensity, yet somehow tender. Traveling to the dark curls, he delved finger in, stroking her clit. He moved one finger in and out, back and forth; her body's immediate reaction was unbelievable, wearing the edge of her control to nothing.

"You're so wet for me, *Charma*. God, I want to please you."

He tweaked her clit. Sensations burst through her. She arched. "Yes."

"Come for me, *Charma*, come for me."

His statement made her heart pound. She wanted to come for him, she wanted to satisfy him.

"Taban, oh God," she moaned against his lips.

"Yesss," he murmured, as she in turn, cupped him.

His groan, his hitched breath, and the heated perspiration covering him, drove her forward. His body's powerful reactions urged her to continue her explorations. His mouth took hers in a deep kiss. His tongue lapped in rhythm to his fingers encased in her heat.

"Come for me."

Her body became pliant in his hands, pleasure building, heart racing, and breathing rapid. Her legs fell open, giving him better access to her nether lips, her body his now. She watched from outside herself, his hands possessing.

Her breath sucked in, she felt the heat of excitement sweep across her skin, tempered by the dewy spread of perspiration. "Don't stop," she begged, the pleasure building, taking her higher and higher.

His fingers set a seductive rhythm, her slick heat fueling him on. She was sopping wet for him.

She was going to explode.

A need built inside her, for what she wasn't sure. She only knew there must be some final release, something spectacular coming. Her muscles drew taut, sensation rolled over her, blinding, incredible pleasure like she'd never known. Her hips moved of their own volition.

She rode the bliss he created, her hips pumping in a natural rhythm to his touch. White light exploded behind her eyes.

"That's it. Ride it out."

His lips claimed hers as his fingers left her body. She cried out, but he quickly pulled her legs around his hips, locking them behind his ass. He lowered her onto her back. For her there was only this man now, his cock at her entrance, hard and unyielding, his hips spreading her wide. His body eased down on hers, a wonderful heaviness.

She whispered his name as he entered her. Absorbing her initial murmur of pain when he breached her, he clasped her hands, his thumb soothing the rapidly beating pulse at her wrist. It wasn't possible to want more, but at that moment she did.

The deeper arousal shocked her. She thought when she lost her self to a man she would be scared and it would be painful. But the reality was neither. It was a profound joining, making her one with him.

Tears of joy formed in her eyes. She tightened herself around him.

"Oh God, Lakota you're untaken? Why didn't you tell me? I could have made it easier."

"No, Taban, it's fine, it's wonderful. I need… more… don't stop…" Her voice trailed off.

Taban wanted to stay buried inside her until there was no tomorrow. She was so tight and wet, sucking him in, allowing him to sink himself to the hilt. They fit perfectly.

He nibbled her mouth until his rapid breathing forced him to lift his lips from hers. Untaken. How incredible, how lucky.

He closed his eyes, savoring the enormity of her gift to him. She was sweet, succulent. He breathed in her scent, the one that drove him wild, and need tore at him. Desperate for release, his cock pulsated, but he knew he needed to take it slow and easy.

"Thank you, *Charma*. Hold onto me now, stay with me."

Lakota sighed at his words and his warm breath at her throat. With his cock buried inside of her, she had never been so whole in her life. He was a part of her now. She squeezed around him and moved with him.

He slid in and out, slowly at first, then pumped with a determined urgency. With each stroke, Lakota's breath caught. Her body reached.

She bowed into him, panting, her heart hammering, compelled to meet his thrusts with her own, enhancing her enjoyment. Their bodies slipped against each other, a sheen of perspiration glistening on their skins.

She was burning up. As her lips latched onto his, he moaned. She tasted herself in his kiss; it was exciting, an intimate sharing that could only happen between lovers.

She ran her hands down his back and stroked his ass as he pumped into her. Her head fell back and she arched, her sighs released. As her second orgasm built, every muscle in her body tensed.

Her legs tightened around him. "Taban!" she cried.

He groaned and stiffened. Her body trembled and shuddered in unison as they climaxed together.

❦

Taban's head rested against hers as his breath slowed. His eyes still closed, he tipped his head to the side and kissed her lips, sipping gently as he eased their bodies side by side. Reaching down, he pulled the blanket over them.

His legs tangled with hers. He pressed her head against his chest. Her breathing slowed as her body finally lost its battle to stay awake and she burrowed into his warmth.

The evidence of their coupling smeared Taban's penis. He knew he would find the blood from her woman's barrier there. He puffed out a proud breath. Lakota was his now, body and soul. He had been her first man, and he would stop at nothing to ensure he was her last.

He tightened his hold on her slumbering body, resting his chin on top of her hair. Her distinctive sweet perfume had his prick rising again. He tried to calm himself.

He couldn't take her again so soon. She needed time to recover. He closed his eyes.

"You are my mate now, Lakota."

At the sound of his voice, her small, callused hand slid around his waist to rest on his ass. She snuggled closer.

He smiled at her unconscious action. Yes, even in her dreams she knew she was his. He chuckled and settled down to join her in sleep.

Chapter Six

Water drops dripped slowly over Lakota's breasts. She moaned, running her hands over her face and down her body, delighting in the simple joy of washing. The creek was warm, like a tepid bath on a heated July day in Scotland, reminding her of home. Not wanting to wake Taban, she had slipped away to bathe. He slept so peacefully, an expression of child-like innocence on his face, she was captivated with him. Last night he had introduced her to the world of love, and she had enjoyed every minute of the induction.

"Here, let me help you with that."

Lakota squeaked out a startled cry when Taban stood in front of her naked as the day he was born, and glorious. The lines of veined-muscles flexed as he neared her, so finely crafted, her Taban. He could arouse her with a simple step. She remembered well running her fingers over the contours of those very muscles, reveling in the hard, sleek shape of his body.

"The water in this river is so warm," she said as she rubbed some sand on her leg and washed it off.

"It's from the mountain, the underground lava heats the waterways. Are you okay, sore at all?"

"No, I feel wonderful."

Despite the fact they had loved all night long, she still craved him in the sexual sense a woman did her only man, needed to have him buried deep inside her; connected in an elemental way, and straining toward the ultimate pleasure.

He walked around and came up behind her, his erection pressing against her back, his hands replacing hers. He played, his fingers lowering, gliding over her wet flesh.

"I woke and you weren't there. This troubled me."

His finger delved into her slit and his other hand tweaked her breast. Pressure built inside her as she strained to her toes instinctively urging her channel closer to him, her panted breaths turned into a long groan as her hips rocked against him. At the same time he entered her from behind, his hard cock slipping into her wetness. His teeth bit down on her shoulder, intensifying her orgasm, as the pain led to pleasure.

"Say you're mine."

She tipped her head back against his chest. Her voice throbbed with want as she groaned, "Taban, yes." Her head lolled from side to side as their wet bodies began to slide together. "Yours."

Pumping faster, his hands touched, worshiped, and loved her. His lips shimmied along her neck, soothing his bite with his tongue while his hips worked in a slow steady rhythm, sinking in and out until she reached for another climax. His body became rigid against hers. "Mine," he declared, panting, until his breath evened, his muscles relaxed. He began washing her again, wrapping his arms around her chest, anchoring her to him.

Lowering his chin into the crook of her neck, he sucked in a slow breath. A noise emitted from his throat, somewhere between a growl and a snarl.

Claimed—was the primary emotion coursing through her. He stirred her in ways she'd wouldn't try to reason, made her want to lock herself in his arms and throw away the key.

Dropping her neck a little to the left she gave him better access. She felt him smile against her skin. He ran his tongue down the slant of her throat to her shoulder, where he lightly kissed.

"In the future. Don't leave like that without waking me," he said as he cuddled the side of her throat.

She stiffened at the command in his tone. "I can take care of myself."

"I'm aware. Please, Lakota. Grant me this. These woods are dangerous." The catch in his voice took her off guard. She'd never had anyone care about her at this level before.

"I'm sorry. Of course, I will. I promise."

"Wash me, *Charma,*" he ordered.

Turning, Lakota scooped water into her hands and slid them over his chest, outlining his pec muscles; she touched the warmth of his flesh. She journeyed, her hands caressing his back, down to his hard buttocks, legs, then back up to his chest. He pressed in and kissed her, sliding his hand behind her head, he locked her to him and ravished her mouth. She came up for air on the tail end of a moan. He tasted so good, that tangy flavor of salt and sugar at the same time, addicting.

Leaning down, he lifted her into his arms. "I'm going to take you back to my tent and love you all day and night."

Not waiting for an answer, he took the rocky trail at a quick march. She laughed and caressed his hair.

"You just loved me all night. So what you're saying is… you want to do it all over again?"

His eyes met hers, and he grinned. "Oh yeah, that's what I'm saying." His voice came out in a throaty rumble.

"I think I'd enjoy that. There is much I'd like you to teach me."

"Oh, I think I'll enjoy teaching you for a change."

⁂

The familiar high-pitched squeal of a MAZ missile woke Taban.

Instinctually, he rolled his body over Lakota's. The ground shook, and the tent collapse with a *whoosh*. The sonic boom of the explosion was deafening. He took in the familiar smell of the discharged ordinance.

What the hell! Are we under attack?

Chapter Seven

"Are you okay?"

Lakota's eyes snapped open at Taban's question, her ears ringing.

"Yes, what was that?" Taban had her pinned, protecting her, his breathing rapid. By the sound of that explosion, something bad was happening. Her warrior instincts immediately kicked in.

"A MAZ missile. Hard to get, illegal actually. Accurate and deadly. I'd know that sound anywhere. Haven't heard one for a long time, since the war."

"I assume we're under attack?"

"So it would seem."

"Let's get out of here and find cover," she yelled.

"Excellent idea." He rolled to her side, lifting the collapsed tent as she shimmied out, grabbing her clothes and boots as she went. Crawling one foot at a time, hand over hand until she reached the end, she surveyed the area. A huge hole was opened next to the tent. She didn't see anything hovering around them.

"That was close." A battle calm reverted through her system. They were in trouble, and she needed to think like a warrior right now, not a woman in love. Taban scrambled out behind her, a laser blaster and pack slug over his shoulder.

"Too close. Run for the trees."

She jumped up and sprinted to the surrounding trees. The pounding of feet followed behind her with Taban on her trail. Striker came tearing up from the side. They all raced into the thick foliage of the forest. A *thump thump* noise made her stop, turn and tuck behind a huge tree for cover. She quickly pulled on her clothes.

"Striker find help." She silently commanded her wolf. He gave a single bark and dashed back off through the trees.

"What is that noise?"

"Turbo helo copter."

Taban's motions followed hers as he tugged on his clothes. "Can I assume this isn't a pick up party?"

She endeavored not to watch him slide his form fitting exercise pants and tight shirt over his naked body, tried not to be aroused, and failed miserably. He was an incredibly striking man. His blue eyes met hers as he drug on his boots. His black hair fell into his face. He finished and tucked the strands behind his ear.

So sexy. Even in the dangerous situation they were in, he stirred her. She remembered the thrill of running her hands over his body, of feeling him buried deep inside of her.

"No, I think we can safely assume this is a killing party, not pick up." Hearing the copter again, she backed herself against the bark. Taban stood, his arms falling to each side of her as he pressed his body against hers. She wrapped her arms around his back and held him close. For just a millisecond, she laid her head on his chest and enjoyed his warmth, his fresh smell, the feel of him touching her. The rapid beating of his heart thundered under her ear. He stroked her hair.

"You're mine, Lakota. No matter what happens today, know that." She leaned back and met his gaze. His declaration warmed her.

"I'm yours, Taban." She stroked the side of his face. He closed his eyes and pressed his cheek into her hand. She kissed him, gently at first, sipping, telling him how much she loved him. His hand fisted in her hair as he tugged her closer, taking the kiss to the next level, his tongue dancing with hers. God, he could spin her up so fast. She ran her hands up his back and buried them in his hair, letting the kiss go on and on, wishing they had all day to learn the feel of each other. Finally, he broke off, his breath panted out.

"We have to get out of here."

An explosion behind him made her flinch. She covered her ears as a screech filled the area. Taban grabbed her close, his body shielding hers.

As the noise tapered off she peered over Taban's shoulder.

"What is that?" An unexploded ordinance was lodged into the ground.

"Finding beacon. The noise is the ram radar. It will transmit our exact location to the copter. Come on. I know a place we can hide until we get in contact with Reack." He yanked her by the hand, tearing out of the area. She trusted him to know where they could be safe.

They ran full-out for close to thirty minutes, weaving in and out of the trees, before Taban allowed them to take a break. Lakota panted and rested as Taban walked to the edge of the clearing, a valley of trees spread out below them. He froze, pulling a device out of his pack; he raised it to his eyes, his posture stiffened.

"What is it?"

She stood and walked to his side. The copter hovered, something flickered, the trees vanished and formed into a solid display of machinery, then it simply disappeared. It was as if the copter had landed directly into the grove of trees, but that was impossible. He handed her the binocs.

She focused so she could get a better look at what was below. Again, all she saw was trees.

"What the hell?"

"That was a cloaking device, hologram driven. It flickered off when the copter landed. The device can disrupt EMP emissions so it would have to be disengaged for a landing. Under that illusion is a well maintained land mining operation. They're pulling something from the earth. Obviously, from the elaborate and expensive cloaking mechanism they've installed, it's not supposed to be there."

When the patter of another copter drew closer, he grabbed her back from the edge.

"Come on, we've got to keep moving."

Chapter Eight

Lakota huddled against the cave wall. Wrapping her hands around her legs, she dropped her head against her knees and tried to catch her wind, taking in deep soothing breaths. It seemed as if they had run forever, Taban never letting up until he found the cave he searched for. He showed his true warrior skills in the last few hours. He was experienced at being hunted and high evasion tactics; his skills were invaluable. For now, they had managed to ditch the copter.

"Where are we?"

Taban dropped down across from her and began rummaging through his backpack.

"This is the pack cave." As soon as he said the words, the wolves that had been haunting them all week came trailing, one by one, into the cave. There were four of them, ranging in color and size, beautiful creatures. The alpha male approached Taban. Taban threw his arms around the wolf and hugged him as the animal licked his face.

"This is your pack?"

"Well, as close to mine as a wolf pack can get. I saved this pack during the war. Found them sanctuary from the hunters and protected these woods after, the woods the council is trying to populate. We've been sort of bonded every since. They will let us hang here, until we can find out what's going on."

He pushed the wolf away and smiled.

As a guarded personality style, he rarely showed amusement, so it was nice to see him happy. She just wished the danger of the situation didn't loom over their heads. Before he took over leadership of the planet, he had obviously lived a hard life, just like her own youth. *No wonder we connected so quickly in every way.* He dug into the pack and took out some sort of watch.

"This was the treaty I was to help you negotiate, for this land?"

"Yes, and now I'm beginning to understand why someone wanted it. With the wolves here, rangers are sent out to watch, make sure there is no treaty violations, people hunting. Whoever desired this land cleared, they must be funding that illegal mining operation. We haven't been out here for a while. The rangers come every six months, plenty of time to construct a mining scaffold. If they were to acquire the land to residentialize it, it could take years to build housing. They could have mined all they want, hold off on the housing. That equipment is pretty deep into the forest; you couldn't see it from over head. The hologram camouflaged it well."

"Who would want to do this?"

"That I don't know." He fiddled with the watch; opening the top. It had a flat gray pad under the face. It began to emit a long set of short beeps.

"What is that?"

He held up the watch.

"Coder, it will send a set of vibrations, silent beeps if you will. Only Reack can feel the vibrations. He has a receiver on his watch. Another one of those stupid devices he made for me, in case of emergency, like the tracking beacon in my bracelet. Never thought I would need it." He started flicking his finger over the small touch screen.

"How does he know what you're saying?" She moved closer, watched him operate the transmitter. He tapped a series, then stopped and tapped again, three small taps, one long, two, pause, then three again.

"It's a code we set up to talk with. He knows what word each tap represents. He made me memorize it. If he can respond, he will."

He waited, then the unit began vibrating. "He's okay. He's asking for our location so he can send a rescue copter."

"You ditched your bracelet?"

"Oh yeah, left it back at the camp as soon as that missile hit. Figured if someone was able to locate us, they must have gotten to Reack. I'm relieved that's not the case."

He tapped the watch. "I'm transmitting our location."

The watch vibrated. "He says a couple hours."

"Come here." He opened his arms. Lakota sank down into him.

"Striker is out there." She chewed on her upper lip.

"Don't worry. Striker is a tough wolf and he knows how to take care of himself. He'll track your scent."

"Yes, yes, he is. Thank you for reminding me." She sighed and rested her head on his chest.

"Let me show you the best part of this cave." He rose and led her further back into the cavern. It was dark, the walls closed in around them.

She squeezed Taban's hand. "Hope you know where you're going?"

"Oh yeah, you can trust me, I know these caves by touch."

"Glad you do."

They walked further back; the walls began to loom down. Lakota reached out and made contact with the stone. Then the rocks literally opened, the sound of rushing water greeted her.

Picking something up from the wall, Taban slammed it against another rock and started a spark, then touched it to a bundle. A torch bathed the space in gentle light. He fitted the handle in a holder attached to the wall. Steam floated around them. Taban began to undress. Raising a single brow, he smiled and reached forward to remove her clothes; she was naked in no time.

"What about Reack?"

"He'll be hours." He lifted her into the water. It was warm, the level coming to her waist and gently swirling around them both. "Hot, nice. Lava, again?" she asked as she sunk down into the wetness, letting the heat soothe her sore muscles. She sat against the bottom and felt the smooth surface of rock.

"Yes." Taban descended with her. He reached out and smoothed his hands over her shoulders caressing her, running his thumb over her breast, he fingered her nipple, played, aroused. She sighed. He floated her to him. Straddling her legs over his, he kissed her, slowly, softly, their lips clinging at first, his cock poised at her entrance, probing, but not entering, exciting her. She fingered him, teased his hardness, running her hand up his length, she pumped him. He pushed into her hand, made a noise that couldn't be mistaken for anything less than impatience. She smiled against his lips.

"You smell so good," he said as he angled his head the other direction, buried his hands in her hair and ate her mouth as if he was starving, the kiss getting as hot as the water. Lining her lips with his tongue, he pushed in, tangoing them together. She wrapped her hands around his shoulders and held on. He reached out and grabbed her ass. Lifting, he impaled her onto his cock, sliding in hard and fast, marrying their bodies.

"Need you," he murmured as he anchored her hips and pushed up. She gasped, and arched, her head falling back, her hair cascading into the water. Felt so good, so right. This was where he was meant to be, inside her, stroking her.

"Taban," she whispered when he latched onto her throat while moving her up and down on his shaft. His mouth traveled to her breast, sucking, teasing her nipples with his tongue.

"God," he growled as he thrust faster, harder, with more sense of urgency. She rubbed her hands down the solid muscles of his back. She loved touching him; the amazing contrast of his hard body compared to hers. He smelled so good, like her favorite cologne wrapped up in one sexy package. Eyes closed, breaths straining out, the passionate expression on his face one of pure pleasure, the sight aroused her. The friction of their union sent her over the top, she moaned, sucked in a breath and flew. He groaned, after one final drive up, he joined her.

"Ahhh," she floated down, coming back to earth. He took her to places she had never been. She was content to be in his arms forever.

"Sorry, meant to go slow. Couldn't, the minute you get close to me, I'm lost." He released her hips and ran his hand up her sides, and folded her into his arms.

"It's okay."

They stayed that way, wrapped in each other, until the heat of the water drove them out. Taban hopped up and sat on the edge of the springs, his legs spread. He offered her his hand. Lakota moved forward, resting her hands on his legs she ran them up and down his thighs as she stood between them. She reached out and teased his cock, watching in amazement as it began to harden. She stroked it, surprised at the velvety texture; he was so soft there. His eyes fell to half-mast, desire apparent. She wanted to please him.

"May I kiss you, there?" She tried not to blush, she had never been so bold, but she wanted to taste every inch of his body.

"You can do anything you want to me, *Charma.*"

She smiled and settled herself between his legs. She started slow, kissing him, then licking. Wanting to completely sample him, she took him fully into her mouth. His pants and groans told her to continue so she pumped him with her hands as she sucked the tip. Using her tongue and teeth, she explored, learning the texture of him. He tasted salty. She worked him into her mouth, taking him in as far as she could. His hands fell to her hair, caressing as his hips pumped his cock in and out of her mouth.

"Lakota, I'm going to come." His voice was low, sounded as if someone yanked his words out of him. She wanted to satisfy him, so she kept going, stroking. He closed his eyes; his head dropped back as sweat glistened on his chest. He was so beautiful this way, under her control. She loved his hardness until he moaned and thrust up, his seed spilling down her throat. She licked, taking all of him. He pulled her out of the water, and kissed her, hard, their mouths mating.

"Thank you, *Charma,* that was incredible," he whispered as he softly kissed her lips.

"What does *Charma* mean?" she asked

"It means, my love, in my language."

"In my language *Ohkiimaan,* means my most loved one," she caressed his shoulder.

He drew her out of the springs, wrapping her into his arms.

"We better get dressed," she murmured. She hated to leave, but they had to be ready for anything.

"I know."

Chapter Nine

Concealed by the overhang, Taban stood at the entrance to the cave. It had been three hours since he called Reack.

"What's wrong?" From behind, Lakota slid her arms around him and laid her cheek against his back. He sighed and dropped his hands over hers, linking their fingers. He could die a happy man in this woman's arms.

"I don't know. Something's not right. He should have been here by now."

He turned and walked her back, pinning her against the side of the cave.

"If anything happens to me, you need to run, get away."

"Taban, I'm a warrior. I fight until the death, no matter what. And I won't leave you."

His heart dropped. He wouldn't see anything happen to her. He lifted his hand and caressed her cheek. His mate.

"If we get through this, will you consider being my chosen mate, *Charma*? Forever." He held his breath while he awaited her answer.

"As in marriage?"

He nodded. "Yes, our mating ceremonies are much like Earth's marriages."

"So, you're asking me to marry you?"

"Yes, I'm asking you to be mine."

"Oh." She smiled and rubbed her thumb along his lip.

"I would consider it an honor to become your mate, Taban." The certainty in her reply settled Taban's doubts. He puffed out a stream of air and kissed her thumb.

She laughed. "Did you worry I would refuse you?"

He shook his head and ran his thumb down her halter top, fingering the leather. He wanted to push it off her shoulder and take his sweet time loving her. He kissed her neck. She made that little mewling noise and melted into him, nearly driving him crazy. He wanted her again.

"Well, maybe, a little."

She rolled her eyes. He chuckled.

"Well, isn't this a cozy scene?"

"Reack." Taban turned and met the gaze of his best friend and the wrong end of a blaster. Betrayal nearly shocked him senseless. He immediately moved in front of Lakota and slowly raised his hands.

"What's this about, Reack?"

"This is about doing a job those I paid couldn't finish. This is about ridding our planet of these wolves and using the natural resources God gave us, Eiknar."

"So, you're the one who's built the mine?"

"Taban, you're so short sided. How the hell do you expect us to pay for anything on this planet when you shut down all the Eiknar mining operations? We're not an animal preserve." He waved the blaster back and forth sporadically, then aimed it back at them. "We have to live on money. Eiknar's fuel is needed in the interstellar community, and we have it." He lifted one finger and pointed at him. "You've grown weak in your leadership, your need to save the wolves has blinded you. You won't listen to anyone."

"So, this is why you wanted to drive the resolution of this land treaty dispute?" Taban stepped closer, one foot at a time, hoping to catch Reack off guard and snatch his weapon.

"Yes. I pleaded with you. I tried to do this without violence, but you wouldn't listen."

"Reack, we have been friends since birth, you saved my life once. Are you sure you want to do this?" Taban positioned his hands high, hoping to lull Reack into a false sense of security then he would make his move. He heard Lakota shifting behind him. He couldn't let anything happen to her.

"I tried everything. Even sent a mediator to you. And look what happened? I have deals, obligations. If I don't deliver this fuel, they will kill me."

Reack's voice cracked on the word "kill". To Taban, this was a sure sign of his nervousness. If he could only reason with Reack, he might be able to get Lakota out.

"Okay, listen we can work this out—"

"No," Reack screamed and directed the blaster toward Taban's chest. The weapon swayed in Reack's trembling hands.

"This is the only way." Tears coursed down his friend's cheeks. God, is this what politics and greed had driven his people to? He wasn't close enough to get the gun. What would happen to Lakota if he fell? All of these thoughts went flying through his mind as he faced his executioner.

All of a sudden, a blur of black came flying through the cave entrance. Striker took Reack down in a flash of fur, teeth and growling, jostling the blaster right out of his hands. Four wolves followed Striker and they pounced on Reack. His screams were silenced when Striker sunk his teeth into Reack's jugular and shook him until he didn't move anymore. Taban rushed forward and grabbed the weapon as Lakota commanded Striker back. Taban handed her the weapon and knelt next to his friend. Reack gasped, blood gushing from the wound at his neck. Taban soothed his hair back from his brow. There was nothing he could do for him. Reack took one final breath, then stopped. Pain radiated through Taban's heart.

"I'm sorry, Taban." Lakota laid her hand on Taban's shoulder. He pressed his hand on hers, surprised to see it shaking.

Standing, he grabbed his pack and indicated for Lakota to follow him.

"Let's get out of here," he said as he left his former friend to the wolves; let him be buried by them.

Chapter Ten

"There will be no further negotiations on this treaty until a full investigation into Reack's dealings can be completed. This meeting is adjourned." Taban knocked his gavel on the table to dismiss the room. Everyone on the council rose and filed out.

Lakota, in her full warrior gear, stood to the side of the table. She looked fantastic, black leather from head to toe, her weapons strapped to her back, and thigh, various honor badges pinned to her jacket. He approached her.

"Solarian Wolf Warrior Lakota Blackson."

"Yes, sir."

She looked so serious, her expression closed.

"I will notify Solaria you will not be returning anytime soon. I have need of your services, indefinitely."

"Yes, sir." Then she smiled, the somber lines of her face softening. This was his Lakota, tender, and giving. God how he loved her. He tucked her black silky hair behind her ear and caressed her cheek.

"I love you, *Charma*," he whispered as he took her into his arms.

"I love you too, *Ohkiimaan*." She melted against him, her leather clad arms hanging onto his shoulders as he snuggled her body against his.

"Do you want to marry on Solaria?" He knew how important her people were to her.

"I would, I have someone there I want you to meet. He is a great man, the leader of our security forces, a person you long thought dead. Someone who should remain a legend to the Elnarians."

"Kabe." His heart pounded at the implications of what she said. He had known his mentor and the former leader of the rebellion hadn't fallen. He had felt it deep down.

"He will be very glad to see you." She ran her hands into his hair and rose onto her toes to kiss his cheek. He held her against him; her smell sent a shiver down his spine, his erection sprang to life. She was his woman, everything he would ever need in life was now in his arms.

"I will not tell anyone of this," he said.

"Thank you."

"No, *Charma*, thank you." He kissed her then, gave her the passion that lay in his heart. She tilted into his body, her arms wrapping fully around him. He took the kiss deeper, loving her with his mouth, she moaned. He pulled back and smiled.

"Is Striker okay?" Her wolf had saved their life, for this he would be eternally grateful.

"Yes. I told him to stay with the pack if he so desired, for now. He was actually having a really good time. Sort of strange, he's usually so disciplined in his job."

"Everyone needs time for recreation," he said as he unbuttoned her leather coat.

"Yes, I think you're right." She moaned when he covered her breasts with his hands.

"I have a bed here, you know, might be nice to see how that works for us."

"I'd like that."

He lifted her into his arms.

"I'm glad you decided to join my world, Lakota, and tried to tame me." He carried her down the hall to his chambers.

"So am I, Taban, so am I."

"There's a political ball tomorrow night. There will be dancing. Will you be my partner?" He let the suggestion in his voice speak for itself.

"Dancing, oh how can I refuse an offer like that?"

"Actually, you can't... as my future mate, you're expected to be there."

She kissed his cheek and smiled. "I will be there for you, *Ohkiimaan*, any time you need me."

"Now there's an offer that can't be refused."

About the Author:

Rae is a multi-published, award winning, sensual romance author and speaker. She is former Air Force, FBI Agent and now is a licensed Private Investigator as well has having Bachelor and Master Degrees in business. Rae loves to write strong female characters, lots of action, and hot romance. Please come explore her other books on her website, RaeMonet.com.

Flesh to Fantasy

by Larissa Ione

To My Reader:

Have you ever been so overwhelmed by life that you wanted to withdraw, to barricade yourself behind closed doors and never have to deal with life's complications again? I know I have, and Kelsa Bradshaw, the heroine in Flesh to Fantasy, has done exactly that. She lives in a safe, carefully-crafted world where nothing bad can happen—except to her computer-generated game characters. But, like anything, too much of a good thing isn't always best. It takes a hot paramedic who is as lonely as she is to pull her out of her fantasy world and into his very real one... where they can both live out their wildest dreams. I hope you enjoy Kelsa and Trent's story.

Chapter One

"Your neighbor is so hot, he could melt a glacier in January."

An involuntary shiver raced through Kelsa Bradshaw at her friend's breathy words. She wholeheartedly agreed. She stepped away from her apartment door to peer over the walkway rail at the object of Melanie's lust, Trent… something-or-other, as he fetched a backpack from the bed of his pickup in the parking lot one story below. Mmm, sin in a uniform.

Broad shoulders flexed beneath his white Portland, Oregon, paramedic shirt, which was tucked into the waistband of black fatigue-style pants that hugged his ass in a fit so perfect, her mouth dried up like desert sand. She could use a sip of the soft drink he'd set on his truck's roof.

"He can melt anything of mine anytime he wants," she sighed to Melanie.

When the "he" in question grabbed his drink and strode away from the vehicle, the summer sun glinted in his tousled blond hair. His eyes, which she knew to be blue, hid behind sunglasses that didn't diminish the intensity in his tanned, chiseled features. The man was a god. A god who just disappeared into the stairwell. Crap! Juggling her mail and gym bag, she fumbled around in her purse for the keys to her front door.

"What's wrong?"

"I don't want to talk to him." Kelsa grasped her keys but dropped a magazine on top of a milk crate-sized package the mailman had left at her door. "Mel, would you grab that?"

Melanie retrieved the box and magazine. "Why not talk to him? Now's the perfect time to introduce yourself. You know, drool over him to his face instead of behind his back. Not that his back isn't drool-worthy."

The key slid into the lock, but the tangle of key chain and purse and gym bag looped around her wrist made it impossible to turn the knob. "Perfect time? After sweating for two hours at the gym?"

Melanie shrugged. "Sure. Give him a preview of what you'll look like after two hours of sweating beneath him."

"Oh, you're a riot." Kelsa placed the bags at her feet and unlocked the door. Just as she reached for the purse and duffel, footsteps thudded on the walkway. Great. Hot Paramedic Guy was going to get an eyeful of bubble-butt squeezed into sweaty shorts.

Quickly, she straightened and offered a blinding smile. Better to present a smile than butt crack.

Too bad it wasn't the hottie. Well, good thing it wasn't the hottie, but bad thing it was the accountant with a serious lack of social skills who lived three doors down.

Apparently encouraged by her smile, he grinned and stopped, looking at her feet. "I like your shoes," he said. "May I touch them?"

"Um, not today, Steve. Thanks anyway."

He just stood there, the goofy grin still on his face. How did the guy function in the world? Not that she had any room to talk. She didn't operate in the real world either, and wasn't sure she'd want to even if her job didn't keep her indoors and inside a realm of virtual reality.

Melanie huffed. "You can go away now."

"Oh, okay." Steve shuffled off, and Kelsa glared at her friend.

"Really, Mel. Did you have to be so rude?" She twisted around to enter the apartment.

"You're too nice. That's how you get stalkers."

"You've got a stalker?" A deep voice rumbled behind them, and Kelsa knew before she looked that the voice belonged to Trent.

She knew because she'd heard him talking and laughing in the pool off her balcony. She knew because that voice had a way of whispering to her in her dreams.

Pulling in a breath, she turned, struggling to find words appropriate for speaking with someone she'd only fantasized about. And as her gaze swept from his generous mouth to his fingers that now held his sunglasses, and right on down his slim physique to the impressive bulge at the base of his pants' zipper, she knew instinctively that the orgasms those fantasies brought would pale in comparison to orgasms the real man could give her.

She dragged her gaze back up to his face, giving herself a mental kick in the butt for even thinking such a thing. Sex with Trent Something-Or-Other wasn't in her future. It couldn't be. "Uh... no. I don't have a stalker."

Trent smiled. Nice teeth. Very white. Very straight. Wouldn't those teeth feel good as they nibbled and nipped their way to —

"She doesn't have a stalker right this minute," Melanie chirped. "But, that guy down the hall is obsessed with her—"

"Shoes," Kelsa broke in. "Not with me. With my shoes."

Melanie rolled her eyes. "And that's better... how?" She leaned close to Trent and gave him a conspiratorial wink. "She needs someone to keep an eye on her. So maybe you could, you know, check in on her sometimes."

"Mel," she warned, but her friend merely grinned. The traitor.

"I'd be happy to," he said in a sin-with-me voice that turned her insides to mush. "Anything for a neighbor."

Kelsa smiled. "I appreciate that, but really, I can take care of myself. I don't even know you, and—"

He extended his hand. "Trent Jordan."

She grasped his hand with her empty one and tried to ignore the tingling prickles that skittered up her arm. "Kelsa Bradshaw."

"Now you know me." He held her hand in his firm grip, the pad of his thumb brushing over her knuckle in slow, sexy strokes. She doubted he realized what he was doing, but every erogenous zone of hers sat up and begged for the same attention. "I've been wanting you for weeks."

"Excuse me?" Had he just said he'd been wanting her? Selective hearing on her part, or Freudian slip on his?

"I said I've been wanting *to meet* you for weeks."

Was that fluttering sensation in her gut relief or disappointment? It had better be the former. With her luck, it was the latter. "Oh. Right. Well, I'm not around much."

He arched a tawny eyebrow. "I see you on your balcony almost every day."

Her heart skipped a beat. She hadn't thought he'd noticed her, even though she often worked outside with her laptop when she wanted to escape the confines of her apartment.

Or when she wanted to get a look at his sleek body covered by nothing but skimpy swim shorts.

"I'm not the only woman who sits on her balcony." Not when he was in the pool, anyway. Women flocked to their verandas like cats in heat when he came outside and strutted his stuff. And what nice stuff it was.

"No, but you're the only one I pay attention to."

Oh, my. A thrill of sexual awareness swept the length of her body at the honeyed drawl in his words. Then her brain kicked in and countered her raging hormones. She pulled her hand free of his grasp. "Surely you can come up with a better line than that?"

He flashed her a bad boy smile that said gobs about the lines he could come up with. "Yeah, I could, but it's no line. Your balcony is the only place I ever see you, so I gotta look when I can. You must work some crazy hours."

"My hours are very flexible." He raised an eyebrow, and she added, "I work out of my home playing video games. RPGs mostly. Gaming takes up a lot of my time, so I don't get out much."

"Obviously you do get outside sometimes," he said, raking his gaze over her grimy gym clothes.

Great. She'd made one hell of a first impression, what with her conversationally-challenged ramblings, sweat-drenched armpits, and crotch-gawking. Not that it mattered. She didn't need to make a good first impression. She wanted to admire Trent from afar, not up close and personal. She didn't *do* up close and personal. Not ever.

Trent shifted his weight in his rugged black military boots, and suddenly "not ever" took a dive right over the iron railing because he *was* up close, so close his salty-clean masculine scent wrapped around her, and her body reacted in ways that were *very* personal.

Her skin itched, too tight for her body. Her nipples tickled and her lungs struggled for every shallow breath. And when he cocked his head to watch her with eyes that seemed to see inside her, sweat dampened her skin. A strange whirring noise joined the thumping of her heart in her ears, and damn if she didn't grow lightheaded.

She glanced at her door that was wide open and letting out the air-conditioned coolness into the summer heat. The door was more than a barrier against intruders; it was a barrier against the real world, which seemed to close in the longer she stood under Trent's intense gaze. Time to go.

"Nice meeting you, neighbor."

With that, she fled into the apartment, Melanie on her heels.

"Shut the door," she called back to her friend as she darted into the kitchen and tossed her bag and purse to the floor.

Melanie slammed the door and followed. "What was that all about?" She dropped the box and magazine on the dining room table.

"I was going to have a panic attack."

"You've never had a panic attack."

"It was going to be my first," Kelsa said with a sniff.

Melanie sighed. "You're such a wuss. You're going to die alone if you don't learn to meet real guys, not virtual weirdos. That last guy, he thought he was a hobbit or something, right?"

"Half-orc. His character was a half-orc."

"What?"

"Nothing."

Melanie muttered something under her breath that sounded suspiciously like "geeks" and grabbed a pair of scissors out of the basket of crap on the table. "Can I open the box?" she asked, already wedging a pointed scissors edge under a flap.

Kelsa shrugged and searched the fridge for a bottle of water. "It's from Grandma Sally. Her newest jams and jellies for the B and B."

"Ooh, her quince jelly is to die for. She sent me some last week and it's almost gone."

Not a shock. Her friend ate the stuff right out of the jar and had been for the twelve years they'd been best buds, ever since Mel's family had moved next to Kelsa's grandma's bed and breakfast when both girls were thirteen.

A loud thump from next door reverberated through the room. Trent on his Nautilus set. She'd seen it when he moved in, and she'd grown used to the rhythmic sound of his workouts. She could picture him working with the weights, bare-chested, sweat glistening on skin that stretched taut over rippling muscles. Mmm. Talk about to die for.

Those were the fantasies she clung to, held in her mind, which was the only place Trent Jordan belonged. He needed to stay there, trapped in her head because as beautiful as he was, she couldn't deal with the real man. Reality was not something she did well.

"Um, Kels?"

"Um, Mel?" Damn, she was out of water. But the two watermelon wine coolers behind the piles of fruit and vegetables and tofu looked pretty tasty, even if they weren't the ideal after-workout drinks. She yanked them from the fridge, mouth watering.

"I know you haven't been getting any lately, but is there something you'd like to tell me?"

Kelsa twisted the top off both bottles and tossed them in the garbage. "Why?"

"These aren't jams and jellies."

She turned around and nearly dropped the drinks. The box Melanie had just opened most assuredly did not contain jars of quince jelly. Instead, it was filled with an interesting collection of sex toys and packs of batteries. She rushed to the table and put down the wine coolers, one in front of her friend.

"Those are so not mine."

"Suuuuure." Melanie lifted a rabbit-shaped vibrator from the box. "I've heard this one is like, uber-amazing." She slid a sly glance at Kelsa. "You'll have to let me know."

"They aren't mine," Kelsa ground out as she spun the box around to get a look at the address on the flap. *Oh, crap.* "Mel, you aren't going to believe this."

Melanie looked up from digging through the box like a kid on

Christmas morning. "What?"

"They're Trent's."

The other woman's mouth fell open. "Seriously? Oh, girlfriend, you need to get to *know* this guy."

It was Kelsa's turn to gape. "You're kidding, right? Why would any guy order this stuff? He's a freak!"

"Says the woman who screwed a hobbit." Melanie smiled wickedly. "You'd better take the box to him."

"I don't think so." She pushed the box toward Melanie. "You're the one who's fascinated by him. You do it."

Making a big production of looking at her watch, Melanie tsked and shook her head. "I would, but I'm in a hurry. I'll get my blender from you another time. Gotta go feed my dog. Later!" She swept out of the apartment without so much as a glance back.

"You don't have a dog!" Kelsa shouted, but Mel slammed the door.

Crap. She looked at the box of toys, and heat seared her cheeks. She couldn't possibly face Trent with this. Talk about awkward. *Hey, neighbor. Thought you might be wondering what happened to your butt plugs. Need to borrow some lube? Oh, wait, they're fifteen different kinds in the box. Have fun.*

Ugh. She did *not* need this. She had enough to deal with now that the gaming company she worked for, Dream sOFT, had begun to shift its focus from fantasy role-playing games to reality-based, real-time strategy games. She'd tested a couple of the new products, without enthusiasm, and her lack of excitement had shown in her work. Her employer had demanded better performance from her or they'd cut her loose, but she wasn't sure she could comply. War games and graphic first-person shooters made her uncomfortable, and at times, physically ill.

There was a reason she didn't watch TV or read newspapers. Thanks to a childhood spent isolated from normal civilization, the big, bad world beyond her peaceful suburban neighborhood scared the bejeezus out of her. Or it would if she allowed herself to think about it, which she didn't.

She did, however, think about her neighbor. Melanie was right; she was a wuss. She could handle leaving a simple box on the doorstep.

Except what the box contained was far from simple.

No, the contents of the plain brown package excited and disgusted her. Made her think things she'd never considered, even though she was far from a virgin and enjoyed sex as much as the next girl.

Made the man who'd ordered them more thrilling in real life than he'd ever been in her fantasies.

Damn, but she was in trouble. And this time, no amount of experience points, twentieth-level wizard potions, or enchanted broadswords were going to get her out of it.

Chapter Two

The damn fan was broken. As if finally meeting Kelsa hadn't made Trent hot enough, working out without a fan had nearly sent him into heat stroke. Time for a dip in the pool.

Hopefully, he'd catch a glimpse of Kelsa sunning herself on her balcony above the deep end. He loved how she chewed her lip while she worked, how she sometimes threw her head back and smiled at the sun, loved how different she was from the slinky blondes of his past.

He'd been determined to make changes in his life, and as far as he was concerned, lusting after a short brunette with a little meat on her bones and breasts that weren't altered by a surgeon's scalpel was a damn good start. Correction, end. He'd made the biggest changes already. Now he just needed a woman with whom to share them.

Not that Kelsa seemed inclined to want to be that woman. She'd been polite—at least, until she'd run off like a scared rabbit—but she hadn't been flirtatious or even overly friendly. Still, he'd been around the block, and he recognized the signs of attraction: flushed skin, rapid pulse and respirations, dilated pupils... Oh, yeah, she'd had 'em all, and then some.

Quickly, he changed into swim trunks, grabbed his towel, opened the front door, and came face to... crotch with the very woman he'd hoped to see as she bent to place a box on his doorstep. She froze, the widening of her brown eyes her only movement. He didn't think she even breathed.

"Hi," he said, fighting a smile as she gulped, glanced at his crotch—she did that a lot, to his amusement—and then straightened, still clutching the box. She'd changed into khaki shorts and a black tank top that outlined the distinct curves of her free-range braless breasts, and judging by the damp strands of her dark shoulder-length hair, she'd showered as well.

"The mailman delivered this to my door by accident." She held the package out to him, but he didn't reach for it. She'd taken off so quickly earlier that he wanted to drag this meeting out. "I opened it. I'm sorry. I thought it was mine. It wasn't. I wouldn't order... not that you would..." She snapped her mouth shut and rolled her eyes. "Just, here."

Her nervousness was as adorable now as it had been on the walkway, but this time, he wouldn't let her get away so easily. She was far too fascinating, this woman who rarely emerged from her apartment and who nobody in the complex knew as anything other than "Hermit Chick."

He stepped aside with a gesture. "Come on in. I don't remember ordering anything, but you can put the box on the coffee table."

"You can't just take it?"

"My hands are full."

"You're holding a towel."

He shrugged. "It's a big towel."

With a dramatic huff, she stalked inside. "You must have ordered this. It's got your name and address on it. Not mine."

She placed the box on the table, giving him a mouthwatering view of her luscious ass as she bent over. She straightened and turned, and her knee struck the box, knocking it to the floor. Small colorful packages spilled out onto the carpet.

She let out a strangled squeak, her exotically almond-shaped eyes flared wide.

"It's okay," he said, walking toward the mess. "It's just a box of—" he picked up a small package of ben-wa balls. Holy shit. "—sex toys."

He must look like a sex fiend. He held the silver balls out to her. "These aren't mine."

Her skeptical gaze bounced from his face to the package and back. "I'm sure they aren't."

He chuckled. "Seriously. What would *I* do with ben-wa balls?"

"I don't want to know," she said, shaking her head but squatting down to help him pick up the dozens of items that had scattered around his living room.

"What did you plan to do with these?" she asked, holding up some jeweled items that looked like medieval torture devices.

"I don't even know what they are."

She flipped the package over, making the little gold dangly things jiggle. A harsh intake of breath whistled through her teeth. "Clit clamps. Ow." Her eyes narrowed to slits as she aimed a glare at him. "Perv."

"You say that like it's a bad thing."

He shot her a wink and inserted a couple of batteries into a vibrator-shaped thing with a tongue on the end. The tongue came to life and lapped at the air. Holding her gaze, he slowly reached out and rested the device against her ankle, just above the leather strap of her sandal.

She went rigid, her lips pressed into a tight bow and her eyes glued to the vibrating tongue as he moved it slowly up the gentle curve of her calf. It tasted her smooth, tan skin, and he gnashed his teeth in jealousy that a damn toy was tonguing her there and not him. A small squeaky noise escaped her mouth, which no doubt could make a man beg, and then she let out a ragged breath that seemed to release the tension in her body. Tilting her face up at him, she gave him a deceptively sweet smile.

"Two can play that game," she said, sounding as breathless as she did teasing. "Shall we see what we can do with this?"

She lunged at him with a butt plug. A freaking *butt plug*. He rocked back, feeling instantly foolish since it wasn't as though she was actually going to do anything with the thing—no way in hell—but he flinched nevertheless, losing his balance and landing flat on his back next to his beat-up recliner.

"Oof."

She laughed, and the rich, throaty sound shot straight to his groin. Then his entire body clenched when she leaned over him, her laughter vibrating her body and his thigh where their bodies touched. He gently grasped her wrist to keep the black rubber toy out of his face where she dangled it. Her smart-ass smirk told him she didn't realize exactly how precarious a position she was in, so he showed her with a light tug that pulled her on top of him.

Her small breasts crushed against his chest and her thigh rested between his, cradling his hardening erection. He hadn't been in this kind of position in a very long time, and if her reaction—smile fading and throat working as though swallowing a large, stubborn lump—was any indication, neither had she.

Damn, but he wanted to kiss that slender neck, right there where her pulse drummed beneath delicate, smooth skin. Her clean, co-conut scent drifted to him, making his own pulse leap and brought to mind images of tropical beaches and fruity drinks and hot sex in the sand.

"Now this," he said softly, "is what I've wanted since the first time I saw you on your balcony above the pool."

"You wanted to lick me with a sex toy?"

"Yeah, I—what?"

"My thigh."

He realized he still held the battery-operated tongue, which was doing obscene things to her leg. It'd be funny if it weren't so sad that a toy was getting more action than he was.

"Oh, I want to lick you," he breathed, shocked at just how intensely he desired to do that very thing, "but with my own tongue."

Beneath her shirt, her nipples pebbled, burning his bare skin. Her breathing became unsteady. Her lips parted for her tongue that flicked over them, nearly wringing a groan from him. She was as hot for him as he was for her.

Her eyes, however, flickering with hesitation behind the lust, told another story. Physically, she was there. Mentally, though… Not will-ing to lose her, he dropped the tongue-toy and drew his hand up her back to the nape of her neck. She closed her eyes, digging into his biceps with tense fingers. Her other hand, the one he held firmly in his grip, dropped the butt plug.

Slowly, he wound his fingers through her damp, silky hair and held her head while he arched his neck and brought his lips to rest against hers.

Her firm, unyielding mouth struck a helluva blow to his ego. She hadn't run away screaming yet, but neither had flung herself into the kiss.

He flicked his tongue along the seam of her lips, wondering if she'd react more favorably to that stupid tongue toy, but then she relaxed against him, her lips softening, opening up. With a groan, he sank deeply into her mouth, driving his tongue against hers. She tasted sweet, like watermelon and wine, and he wanted to drink her in until he was intoxicated.

Her free hand moved up his side, over bare skin that quivered with each stroke. She caressed his ribs, tracing the intercostal spaces between that he'd never thought were sensitive, but now tingled and contracted even as his heart banged almost painfully against them. She shifted the leg that pinned down his hard cock, and he stifled a moan. No way could she miss the bump under her thigh, not when the only barrier between them was a paper-thin layer of swimsuit fabric.

He trailed kisses along the edge of her jaw and down, to the soft skin in the hollow of her neck. "You feel good, Kelsa. Finally, after all the daydreaming, you're right here in my hands."

"Daydreaming," she echoed, her throat humming against his lips. Then her hand stopped its glorious exploration of his chest. "You daydreamed about me?"

Releasing her wrist, he brushed her hair away from her face so he could look into her eyes as he pressed his erection into the soft flesh of her inner thigh, where he found both relief and an intense ache as he pulsed against her.

"Every waking hour. The real woman is better. Scorching. Wicked sexy."

He smoothed his fingers down a chestnut strand of hair and toyed with the end, but she shook her head and pushed to her hands and knees. "No."

"Yes." He sat up and reached for her, but she scrambled to her feet.

"I don't do real." She spun toward the door. "I have to go."

Why did she keep doing that? Frowning, he jumped to his feet and grabbed her elbow as she reached for the door knob. "I want to see you again."

Her expression softened, her eyes conveying regret. "It'll ruin the fantasy."

"The fantasy of what? How sex between us would be? You've fantasized about that too?" A tinge of red streaked along her softly sculpted cheekbones, and she nodded.

He pulled her closer and traced her lips with his thumb, and his gut did a slow, pleasant roll when she closed her eyes and moaned. "The reality will be better than the fantasy," he promised, his voice sounding rough and strange to his own ears, and he realized how long it had been since he'd been with a woman, how rusty he was at this.

Thick, dark lashes flew up, revealing eyes that glittered with panic. "That's the problem." She jerked away and darted outside, slamming the door behind her.

The noise echoed through his apartment, an audible reminder that he was alone, mentally and physically. He jammed his fingers through his hair and wondered how to bring himself down from the high he was on after the steamy encounter with Kelsa. His body still hummed with unquenched desire, his muscles still pulled taut with lust, and the toys scattered about the room only made it worse.

Turning, he stepped on the butt plug and swore. Only one person could possibly have ordered the toys. He dug his cell phone out of his work pants' pocket and dialed.

Adrienne answered her hotel room phone on the first ring.

"Yo, sis."

"Trent! Are you coming tonight? You never RSVP'd."

"That's because I don't want to attend a rehearsal dinner with people I don't even know."

"You know both me and the bride."

Yeah, he knew the bride. Becky had been his sister's best friend all through high school and college, and now that Becky was getting married to some accountant she'd met in Portland, Adrienne had come to town as the maid of honor.

"Fine. I'll be there." He ran a hand over his face, wondering if his five o'clock shadow had scratched Kelsa's supple skin. "By chance, did you order enough sex toys to supply a brothel and have them shipped to my apartment?"

"You got the package! Thank God! I was just getting ready to call you. I was getting desperate."

He glanced at the dozens of packages dotting his living room carpet. "Apparently."

"They aren't for me, silly. They're for the bachelorette party. I'll drop by and pick them up in a few minutes."

"Hurry. Some of them scare me."

He hung up and returned the toys to the box. Some really were disconcerting—a Deep and Dirty *Invader?*—but others looked like they could be a lot of fun with someone like Kelsa. Now he needed to devise a way to convince her of the same. He had to figure out what made her tick.

The first time she'd run, when they'd been out on the walkway, she'd gotten squirrelly after he said he'd noticed her. Just a few minutes ago, things had been going well until they'd started talking about fantasies. So she apparently liked fantasies, but not the real thing. Why?

There was only one way to find out. He'd have to get to know her better, something he'd wanted since he'd moved in eight months ago and had seen her on her balcony wearing a skimpy swimsuit while smoothing suntan lotion on her skin. Unfortunately, he'd never had a chance to meet her because his crazy rotating shifts and her reclusive nature had kept them from coming face-to-face.

Until today.

And he'd never been one to shy away from an opportunity that presented itself. Not when he'd spent the last few months alone in a new city and on a new job. He was sick of being alone.

How screwed up was that, given that he'd left Los Angeles in order to *be* alone? At twenty-eight, he'd grown tired of the partying and hangovers and one-night stands that rendered him unable to perform his job properly. One huge scare, one *huge* near-tragedy, had been enough to make him see the need for a life-altering change.

So he'd moved away from the bad influence of the friends he'd grown up with, away from the wealthy family who had coddled and protected him from the consequences of his own actions for far too long, and he'd put down roots in a town where no one knew him and where working as a paramedic instead of a lawyer like his father was a real job and not a rebellious statement.

Thing was, he was happy, crazy as that seemed. Happy, except for the gaping hole in his life; a relationship. For once, he wanted something real, something tangible, something challenging.

He wanted Kelsa.

Chapter Three

The knock on Kelsa's front door came exactly twenty-four hours to the minute after she'd fled Trent's apartment. No one ever knocked on her door. Her only friend, Melanie, simply walked inside, and the FedEx guy rang the doorbell when he brought her computer software.

So she had a pretty good idea who stood on the other side of the door.

Trent.

The one person she didn't want to see but whose image she conjured in her mind every thirty seconds. She kept replaying what had happened yesterday in his apartment, the kissing, the touching, the way she'd felt while she sprawled on top of him, her inner thigh rubbing against the thick length of his erection.

Even now, her breasts flushed with heat, and dampness bloomed between her thighs when she thought about him replacing the strokes made by the tongue-vibrator with that of his own tongue. His tongue that had pleasured her in so many ways in her fantasies, the tongue that could never pleasure her for real.

Hand shaking with both dread and anticipation, she opened the door, and her heart did a flip-flop when she saw Trent standing there in faded Levi's and a white T-shirt that did nothing to hide the sculpted muscles beneath.

She'd admired men before, but this particular man, well, he "stirred her innards", as her grandma would say. Her ability to judge height and weight sucked, but she knew he was six-foot-something and wasn't so thin he'd blow away in a strong gale, but wasn't so heavy he'd crush the lucky woman who got to bear his weight between the sheets.

No doubt about it, Trent Jordan had gone through the line twice the day God had handed out sex appeal.

Say something not stupid. "I didn't know you were coming by." That didn't qualify as not stupid, but it was better than standing there with her tongue hanging out.

"That's the beauty of not calling ahead." He grinned. "Not that I have your phone number."

"There's a reason for that," she sighed, wishing she were immune to his charm, but holding the door wider and gesturing for him to come inside. "Can I offer you a wine cooler?"

He stepped over the threshold and moved inside. "Thanks, but I don't drink."

"You entertain yourself in other ways, then?" She waggled her brows. "Did you have fun with your toys after I left yesterday?"

"Sadly, no. My sister picked them up for a bachelorette party."

"Likely story."

Laughing, he cast a glance around the living room at her three pieces of furniture; two bean bag chairs and a coffee table. Instead of commenting on her lack of furnishings and television, he swung back around to her. "Why did you leave so suddenly?"

"Not one for beating around bush, are you?"

"I like directness. I like *real*."

His smile faded, replaced by an intense expression she'd expect to see when he was on the job. Or working out. Or making love. She gave herself a mental slap. She didn't need the latter image bouncing around in her head right now.

He studied her for a moment, and then took two long strides toward her, driving her backward until her spine smacked up against the wall. "Which is exactly what you hate, isn't it?"

"What makes you say that?" she asked, making an effort not to squirm and failing.

"Your job. Your lifestyle. The fact that it's okay to fantasize about us having sex, but the moment it looks like it might happen, you freak."

She clenched her fists until her stubby nails—kept short so as not to interfere with gameplay on the computer keyboard—dug painfully into her palms. "You have no idea what you're talking about."

She brushed past him, ignoring the heated energy the contact had sparked, and headed for the kitchen. For what reason, she had no idea. She only knew she had to get away from him and his accusations that hit too close to home.

Apparently, the man had no concept of "needing space," because he followed her, his heavy footsteps spurring her past the kitchen to the personal safety net of her office. She stepped inside the converted second bedroom, the dark space lit by the green glow of her thirty-inch plasma-screen computer monitor and the neon red of the three-foot tall lava lamp in one corner.

She flicked on the stereo and found instant calm in the Celtic melodies preprogrammed to start.

"Jesus." Trent stood in the doorway wearing a stunned expression she doubted people often saw. "This is unbelievable."

She shrugged. "I like it."

"You have bean bag chairs in the living room, but you have this—" he spun the desk chair around "—in here? It looks like something from NASA." He frowned. "Or a mad scientist's torture chamber."

"It's a gaming chair. I'm testing it for the manufacturer." She pointed to the speakers on either side of the head rest and the one beneath the seat. "It connects to the computer to provide vibration and surround-sound." She knew her enthusiasm made her sound like a giddy child, but so what? This was her realm.

"And see here?" She flipped a board up from the right arm rest. "I can put a flightstick and throttle here, and then when I attach the foot pedals, I can settle in for flight simulators that feel real. The chair vibrates and shudders with every explosion, every impact. It's awesome."

She gestured to the steering wheel on a shelf near the window. "Or I can play racing games. It's like being in a real car."

Not that she knew what driving a car was like since she'd never learned. No need. No desire. Besides, if she wanted to go anywhere that took her out of walking distance, she had Melanie, her faithful friend without whom Kelsa would never have learned about the birds and the bees, pop music, or romance novels.

Heck, if not for Melanie's encouragement, she'd probably still be a virgin living in her grandma's attic and preparing meals for guests.

Shaking his head, Trent ran a finger over her state-of-the-art CPU. "This stuff must cost a fortune. No wonder you don't have any other furniture."

She snorted. "I don't have other furniture because I spend all of my time in here. Most of this was free. Companies send me their products to try out and review for *Gamer Chick* magazine."

"I thought you tested games."

"I do. My employer makes games and I play them, find the bugs, and report them. On the side I review products."

"You like being locked up all alone staring at a computer screen. Honestly?"

"I love it. I can sit in here for days on end just playing games. Who wouldn't love that?"

Trent said nothing, but she got the impression he wouldn't love that. He glanced around the room at the stacks of jewel cases in her bookshelves and at the game posters that covered every inch of wall and ceiling space.

"A few months back I answered a call to an upscale apartment for an unknown malady. Turned out the patient was some sort of gamer geek. He'd been playing a sword-and-sorcery thing for days. Didn't eat. Snorted cocaine to stay awake." He turned to look her in the eye. "He was hyper, suffering from dysrhythmia, dyspnea, and hallucinations. The guy thought we were warlocks. Kept telling us he was immune to our spells. He beaned my partner with a beer bottle, said it was a potion of acid."

"That's awful," she said. "Acid potions are green, not brown. Duh."

His hard stare looked more than a little concerned.

Shaking her head, she pushed her chair back into place beneath the desk. "I'm kidding. The guy was clearly a nut. I don't do drugs, and I do get sleep sometimes."

"What else do you do?"

She rolled her eyes at the interrogative edge to his question. "I work out. You saw me yesterday in my workout finery." He'd probably smelled her, too. "And I shop." So what if the gym and grocery store were both within two blocks of her apartment?

"Do you go out with friends? Do you go to movies? Go on dates?"

Her hackles rose. None of this was any of his business, and his questions had become a little too personal. "I don't have time."

"No," he said, his voice gentle yet undeniably sure. "You're afraid." He came closer, so close she could smell his woodsy aftershave, and she couldn't deny his accusation. "Of what?"

It occurred to her that she should flee right now. Just bolt out of the room, out of the apartment, but her feet wouldn't obey her brain when he reached out to caress her cheek. Heat curled through her insides, and oh, she wanted to spill all her fears. Wanted to confide in him like she'd never confided to anyone but her brother who had grown up like she had, victims of their parents' cult-religious beliefs and lifestyle that had removed them from the rest of the world. Even Melanie didn't know everything.

"I can't," she whispered, because she didn't know Trent well enough to tell him diddly squat, and she didn't want to know him in any more intimate ways than she already did.

He dipped his head a fraction of an inch and hesitated, letting the air between them crackle with electric undercurrents, and then he brushed his firm lips over hers. "Tell me."

The echoes of his voice, deep and soothing, shimmered over the suddenly sensitized skin of her lips, and then spread over her entire body until fevered goosebumps pimpled every inch of her flesh. Her breasts ached, her nipples puckered, and she grasped his arms, pulling him against them even though she should be pushing him away.

The computer monitor's screen went black, but red light from the lava lamp bathed the room in a soft glow that created rippling effects in the posters, bringing them to life. The wizards and knights fought to the melody of Celtic harps. Dragons and orcs snarled to the whistle of Irish flutes.

Trent's hard body crushed to hers, a wonderful but too real experience in the room she'd designed to transport her into a virtual realm of fantasy that kept her sane.

Panic wrapped around her, squeezing the breath from her lungs, and she shoved against the solid muscles of his chest and fled into the hall, where she sagged against the wall and sucked in huge gulps of air.

Trent joined her, his brow furrowed. "Kelsa?"

"Don't."

He shoved his fingers through his hair, leaving behind adorably unruly tufts. "Listen to me. There's something between us. I can feel it, and I know you can, too."

Oh, she could feel it all right. In every organ, every bone, every cell—including those that should be functioning in her brain, telling her to give him the boot, but good. "You don't understand. You can't."

"Try me."

She met his gaze, and for a moment, all she could think about were his gorgeous eyes. Magnetic, warm, patient as he waited for her to speak. Too bad it wouldn't happen. She couldn't answer his questions because then he'd know her too well and things could get too serious. No way she'd let that happen. Her world was games and toys and make-believe. To step into his world would shatter the one she'd so carefully created.

Even now, as he propped a shoulder against the doorframe of her game room and watched her, his very presence threatened to transform her environment. The power of her fantastical surroundings couldn't match up to the force of Trent's masculine, physical presence. Her room, her pride and joy, looked small, insubstantial.

Different.

She pushed away from the wall. "Come into the living room."

"Away from your game room."

Bingo. "No. I just want to be comfortable."

"Because bean bags are so relaxing."

"That, Mr. Smartass, depends on how you're using them." She hadn't meant her remark to sound sexual, but when heat flickered in his eyes, she knew she'd found a way to get him away from her precious game room.

"I can think of several practical applications for bean bag chairs," he suggested.

"So can I."

He laughed and followed her down the hallway. "Now I *know* you're trying to distract me."

"Oh? Why's that?"

"Because you've been fighting my advances with everything you've got, but suddenly you're flirting."

She stopped in the living room and turned to face him again. "I'm not fighting." Not fighting him anyway. Her struggle was with herself and her own desires.

He took her hand, pulled her to him in an embrace that felt better than anything she'd ever experienced—and which frightened her beyond belief. "You are, and you know this thing between us won't go away."

"It might." And dragons might fly out of her butt.

Chuckling, he stepped back. "Silly woman. Go to dinner with me."

"Sorry. I don't date."

"Ever?"

"Ever."

Why did he have to look at her like that, like she was a puzzle to solve? Probably because she felt like a thousand-piece jigsaw puzzle with more than a few pieces missing.

"So we're doomed to fantasizing about each other? Doesn't that seem like a waste?"

"Only if you aren't fantasizing properly."

"Oh," he murmured in a dark, seductive voice that made her breath catch, "I assure you, there's nothing proper about what we do in my fantasies."

The air in the room thinned and electrified. Her scalp tingled, her lungs couldn't take in enough oxygen. She couldn't speak for fear the only words that would come out would be, "Show me."

He reached out, touched her chin with his finger, and tipped her face up to his. "Be with me. On your terms. I'll take you any way I can get you."

She melted, flattered and tempted. In the past, she'd been with men for a mutually satisfying good time that didn't involve any kind of relationship, but she wasn't sure she could do that with Trent. She was already too attracted to him to allow for complete detachment. Plus, he lived next door. She wouldn't be able to go anywhere without seeing him or something that reminded her of him.

Heck, even the pale blue sky would forever remind her of his eyes, eyes that welcomed her like she'd come home. Which was odd, since she'd never really had a home to call her own and had no idea how it felt to be welcomed into one.

She and her brother, Michael, had lived the life of nomads in a cult that raised the children as a unit. She'd known who her mother was, even if she hadn't lived with her, but her father could have been any of the members. The day Michael turned eighteen, he'd stolen Kelsa away from the compound in the Utah wilderness and had tracked down their maternal grandmother, who had taken them in and had given them as normal a life as possible.

Still, Grandma Sally's bed and breakfast hadn't felt like home. More like the hotel it was.

"Kelsa? Are you going to answer?"

"I can't do what you're asking."

He used the edge of his finger to draw a line from the tip of her nose, over her lips, down her chin, her throat, and then lower, to the scoop neckline of her fitted tee. Her skin prickled beneath his fingertip, and some traitorous part of her hoped for his touch to continue beneath the fabric.

"You're a challenge, lady. I never back down from a challenge." His expression one of savage determination, he spun on his heel and stalked out, leaving her trembling with desire and dread. This man was going to rock her world whether or not she wanted it. Somehow, she had to go on the offensive and take the upper hand before she lost everything. But how?

Chapter Four

Four days. It had been four days since she'd seen Trent. Four days of strange mail deliveries, all the while wondering just what the sexy paramedic was up to.

Kelsa plopped down in a bean bag chair and opened the latest package that had been over-nighted to her. On her coffee table, the three previous days' gifts were lined up in order of size.

A jar of chocolate body paint. A box of flavored condoms. A battery-operated tongue that gave her palpitations every time she looked at it and thought about the way Trent had used a similar one on her. She tore into the newest box, smiling in spite of herself. Edible underwear.

She gave the box a sniff. Cherry. How shocking.

She tossed the box onto the coffee table with the other toys and fell back into the soft, squeaky bean bag, smiling like a fool. Trent hadn't shown his face for days, but she knew he was behind the gifts.

What was he thinking? That she'd change her mind about sleeping with him just because he'd sent her toys they could share? Toys with which they could satisfy their cravings for each other in fun, creative—

Oh. My. God. That was it. The toys were for play. Play was fantasy. He was giving her a way to enjoy sex without realism. He'd also given her the opening she needed to take the upper hand.

Temptation beckoned. Ever since her last encounter with Trent, she'd been stewing in a heated pool of desire, and she was ready to explode. Even her skin felt stretched and tight, as though on the very brink of cracking under the pressure of the sexual frustration that filled her.

She took a deep, steadying breath. It was time to play.

"Okay, here's the thing." Kelsa stepped through Trent's doorway and shut the door behind her.

"Hello to you, too," he said, jazzed by the unexpected visit after a day that had gone so badly at work. He hated losing patients, hated the feeling of helplessness that went along with it.

A soft pink blush that matched the color of her tank top crept into her cheeks. "Sorry. I sometimes forget manners. Hazard of working alone."

"It's okay. You're sexy when you're rude." Hell, she was sexy anytime, but especially when she was agitated. Her chin jutted out stubbornly, color rose in her face, and her breasts lifted, the nipples clearly outlined beneath the fitted tops she favored.

She rolled her eyes and propped a fist on her hip. A fist holding the box of flavored condoms he'd sent her. Hopefully she'd come to use them and not throw them at him.

"Anyway, as I was saying." She held up the condoms. "Let's fuck."

He nearly choked on his own larynx. "What?" People rarely surprised him anymore—he'd seen a lot in his years as a paramedic—but she had him wondering if he'd stepped into the Twilight Zone.

She brushed past him and tossed the box on the couch before turning to face him. Now that his initial shock had passed, he noticed her flushed cheeks. She wasn't used to being so forward or speaking so boldly.

"Fuck. You know, your penis in my—"

"I know what it is. I'm just surprised."

"Why?" She bit her bottom lip, her expression pensive. "You sent me the... gifts, for a reason."

"Yeah, but I still figured that us getting horizontal was a long shot." He made a mental note to thank his sister for the idea of sending fantasy materials to Kelsa.

"Right. Well, that's what I came to tell you." She looked down for a moment as if gathering her guts to say whatever was coming next.

When she looked up, the steely resolve in her eyes hit him with the force of a shock from a defibrillator.

"You said yourself we both want it, so there's no point in denying ourselves." She cast an appreciative gaze at his bare chest and then cleared her throat. "Here's the thing. We're going to have sex. We're certainly not going to make love. We're going to get sweaty and physical and then part ways without any deep conversation and emotion. Got it?" She lifted her chin and locked her heated gaze with his. "We're going to fuck."

Got it? Oh, yeah. No woman had ever spoken to him like that, and hell if it wasn't a major turn-on. He was aching and hard already.

She stood there waiting, her expression a mixture of hope and lust and fear, as if there was any doubt about what his answer would be. Heart pounding, he crossed to her, grasped her shoulders, and crushed his lips to hers. Her lush curves form-fitted to his body as if she were made for him and only him, and he flexed his fingers, savoring the feel of her firm flesh and smooth skin. She hummed her approval into his mouth and slipped her arms around his back.

"Those are words men dream of hearing," he murmured against her lips. Damn straight. What man didn't long to hear a woman tell him she wanted to slap skin but not engage in mushy conversation? Hell, he'd prayed for such a thing all his life.

So why was he not as thrilled as he should be? Sure, he was turned on, but was that enough?

He'd wanted his daily deliveries to wear her down, bring her to him, but he hadn't expected the demand for a purely physical relationship. He'd hoped for more than fantasy, that she'd allow even a small amount of emotion to play a part of what they did. He'd had enough of wild rides with no commitment. He'd grown tired of women who wanted him for his money or lifestyle or family connections. Still, only an idiot would turn down Kelsa's offer, and he wasn't an idiot.

Her hand dropped to his ass and squeezed as her hips ground against his erection, and he decided that yep, exchanging bodily fluids but not conversation was enough.

For a price.

Kelsa's body screamed with need even as her head screamed that this was a mistake no matter how agreeable Trent seemed at keeping their relationship all about fantasy. How strange that in her daydreams she longed for the real thing, but now that she had it, she tried to pretend it wasn't real, that the fantasy—Trent and not the living, breathing man was responsible for the sensations streaming through her body.

"Don't think," he said into her ear, and before she could ponder how he even knew she *was* thinking, he nipped her lobe and then laved it with his tongue, soothing the skin and effectively squashing the voice that told her to stop this insanity. "Just feel."

Oh, was she ever feeling. She was feeling fire burn her up. She was feeling her lungs ache with a held breath. She was feeling a low, throbbing pulse between her legs as he widened his stance and pressed his erection into the swell of her belly through his denim shorts.

His lips kissed a path down her throat to where his fingers massaged the bare skin of her shoulders. She barely resisted the impulse to tear off her clothes so he could massage the bare skin of her everything.

"I want to feel." She dropped one hand low, to the back of his thigh, and dragged her short nails up very slowly. "More."

He made a sound deep in his chest and drew back, and the intensity of his gaze threw her off balance. In her fantasies, he burned for her, but not like this. Not like a man who might die if he didn't take his woman that very moment.

His woman. For a moment she savored the thought, knowing that belonging to him would mean she'd never be lonely again.

"Kelsa," he whispered, and she tore her gaze away, shoving those rogue thoughts back into the dark recesses where they belonged.

Looking into his eyes was a mistake she wouldn't make again. The eyes gave too much away, and if she wanted to keep reality at bay, she had to keep from seeing into his soul.

He broke away from her to grab the box of condoms, giving her what should have been a moment to catch her breath, but instead did the opposite when she couldn't help but watch his sleek, strong body in motion.

Taking her hand, he led her to his bedroom, where the soft glimmer of the pool-area lights through his open window cast just enough illumination in the evening darkness to allow her to see the bed—all twisted sheets and no blankets—and a tall dresser piled high with clothes.

After tossing the condoms on a pillow, he turned to her, the ropey muscles of his bare upper body sharply defined in the dappled light and shadow. "Strip."

"How romantic," she commented wryly, already lifting the tank top over her head. Her naked breasts pulled tight, and her nipples beaded as the cool air-conditioned breeze blew over them.

A low growl rumbled in his chest as he took in the sight of her bare breasts, and then he dropped to his knees in front of her to nuzzle the sensitive flesh of her belly. "You don't want romance, remember?"

Tension coiled inside as he kissed her stomach, swirling his tongue through her navel. "I remember," she murmured, heat blossoming in her cheeks at the memory of how she told him what she wanted.

Hooking his fingers on the waistband of her shorts, he tugged them down to expose the red triangle of edible underwear she'd donned after bolstering her courage with two wine coolers. He rewarded her efforts with a smile against her skin.

"How did you know I'd want to eat?" He leaned in to fasten his teeth on the licorice ropes that held the candy in a low-slung fit around her hips.

Her breath hitched, but she managed a weak, "Lucky guess. Now stop talking."

"Mmm, why?" He dragged his tongue along the fruity string, and then his lips tickled as he chewed through the candy until the novelty fell away.

She was no stranger to sex, but she still felt exposed, embarrassed, and excited all at once when his gaze settled over her mound. No man had been this close with his mouth, and she groaned with apprehension and anticipation as he skimmed his hands up her legs.

"Because," she gasped, unable to say anything more.

His palms drifted higher, higher, until his thumbs stroked the lips of her swollen sex before parting them, exposing her moist flesh to his warm breath. "Because you want to fuck."

She shuddered at the way he said it, like what they were going to do would be more than that, like it would be rich and decadent, and oh, God... his tongue was the epitome of decadent as it dipped inside her and then dragged along the length of her slit. Nothing had prepared her for this; nothing could have. No number of fantasies could have readied her for the reality of what Trent was doing, how he flicked the tip of his tongue over the pulsing knot of nerves at her center and then sucked it gently between his lips so her hips jerked toward him.

"You taste good," he murmured. "Salty and warm, a hint of sweet cherry."

Hands shaking, nerves fluttering in her stomach, she speared her fingers through his hair, holding him there. Knowing she shouldn't look, she did, watched his tongue dart in and out, noted his closed eyes, that his shadowed expression was one of feverish ecstasy. When he opened his eyes, she looked away, licking her lips as he slid his finger through her folds, circling the sensitive rim of her entrance, drawing her closer to his mouth.

"Does this feel good?" he asked, his voice breathy and deep.

No words would come, so she moaned her response, and he added a finger, pushed them both into her core. She cried out, already so close to the peak that her buttocks tightened and her knees shook until she could barely support her own weight. He was ruthless in his technique, sucking her clit and thrusting into her with his fingers in a slow in-and-out-circular motion that kept her on the brink and struggling for each breath.

It was torture, luscious torture that had to end. She ground against his mouth, rode his hand until he took the hint and worked her hard, increasing the pace and rhythm of his strokes. Long fingers massaged the pillow of raw nerves deep inside, and his tongue lapped at her flesh until he took one long, hard pull on her clit and—oh, yes, yes... she came apart in a hot rush of release that left her gasping for air.

He eased her down with slow, soothing licks of his tongue, and then, just before her rubbery legs collapsed, he stood, effortlessly swept her into his arms, and settled her on the bed. In the shadows she saw a flurry of movement, heard the rustle of clothing, and then he was beside her, his naked skin against hers.

"You're beautiful," he whispered as he caressed her hip and leaned in to taste her throat where her pulse still beat madly.

Reaching between their bodies, she ran the flat of her palm down the soft line of sandy hair that stretched from his chest to the hot juncture between his thighs. She grasped his cock, squeezed, and he sucked in a harsh breath.

"Don't," she said. "Don't say things like that."

He stiffened, though she wasn't sure if his reaction was a result of her fingers gliding over the velvety skin of his erection or from her words. "Right. Wouldn't want reality to intrude."

"Exactly."

Still stroking him with one hand, she used the other to grope the mattress in search of the condoms. Her fingers closed on the box as his mouth closed around her nipple. Jolts of sensation arced from where his wet lips met her skin and all the way to her womb. His tongue circled the stiff peak while his big hands expertly kneaded the aching flesh of her breasts. Fire consumed her, hot, stinging, and she writhed against him, wondering why she hadn't introduced herself to him months ago. So much time wasted alone in bed when she could have been with him...

"Mmm," she groaned. "You're better at that, at *this*, than I'd dreamed."

"Did I do this to you in your fantasies?" he asked, running his hand down her side, over her hip, and then dipping his fingers into the slick moisture between her legs.

"Uh-huh."

"And this?" His warm breath tickled her breast as his thumb circled her clit, and need surged through her veins, sparked her nerve endings, and collected in a single ball of desire at her center.

"Yes," gasped, "yes."

A finger pushed inside her and then trailed slowly back, exploring vulnerable areas she hadn't dreamed of him touching. "What about this?"

Hot, electric tendrils of sensation gripped her, stripped her of her ability to speak. She tossed her head from side to side, not caring that her hair stung her eyes, caught in her mouth. She was a heartbeat away from her second climax and they'd barely even begun. No fantasy could match this, or even come close.

Drawing a ragged breath, she tore open the condom packet with shaking hands and inhaled the fruity scent of banana that would have made her giggle if not for the fingers expertly caressing her, stroking her to fever-pitch, preparing her for more.

She reached for him again, skimmed her thumb over the bead of moisture that seeped from the tip of his erection.

"Kelsa..."

His voice trailed away on a groan as she spread the moisture around the silky mushroomed head and then sent several firm, slow strokes down the length of his shaft. Never had she enjoyed the feel of a man so much. She'd always taken her pleasure selfishly, wanting release through the quickest and most direct method that didn't require intimacy and the messy complications that came with it. Now she reveled in every one of Trent's reactions to her touch, the way his muscles leapt under her fingers, the way he made rumbling noises deep in his chest when she caressed him.

Clenching the condom packet between her teeth, she pushed Trent from his side onto his back, and then spread his legs wide to kneel between them. As his hands stroked her arms, she let her fingers linger on his thick thighs, let her palms massage and knead the firm muscles beneath the skin. His gaze seared her but she dared not look. Instead, she plucked the condom from its wrapper and concentrated on rolling it down over his cock to create the required barrier between them—not the pregnancy one, but the reality one.

"I've wanted to do this for so long," she said, and starting with a kiss on the broad head, she tasted him, or rather, she tasted the condom. The latex smelled like bananas, but it didn't taste like them. Not unless the bananas had first been dipped in rancid motor oil.

Suppressing the urge to tear the thing off and savor Trent as she did in her dreams, she closed her mouth over him and felt his moan all the way to the back of her throat. He twined his fingers through her hair, making her scalp tingle.

"Sweetheart, you have no idea how good that feels."

She smiled around his thickness and ran one hand up the shaft and dropped the other to cup the puckered, tight skin of his balls. Their heavy weight filled her palm as she rolled them gently between her fingers.

Adding suction, she increased the speed of her strokes along his cock, but seconds later he levered up with another moan to hook his forearms under her armpits and pull her on top of him.

"I can't take any more."

"How unfortunate," she said, teasing his nipples with her fingers and planting kisses over pecs that twitched under her lips, "because I can do that for a long, long time."

His audible swallow practically echoed off the walls. "What every guy dreams of hearing."

"I'm saying all the right things tonight, aren't I?"

In answer, he tumbled her onto her back and drove his thigh between her legs. The hard muscle created the most delicious pressure there against her center, and the beginnings of another powerful orgasm coiled inside her.

Trent caressed her breasts with his hands and mouth as he positioned himself between her legs. The tip of his cock tantalized her, rubbing up through her folds to her clit and then back down to the sensitive rim of her entrance. She arched against him, desperate to feel him inside her, but he held back. Where did the man get his patience?

Bracing himself on his elbows, he framed her face with his hands, holding her for his kiss, for the sweep of his tongue inside her mouth. He seemed to be pouring every ounce of himself, his passion, into her, and suddenly the extreme intimacy became cloying, suffocating.

She needed release, not affection. She tore her mouth away, breaking free of his hands to sink her teeth into the corded muscle between his neck and shoulder.

He grunted, but he got the hint and finally—*finally!*—eased inside her with an agonizing slowness that made her want to scream in both unbearable pleasure and frustration.

"How do I do this in your fantasies?" he whispered, his breath hot against her ear.

"You don't torture me, that's how."

His smile tickled her cheek. "I haven't even begun to torture you."

"You need to work on your bedside manner," she growled, wrapping her legs tightly around his waist and digging her heels into his hard buttocks to pull him deep inside her. She lifted her pelvis, moving her hips in slow circles, smirking with satisfaction when he clenched his teeth in a battle for restraint.

"Not fair," he said, and gave her two sharp thrusts, bringing her to the very brink. "Are you close?"

She could hardly speak, could hardly think. "Not... telling." No way. He'd probably turn up the torment a couple of notches.

"There's a price for this, you know." Two more thrusts.

"Anything." She licked her lips, knowing on some level she shouldn't have spoken those words, but unable to care.

One more thrust, deep and slow, and she twitched as her womb contracted with something that wasn't quite the relief she needed, but was so close she could cry.

"Anything?"

"Yes! Just. Keep. Moving." She ground harder, encouraging him to do something, anything but hold her on this precipice between misery and ecstasy.

He pulled out, the blunt head of his erection hovering at her entrance, and she whimpered with wild need. "Go on a ride-along on my ambulance," he said, his voice tight and more than a little winded. "See my world."

"Fine. Whatever. Just make me cum."

With what sounded like a relieved rush of breath, he plunged deep, filling her with quick, hard strokes that sent her over the edge and into a place he'd never taken her in her fantasies. Oh, this was so much better.

And, somehow, so much worse.

He shuddered and stiffened against her as his own silent climax took him, and as he kissed her neck, caressed her body like no one ever had, she wondered exactly what she'd agreed to and how much of a price she'd pay for the best, most intense sexual encounter of her life.

Chapter Five

She was surrounded by ice trolls. Poisoned by giant spiders. Cursed by a wizard's spell. Her entire party had been butchered, and her life points were draining faster than she could replace them with healing potions.

To top it off, she had only one remaining magic scroll. A wimpy fourth-level scroll, at that.

Exether, a twelfth-level fighter-druid, removed the scroll of Flame Strike from her pack and cast the spell. Fire erupted around her, searing her enemies, but at the same moment, the wizard's lightning zapped her. Electric shocks winged through her body.

In the distance, a bell pealed. Funny, she didn't remember passing any churches when she and her party of adventurers had trudged through Blackheart Forest.

Another bell. Not a church bell. Doorbell. *Doorbell.*

Kelsa blinked, momentarily bewildered by the sudden expulsion from the virtual world into the real one. She tapped a command into the computer keyboard, pausing the fantasy role-playing game in time to delay Exether's death.

Leaping from the seat that still vibrated with the shock of the lightning spell, she nearly tripped over the package she'd received from her employer today, a package containing a new ultra-violent first-person shooter game called "City Streets: Thugz Rule." The gory pictures on the outside had been enough for her to drop it back into the box as though it were diseased. How was she supposed to play the game if she couldn't even open it? She kicked the box into the corner, aware that she'd have to find a way to play the game if she wanted to keep her job.

The doorbell rang again, and she hurried, knowing before she opened the door that Trent would be on the other side, but what made her draw in a harsh breath was how different he appeared to her now that they'd been intimate.

Before yesterday, he'd been hot. Sizzling. Today, every inch seemed altered. Hotter. His starched white paramedic shirt contrasted with tan skin that had been salty and tangy and male. Black fatigue pants stretched over slim hips she'd wrapped her legs around. Her fingers practically cramped with the need to trace the patches on his shirt until he begged her to flick open the buttons and expose the hard planes of his chest to her hands.

"Hey."

"Hey." This was the first she'd seen him since she'd slipped out of his apartment while he was in the bathroom cleaning up after sex, and if this wasn't the most awkward thing in the world, she didn't know what was.

"I'm heading to work for a swing shift, so I won't be home until after midnight—"

"I'll be busy," she blurted, a twisting sensation in her gut. This was exactly what she had been afraid of; him thinking sex equaled a relationship.

He raised an eyebrow. "I wasn't going to suggest we get together."

"Oh." Embarrassment heated her face, but worse, disappointment raged through her. Why should she feel let down? She didn't *want* to get together with him again. Hormones. Had to be hormones. Which was crazy, since they'd satisfied their lust for one another. There was no need for round two in the sex ring.

"Not that I don't want to," he added, which made her feel better. *Stupid hormones.* "What I was going to say is that I won't have a chance to talk to you until tomorrow, and you need to be ready to go by one o'clock."

"Go? Where?"

"On the ride-along."

"The what?"

He stepped inside, invading her personal space and charging the atmosphere like the lightning strike to her fantasy game character couldn't. "You said you'd go to work with me. Ride in the ambulance. See a little of my world."

Dimly, she recalled he'd mentioned something about that. "In case you hadn't noticed, I was a little... distracted when I agreed to your demand."

The cocky smile that lit his face was her only warning before he folded her into his arms and hauled her up against his him. "I distracted you?"

"You know you did." She breathed deeply, savoring his clean, soapy scent and trying to put out of her mind the image of the last time they'd been in this position; naked, sweaty flesh on naked, sweaty flesh. "You cheated."

"I would never," he said, sounding theatrically shocked.

She pushed away from him and stepped into the living room, needing space. Lots and lots of space. Her brain had a tendency to clog up when he touched her. "You're doing it now. We had a deal. Just sex. No personal involvement."

The jerk's smile grew cockier, if possible. "So it's sex now? Sounds like we took it up a notch."

"Just because I don't feel like being vulgar—"

He moved toward her again, not so much walking as stalking. "Come on. I got to you. Admit it."

Damn him. He had gotten to her, but she'd never admit to it. Voicing it would make her feelings real. "Look, it's clear we can't have just a physical relationship, so let's just stop this whole thing now."

"Like hell," he growled, but the sound was more playful than harsh. "I'm not stopping anything."

"Then don't ask me into your world. I don't want to see it. I don't want to know you that well."

His luscious mouth turned into a naughty smile. "The ride-along isn't about getting to know me. It's about *my* fantasy."

"Your fantasy is to have a woman ride in an ambulance with you while you work? You need help."

He laughed. "Trust me. It'll be me and you alone, and I promise to make it everything a fantasy should be."

Oh, when he put it that way, in a voice that had gone all low and smooth, like warm maple syrup, how could she refuse? Somehow, she had to. As promising as his words were, venturing into the world with him would be too much. She'd invested a lot of time and energy to make her world safe and disconnected from the outside, and she couldn't allow one sexy man to destroy everything she'd worked for.

"I can't."

His eyes narrowed, and his expression became a mask of professionalism she hadn't seen before. "Are you agoraphobic?"

"No. Of course not. I go outside."

"Right. To the gym. Shopping."

Infuriating man. "More than that. I see movies."

He cocked an eyebrow. "Let me guess. Lord of the Rings?"

She hoped the blush heating her cheeks wouldn't give her away. So what if she only liked movies set in other worlds or other time periods? "Smartass. My point is that I do go out."

"Then what's stopping you from going to work with me tomorrow?"

Infuriating, *persistent* man. "Don't you have to go to work now?"

He glanced at his watch and nodded. "Yeah. My sup is going to kick my ass if I'm late again."

Without warning—she hated when he did that—he hooked his arm around her neck, drawing her close once more. She wanted to resist, but being near him felt so good and right. Which was wrong.

"What do I have to do to get you to agree?" He nuzzled her throat, and she groaned.

"That's a good start." Then she shook her head, which didn't do enough to clear the lusty haze clouding her thoughts. "You aren't plying me with sex this time."

"Not even sex in an ambulance?"

"Not even—" she blinked up at him "—did you say sex in an ambulance?"

"Yeah. My fantasy. What did you think I was talking about? I don't want to have a woman riding in an ambulance while I work. I want to *have* a woman in an ambulance." A naughty smile played on his lips, and the room spun. "I want you to be that woman, Kelsa."

Oh. Oh, my. The spinning room shrank and grew warmer. Sex in an ambulance was something she'd never dreamed of doing, but wow, she couldn't think of a better way to keep sex between them as fanciful as possible. Still, what would happen when they finished? She'd be stuck going with him to gory accidents and to violent crime scenes—the very things from which she'd shielded herself. Yes, she was a weirdo, but why ruin the life she had when she was perfectly content?

Mostly content, anyway. Fits of loneliness attacked her sometimes, especially when Melanie mentioned things like how Kelsa was going to die alone if she didn't meet someone. Then there was the fact that her employer claimed her work on reality-based games was substandard—and career-threatening.

So maybe getting out this once wouldn't kill her. The experience might even give her a different perspective with which to work with those stupid games Dream sOFT had been sending.

Still, she wasn't going to make this easy for Trent no matter how much he nuzzled her neck—oh, yes, just like that. Not after the way he'd tricked her earlier, getting her to agree to something while in the throes of ecstasy.

"I'll do it," she said in a voice that sounded strangled by lust, "but on one condition."

He lifted his head from where he'd been nibbling on her collarbone. Suspicion glittered in the remarkable blue pools of his eyes that made her want to jump in and put out the fire flaring up in her veins. "What?"

"Do you have a computer?"

"Yes..."

"Are you online?"

"Uh-huh." Excitement replaced the suspicion in his gaze. "Are we having computer sex? Cool."

She laughed. "It's a surprise... if you trust me with your apartment key. Call me when you get home, and I'll have everything set up."

"So, no computer sex?"

"No need to pout. If you want to have sex with your computer, I won't stop you." His snorting laughter followed her to the phone stand, where she dug out a sheet of paper and pen. She jotted her phone number down and handed it to him.

"Baby," she said, "I'm gonna blow you away."

Chapter Six

What. The. Hell.

When Kelsa said she was going to blow him away, Trent had assumed she'd meant something very sexual involving her talented mouth and his body parts. Instead, she was in her apartment and he was in his den, his butt planted in the NASA techno-chair she'd brought over from her computer room, and playing some nerdy online role-playing game with her and her disturbingly sexy elf-character, Exether.

Damn, she was blowing him away, all right. With spells called "Cone of Wind," and "Sunscorch." They were supposed to be fighting evil forces together, but somehow—and he had a feeling it was intentional—her spells kept catching his character, Tristan, in the crossfire.

A dialogue box popped up on the screen, and Kelsa's message flashed at him.

Exether: What's the matter? Can't keep up with me?

He watched Tristan, a stumpy dwarf fighter—Kelsa's sense of humor at work—drink a healing potion and then lumber toward the scantily-clad Exether.

Tristan: Why don't you invite me to your place, and I'll show you what I can keep up.

Exether: LOL!

Tristan: What the hell is LOL? And is it wrong to think your elf is hot?

Exether: LOL = Laughing Out Loud. And if you want to lust after me, you can.

He frowned, unsure how to handle that last bit. Did she say he could lust after her *character*, or her? Did she see them as one and the same? Just how involved was she in this fantasy stuff? He knew this was her job, running games through every scenario imaginable to test for glitches, and in fact, she was right now testing the online program they were playing, but was this more than a job to her?

Exether: Helloooo? Are you so busy lusting after me or Exether that you can't type? Hmm. Maybe your hand is too otherwise engaged to push the keys?

Thank God. She wasn't so immersed in the game that she was referring to herself as Exether.

Tristan: LOL! (That is so lame.) And no, my hand is not too busy. But why don't you come over and let it get busy?

Exether: Tsk-tsk. We still have wyverns to slay.

He sighed, and on the screen, Exether whacked Tristan with her golden mace. A sharp vibration jarred him in ass. She certainly knew how to get his attention.

Exether: Did you feel that?

Tristan: Like a kick in the butt.

Exether: Wanna get lucky?

It was too much to hope she meant that like he wanted her to mean it, but he typed in a quick yes. At least, as quick as he could type with two fingers. She didn't reply, but on the game screen, her character asked Tristan if he wanted to "lay together."

Surely it was a trick, but he looked over the three multiple choice answers he was given, and picked the one that amounted to a grumpy dwarf "sure."

Next thing he knew, Exether had peeled off the skimpy animal skin Zena-thing she'd been wearing and stood there, bare-assed in the middle of a forest. Tristan, being a cave-dwelling dwarf with zero social skills, pounced on her. There was nothing graphic about what happened on the screen, but damn if his NASA chair didn't start vibrating in rhythmic throbs that shot down his legs and up his spine and into his balls.

Tristan: Now I know why you spend so much time playing computer games.

Exether: *giggles* You like? Now imagine me sitting on your lap while the chair vibrates. Taking you inside me, rocking back and forth...

Oh, he imagined, all right. He imagined her tight inner muscles clenching him as they had the other night. He saw in his mind how her toned legs wrapped around his waist, guiding him to bliss as he suckled her small, firm breasts. He could practically feel her hand reaching between their bodies to cup his balls as he exploded. To experience all that while sitting in this vibrating chair... Jesus. He wasn't sure his heart could take it.

Tristan: Get over here. Now.

Exether: Sorry. Can't. Gotta finish the game.

Trent swore, long and hard. Like his dick was at this very moment.

Tristan: How long are our characters going to be getting it on? Don't you think it's a little awkward for them, him being three feet tall and all?

Exether: You don't think he's the perfect height for a few things? He doesn't need to get on his knees.

He nearly groaned at the memory of being on his knees, his face buried in Kelsa's sweet folds.

Tristan: If you come over, I'll get down on my knees.

Exether: Maybe I'd get down on mine. Play with your joystick a little.

His joystick strained against his jeans like it wanted to dive right through the computer screen to get to her.

Tristan: You're killing me, here.

Exether: Poor baby.

Tristan: I appreciate the sympathy. How did you get this job, anyway?

Exether: My brother is a programmer for Dream sOFT. He got me the job when I was sixteen.

Tristan: While you were still in high school? How'd you find the time?

Exether: I was home-schooled.

Now that was interesting. Finally some personal information. Should he press for more? He shrugged. Why not?

Tristan: How many brothers and sisters?

Exether: One brother.

That she didn't ask about his siblings didn't escape his notice.

Tristan: I have one sister. She lives in L.A. near my parents. Where do your parents live?

Exether: What time did you say we had to leave tomorrow?

He blew out a frustrated breath.

Tristan: One. And hint taken.

The chair stopped vibrating, to his mixed relief and regret. Apparently the slinky elf and stumpy dwarf had gotten their fill of each other and were now ready to go slay some sort of creature in lieu of a cigarette, Exether with her spells, and Tristan with his broadsword.

Damn, the wounds that blade would cause… lacerations, avulsions, amputations, through-and-through punctures. If the victim was wearing armor, the blunt-force trauma injuries could be devastating. As far as he could tell, the only medical treatment the characters received was in the form of healing spells and rejuvenation potions that sealed wounds and repaired damage. Then there were the scars. Did the magical treatments heal without leaving permanent disfigurement?

Exether: What are you doing?

He realized that Exether had walked to the edge of the screen to wait for Tristan, who stood like a stump in the middle of the small clearing where they'd knocked troll-skin boots.

Tristan: I was analyzing the medical implications of a broadsword attack.

Exether: Um. Okay. You coming?

I wish. He could have typed the sentiment, could have played the pervert she expected him to be, but he was tired of playing both the guy who was happy with a purely sexual relationship and the dwarf on the screen. He simply couldn't immerse himself as wholly into a fantasy realm as she could. The fact that he'd been thinking about ways to treat sword wounds was proof. He lived in a very different world than hers.

This fantasy crap wasn't his style. This internet thing didn't work for him. Sure, the chair was cool, and yeah, teasing chatter was fun, but he could only take so much virtual stimulation. He wanted Kelsa here in his arms where he could feel her and taste her and smell her. Where he could talk to her, laugh with her. Sex was fine—hell, it was awesome—but he wanted more than that, and tomorrow was the key.

He'd invited her on the ride-along so she could see his world, which was a place where reality didn't just stare you in the face—it slapped you upside the head and then puked on you. Unfortunately, she didn't want anything to do with reality.

Enter ambulance sex. It had been a stroke of sheer genius to bring that up—he'd always wanted to join the Code Three Club—and the suggestion had been exactly what he'd needed to tip her scales.

He'd give her the fantasy fuck, and then maybe, just maybe, she'd let her guard down enough to want more.

Exether: Tristan! What are you doing?

Tristan: Thinking about going to bed.

Exether: Just drink a rejuvenation potion. We don't need to rest yet.

He sighed and rubbed his hand over his face, now rough with stubble.

Tristan: For real. It's three o'clock in the morning.

Exether: *pouts* I suppose I can handle things without you.

Tristan: But do you want to? Wouldn't you rather have me by your side?

He held his breath as he waited for her reply, his heart pounding at the same rate as the cursor that flashed in the space beneath his dialogue.

Exether: I've done okay on my own so far.

Tristan: Is "okay" enough?

Silence stretched over the internet. His pulse raced. This was crazy. Waiting on a typed response from a woman who wanted him only for sex had worked him up to stress levels he usually only felt during a code three call. He should just shut off the computer and be done with it—the game, the woman, the sex. He reached for the power button, but the message that popped up on the screen stopped him.

Exether: It has to be enough. Good night, Tristan.

It has to be. Why? Why would anyone settle for okay?

Trent shut off the computer and dragged his sorry ass to bed. Okay wasn't acceptable. Not in his line of work, not in his life. Nor was it acceptable for the woman who fascinated him, who made him laugh when he hadn't had anything to laugh about in a couple of years, and who made him feel more in a few days than he'd felt in his entire life.

Tomorrow he'd make "okay" a thing of the past. He'd make Kelsa feel something more than okay whether she liked it or not.

Chapter Seven

Kelsa was ready when he knocked on her door. She wore jeans that emphasized her shapely, toned legs, and a T-shirt that stretched tightly over breasts his fingers itched to caress.

Down boy.

"Am I dressed okay?"

His jaw clenched. That word again. He was going to wipe it from her vocabulary. "Not okay. You look great. You need to be comfy."

She gave him a sly grin as she strolled through the doorway. "I'm not wearing any underwear. That's comfy."

Lust clogged his throat until he could barely breathe. He had no idea how he made it to his truck and then all the way to the ambulance bay without pouncing on her like a horny dwarf on a sexy elf, but by some miracle he managed.

"So this is where you work, huh?" she asked as they walked through the oversized garage toward his rig after signing in with the supervisor.

"Yep." He pointed to where his partner walked around the ambulance as he performed a check-out inspection. "That's Jeff. He practically lives here."

Jeff looked up and waved. "Hey. We're ready to go. I already did inventory."

"You must have gotten here early again."

Jeff shrugged. "I have no life."

Trent shot a glance at Kelsa. "Must be contagious."

She punched him in the arm and then turned a million-watt smile on Jeff. The lucky bastard. "Hi. I'm Kelsa."

Nodding, Jeff shook her hand. "Trent told me all about you. Hop inside and we'll roll."

Trent helped her into the box section of the rig while Jeff turned in the paperwork. When Jeff returned, he shut the back doors and left Trent and Kelsa alone. She sat in the jump seat at the front, and he planted himself on the long bench that ran the length of the patient compartment. The door that separated the box from the cab was closed, giving them privacy.

The engine roared to life, and the rig pulled out of the bay.

"So... what do you think?"

She looked around, her fingers squeezing her knees. "It's interesting. Smells like disinfectant."

"You're nervous."

"Nope."

Frowning, he moved to the jump seat and crouched on his heels beside her to pry her hand from her leg. The air-conditioner blasted cool air through several vents, but not enough for her hand to feel as cold as a corpse's. He swept his thumb over her wrist, tracing the delicate veins just under the surface of the skin. "You're lying. I can feel it in your pulse."

She shot him an annoyed glance. "Must be nice to be a human lie detector."

"It's one of my many talents." He tucked a strand of hair that had escaped her French braid behind her ear. "Tell me what's wrong."

"I've just never been in an ambulance before."

"Is that all?"

Her eyes told him everything. She wasn't nervous about being in an ambulance, she was scared of being with him. Of learning more about his life than she wanted.

"This was a bad idea," she said, dropping her gaze to her sneaker-shod feet. "Could you guys drop me off at my apartment? Or anyplace. I can get a cab."

He drew her hand to his lips, where he kissed her wrist, her palm, the pads of each of her fingertips. Her pulse rate increased, and a surge of male pride that he'd been the cause speared him.

"Come here." He led her to the bench and settled down beside her.

"This is supposed to be fun. Don't think. Don't analyze."

Not yet, anyway. After today, she could analyze all she wanted, and he hoped she would. He wanted her to see him as a person, not as a sex toy or a computer-animated dwarf.

"If I can't think, what do you suggest I do?" She looked up at him through thick lashes. A teasing light flickered amongst the flecks of gold in her brown eyes, and without warning, his cock stirred to life.

"Tell me about the underwear you aren't wearing."

The sultry smile that stole along the edges of her mouth sent his temperature soaring by more than a few degrees. "Oh, you would have loved them. Very skimpy. Black satin. Thong."

He pictured a thin black string disappearing between the plump cheeks of her ass, and he could practically feel his finger hooking under the fabric and following it down until he encountered the creamy moisture between her legs.

"They sound great," he said, "but I like them better in your drawer." He curled his hand around her nape and leaned in to capture her mouth with his.

She stiffened, and he realized that although they'd kissed before, this time they knew each other much better. This was personal, and it bothered her. He smoothed his tongue over her lips, urging them apart.

"Stay with me," he murmured against her mouth. "Just for now."

She sighed, relaxing and melting into the cradle of his body, parting her lips to deepen the kiss.

Her nipples hardened against his chest—damn, he appreciated her habit of going braless—and he slid his hand up her side to stroke his thumb over the fleshy curve of her breast. The ambulance took a sharp turn, and although Trent had long since developed "rig legs," an ability to maintain his balance in the moving vehicle, he took advantage of the opportunity to lean into her, to press her against the padded back rest.

She made a hungry, desperate sound and locked her arms over his shoulders, pulling him closer. His erection pushed into her hip, which she rocked in a slow, rolling motion, telling him exactly what she wanted and driving him nuts.

"Show me your fantasy," she whispered, and caught his bottom lip between her teeth before soothing it with the tip of her tongue.

"This is it, baby."

His lips swept over her cheekbone and into the indention beneath it, to her ear, and as he nipped lightly at her earlobe, the sound of her panting breaths heightened his own need and reassured him that she wanted him with the same intensity that he wanted her. He nuzzled his way down her throat, dipping his tongue into the hollow where her clavicles met. She arched her neck as he licked a trail along the neckline of her shirt, and then he bent his head and took her nipple into his mouth, right through the fabric.

"That feels incredible," she said, tunneling her fingers through his hair, caressing his scalp and applying gentle pressure.

"You taste incredible."

He lifted her shirt to bare her beautiful breasts some might consider small, but he found to be a perfect handful. Open-mouthed, he savored one raspberry-colored bud, wrenching a moan from her, and then he suckled it deeply, taking as much into his mouth as he could, loving how it made her squirm.

"Trent." Pushing his head away, she cast a worried glance toward the front of the box. "What about your partner?"

He ran his palm down her softly rounded belly to the waistband of her jeans. "He's not invited."

She huffed, clearly not in the mood for humor. "Can he hear or see?"

Dipping his head, he flicked his tongue over the skin just above the top button of her pants, and then he tore them open with his teeth. "Nope."

"Oh, good. Nice trick with the teeth."

"I told you I have many talents."

"Mmm, yes, you do." She squirmed again, opening her legs as he moved off the bench to kneel between them. "What does he think we're doing back here?"

"Probably exactly what we're doing."

She sat up straight, squishing him between surprisingly strong thighs. Her workouts must be hell. "What? Did you tell him?"

"No, but he's not stupid."

"You must do this a lot."

The steely note under the velvet of her voice, the tone that made it clear she was more than a little angry, brought a smile to his lips. He *was* getting to her. "Never." She speared him with a skeptical glare. "I'm serious. I've wanted to, but it never happened."

He always wondered why he hadn't done it back in his young and dumb days, when all he cared about was having a good time and getting laid. There'd been no shortage of women he could have gotten into the back of an ambulance, but for some reason, he hadn't been able to bring just any bimbo into a place that had always seemed sacred to him, ridiculous as that sounded.

What had begun as a career designed to push every one of his parents' snobby-rich buttons had turned into something that filled him with worth that had nothing to do with money. He loved his job, loved the adrenaline rush that came with emergencies, loved the fact that for the first time, he had a woman he felt comfortable bringing with him to the job for a fantasy that might convince her she was the only one for him.

She relaxed, and he gently pushed her legs apart so he could breathe again. Just as he reached for the remaining buttons on her jeans, she stiffened once more. "Wait. I forgot the toys."

"We don't need them." He popped a button.

"I do."

Another button. "Isn't the ambulance enough?" Another. "It's moving, we've got the stretcher, I'll keep my uniform on—"

"Not enough. I still know it's you."

Any normal person would take offense, but he understood what she meant, and in her bizarre-o world, what she'd said spoke volumes. She'd grown too close to him, and even the ambulance setting and uniform couldn't shut out the reality of what was going on in their relationship. More than ever, she needed keep a barrier between them, needed to keep things sterile.

Sterile.

He grinned and stood. "Close your eyes."

She lifted an eyebrow and then shrugged and obeyed. Quickly, he pulled on a pair of latex gloves. When he returned his gaze to Kelsa, he took a moment to admire the sight of her sitting on the bench, relaxed, her shirt pushed up over her breasts, her jeans wide open and revealing a light fringe of brown curls. He quivered with the desire to taste all of her, feel all of her, and he wanted to take a long time doing it.

Unfortunately, they didn't have time. Jeff could get a call at any moment.

"Are you ready for me?" he asked, and she nodded, making her breasts jiggle hypnotically.

Unable to wait any longer, he straddled her legs and bent over to settle his mouth over hers. He nibbled her lips until she opened up to the hungry thrust of his tongue. Slowly, he smoothed his hands from her curvy waist to her breasts.

"Wow," she breathed. "Are you wearing gloves?"

"Yep."

She smiled. "I like it."

A woman after his own heart. He grasped the waistband of her jeans and tugged them down, pulling off her shoes with them. Kelsa opened her eyes, watched him through slitted eyelids as he spread her legs and kneeled between them. Her dark curls were neatly trimmed, and her swollen pussy, open to him, already glistened with moisture.

"God, you're beautiful."

"Don't—"

"Yeah, yeah. Don't say things like that." He smoothed his hands along her thighs and down the hard contours of her calves, drawing a soft moan from her.

"That's so erotic," she said, the raspy, needy tone of her voice causing his balls to draw up almost painfully.

He teased her ankles and then massaged his way back up her legs to her inner thighs. Her heat threatened to melt the gloves, and he uttered a curse at the thin barrier between them.

With one hand, he uncoiled the stethoscope from around his neck and hooked the earbuds into place. Taking the bell between his gloved fingers, he positioned it just above her mound.

She inhaled harshly and peered down at him. "What are you doing?"

"I want to listen to how your heart reacts to my touch." If he had his way, *only* his touch from now on.

Biting her bottom lip, she nodded and let her head fall back against the headrest as he eased the stethoscope bell up her abdomen to where her pulse pounded above her navel.

"Feels weird."

"Weird good, or weird bad?" he asked, the echoes of their words vibrating through the device.

"Oh, definitely weird good. Cold, yet smooth and naughty." Her voice deepened, turned husky. "I'll never look at medical equipment in same way again."

"Good." He bent forward and opened his mouth against her sex, not tasting, just kissing, and her heart rate doubled, thundering into the stethoscope.

Smiling, he slipped a finger between her folds, pressed lightly on her pulsing clit. Her mouth fell open on a sexy little mewing sound, and this time, her pulse went wild.

The scent of her arousal, musky and warm, heightened his own, and the urge to taste her overwhelmed him. He tore the stethoscope away, tossing it to the floor, and reached around her back to place one hand against the curve of her spine to lift her and bring her closer to him. With an impatient growl, he buried his face between her legs, kissing her, ravishing her, swirling his tongue around her engorged bud. He dipped one finger inside her, then two, amazed at how her cream coated the gloves, easing the strokes and creating a smooth friction that made her buck.

"Mmm, yes," she gasped. "There."

She was beautiful, so gorgeous with her head thrown back and her throat working to swallow her moans, and because her panting breaths and gush of moisture told him she was close, he scaled back his efforts, selfishly wanting to watch her freeze in the moment. Her fingers clutched the bench so hard her knuckles had gone white, and he wondered how he'd explain any permanent grip marks in the padding to Jeff.

"Trent, please," she begged, "let me cum."

He held her on the precipice a little longer with three long, slow passes of the flat of his tongue through her slit, and then he drew her clit into his mouth and suckled hard.

She nearly jumped off the seat with a sobbing shout, and her thighs trembled against his shoulders. Thank God Jeff was driving the rig and not parked in a lot somewhere, because the power of her climax rocked the truck. Quickly, since he was about to lose it himself, he pulled her off the bench and pushed her gently to her knees. She gave him a contented smile as he bent her over the stretcher so her fine ass cradled his aching cock. He fumbled for the condom he'd stashed in his baggy mid-thigh pocket and ripped the package open with his teeth. In record time, he'd unzipped his pants and smoothed on the rubber.

Kelsa raised her ass and gave it a wiggle, and he nearly groaned at the invitation. "Greedy thing."

"Always. Hurry," she whined, and he obliged.

He sank into her, shuddering at the sensation of her still-clenching internal muscles sucking him inside. She was tight, so tight, and he thrust slowly, pulling all the way out before plunging deep again, the slide of flesh on flesh as exquisite as anything he'd ever experienced. His hands grasped her hips, and though he couldn't feel the texture of her skin through the latex, her heat scorched his palms.

"Touch me, Trent."

He started to reach around to her sex, then pulled his hand back. The gloves were cool—he'd never had sex like this before—but this was about breaking down the barriers between them. He pounded into her with his shaft, distracting her, and peeled the glove off one hand. He dropped the glove and then slid his hand around her waist and over the soft curls to sink his finger between her slick lips.

She bucked against his hips when he circled her clit, and then she shouted his name, her internal muscles clasping his cock until his vision dimmed and he couldn't take it anymore. His orgasm hit him like a summer storm, slamming into him without warning and turned his world upside down and inside out.

He thought he might actually have blacked out for a moment, because he didn't remember falling forward over Kelsa's back, but then he found himself kissing the swells and contours of her neck and spine, which were damp with sweat.

"Damn," he murmured against her skin.

"You charmer of a poet, you."

Chuckling, he eased his weight off her, his arms trembling like he'd carried a four-hundred pound patient down thirty flights of stairs. Chest heaving, he sank stiffly onto the bench and handed her jeans to her, wondering when his strength would return. He found enough strength to remove the condom and zip up his pants, but he hoped they wouldn't have a call anytime soon.

Kelsa fastened her jeans and slipped on her sneakers, and then plopped down beside him on the bench. "You sure know how to show a girl a good time."

"I aim to please."

She dropped her head back against the padded rest and stared up at the roof. Despite the fact that his lust had been slaked—temporarily, at least—he couldn't help but admire the rapid rise and fall of her breasts as she struggled to catch her breath.

"I don't know how we're going to top this. Those toys you sent were great, but…"

He ground his teeth at the mention of the toys. Yeah, he liked messing around with props as much as the next guy, but damn it, he wanted normal, one-on-one, skin-on-skin sex with no gimmicks. No fantasy. He craved a genuine lovemaking session with a woman who saw *him* and not just his dick.

He surged to his feet and tossed the used condom and gloves into the trash, taking care to conceal them.

"What's wrong?"

He swore, tempted to tell her exactly what was wrong, but knowing she needed time to figure it out for herself. He couldn't force her into wanting what he wanted, which was a relationship where they could enjoy each other doing even mundane things, like watching TV or eating greasy onion rings at a carnival. Oh, yeah, he was a true romantic.

Drawing a hard breath, he shoved aside visions of carnies and poorly maintained rides, and managed a tired, "Not a thing."

"You're lying," she said, reaching out to take his hand with hers that was now warm, "and I don't need to be a human lie detector to know that."

"Be careful. You're touching me in a non-sexual manner." Damn, that sounded petulant and childish, but he'd gone past caring.

She bit her lip as if reconsidering, and then she shrugged. "I'm sure this once won't kill me."

No, but it might kill him. Every sexual touch, every sexual look grabbed his gut and brought him to his knees. Far worse, though, was how every time she did something purely out of enjoyment of his company, when she laughed or touched him or shared what little she had of her life, it seized his heart and strung it up.

He sat next to her, twining her fingers in his. "Why didn't you tell me where your parents live?"

He'd never seen a human being—a live one, anyway—go as rigid as she did then. "Because personal questions aren't allowed."

"So you aren't curious about me at all? I'm just a piece of meat to you?"

Kelsa pursed her lips as if annoyed, and then she gave a haughty sniff. "Cucumber."

He blinked. "What?"

"I'm a vegetarian, so you wouldn't be a piece of meat to me. If you were any food, you'd be a cucumber."

For a few thudding heartbeats he stared at her, torn between strangling her and kissing her. "I can't decide if what you just said is erotic or fodder for therapy."

The corners of her lips trembled with the need to smile, and then she did, along with a lively giggle that sounded natural for her, like she should be doing it all the time. "If it's any consolation, you'd be a very large cucumber."

"Aww, that's the nicest thing you've ever said to me."

His tone had been teasing, but her face fell, and she made a squeaky sound in her throat. "You're right," she murmured. "I'm such a jerk. I'm sorry."

Something knotted in his chest, and suddenly he needed to lighten things up again. Too much was at stake to have a serious conversation in the back of an ambulance. Smiling, he squeezed her fingers. "You almost sound like you care."

"I do."

He blinked in surprise; she did the same. Had she just now realized that she cared about him, that there was more to this than just sex?

"Ha! I knew it."

Anger flashed in her eyes, and she pulled away to cross her arms over her chest. "Don't get all excited. I didn't mean anything by it."

"No?"

"No."

Like earlier during sex, when he'd not wanted to send her over the edge, he decided now to avoid the same. Now was not the time to talk or pressure her. Not when he was also on the edge—an edge where he'd never been, one that put him dangerously close to falling head-over-heels.

So he put on his best neutral face and shrugged. "Okay. Can't blame a guy for getting his hopes up, though."

Smiling to himself because his hopes *were* up, he opened the window in the door separating the cab from the box just as the radio squawked. He turned back to Kelsa with a grin. "Looks like we have a job."

Chapter Eight

Kelsa sat in the jump seat, staring out the ambulance's back window. Trent had moved forward into the cab's passenger seat to fill out paperwork as the ambulance sped, sirens blaring, through early evening traffic. Through the now-open door that separated the cab from the rear section, she listened to Trent and Jeff discuss the possible course of action they'd take at the scene of an apparent heart attack victim. His voice, deep and soothing, was that of a skilled professional, a man whom she didn't doubt could ease the fears of his patients with a few confident words.

It was strange how she heard the lover in his voice as well as the professional, how she knew that if all he did was murmur medical jargon into her ear, she'd still become wildly aroused. She stole a glance at his profile, the strong line of his jaw, the tan skin that stretched over well-defined cheekbones, the firm mouth that dealt oodles of pleasure.

The same mouth that spoke things it shouldn't speak. Like that she was beautiful. Or that she cared about him. Damn him! He knew the deal. No intimate conversation, no cuddling, no nothing that might be misconstrued as a genuine relationship.

He hadn't followed the rules. She should be furious. Upset. On some level, she was both, but somewhere deep inside, the knowledge that he wanted more from her filled her with a bubbly giddiness she'd not experienced before. No one had ever wanted more. How could that not make her happy?

It also left her vulnerable.

Maybe she'd contracted a case of after-orgasm bliss. She hoped so, because that, at least, would wear off. Love wouldn't. Not that the emotion gripping her so hard she broke out in a sweat whenever Trent was near could be love. No way. The only thing she felt for that hot paramedic up there was a healthy dose of lust.

Oh, and guilt. Groaning, she buried her hands in her face. She'd said he was a cucumber. Worse, that was the nicest thing she'd ever said to him. How many nice things had she thought in her mind, like the fact that he was patient and sexy and gentle? That he could turn the head of a blind woman. That he made her feel safe and wanted.

The ambulance slowed, and she turned to look through the windshield. Ahead, the rotating roof lights from two police cars flashed blue beams onto an old brick brownstone tattooed by graffiti. Garbage lined the sidewalks beneath the iron-barred apartment windows. Her stomach churned and the moisture evaporated from her mouth, leaving a cottony feeling on her tongue. This was the real world, and already it was ugly.

Jeff parked the ambulance, and then he and Trent rounded the truck to gather equipment from the rear.

"What can I do?" she asked, secretly hoping Trent would tell her to curl up under a blanket on the floor and stay there, and knowing she could never do so even if she wanted to. She needed to broaden her horizons, if only enough to help her keep her job.

Trent smiled, shooting her an easy wink that seemed at odds with the hurried, yet confident manner with which he assembled his gear. "Come with us, but stay out of the way."

She followed them into the building, where they rushed up four flights of stairs because the elevator was out of service. At the landing, Jeff turned to her, panting but still moving at a brisk pace.

"Patients are always on the top floor. No one can have a heart attack on the ground level."

"Stop whining," Trent said, not the least bit winded. "It's good exercise."

"Which is probably what gives them the heart attack in the first place. Climbing all these stairs."

Jeff's irritation left her speechless, but she wasn't sure that Trent's joking wasn't worse. How could they be so detached about something like this? A person could be *dying.*

Two police officers spoke in hushed tones in the hall near the patient's apartment. Trent and Jeff entered immediately to take control of the scene, where two more officers grunted and wheezed as they performed CPR on an elderly lady lying in the entryway, her skin waxy and pale, her lips blue.

Legs frozen, Kelsa slapped a shaking hand over her mouth and stopped outside the doorway. Oh, God, she couldn't watch. Neither could she look away.

After a rapid initial assessment, Trent quickly and efficiently inserted a tube into the woman's throat while Jeff took over chest compressions from one of the officers. Once the woman was "tubed," as Trent called it, Jeff "bagged" her by squeezing air into her lungs, and Trent hooked her up to a defibrillator and began a series of shocks.

Two firefighter-paramedics arrived, breaking Kelsa out of her morbid trance. Stomach churning, she stepped away from the door and found a grizzled skeleton of a man sharing the hall with her. How long he'd been there watching dispassionately, she had no idea.

He jerked his chin in the lady's direction. "Name's Esther. Been a tenant for twenty-five years. What a shame."

She nodded, not knowing what else to do or say.

"Always paid her rent on time. Some punk kid'll prob'ly move in now. Shame."

She blinked, stunned that the man had so casually written the woman off. "She could make it."

He looked at her like she'd suggested he let the next tenant live there for free. "She ain't got no reason to. She's alone. Coupla cats..."

He shrugged and walked away, leaving her wanting to vomit up the falafel pita sandwich she'd had for lunch.

When Kelsa looked again, Trent and Jeff had loaded the woman onto a stretcher and were pushing her out the door. A firefighter-paramedic rode the stretcher, straddling the lady and crunching compressions into her chest while Trent squeezed the bag connected to her breathing tube, his expression intense, concerned. Sweat beaded on his forehead and soaked his shirt. His eyes reflected the fear she felt in her heart, the fear that the woman wouldn't survive. Admiration swelled in her breast as she began to comprehend the amount of inner strength he must possess in order to deal with the multitude of oppressive emotions he experienced every day.

Kelsa followed them down, waiting in the darkness broken by emergency vehicle lights as they loaded the lady into the back of the rig where she and Trent had found so much pleasure.

Her entire body shaking, she climbed into the front passenger seat and then clenched her jaw tight to prevent her teeth from chattering. It was all too much. Reality overload. Emotional overload. If she were a car, her engine, oil, and transmission lights would be lit and buzzing.

Trent took his seat, started the engine, and then spoke with dispatch on the radio as he steered into traffic.

"You don't look good," he said, after replacing the radio mike.

How could he sound so cavalier, as though he hadn't just sweated his ass off trying to save a woman who was, at this moment, fighting for her life in the back of his ambulance?

"That's because I'm not," she said. "That woman could die." Alone.

He nodded. "Most likely."

Most likely. Regret dripped from his voice, but the words themselves... so cold. "Doesn't it bother you?"

"It happens."

"So that's it? You just blow it off? People get hurt and die and you say 'it happens'?"

He gave her a look she wished she could see better in the darkness. "That's the reality. I can't hide from death or pretend it doesn't happen. I accept it and deal with it."

She shook her head, wondering where the Trent whose eyes had been full of concern and fear had gone. "So it doesn't bother you at all?"

"I didn't say that."

"Then tell me if it bothers you," she pressed, unsure why she needed an answer. Was it because she wanted to confirm what she already knew—that he was a rare catch, the kind of man women prayed to find? Or was it because she hoped to uncover a flaw, a reason to pull away before it was too late?

His jaw clenched so hard she expected to hear a tooth crack. "Yeah, it bothers me. I hate losing patients. I hate seeing people in pain. Happy?"

She should have been, now that she'd gotten him to admit he was human, but misery only settled in deeper. Things like this hurt him, and she'd made him fess up, something she doubted he ever did, even to himself.

"Then why do you do it?" she asked quietly. "Why do you do this job every day?"

"Sometimes, I have no idea."

The brutally honest answer sliced at her heart, spilling even more emotion into her bloodstream, and tears stung her eyes. She turned away, looking out the window into the darkness, unsure of what to say and not wanting him to see her distress. Trent's job forced him to see the very things she'd avoided. Perhaps if she hadn't grown up in seclusion, in an environment where chaos wasn't allowed, she'd be better equipped to handle what had happened today at the scene. As it was, she just wanted to go home, shut the door, and isolate herself until she forgot today and Trent and a little old lady who had nothing but her cats.

She dabbed at her eyes and turned back to him. "I'm going to catch a cab from the hospital."

He said nothing, only gave a sharp nod.

"We can't see each other again."

A muscle leapt in his cheek and his lips pressed tightly together. Just when she thought he wasn't going to say anything, he turned to her. "I'm not letting you go."

"It's not your call to make."

He took a deep breath and turned back to the road. "Why can't you accept what there is between us?"

"Why did you want me to come with you today? Don't give me some bullshit story about lifelong fantasies. You wanted to shake me up."

"There you go. You just answered your own question."

Bitter laughter bubbled up like acid. "You are such a jerk. All along you've talked about opening up and sharing, but then you sit there all smug and superior, refusing to do what you insist I should. Nothing shakes you up, but it's okay to do it to someone else."

"I get shaken."

She crossed her arms over her breasts. "When?"

His jaw tightened again, and she nearly smiled. Clearly, he didn't want to talk about it, but not doing so would prove her point.

Finally, he said, "When I screw up."

The way he said it, in a gravelly voice that sounded dredged from the bottom of his soul, made her stomach drop.

"We all screw up."

"Yeah, but when you screw up, you kill a computer character. I kill a real person."

There was something more behind the words, but dear Lord, she didn't want to know what. She'd never wanted to view him as anything but a fantasy, and now that the real man with real feelings and a real job had emerged, the fantasy was dying a slow, painful death.

"How much longer?"

"Until what?"

"Until we get to the hospital."

His hands flexed on the steering wheel. "Five minutes." He slid her a glance. "So why don't you use that five minutes to tell me why you hole up in your apartment and live in a fantasy world?"

"That's not exactly what I do—"

"My ass. Go ahead and tell me how that's not what you do. Tell me how you are any different from that lady in the back of my rig."

Oh. God. She was different. She had her brother and Melanie and her grandma. She didn't have cats. Not yet, anyway. She'd always wanted one. Pets weren't allowed in the compound where she'd grown up, and her grandma was allergic.

"I have family. Friends. I meet guys."

He raised an eyebrow. "Before me, when was the last time you were with a guy?"

She shrugged. "It's been a few months." Ten, to be exact.

"How did you meet him?"

She looked out the window at the cars that seemed to stand still as the ambulance passed them. At the buildings, the road, the street lamps, anything to keep from answering.

"How, Kelsa?"

"Online, dammit," she said through clenched teeth. "Okay? I met him through an online role-playing game."

He'd been fun, they'd flirted online—in character—for months, met every couple of weeks for sex that had been a luxurious break from the monotony of daily life, and that was that. When he wanted more, she'd ended it, which was about the same time Trent had moved in, so she'd spent her time fantasizing about him rather than meeting more online sex partners.

The corner of Trent's mouth tipped up slightly. "Was he a dwarf? Gnome? A wizard with a big wand?"

"Oh, you're hilarious."

"And you need a reality check."

"Again, not your call to make."

Blowing out a long, measured breath, he rubbed the back of his neck. "Tell me about your parents."

Grr. "Why are you so hung up on them?"

"Because you're so dead set against talking about them."

The hospital loomed ahead, and she thought she'd never been so happy to arrive at an E.R.

As Trent pulled the rig up to the emergency room doors, he said, "Don't leave. Not yet. Give me a minute."

She didn't want to, but she'd give him that one courtesy before she took off in hopes of never seeing him again.

So she waited outside while he and the other medics rushed the woman into the hospital, and a few minutes later, Trent emerged, took her hand, and led her to a quiet, grassy alcove with a bench and fountain. Security lights illuminated the little park, but the broad-leafed maple trees softened the glare.

"What are you doing?" she growled as he pulled her down on the cement bench. "If this is another one of your fantasies…"

What? What would she do? Probably give in. Sex with Trent out in the open, in a park where they could be discovered... she shivered at the wickedness of it.

Then she gave herself a mental kick in the butt for even considering such a thing when she was supposed to be giving him the boot.

"It's not," he replied just as gruffly. "I'm going to tell you about *my* reality check."

"I don't want to hear it." She started to stand, but he grasped her upper arms firmly but gently, and held her on the bench.

"Too bad. You're going to hear what happened to me when I thought life was all fun and games."

"Believe me, I don't think life is all fun and... fun."

His mouth quirked and she knew he'd filled in the blank of what she'd not said, that her life *was* games. "Well, I used to. Even my job was a game to me."

She frowned. "Were you a paramedic?"

"Yep. A shitty one. I goofed off. I came to work hungover and half-drunk..." He trailed off, looking away to gaze blankly at the fountain spray.

"I don't get it. You love your job. Why would you—"

"I was a selfish asshole, that's why." He clenched his fists in his lap but didn't look away from the spot where he stared. "Wanna know why I became a paramedic? To piss off my parents. They wanted to send me to some Ivy League school to follow in my dad's footsteps, and I rebelled. One day between the duck liver pâté and minted lamb, they asked what I wanted to do instead, and I happened to see an ambulance whizzing by the restaurant, so I said I wanted to be an ambulance driver."

He shot her an amused glance. "Medics hate being called ambulance drivers, by the way." His smile faded, and he looked somewhere inside where she couldn't follow.

"Anyway, they didn't think I was serious, basically dared me to do it, so I did. I hated it, but I had a point to prove, you know?"

"So I spent years goofing off, doing just enough work to not get fired, pissing off my parents more and more. I was a waste of good blood and organs." He twitched a shoulder in a shrug. "All organs except a liver, anyway. Probably shot that all to hell with the drinking."

Kelsa swallowed dryly, unable to reconcile the man who'd worked so intently to save the elderly lady with the man he claimed to have been. "I'm sure it wasn't as bad as all that."

He gave a bitter laugh. "No? I came to work one day after four days off, four days where all I did was party. I was groggy, probably still drunk." He shut his eyes, his mouth crimped with the pain of a memory she didn't want to hear but was powerless to stop. "My partner hated me, hated how I didn't give a rat's ass about the job. He usually took care of the patients, which was fine with me. I got to drive and not deal with people I thought were beneath me. So on that day I was driving. Patrick had a stroke victim in the back. I dozed off in an intersection. Broad-sided a van carrying a family to a birthday party."

Nausea bubbled up in her throat, and she reached out, took his hand that was still clenched and stiff.

"No one died," he said in a raw voice, "but one of the kids was critical for days, and the parents both had broken bones. My partner cracked a couple of ribs. Me? I got a nick on my cheek. Here." He pointed to the tiniest of scars on his right cheekbone that she'd not have noticed had he not pointed it out.

"So what happened? Did you get into trouble?"

He shook his head, and a blond lock fell forward, begging her fingers to brush it out of the way, if only for an excuse to touch him intimately. "My parents have the best lawyers in the country at their disposal. By the time all was said and done, the family was made out to look like the cause of the accident. Thing is, I was still so fucking selfish that I let it all happen."

"I quit the ambulance company, let my cert lapse, and worked a year with my dad at his firm. I figured I'd head off to college like my parents wanted. Problem was, I couldn't stop thinking about being a paramedic. Every time I heard a siren, my heart went crazy, my adrenaline surged, and I wanted to be the one responding."

"One day, I was driving to work, and I witnessed an accident. I stopped to help. Saved a guy's life. It felt good. Awesome. Man, I missed doing the job."

She finally reached up and brushed the lock of hair back, held her hand there when he leaned into it. Emotion clogged her throat at the simple pleasure she took at giving comfort. Never had something so small made her heart swell so much.

"So what happened?" she asked softly, and he withdrew.

"The whole thing had been a massive wake up call. Reality check. Major kick in the ass. So I sent that family I'd plowed into an anonymous check for what remained in my trust fund, I earned my paramedic certification again, and I moved here. I've never been happier."

"What about your parents?"

He snorted. "They're wondering where they went wrong with me and my sister. They can't decide what's worse; a son who's a blue-collar worker or a daughter who's a business success, but a lesbian."

Kelsa laughed but instantly sobered when he pulled her to her feet and held her hands.

"Don't do what I did. Don't pass up opportunities because you're avoiding something."

"I don't pass up opportunities or I wouldn't have come to your apartment with flavored condoms in the first place."

His mouth twitched in a remembered smile. "Yeah, but that was a safe bet. No guy is going to send you sex toys if he's not guaranteed to sleep with you."

She took a step back from him, needing to keep a clear head, which was impossible when he touched her. "Then I have no idea what opportunity you're talking about."

"I'm talking about us and you know it." He scrubbed a hand over his face. "What's the deal, Kelsa? Did some guy hurt you? Is that why you can't see past the sex we have?"

"I can't see past the sex because there isn't anything to see."

Emotion—anger, hurt, she couldn't tell—clouded his eyes. His jaw tightened, and lightning-quick, he grabbed her hand, pressed it over his heart that pounded into her palm.

"Nothing to see? How about something to feel? I'm here, Kelsa. I'm real." He tugged her fully against him so abruptly she gasped. "This is real. No more playing, no more denying, no more *damned fantasy*." His heart sped up and she wondered how he could stand the way it must be throwing itself against his ribs. "This is what you do to me."

Oh, God, that's what he did to her, too. It was dangerous, the feelings that burst inside her chest. This was definitely real. Too real. It was certainly no longer about fantasy. It was about her world being turned upside down, and about Trent shaking the very foundations on which her life was built.

She wanted him, wanted him with a fierceness she'd never experienced. She simply didn't know if she was ready for an authentic, normal relationship. Heck, she might never be ready. Too many years of pretending the outside world didn't exist had filled her with a sense of rightness in her own world.

Avoidance was so much easier than facing reality.

"I have to go." She twisted away from him, stepping back when he moved toward her. "Please don't." With that, she fled toward the hospital's main entrance and a pay phone.

She didn't look back. She couldn't. If she did, her heart would break.

Chapter Nine

Her heart broke anyway.

Kelsa sat in the dark in her living room, unable to do anything but cry. When had she last cried? It had been so long she couldn't remember. She'd been a teen, probably. Heck, most likely it was the day Michael had dragged her from the compound, hand over her mouth to quiet her protests. Life had been so simple there—dysfunctional, but peaceful.

Dashing hot tears away, she dialed her brother's number, hoping he'd forgive the three A.M. call.

"Hello?" A woman's sleepy voice.

Kelsa bit her lip. It hadn't occurred to her that he might have company. Not her brother who was as reclusive as she was.

"This is Michael's sister. Is he there?"

There was a soft rustling and some static, and then her brother's groggy voice rasped, "Hey. Are you okay?"

"Yes. No. I'm sorry," she sobbed. "I just need to talk."

"It's okay. What's up?"

"I-I'm afraid I'm going to die alone."

"What? Kels. That's ridiculous. You called me at this ungodly hour for that?"

"It's more than that. I met this guy, and I really like him. I think… I think I love him."

"That's great, sis. I'm happy for you."

"Don't be. It's not what I want."

"Why the hell not?"

She blinked. She'd never known her mild-mannered geek of a brother to swear. "You grew up in the same place I did. You should understand."

He heaved a sigh. "No, I don't understand. What I do understand is that you've never given yourself permission to feel anything. You're still stuck in the land of weak-minded disciples who worship space-ships and reject anything based on logic, fact, and reality." He sighed again. "I told grandma she'd made a mistake by home-schooling you and not exposing you to normal kids and normal life. I only compounded the problem by offering you a job that would keep you just as secluded as that damned cult had. It took me a long time, Kels, but I got over the brainwashing and the fear those bastards instilled in us. I'm happy now."

"How," she choked out, "how did you get over it?"

There was a long pause on the other end of the line, and then finally he said, "I told people what happened. I turned in the cult for child abuse. A couple of years ago. I'm sorry I didn't tell you, but I was afraid you wouldn't understand."

His gentle explanation stunned her. "Michael... they didn't abuse us!"

"You don't call making us all wear the same clothing to turn us into androgynous drones abuse? Raising us without parents in a barn like veal wasn't abusive? Or how about forcing little girls to become wives? Come on. You aren't stupid. It was wrong and you know it. The sooner you admit it, the happier you'll be."

She sniffled and reached for the roll of toilet paper she'd brought from the bathroom earlier. "Like you?"

"Like me." He hesitated again, and then said softly, "The woman who answered the phone... that's Linda. She's my fiancée."

"Oh. Um, congratulations. Does she... does she know—"

"She knows everything. She's okay with it."

She congratulated Michael again and hung up, wondering if she'd ever be more than okay about everything that had happened in her life. Maybe he was right. Maybe it was time to let someone in. Hopefully it wasn't too late.

Trent stared at his computer screen, thinking of all the reasons he shouldn't read the email sitting there in his inbox. An email from Kelsa, from whom he'd heard nothing since she took off from the hospital. He'd called, had a charming conversation with her answering machine to tell her that the elderly lady they'd picked up had passed away, but that was it. Well, he'd knocked on her door once, but she hadn't answered, even though he knew she'd been home.

So he'd given her a few days to come around, but just this morning he'd begun to believe she wouldn't, and the pain that stabbed him was sharper than any of the twenty-gauge needles in his medic jump bag. Now there was an email from her, a message that may very well be a sprinkle of salt for his wound.

Oh, what the hell. He was a glutton for punishment.

He opened the email and sat back, steeling himself for another rejection.

From: GamerGirl

To: TrentJordan

Subject: Taking Chances

Hi Trent,

I'm sorry I didn't answer your call or the door when you knocked. I guess I've needed time to straighten some things out in my head and in my home. I've done all I can do on my own, and now I need you.

You're a paramedic because you want to help people, right? Well, I need help now more than I've ever needed it. I know I've hurt you. I've asked you to settle for less than you wanted and at the same time asked for more than you could give. So I understand if you don't want to help me out with this.

But if you do, if you can, I'll be home, and I'll always answer the door to you.

Kelsa :)

Whoa. He jumped up from the seat and paced the narrow strip of carpet in his spare bedroom. What kind of help did she want from him? Did it matter? He told her he wouldn't let her go. So now he had to go find out if he'd made the right decision.

Kelsa's chest tightened as she held the door open for Trent, who looked magnificent in sweat shorts and a white paramedic T-shirt that said *"We don't deserve to be called heroes. But then, we don't deserve to be puked on, either."*

Boy, had she puked on him.

Always before he'd been an open book with eyes that sparkled with life, but today they were hooded, unreadable, and it pained her to realize just how much she'd hurt him. He looked wary, like he expected a sucker-punch at any moment.

He brushed past her, and little flutters shot across her skin where their arms touched. She'd missed that. She'd missed *him.*

"You got a TV," he said, a touch of surprise in his voice.

"I've even tried watching it. Sitcoms. I can't bring myself to watch dramas or the news yet."

He turned, looked her over from her bare feet, up her jeans-clad legs, to the baggy T-shirt she'd thrown on. Despite all the clothing, she felt naked.

"So, what can I do for you?"

She nearly shuddered. So professional. So emotionless. He wasn't going to make this easy on her. She deserved nothing less.

"I need—" she took a deep, calming breath "—I have to get something off my chest, and I think it'll explain my need to live in a fantasy world."

Most of the tension drained from his face, and he nodded. "I'm all ears."

She sank down in a bean bag chair, and he did the same. She told him about growing up in a cult, about sleeping with dozens of other children in a large, one-room barn where they slept on mats on the wooden floor, about how they'd lived without electricity or modern conveniences.

How, when Michael spirited her away in the middle of the night, she hadn't wanted to go. She'd kicked and screamed, aware on some level that had he been caught, his life might have been in danger. And yet, until she spoke with him two nights ago, she'd still protected the cult members in her mind, still made excuses for their behavior.

"You were brainwashed," Trent said, as if that made what she'd done okay. "And it explains a lot. Hell, I can't believe you're as normal as you are."

"Normal? Not a word I would ever have associated with me."

Trent leaned forward in his bean bag chair, braced his forearms on his knees. "So what does all this mean?"

She shook her head. "I don't know. I guess I'm just ready to blend a little reality with fantasy."

"Do you really think you can do that?"

She gestured to the TV. "I bought that, didn't I?"

"Doesn't mean much. Who says you have to turn it on?" He fixed her with a narrow-eyed, suspicious stare. "What does all this have to do with me? You said you needed my help."

Nodding, she stood and held out her hand. He took it, cautiously, and allowed her to lead him to her computer room, where she stood at the threshold, staring into the darkened space.

Taking a deep breath, she squeezed his hand and stepped inside. She flicked on the lights—the harsh overhead lights she'd never used. The room had never been lit by anything but the computer screen and lava lamp during the night, and the sun streaming through the window during the day.

"What are we doing?"

She turned, placed a hand on Trent's breastbone, over his heart. "We're going to make love. No gimmicks, no toys." His breath hitched, and she smiled as she trailed a finger down, over the washboard muscles of his abs, over his navel, to the waistband of his low-slung shorts. "We're going to do it in here, in my sacred place." She dropped her hand lower and found him hard already. "You brought fantasy to your workplace. I'm going to bring reality to mine."

His hands lifted to her upper arms, where ran them up and down in long, soothing strokes. "I've never wanted anything more than to make love to you, but are you sure you want to do this?"

She kicked aside the box containing the violent computer game from Dream sOFT, knowing that after this she'd be able to play the thing, though never enjoy it. Looking into the heated depths of Trent's eyes, she nodded.

"I love you. I may not be ready for parties and concerts and amusement parks, but I'm ready for you, and I want you in every aspect of my life."

His loving grin wrapped around her heart. "In every aspect?" he teased, his grin turning wicked. "How about in that NASA chair?"

Desire pooled her blood in all the right places and made her lightheaded with the need to have Trent inside her. "You read my mind."

He took her in his arms and pulled her roughly against him, and this time when she thought he felt like home, she knew what home was. It was being in Trent Jordan's embrace as he whispered that he loved her over and over.

Home was being in a room of fantasy with the man of her dreams who was all too real.

About the Author:

Larissa Ione is the author of spicy paranormal romance and sexy contemporary romance with a medical slant. An Air Force veteran, she has lived all over the United States and Europe, and she now lives wherever her Coast Guard husband's assignments take her, their nine-year-old son, two cats, and two mice.

You can contact her and learn more about her writing at Larissalone.com.

Heart Full of Stars

by Linda Gayle

To My Reader:

Three emotions have united people throughout time: love, hope and passion. *Heart Full of Stars* is set far in the future, but these emotions still resonate as two lovers race against danger and rediscover desire.

Chapter One

Mars Outpost
Earth Year 2118

"Get this thing off me!" Fanta slung an angry glare at the bartender as she plucked at the slimy, segmented tongue lapping around her forearm.

The bartender tossed his shaggy black mane and laughed. The sound chimed through the air like a chorus of crystal bells. Only pretty thing about Vuilites, Fanta thought glumly. Beside her, the mammoth Triclops unfurled a second tongue around her shoulders, and she almost leapt out of her skin.

"I said I'm not interested, you troglodyte!" The frantic waving of her hands toppled her glass, splashing liquor into the Trike's mucousy eyes. All three blinked furiously. The Trike growled, a basso complaint more felt than heard.

Pinned to her barstool by the creature's bulk, Fanta pressed back against the counter. "Look, buddy, you asked for it."

"Back off, Quask."

The Trike swiveled his elephantine head toward the source of the command. A dark-haired man stared down her suitor. He stood with his legs slightly apart, his stance relaxed. The fingers of his right hand casually stroked the duct tape-wrapped butt of a blaster protruding from a holster slung low on his hips. Quask hesitated, snarled, then, to Fanta's unending relief, backed away.

"Thank you," she sighed. The man eased up next to her. She scooted her chair over to make room.

He raised two fingers to the bartender, who brought him a shotglass of dark liquor. "Figures Quask would be the first one to sniff you out," he said, then downed his drink in one gulp. He waved over another, ordered one for her as well.

"He did more than sniff." She dabbed slime from her sleeve with a cocktail napkin. "Do you know him?"

"Wouldn't be the first time I'd toasted his tentacles." He turned to her, eyes inscrutable, and held out his hand. "Decker, security. What's your business here, Miss... ?"

"Rae. Fanta Rae." Clasping his fingers, she offered her best smile. He seemed immune. The drinks came and he appraised her solemnly.

Whatever he'd ordered stung her lips and dove down her throat like a swarm of hornets. Gagging, Fanta dropped the glass. That, at least, elicited a fleeting smile from Decker. She gazed at him over a napkin pressed to her lips.

True, he was the first man she'd seen in years, but even back then, before she'd left Earth, she would have found him wickedly hot. Eyes the intense blue of a clear winter sky just before dusk, black hair razored in a buzz cut, dusted with silver at the temples, a strong, shadowed jaw that jutted when he clenched his teeth. The hand he curled around the shotglass was large and calloused. With an unexpected tremble, Fanta imagined the delicious, rough feel of those hands dragging over her naked skin. Then she shook her head. God, it had been a long time.

He waited while she cleared her burning throat. "I'm here by accident, actually," she rasped. "My hopper broke down. It's in the shop, you can check it out yourself."

He nodded. "I saw it."

"Then you know I'm on my way home."

That iron jaw tightened. "Recolonizing?"

"Yes. I should have landed at New Ellis, of course." She rolled her eyes. "Would have, if my generator hadn't given out."

He produced a palm-sized gray instrument from under his jacket. "I'll still need to run a proof."

"Sure, of course." Fanta waited while he made adjustments to the Identicom, then pressed her thumb on the pad. When the minute needle broke her flesh, drawing a drop of blood, she flinched. A light blinked green. Decker put the scanner back. "It'll take a few minutes. Where've you been since?"

Since. She knew what he meant. Since the Aggressions, the series of wars that had wiped out three-quarters of Earth's population and driven the survivors into the cold and empty arms of space.

"All over. Star cruising. I'm a singer. I got some great gigs cross-galaxy. In some parts of the universe, I've sold more recordings than Elvis and the Beatles combined." She smiled, and he grunted.

"Sing something," he said.

Glad for the distraction, she slipped off her stool. "Okay. Let's see. Oh, this was a big hit on Pegasus Nine." Tapping a complex rhythm against her hips, she sprang into a peppy tune, showing off with twisting trills up and down a scale that would daunt most vocalists. The language, of course, added to the difficulty of the performance, but Fanta prided herself on her mastery of Guifpegn.

Decker, watching with a look of bemusement, nursed his drink while a few offworlders paused to listen. One, a blue skinned Pegian, her aural tubes vibrating, burbled in admiration.

With a modest grin, Fanta bowed. The Pegian snapped her appendages appreciatively and moved on.

Decker finished his drink. "No, something from home. From before."

She searched her memory, thrust her fingers through her spiky hair.

"I, uh, I'm sorry, I don't remember..."

A corner of his mouth quirked. "S'okay. Don't worry about it."

Regret nudged her, and a little shame. "Hold on, I do, I think." She cast a glance ceilingward, blurred the gleaming silver ductwork in her vision and let her lids droop. Started singing, "With a heart full of stars, I wait for you..." Her head rolled down. She kept her eyes closed, kept her voice low and sultry. "In a world without hope, I reach for you..." Then, feeling her tenuous hold on the lyrics slip, she hummed a few broken bars through a rueful smile. She shook her head, shrugged. "That's all I… Decker?"

Eyes wide and dark with shock, he stared at her. Then he blinked and passed his hand over his mouth, down the coarse stubble of his chin. "Jesus," he said, his voice edgy and harsh. Something out past the fabriglass dome seemed to catch his attention and he turned away from her, toward the flat, featureless Martian landscape. He drew a cigarette from his pocket, clamped one end in his mouth. His hand shook a little as he lit it and took a heavy drag.

Fanta caught her lower lip between her teeth. "Sorry, guess I'm rusty."

A veil of smoke fogged the view as he exhaled. The eyes he turned on her were glossy, blue as despair. "After all these years. After all these years, it still hurts."

Fanta dropped her gaze to the floor, studied the gridwork beneath her boots. A sharp beep made her look up. Decker flipped open the Identicom and raised a brow. "You check out, Fanta Rae." His expression of reserved detachment had returned. Baring his teeth around his cigarette, he snapped the Identicom shut, thrust it in his belt, flicked a waste of ash into the grids. "You're free to go. Have a nice day."

Pushing away from the bar, he took a step. Fanta's hand shot out, grabbed his. Fingers closed around warm, real, human flesh, and her breath snagged in her throat.

Decker said, "Something wrong?"

The big Trike slouched past them. Its rheumy amber eyes rolled over Fanta with a damp gleam of unmistakable hunger. She flicked a desperate glance toward Decker.

"He likes you," he said in a dark, softly teasing tone. When Fanta swallowed hard, he asked, "You got a place to stay?" Though he took back his hand, he gave her fingers a parting squeeze. Her limp hand felt impossibly cold as it dropped to her side.

"I hadn't thought that far ahead." She managed a wan smile. "I wasn't even supposed to be here."

"Right." He pitched the smoldering cigarette butt onto the floor.

"Sorry."

"Stop apologizing." Decker squinted into the muted ultra-violet lights and for a moment, Fanta thought he was going to walk away after all. But then he turned back to her, his face set as if he had reached a decision. "Guess you'd better come with me."

Grateful, she flitted to his side and followed him from the bar. "If you'll just point me toward the Human Sector—"

"Didn't you notice?" He jerked his chin at the multi-hued crowd pressing around them.

The mall area jammed with life. Blue-skinned Pegians, other trikes, a few races Fanta didn't recognize.

"Mars is all offworlders now," Decker answered for her. "You and me, we're the only humans in town."

She eyed him with new appreciation. "How long have you been here?"

"Since."

"Why?"

He pulled out his cigarettes, offered her one. When she shook her head, he lit one for himself and led her down a less crowded corridor.

"Aren't you going to recolonize?" she asked. "They say Earth's beautiful now. Clean and fresh and safe. You could start a new life."

"No."

With a sideways glance, Fanta took in the stubborn set of his profile. "You must get lonely."

Pausing at a slight indentation along the wall, he wiped his palm over the wavelength reader. The door slid open. Fanta hesitated only a second. She'd learned to rely on her instincts. The only alarm Decker set off was her libido, which clamored for an end to the drought of human contact. She'd survived nine years of alien hands, claws, paws on her skin... Fanta barely checked herself from reaching for Decker again. She followed him into the sparsely furnished apartment.

He pulled a rumpled blanket off the sofa, pushed the cigarette butt into an empty beer can. "You can hang here. No one'll bother you. There's a photophone in the kitchen, if you want to check on your hopper. Food, too."

"Thanks."

The room smelled of smoke and booze and old blankets. Should have been off-putting, but Fanta found it oddly comforting. Human smells. Male smells. The touch of the Y-chromosome everywhere in evidence. She watched Decker fuss about the room, picking up litter.

Arms overburdened with papers and dirty laundry, he looked around, apparently searching for some place to dump his load. Fanta followed him to the tiny kitchen where he propped open a closet with his foot, packed in the garbage, then quickly closed it. Flattening his palms against the door, he slanted an apologetic grin. "Place is a mess. Never noticed it before."

"That's okay." She smiled back. He was younger than he'd looked in the dim lights of the bar. Mid-thirties, tops. Going gray early. She reached out and touched his hair, stroked her fingers down the rough plane of his cheek.

Decker sucked in his breath as if she'd slapped him. "Don't."

The stark vulnerability in his eyes lanced her. "You've been here alone, all this time?" she gently asked.

"Way I like it." But his voice guttered out and his gaze slipped from her lips to her breasts. Her nipples hardened as if he'd touched them.

"I haven't seen a real man in nine years," she said. "I... Thank you for protecting me."

"My job," he said.

"Your job to bring me here?"

"No."

"I feel safe here," she whispered, pleading with her eyes, with the soft sway of her body as she stepped closer. "I trust you."

"You don't know me."

"You're human, like me. Alone, like me."

She lifted her hand to his face, fingers placating, tracing the line of his jaw. "You can't run forever."

He caught her wrist. "Can."

But his thumb, seemingly of its own volition, made tiny circles over her pulse. When Fanta moved to press her palm against his face, he let her. With a soft groan, eyes closed in surrender, he leaned into her hand.

"Hold me, Decker," she whispered. "I want to forget, to feel alive again..."

She brushed her lips across his mouth, felt him shudder. An answering shudder quaked through her body. On the second pass, he slid his arms around her waist, pulling her close. The hard evidence of his desire pressed against her thigh. Hands twined behind his neck, she drew him down, tasted the bitter liquor on his tongue.

Then he pulled back. His eyes glittered with his own sharp need. "It's too soon. We should wait."

"For what?" She stroked her body against him, and his lashes twitched.

"For something. Nothing. I don't know." With a hungry growl he took her mouth again. "Fanta..."

He tasted of smoke and desire and desperation born of long years of loneliness. His hands roamed everywhere, slid down her spine, cupped her bottom, squeezed, yes, just right. His kisses explored, teased, tested. She felt the price of his restraint in his rigid biceps and tense shoulders.

"I don't want to hurt you," he said, but his hand closed over her breast and his thumb found her nipple beneath the slippery fabric. "We won't see each other again."

"I'm not a sensitive girl." She slid her hand down and squeezed his cock through his pants so his eyes rolled in his head. "Hurt me, Decker. Use me. I want you, want you..."

His mouth slamming down on hers muffled her pleas. The strength of his grip bent her over his arm, made her clutch at his shoulders. She opened her mouth for him as her body thrummed and ached. Her nipple peaked beneath his stirring thumb. He kneaded it, plucked at it, then his hand moved to her throat and down to the fasteners on her blouse.

She was wet and hot and needed to rub her clit against that thick erection beneath his jeans. When he finally found his way under her shirt to her skin to her naked breast, she cried out.

He pushed her back against the wall and stripped away her top. Glorious cool air rushed over her skin. His jaw was tight, his eyes burned. Almost roughly, he spun her, gripped her wrists and brought them up over her head, held them to the wall. Fanta gasped. For a moment, fear touched her. Maybe he took her "hurt me" too literally.

Then one rough palm came up to massage her breast and Decker's hot breath moved against her ear. "One night, Fanta Rae. With a heart full of stars."

Her dark, scarred lover was a romantic. She wanted him all the more. His hand shook a little as it traced the curve of her breast and the sweep of her hip. This meant something to Decker. Not just a quick fuck. No random meeting of strangers reaching through the darkness to pass into forgotten memory.

Fanta stilled under his caresses. She didn't fight his grip on her captured wrists, but trusted, listened to the meaning of his touch, tasted the emotion in his movements.

And he moved slowly. His fingers rasped her nipples, drew on them until her womb throbbed in time to his tactile rhythm. Her hips nudged in synchrony. She wanted his mouth, there, everywhere. She tried to turn. He held her tight. Fanta groaned.

His hot, hard body covered her back as he leaned into her. The iron bar of his cock rode between the cheeks of her ass. His roughened palms stroked her from throat to breast to hip. Sensation flushed over her skin. Her pussy wept for him, lips swelling.

"Please, Decker."

"Stay."

Releasing her wrists, he hooked his thumbs into the waistband of her silver skirt and tugged it down, slowly, over her bottom and her thighs. His mouth followed, licking, nipping at her hot flesh. As soon as he got it past her knees, she spread her feet apart and whispered "please" again.

His palm burned a path up her inner thigh. She wanted to see his face, but his harsh command and this strange trust held her. She panted against the wall, focused on feeling.

Thick fingers stirred her juices. A shuddering cry tore from her. He twisted a finger up into her and she bore down on it, balling her fists up above her head, eyes closed tight before the pleasure and need sucked her will away.

"God, Decker, I hate you. I want you. Don't do this. Do more." She started to turn again, but he held her fast with a hand on her hip.

"Not yet. Spread your legs more."

Slave to his graveled voice, she did.

He touched her everywhere, with more tenderness than she could bear. If he'd been rough, fast, she could have screamed, exploded, been done. Instead, he drew the pleasure out like a chain of gold, building link upon link.

He circled her clit with a butterfly touch, slipped his fingers between her swollen folds, plunged inside her to press and stroke and make her squirm. He kept her balanced, damn him, on the silver edge of ecstasy. Sweat sprang on her back. She trembled. Her pulse beat in her nipples. She pressed them against the cool wall for relief and found her pleasure impossibly heightened.

"I want to see you," she gasped.

"Yes. Now." He turned her and she looked down where he crouched. Winter blue eyes held hers even as he leaned forward and swept his tongue across her distended clit.

Fanta screamed.

He caught her as she fell, limp with the pleasure that strummed through her in wave after glistening wave. Yet her clit still ached, her pussy felt empty. He caught her up in his arms and kissed her slack lips. Fanta laced her fingers through his damp hair. He'd been sweating, too.

"You're too good at that," she whispered.

"You're beautiful, Fanta. Like starlight in my arms."

She touched his jaw. "You're a poet."

"There once was a girl from Nantucket—"

She laughed at the unexpected humor and pressed her fingers to his mouth. "Okay, maybe not such a poet after all. You must have other talents." She stroked her hand over his still-hard cock. "That wasn't all, was it?"

"Hell, no."

Decker hooked his arms under her knees and carried her small
weight to the sofa in the cramped living room. Fanta Rae's wide eyes
glowed with trust and the embers of her come. What a gift she was,
to him, the last man who deserved anything, let alone this shining
star of a girl.

He set her down gently on the tattered couch and knelt beside her.
Her skin was pale, peppered with freckles. Cuffs and collar didn't
match, he noticed, smiling as he feathered his fingers across her bare
thigh. Her hair might be fuschia, but a neatly trimmed patch of downy
blonde covered her mound.

Her knees relaxed apart in silent invitation. Her pussy lips were
slick and swollen, flushed deep pink from his caresses. She smelled
like... like nothing he'd known in a long time. Flowers, maybe. Falling leaves.

He almost lost it right there.

She pulled at the collar of his shirt. "Kiss me."

He put a hand on the soft curve of her knee and hesitated.

Her brows knit. "What's the matter? Something's the matter."

"I haven't..." He took a deep breath to stop his trembling, inhaled
her sultry scent instead. "Not since my wife."

She rolled to her side and wrapped her arms around him. Gentle
hands caressed his shoulders.

"Tell me," she said.

"No."

Feathery kisses drifted over his face and throat while she pushed
off his jacket and loosened his shirt. She was naked, while his clothes
still provided one last barrier between them. He rolled onto the sofa
and pulled her on top of him.

She seemed to understand he did it to stop her. Propping her chin
on her fists with her pointy little elbows digging into his chest, she
stared down at him.

"I didn't lose anyone like that," she said, her voice quiet. "Friends.
Neighbors. My dog. I barely escaped." She rubbed at her nose. "I

guess anyone could say that."

"Where'd you go?"

"Ursula Seven. I left on a stellar barge on the very last day. I had a bankable talent. Otherwise..." She shrugged.

His gut went cold. She'd have been left behind to die, like so many others. Millions.

"You signed a contract?" he asked.

"Yes. It's over now."

But her gaze slid away as if the retelling was too much to bear. Or she wasn't telling the truth. Neither would surprise him. The Aggressions had brought out the worst in humanity, and toward the end, cutthroats who operated off-world sold barge space to the highest bidder. If the refugee had no money, they took life instead. People sold themselves into slavery to escape. Driven by terror, they signed shady deals. Some wound up shackled in Krackus mines or in the sex slums of alien worlds.

If the contract was breached, people died. Or worse.

"I've seen contract hunters pass through this station," he said. "Gets ugly."

"I made lots of money for them. They can't complain."

"What about you?"

"I started out with nothing and I still have most of it left." She gave him a grin that tugged at his heart. "Your turn now."

"I was a Marine," he said. "Stationed around the moon. I saw it. I was looking down when the assholes did it." The barrage of red flashes across the continents, lighting his cabin in eerily silent pulses.

"Your family?" she asked.

"Gone. All gone."

"Your kids—"

"No." Gray pain churned inside and he shoved it down deep as he'd done so many times before. "No more talking."

Fanta pressed her warm cheek to his jaw. He let out a long breath and threaded his fingers through her soft halo of hair.

"We made it, Decker." Her soft kiss offered absolution. "We're alive, here, now. You and me."

Her hips moved over his belly, and his cock leapt to life again. She slid up so her taut, pink nipple hovered over his lips. "Take what you need."

He needed so much—to lose himself in her. To find himself. She knew somehow. Unleashed lust roared through him. He closed his eyes and cradled the soft weight of her breast in his hand. He drew her sweet offering into his mouth. She stroked his hair while he rolled her nipple over his tongue. Fanta's breathy mewls of pleasure blotted out all thoughts.

Alive. Yes. For the first time in forever, life stirred in him.

He stood and unbuckled his pants. She sat up and did the rest. Bold as could be, she reached for his cock. A fever flush gripped him as her fist closed around him. Then her warm lips wrapped around the head, and the world went up in white light.

She sucked him ruthlessly, dragged her tongue up his length. Her nails scraped over his thighs and his balls. Twisting, primal desire drummed through him. Heat gathered in his groin. He gripped her slender shoulders and groaned. So close, too soon—

He tore from her delicious mouth and sank to his knees.

"What—" Her surprise ended in a yelp of delight when he spread her legs and thrust his tongue deep into her pussy. Her fingers knotted in his hair. Her thighs would strangle him, but he held them open with his hands.

She tasted of dusky spice. Fire and earth.

Her panting cries made his blood burn. He fingered her, driving into her sopping, tight passage while his jealous cock ached. His tongue swirled the moist bead of her clit. He felt her orgasm building in the clench of her cunt around his knuckles. He was as merciless as she, pushing her farther, harder.

At last she broke with another scream. Her come flowed over his tongue, sweet as rain.

He pushed her back on the sofa and covered her with his body. She needed to regroup, he knew, but his muscles trembled from holding back, and if his dick got any harder it'd break off. He tried to touch her face gently, ended up slipping a finger between her parted lips.

She wrapped her tongue around it and sucked.

"God," he growled.

"Yes, I think I just saw Him." She smiled up at him, tousled and sexy as hell. What a woman.

"I stopped taking shots a long time ago," he said. He could get her pregnant.

She shook her head. "It's all right."

Good. Because he couldn't wait one second more. Just as he put his hand between her thighs to part them, she pushed him over and swung a leg across his torso. Gleaming eyes gazed down at him.

"My turn," she said. She took his wrists in her small hands and held them above his head. Her breasts swung temptingly just out of reach, making his mouth water. Then she lifted herself and, using one hand, slid his cock into the molten confines of her cunt.

"You're going to kill me." He sucked in a breath. "I survived this long, and now I'm going to be fucked to death."

She pouted prettily. "I can stop."

"No, no. I'll be brave and accept my fate." He wrapped his hands around her waist and lifted her a little, then let her slide back down his shaft. Dark pleasure flowed into his bones. He crossed his eyes and groaned in ecstasy to make her laugh. The reverberations trembled through him and made his breath hitch. "You're so sweet and tight, like hot cream, like heaven."

His praise pleased her. She wiggled her bottom and bathed his nuts with moisture.

"Look at us," he said, lifting her again.

She looked down to where their bodies were joined. His shaft glistened with her fluids, her love lips glided over the thin, veined skin. He held her just so the blunt head of his penis touched the mouth of her cunt, then he pushed up with his hips and buried himself in her again. Fanta threw back her head and moaned.

"Touch yourself," he growled. "For me. I want to see."

Eyes glossy, she lifted her fingers to her breasts and pinched her nipples. She bit her lip and panted while he built up a rhythm inside her.

He felt the now-familiar tug of her pussy working toward climax. He angled his thrusts to hit the sensitive spot inside her. White heat poured through him. Blood bolted to his cock. Fingers dug into the yielding flesh of her hips and thighs. He pounded into her. Now she moved, leaned forward, hands on his chest, eyes closed. Her head swung back and forth while she whimpered and circled her hips.

"More." He knew she danced on the edge. "Do it."

She reached between them and rubbed her clit.

Yesyesyesgodyes— The pressure built, rose. Flashed. He gushed into her, fucked her hard while she came and came and came…

And the world went away.

Moments later, long moments later, with her limp arms and legs tangled in his, Decker felt the first wash of guilt.

Everything slid back into place in his lust-blurred vision. The cramped apartment. The dingy lighting. The smell of sex and sweat and stale cigarettes.

He could use one now. Careful not to disturb Fanta, whose head lay on his chest, he reached behind him for his pack and lighter. The first drag burned away the taste of her and he instantly regretted it.

She stroked his chest. "Aren't those things bad for you?"

"Dunno. They're Vuilian. Made out of… something else. They say they're okay."

"Who says?"

He breathed out a pale gray cloud, shrugged. "The Vuilites."

She gave a sleepy snort and nuzzled against him. He cuddled her close. What the hell did he have to feel guilty about? He'd gone almost nine years without a woman. Only a few cold-blooded aliens to call friends. Alone on this rock. Still, it jagged at him. His family. He'd sworn his life to them and failed. Was he forgetting them now?

He wanted to get up.

"Want a shower?" he asked her.

She murmured a protest and twined herself around him like a vine. "Stay with me, Decker." She peered at him. "Is that your first name?"

"Last."

After a silence, she said, "Well?"

He pulled in smoke and narrowed his eyes. "I'm not sure I know you well enough to share my first name."

She punched his ribs and he laughed.

"Bastard," she muttered.

"You guessed it. My name, it's Bastard."

"I bet it is." She bit his nipple so he yelped.

"Ow, you." He gently pushed at her shoulder to roll her onto her back. Fanta stretched out in all her considerable, naked glory. He rubbed slow circles over her bare belly. And felt guilty.

"I have to go back to work," he said.

"Come with me," she whispered.

"Didn't I just?"

"Not that. I mean, come back to Earth."

He stared into her serious eyes. "There's nothing left for me there."

"We all lost in the war." Her hand trailed over his bare chest and settled over his heart. "There's no going back. But we can go forward. Together."

"You sound like a recolonization commercial." He gave a harsh, bitter laugh and plowed his fingers through his hair. "It's not that easy." He stood and snatched his shirt from the armrest. "Forget it, Fanta."

Chapter Two

Despair pooled in her gut. She drew her knees up under her chin, watched him dress, didn't try to stop him when he headed for the door.

"Get some sleep," he said, buckling his gunbelt. "My shift's not over 'til dawn. Help yourself to... whatever." Their gazes locked and he hesitated as if he might speak, might give her a thin thread of hope. Fanta's pulse skittered. Then the door shushed open and he was gone.

With a heavy sigh, she curled into a ball on the sofa. The ragged blanket, hand-knit probably by some long-gone aunt, provided little warmth, and she tossed beneath it for a few minutes before she got up and took a shower.

Decker's come washed down the drain, but the echo of his cock inside her remained. She felt expanded. Whatever emptiness she'd felt had been filled, and then left emptier than ever all over again. She thumped her fist against the shower door and wept.

Eventually, she gave up, dressed, and dialed the garage on the photophone. The Pegian mechanic shook his head at her through the screen. "Hopper's fucked," he said in a watery voice.

"What do you mean?"

"Can't get the parts. It's an old machine. I got a call in to Northside—"

"You said you could fix it."

The Pegian mumbled and glanced away.

What did he care, there was nowhere else for her to take her business. Shit. The back of her neck prickled. Something didn't feel right. The way he kept glancing aside. "How much longer will it take?"

His appendages drooped. "By morning, maybe."

She cut him off with a wave of her hand. "All right. Do what you can. Call me at—" Aw, double-shit. She didn't want to drag Decker into this. And she didn't want to give away her location. Just in case.

Her mouth felt dry and she rubbed her palm across her forehead.

"You in a hurry, you can take a rental," the mechanic burbled.

"Rental?" Yes. Any way to get to Earth faster, where aliens were not allowed, where she could forget and be forgotten. "I'll come down."

The Pegian had already bent to jot on a clipboard. The connection winked out.

Fanta slumped against the wall and put her head in her hands. Her mind played tricks on her. The mechanic was busy, that's all. No way Tirrell would have followed her here. Whether he liked it or not, she'd closed her contract. She'd paid for her freedom a hundred times over.

She paced back to the sofa, folded the blanket, draped it across the armrest. Someone had once loved Decker well enough to knit a little red heart into one corner. She hadn't noticed it before. Her hand smoothed the tired yarn and her eyes closed against fresh tears.

Decker would find her gone when he returned. She wondered if he'd be glad.

"You're late," the big blue lizard said.

Decker nodded to Wejar, his shift partner, and joined him at the bar. With a scaly claw, Wejar delicately peeled back the top of his cup of kava and lapped at it. "Fook, no sugar. What's a body got to do around here to get some sugar?"

"Here." Decker tossed him a few packs from a bowl.

Wejar's yellow eyes narrowed as he dumped the sweetener into his bilious black drink. "Eh, what's going on? You look like you been dragged around some."

"Don't I always look this way?"

"Good point."

Decker patted his breast pocket. "Got a smoke?"

Wejar tossed him a mostly empty pack and Decker shook out a cigarette. He'd forgotten his at the apartment. The way his mind latched onto the excuse to go back irked him. Since he'd taken one step from the door, he'd wanted to turn around and lose himself in Fanta again. Not good.

"What's going down?" he asked, more for distraction than for the information.

"The usual. Some fool in Quadre got his head blown off over a baro game. Coupla fights in Wikki. Hey—" He flicked out a cigarette for himself. "Turn on your com. Brass is looking for you. Wants to know what happened to that human intro you ID'd."

"Why?"

"Got some news on her. She broke contract."

Decker nearly swallowed his cigarette. "What?"

"Coupla real bad guys shipped in from Ursula Seven. Mob connected. Looking for her."

"Shit." He should've listened to his instincts.

Ganas couldn't raise their eyebrows—they had none—but Wejar's primary spines raised a few inches, revealing his interest. "You know where she is?"

Had she lied to him? Shit... He ignored Wejar's question. "Her ID checked out. No open contracts."

"No matter." He rubbed two claws of one hand together, meaning their bosses had taken a bribe to deliver the girl or stay out of the contractors' way, whichever came first.

A chill settled at the base of Decker's spine. He took a sour drag on his cigarette, tried to maintain an aura of detachment. "So, who's here to collect?"

"Coupla Tarsians. Seen 'em sneakin' around the mall, but they don't cause no trouble yet."

Tarsians. Nasty. Now what? Even if Fanta hadn't lied, in the big, dirty scheme of things, truth became irrelevant. She'd seduced him into her situation. If brass found out he'd sheltered her, slept with her—Christ, he'd be out on his ass, too. Maybe this rock wasn't paradise, but it was all he had, and it beat a Krackus mine all to hell, which was where he'd probably end up.

Decker waited for the anger, tried to convince himself to grow cold toward her. Not his problem. Right? He could pretend he didn't know her. Unless, of course, she still slept in his apartment. He almost groaned.

Wejar lowered his head. Smoke drifted from his nostrils, dragon-like. "Better if you find her first."

Damned perceptive Gana. Decker crushed out his cigarette and scrubbed at his eyes. "Maybe better for her if they do. I might do something I'll regret."

Like he had already. Worse, his stupid heart thumped against his ribs and all he could think about was dragging Fanta to safety and screwing her until this hard, bitter world disappeared again.

Ganas couldn't laugh, either, but his friend's rattling wheeze sounded close enough to a snicker. Decker shot him a scowl then sighed.

Wejar seemed to expect the favor Decker asked. Not a single spine raised when he began to talk.

"Crap. I am so lost…"

From the apartment, it should have been only a few turns to the garage. Instead, Fanta found herself jammed shoulder to tentacle in a crowded corridor headed who knew where. The clicking, burbling mass of life carried her along like a leaf in a stream. Panic began to swamp her.

"Garage? Which way to the Southside garage?" She asked it in Guifpegn, Tarsus, Almeika, and got only rude stares or grunts in return. Over a sea of heads, one pair of alien eyes singled her out. A tall indigo lizard-thing fixed a flat gaze on her. Didn't look friendly. She used to have nightmares about dinosaurs. Big teeth. Sharp claws.

Her nerves buzzed. She spun to bolt and shove through the mob. T-Rex nails hooked over her shoulders and bit into her skin. Fear ripped her. She slammed her elbow into the overgrown reptile's gut and heard it bark out in surprise.

The claws latched around her arms in a merciless grip. The thing hissed, "Escaping?"

She twisted to look up into the scary, scaly face. A cigarette dangled incongruously from between spiky teeth.

"I was checking on my hopper, as if it's any of your business. Let me go."

"Yeah, yeah." Sharp claws slid down to her wrists. He held them with one... hand... while the other reached around to his belt. The sight of silver cuffs shot a bolt of fear through her.

"Please, no," she gasped, fighting him. "What are you doing?"

"Fanta Rae, you're under arrest for breaking your contract."

All the air left her lungs. "It's not true."

"Not what I heard."

"Please, listen—" She searched the crowd for a rescuer. Indifferent alien faces stared back at her. The cuffs clicked around her wrists. Desperate, she scanned the dino's uniform, recognized the same sort of badge Decker had worn. As he pushed her into motion, she said, "You're security?"

"Yeah."

"Ask Decker, he knows."

"Decker who?"

She almost swore. "He's human, like me."

"How unfortunate."

"Where are you taking me?"

Her captor clammed up and shoved her along, into a shadowy passage that smelled of old oil and rust. They were alone. *She* was alone—with a T-Rex. Fanta broke into a cold sweat. She tried to jerk away. "Let me go, you Godzilla! Help!"

The lizard spun her around and pushed her back against a closed door. "No one will help you now." Bristling yellow spines sprang from his neck in a nightmare display.

Fanta squealed, "Don't eat me!"

The door slid open and he shoved her into a room.

Chapter Three

The door hissed shut and something grabbed her by the arm. She was pulled back hard against a solid body. Fanta lunged forward, kicked and, the hell with her precious vocal chords, screamed like a scalded cat.

"Hey!" A human shout cut through her terror. "Fanta, quit!"

"Decker!" *Thank God.* Despite his iron grip, she whirled to hug him. The damned cuffs— She pressed herself against him instead and buried her face against his neck. Safe, warm, familiar. Human.

He seized her upper arms and lifted her up on her toes. His glacial gaze brought all her fear tumbling back.

"You were supposed to stay where you were." He'd been angry when he left. Now, in the pale amber light glowing through the single window, he looked truly pissed. "I went back to my apartment to find you. Where the hell were you going?"

Her relief snuffed out. "I just wanted to check on my hopper."

"You could have used the phone."

"I did. It wasn't ready. They couldn't get the parts."

"Then why go and check?"

"To get a rental."

"To beat the contractors?"

"What contractors?" She wanted to be brave, hated the way her voice shook. "You and that lizard, you're wrong. There *is* no contract. I'm free."

He set her down roughly. "There're Tarsians here to collect."

"God." His news hit her like a punch in the gut. Slender black Tarsians with their drugs and darts. Masters of torture. Only Tirrell would hire such mercenaries.

Her knees went watery. Decker caught her before she fell. He put her in a chair and stepped back again as if he couldn't stand to touch her.

She leaned forward, tried to catch his indifferent gaze. "Please. I told you the truth."

"You don't get it," he said. "The truth doesn't matter. Even if I do believe you, there are still Tarsians hunting for you, and enough money behind them that no one is going to care."

"Not even you?"

His dark brows lowered.

Fanta balled her cuffed hands into tight fists. "After all, the only thing binding us is an hour's sex? Is that it?"

"Not even that."

Hot anger strangled her. "You selfish jerk."

"Me?" His voice rose. "You just screwed up my life, lady. There's a dozen witnesses who saw me leave the bar with you this morning, including Quask, who would trade his third nut to see me hang. All anyone has to do is a DNA scan of my apartment—"

"I'm sorry!" Her shout exploded in the small room.

Her outburst shocked them both into silence. Fanta could have sworn she heard her heart beating. Decker stared. He ran his hands over his hair and closed his eyes.

At last, he let out a heavy breath. "Stop apologizing."

Shivering with adrenaline, Fanta sniffled. "I need a tissue."

He went to her, muttering obscenities. Crouching beside the chair, he reached around back and undid the cuffs. As soon as her hands were free, she slid them around his neck and held on tight.

And he held her back.

His hair smelled of smoke and soap and the shadow of sex. She rubbed her tear-dampened cheek against it, imprinting him forever in her memory. "I never meant to get you in trouble."

"You can't help it. You're a woman."

She drew back, ready to snap, but his crooked grin diffused her temper. She took his hands in hers. "Tarsians, huh?"

"Mm hm. Know who sent them?"

She nodded. "My manager. *Former* manager. Tirrell."

"The guy who had your contract."

"Yes. *Had*." Thank you, God, he did believe her. "He never wanted to let me leave. Threatened me if I tried."

"Why?"

"I told you, I sold more recordings than Elvis and the Beatles combined." An awful thought occurred. "I made him rich enough to be able to hire Tarsians."

"Well, hell, that's a sad irony." He rubbed his thumbs over her knuckles. "How'd you get away in the first place?"

"I had friends, they helped me escape. Earth is about as far from Tirrell as I can get. I thought with the security grids, I'd be safe. But…" She shrugged. "My stupid hopper broke down."

"And here you are."

The shivers returned, spinning through her. She gripped his fingers tighter. "What am I going to do?"

"Find another way. There's always Plan B." He slid his palm around the back of her neck and pulled her to him. His lips covered hers, firm and real. She moaned with the relief of it, and sank into the kiss. Tongues touched, and heat raced through her, burning away her fear.

Maybe one hour of sex didn't mean much to him, but her body responded as if they'd never left off. This man, this moment—she clung to him like a lifeline.

He drew back and smoothed her cheek with the back of his knuckles. "Wejar's buying us time."

"Wejar? The lizard?"

"He's a Gana. And a friend."

"Then you do have a plan?"

"Kind of. He's keeping an eye out for the Tarsians. When the coast is clear, we make a run for it."

She kissed him again, lingered against his lips. "You do care."

He scowled and stood and pulled her to her feet. "You'll be the death of me."

But nothing he said really mattered. His actions counted. The way his eyes scorched a path over her. The strength in his grip still holding her hand. His harsh groan when he pulled her to him again and smothered her lips with his own.

She opened her mouth to him and his tongue dove inside, caressing the way it had once teased her pussy. Her inner muscles clenched and rippled. She slid her hand down his thigh and found his cock already hard, straining against the fabric. He hissed in a breath. He wanted her, too.

"We really shouldn't do this," he muttered, as he worked his way under her shirt to cup her breast.

She tugged at his uniform buttons. "Not much time."

He kissed her eyebrows, her cheeks, her throat. She tipped back her head. Her pussy pooled with desire. His fingertips teased her nipple and she gasped. "So good, so good."

"It's the adrenaline." He pulled her shirt over her head and slid his hot mouth over the curve of her breast. "Danger makes you horny."

"I'll get in trouble more often."

His blue eyes rolled up at her. "Please, don't."

He kissed his way down her bare belly and circled his tongue in her belly button so tremors wracked her. She clenched her fingers in his hair and thrust her hips forward, craving contact. Never had she burned so bright for any man.

She needed him now, needed the solid, real strength of him inside her. Her lover, her dark protector. He tugged down her panties and slid his fingers through her soaked slit.

"God, I missed you," he groaned.

No words could have been sweeter. She whimpered and ground against him. "Don't make me wait any more."

He swore under his breath and ripped his zipper down. He pulled out his thick cock. The sight of his big hand around the heavily veined shaft made her pussy weep even more.

"Where—?" The room had no bed, no sofa, not even soft carpeting.

Decker turned and dragged her toward the lone chair. He sat with a thud and pulled her onto his lap. His palms beneath her thighs helped steady her. His breathing came fast. He bit her shoulder, urgent, feral. Lust shivered through her. Her nipples grew so hard they ached. His lips clamped onto one as he pushed her down onto his cock. The imposing breadth of him made her cry out.

"Rock, baby," he urged.

She moved her hips, gripped him inside her. The fabric of his jeans chafed her inner thighs, heightened sensation. Oh, the sheer size of him, the stretching, the head of his penis pushing against her tender inner walls. He kissed her deeply, sucked at her lips, dragged them between his teeth. He was different now—possessive, fierce.

He clutched her bottom and coaxed her into a steady, urgent rhythm. One hand shifted to her thigh and his thumb found her clit. Circled. Stroked. She leaned back, hands on his knees, and pumped hard. Fiery sensation spiraled. Her breasts bounced. She felt his wicked gaze on them and reveled in it.

He grew impossibly thicker and heavier inside her. His guttural groans spurred her toward her own climax. It grew like a storm. Then—

"Decker? Decker, you there?"

He grabbed her waist and pushed her down hard on his lap. Held her still. Sweaty and out of breath, they stared at each other. The voice came again.

"Fuck me..." Decker muttered. He reached down to his shirt on the floor and found the com. "Yeah, Wejar."

"You're about to have company. There's a Tarsian heading toward your corridor."

Timing was everything.

Decker zipped his pants and adjusted his gunbelt. Hell, he hadn't even had time to take that off. How could two people, still mostly dressed with assassins stalking them, get into so much trouble? Fanta's fuchsia hair popped out of the top of her shirt as she tugged it back on. Her short silver skirt already hid her sweet pussy that had been so close to coming.

After checking his blaster, he seized her hand. "There's a back way out. It'll take us under the mall and toward the launching port."

"They'll be waiting for us, won't they?" Her kiss-swollen lips looked deliciously damp even as she frowned. "My hopper. They must have gotten to the mechanic and told him to lure me there."

He forced his gaze up, only to be caught in the beauty of her thickly-lashed eyes. "Makes sense, but…" But what? Hell, all his blood concentrated in his other head, leaving his brain with nothing but cobwebs. He pulled her toward the back of the room, to a secret door. "Don't worry. Between me and Wejar, we'll get you out of here."

She tripped along behind him. "He said he didn't know you."

"We figured it'd be best if it looked like he arrested you and kept me out of it."

"Tried to make it look like you really didn't know me."

"Yeah." He felt vaguely uncomfortable with that now. "Nothing personal."

"Sure." But he heard her bruised tone.

Hadn't he warned her? Hadn't he been the one to say someone would get hurt? Yet would he fuck her all over again? Hell yeah. His grievously disappointed cock remained half-hard, and her sultry taste lingered in his mouth.

He'd never forget the jolt he'd felt when she'd turned into his waiting arms. Like the sun had come up. Like someone had breathed life into his soul. Shit, this was a bad way to be thinking. He didn't want any attachments.

The door opened a few inches and he had to put his shoulder to it to get the rest done. It took all his strength to shut and bolt it from the other side. He stood back and looked at the rusty controls. "Stand back and I'll blast it."

"Allow me." Fanta reached out and ripped the wires from the box. Yellow sparks popped then died.

He grinned at her. "Nicely done."

She moved to his side, her sweet mouth pressed in a worried frown. "Where are we?"

Ancient ductwork rose just above their heads. Portholes placed about two meters apart let in dusty Martian light. "In between the walls, basically." He pointed into the gloom. "If we go that way, we'll walk under the entertainment sector, around the perimeter of the dome. The shipping ports aren't far from there."

"I can't take my hopper, they're watching it."

Her voice trembled, and he slung an arm around her for comfort. "If Wejar can't secure passage, I'll get you out on my own. Don't worry, sweetheart."

"I don't know what to say. You're risking a lot for me."

"Hey. Birds of a feather get shot together. Right?"

Fanta threw her arms around him. She probably didn't know how the feel of her awesome breasts against his chest made his cock stiffen. Or maybe she did, because her lips found his and before he knew it, he had her back against the wall with his tongue in her mouth and she wasn't exactly protesting.

Her talented hand took a dive toward his zipper and he had to grab her wrist. "Whoa, darlin'. We have to move, really." Not that he wanted to. Not that way. Plenty of other ways he'd like to move, though.

Her lashes fluttered. "I'm just so… grateful."

"Grateful. Yeah." He laughed as best he could through the pain of his frustrated erection. "Me, too. This has been a good day. Let's not ruin it by ending up dead."

That seemed to shock some sense into her. They started down the dim passageway.

⁂

Fanta stayed close to Decker. He knew where he was going. Right? She kept convincing herself he did. They groped through a section so dark and cramped she kept up only by holding onto his belt. Her boots swished through fetid, shallow water. Something rubbery slid over her cheek and she yelped.

Decker reached back and put his hand on her hip. "Okay?"

"It touched me," she squeaked. "Slimy, like a tentacle."

"Sewer squids. Harmless. Mostly."

"Great…"

She concentrated on the dim glow of his com. He spoke quietly into it. Wejar answered. The Tarsian had gone room by room down the corridor and spent a great deal of time in the room they'd occupied. Wejar had been able to distract the assassin with some excuse to close up the area for security, but she knew the mercenary wouldn't be put off so easily.

Tarsians hunted by aura. They picked up the psychic echoes of a life-force and tracked them like crumbs. She shivered. God knew what a powerful aura she and Decker had left in that room.

Her heart beat in her throat as the overhead ducts seemed to drop lower and lower. Her shoulders brushed damp metal on either side. Claustrophobia pressed down on her. "Decker." She tugged at his belt. He could barely squeeze his hand back to touch her.

"Hang on, honey. We're coming to an open area."

She couldn't breathe. A scream clawed its way up Fanta's throat. The many tons of alien metal pushed down at her. "*Decker.*"

"Here." He grabbed her wrist and pulled her forward.

At last, she could stand, and the concrete ground was dry. But the soggy, warm air clung to her and the chamber they'd entered was as black as deep space. The repetitive thump of a ja-ja band far above them rumbled like a huge animal heart. She felt like a rabbit trapped in its hole.

"This isn't much better."

He pulled her into the protective circle of his arms and rubbed her back. "We're almost there. We're under the entertainment sector. Hear the music?"

"Yes. How much farther?"

"Another fifty meters."

"Let's keep going then." She needed light, air.

"Can't. Wejar says the Tarsians are right overhead."

"What?" She reflexively stared up into the pitch black.

"They've managed to track us, but they don't seem to know exactly where we are. We're safe for now. Wejar's going to try to draw them away."

"How? They'll never give up. I've seen them bring in people who tried to escape. They were... changed. Half-alive." She turned her face into Decker's shoulder and shuddered. "I can't take it. I'm scared."

"Shh. I know."

Panic rose on midnight wings to beat in her chest. "I have to move. Have to get out of here." She tried to pull away. He held her tight.

"Ten minutes, Fanta. Twenty, tops. If we move ahead, they'll find us. We're right under a concert hall. All the life forms up there will confuse them."

Her legs felt rubbery. She clutched at his shirt. "Decker, promise me. Promise me you won't let them take me. If they get me, you have to... have to..."

His strong hand cupped her jaw. "Quiet."

He held her in the darkness. She struggled at first. He murmured, "Easy. Focus. Focus on my voice," until at last she began to listen.

"All right now," he said, running his thumb over her lower lip. "We'll have to think of something to do for the next few minutes to keep your mind off things."

Quivering against his chest, she nodded. Not that he could see the gesture. "Okay," she said, her voice small.

"Tell me," he said, "where you want to go on Earth, what you want to do."

"I... I thought I'd go west. I grew up in Massachusetts, on the shore." She wrapped her arms around his waist and listened to his heart. "I wanted to try something different, something brand new. Where were you from?"

"Idaho."

"Farm boy?"

"Yeah. We grew corn, had chickens." He rubbed his hands over the small of her back. "Ever seen Gwalens? They kind of look like chickens."

"There's not much I haven't seen since," she said. "Except for humans. Once and a while I'd see one. A man or some poor woman, down at their master's feet." She swallowed hard, remembering the pleading stares cast up to her as she sang to wealthy alien patrons, the hollow feeling of powerlessness. "I tried to help a girl once, tried to help her escape. The Tarsian bounty hunters who caught her, they..."

Her voice hitched and Decker held her tight. Fanta shook her head. "They lobotomized her, with drugs. I saw her again, at the end of a chain, and there was nothing in her eyes, nothing..."

"Fanta..." He brushed his lips across her ear, stroked her hair. "That's not going to happen to you."

She squeezed her eyes shut against the darkness. "Is it all a dream? Am I being stupid, thinking I can ever be free? This nightmare, it won't end, I'll be running forever."

"No," he said. "There's hope here."

Here? Where? In his words, in his arms... Fanta wanted so badly to believe it.

He pressed a kiss into her hair. "Well, so much for cheering you up. Maybe we should talk about something else." His voice dropped as he rubbed his cheek against hers. "Or do... anything else you want."

"Just hold me..."

The way he rubbed her soothed her. She relaxed against his chest. He massaged the nape of her neck, her shoulders, her lower back. Strong fingers worked over tense muscle.

Danger made you horny, he'd said. Whatever it was, she felt it now, a flame of need licking between her thighs, demanding her attention. With a helpless whimper, she touched her lips to his throat. Decker cupped her face again and slid his mouth over hers. Gentle at first, the kiss deepened. She sucked at his tongue, abraded her cheek with the rough stubble on his chin. Sensation, even this slight pain, grounded her to reality. Losing herself in lust kept the nightmares at bay.

He lifted her arms to twine around his neck and his hands slid down to her skirt. He tugged, then the hem lifted over her butt. His palms cradled her ass cheeks, spread them, squeezed them. Moaning into his kiss, she pumped her hips softly. In the absolute black, with the drum beat pounding in her bones, Fanta floated in a weightless sea of desire.

She knew he'd find her pussy dripping when he touched her there. The orgasm she'd almost reached in the other room still hovered, trembling, waiting for him to coax it from her. His low rumble of approval told her all she needed to know. He angled a finger inside her, dipping into her hole, touching damply at her clit, back again. Shudders wracked her. She ate at his mouth. His tongue slid deep against hers as his fingers worked her to a frenzy.

Their ragged breathing filled the void. His mouth moved close to her ear. "I'm going to fuck you now. Don't cry out."

She nodded against his cheek. He turned her, put her hands against the warm wall and pressed between her shoulder blades. She knew what he wanted. She wanted it, too. Right now, nothing mattered more than satisfying the ferocious lust he stirred in her. Spreading her legs, she bent forward. His palms ran over her ass cheeks and her back. She presented herself for the thick invasion of his cock.

The blunt head stretched her, pushed into her, all the way to her womb. Fanta gasped. In this position, it felt so different. Sharper. Harder. More intense. When he began to move, she yelped with pleasure-pain. His hand came over her mouth. "Shh." He slid a finger between her lips and she sucked hard, tasting herself, wishing it was his cock. Not that she didn't love it where it was.

He bent closer and nibbled the back of her neck and her shoulder where her shirt had slipped. Sharp little bites that sent shivers over her skin. He reached beneath her bra and played with her nipples, twisting them hard, flicking the tips. And all the while her body bucked and burned with desire, she focused on not screaming, not exploding. The pleasure focused like a laser. Decker became her world. His smoky scent, his rough fingers, his cock. He found her clit unerringly, circled it with the pads of his fingers. Her climax swirled, gathered.

She kept her promise not to scream—barely. She clamped her hand over her mouth to keep from shouting out her pleasure as he slammed into her and snarled out his own climax. His breath burned on her nape. His come filled her cunt. The ripples of her orgasm carried it into her body, the primitive flow and power of life. She wanted to hold him there forever, keep this feeling forever.

Of course, she couldn't. She floated slowly back to reality. They stayed joined. Fanta, still bent into the wall, breathed hard through her mouth. Decker wrapped his arms around her waist and rubbed his face between her shoulders. His cock inside her had barely diminished. If they weren't running for their lives, he could probably do it again, and again. Amazing man.

Above them, a wave of applause rippled through the walls.

"Thanks, folks, we're here all week," Decker said, his voice gritty with sex and humor.

Fanta gave a dry chuckle.

Decker asked, "What?"

"I was just thinking," she said, "maybe we could live down here forever like the tunnel people in old New York, just screwing and hiding."

"That's the best idea I've heard all day." His cock slid out when he straightened. She sighed her disappointment, but turned in his embrace and found his mouth for a gentle kiss. It really wasn't so bad after all, this little dark cradle of space they'd created.

"Feel better?" he asked, stroking her back, her hip, the naked slope of her bottom.

"Can't you tell?" She sighed, loving the heat and strength of him.

"We shouldn't have long to wait."

"I don't mind it so much now. It's like being in a womb. The warmth and the humidity."

"Can't say as I remember."

She laughed softly. He felt so good to hold. His damp cock pressed against her bare thigh. Her skirt was still around her waist. Her underwear braceleted her ankles. Neither of them was in any hurry to rejoin the world.

After a long moment, his hands moved over her in the darkness to pull up her panties, straighten her skirt, brush her hair from her face, as gently as if she were a child. Her skin warmed wherever he touched her. Fanta wondered at it. This trust, this innate understanding that she was safe with him—that she belonged with him—glowed inside her like a single star on a cloudy night.

He dressed and sat, pulling her down with him to cuddle in his lap. She rested her head on his shoulder. "Where will you go when I'm gone?"

"Go? Nowhere."

"Is this where you'll spend the rest of your life? On this station, all alone?"

"It's not so bad. I've got Wejar and my fabulous apartment. Don't forget Friday night bingo at the Wikki Hall."

She smiled in the darkness and rubbed his chest beneath his shirt. "You're too good to let go."

He stiffened. Damn, she shouldn't have been so blunt. "Will you visit me, at least?" she tried.

"Fanta—" Of course, the com crackled. Probably for the better. She didn't think she would like his answer.

Decker spoke into it, though nothing more than static came across. "Wejar? Where are you, man?"

A hiss of nothingness. Decker's arm hardened around her waist. "Wejar?"

A wet plop echoed from the corridor they'd left. As if a frog had jumped into a pond. Or someone had set a foot wrong in the water.

Decker stood and pulled her up with him so rapidly that her head spun. Fanta's heart jerked into overdrive. She gripped his waist. "What is it?" she whispered.

"Dunno."

She couldn't see his face, but she imagined him peering, trying to slice through the darkness with his eyes and his instincts. He moved and she knew he'd taken his blaster out of the holster. Fanta held her breath and strained for another sound.

Abruptly, he pushed her toward the next corridor. "Go ahead of me. Hurry."

The urgency in his tone sent her into high speed. Forcing her feet to move, she groped the walls and prayed the other Tarsian didn't wait around the next black bend. Damp steel slipped beneath her palms as she struggled to feel her way. Decker's hand pressed at her back. "I can't see, I can't go any faster," she said.

"You gotta, honey."

Something pinged against the wall, creating a tiny spark.

"Dart!" Decker said. "Go, go, go!"

Terror spurred her into a blind run. Decker pounded behind. "Light ahead," he said, his voice low and tense.

They came to a fork in the corridor. He seized her, yanked her into an indent in the wall. She could see him now, barely, in the sepia glow. His voice was harsh. "Keep going right. If we get separated—"

"No—"

He gave her a sharp little shake. "If we get separated," he repeated grimly, "get to the launch bay. Look for a black KR4 Sprinter. That's mine. The code is four-nine-oh."

"Not without you."

"Don't be stupid. Get lost, get to Earth. You'll have half a chance there."

Whispery footsteps funneled toward them from behind. The quick, light patter of mercenary feet. Only Tarsians moved so fast and so silently. Fear zipped across Fanta's skin. "Don't suppose you have an extra blaster?"

"Not on me." He took a second to glance at her. "You okay?"

She met his steady, steely gaze and found courage there. Fanta nodded. She could do this.

He raised his weapon. "Let's go."

They sprinted down the better lit corridor. Fanta focused on running, not on the monster that trailed them. Finally, the maroon doors of the lower docking bay loomed ahead.

"I have the security code," Decker said. They skidded to a halt. Fanta whirled, her back to the huge doors. Her gaze swung wildly down the hall. Where was the Tarsian?

Decker jabbed at a keypad. His rasped curse made her stomach go cold.

"Not working," he said.

"Of course not," she moaned.

"Wait, there's a—"

A slender shadow slid into view.

Fanta screeched. "Decker!"

"Almost—" He grunted. The door behind her remained closed. Eyes glued on the barely seen form down the hall, Fanta reached to shake Decker's shoulder. And found air.

He lay crumpled on the ground. A silver dart protruded from the back of his neck.

Chapter Four

No...

Nausea gripped him, twisted as if a cold hand reached inside and grabbed his guts. The dart burned in his neck, pumping poison. It came so fast. Fucking Tarsian. He pushed himself up on his forearm, felt the world wobble.

"Decker!" Fanta sounded far away. Scared. Shit. He tried harder to stand. She plucked out the dart. Pain burst through him. *Fanta.* Fear for her made his heart pound, made his racing blood carry the poison through his system. He had to calm down. He got almost upright, enough to slump against the wall.

"What do I do?" Fanta's echoey voice trickled through fog. He blinked. Couldn't feel his legs. So this was how it ended.

Warmth on his cheeks. Fanta's hands. Her luminous eyes filled what was left of his vision. Beautiful eyes. Couldn't let her die. It took all his strength to lift his blaster. "Kill it," he said. His lips felt thick and dry.

She didn't seem to understand. "The door! How do I open the door?"

"Kick it."

She must have thought he still spoke of the Tarsian. Her brows knit. "What?"

"The door," he ground out, fading fast. "Stuck. Kick it."

His head lolled when she let him go. He forced his eyes open long enough to watch her smash at the door with her small, booted foot. Rolling his gaze to his right, he saw the Tarsian's slithery silhouette approaching slowly. The thing must be unsure how dead Decker was. Decker still had his blaster, but not the strength to lift it. He nudged the barrel toward the alien and pulled the trigger.

Fanta screamed at the blast, but the Tarsian spat back into the shadows. It bought them another few seconds. Under Fanta's assault, the doors wheezed open. She reached for him.

Decker shook his head drunkenly. "Get going."

"Not without you." She crouched down and worked her hands under his armpits to lift him.

Decker's heart flopped in his chest, full of fear that she'd die pointlessly trying to save him. He managed to turn his head enough to look at her and tried to make his numb lips work. "Why're you doing this? You're nothing to me. I did my job. All it was."

She stubbornly yanked at him. "I know you don't mean that."

A movement drew his attention. Decker pulled off another blast that skimmed the floor and exploded meters away. This time, the Tarsian kept coming. Growing desperate, he growled, "Take the blaster. Save yourself."

"See, I knew you cared!" She found her grip and somehow, dragged him through the partly open doors.

Freakin' girl! If the Tarsian didn't kill her, Decker would. If he lived.

Fanta pried the blaster from Decker's stiff fingers. The controls went up in a shower of sparks. The Tarsian hissed in outrage as the doors snapped shut in its nearly featureless face.

Fanta got behind Decker and looped her arms around his chest. "Now you're going to walk it off."

"What?" Nuts, that's what she was. "I'm dying here."

"Tarsians rarely kill with darts. They stun. They like to kill more… gradually." He felt her shudder against his back. "Now come on, try. We're almost there, almost to freedom."

Yes. She was right. The docking bay was only ten meters or so down this corridor. Maybe, if he could get her there, she'd be safe. But he had no strength. "Can't. You go."

"Damn it, Decker." She gave one massive pull. "Don't you dare give up on me."

Suddenly, he was on his feet. Unsteady, feeling packed in cotton, but he stood. He slung around to face her. "You better never—"

She waved her small fist at him. "Don't even talk." Her eyes flashed with fear-driven temper. "Just walk. Come on."

Still groggy, he staggered along with her help. With each step, the pins and needles feeling ebbed from his legs. Some warmth crept back into his hands. He eyed Fanta, who strode along purposefully. He should be mad that she'd risked herself to save him. But how could he be? She had guts, even if she was a sentimental fool.

"Which one?" she asked. They'd arrived at a series of doors set along the curved wall.

"I don't know."

"What do you mean? I thought you had a plan?"

He tried to blink the last of the cotton from his brain. "Wejar was going to let me know where the Tarsians were. Now..." He pulled his com. "If they've got him, then calling will only make things worse. That's the only reason he would have lost contact."

Fanta bit her lower lip. "What about your sprinter?"

He shrugged. "Now that that thing has seen us together, they'll be guarding it, too."

"We have to do something."

"Mm." His thoughts began to focus more easily. Fanta had been right about the stun dart. He'd have to put off dying for another day. He scrubbed at his face and considered their options. "I have a second vehicle, one I've been working on when I had time. It's old. Hell, I'm not even sure it'll fire up. But I doubt they'll look there."

Hope lit her eyes. "Where is it?"

"A secondary garage, adjacent to the main bay."

She started to walk, but he grabbed her arm. "Listen to me. It's a dark blue Andromeda, under a red tarp in the far right corner. It's far from the bay doors. You'll have to gun it, but she's quick, you'll make it if you don't hesitate."

"Just me?" Fanta's lips tightened. Her gaze searched his face. "You won't even think about coming back, will you?"

"No."

She yanked away. "What is it about this place that's so wonderful you can't leave it?"

"There's nothing wonderful about it. That's exactly why I do stay."

"To punish yourself?"

He shoved past her. "We don't have time for this."

She clipped along beside him, clearly furious. "You *are* a coward."

"Sure, whatever you say." Brat. He'd like to take her over his knee and spank her. The way his cock heated with interest at that idea only goaded his anger. This woman, this *intrusion*, did nothing but drive him crazy, and he'd still like to push her up against the wall and pound into her 'til she screamed in ecstasy.

Hell, nothing made sense anymore.

He was almost running by the time they reached the lower bay door.

"Talk to me, Decker." Fanta grabbed at his arm. "I risked my life to save you back there. You owe me."

"I'm trying to return the favor," he snapped. "Now zip it before you alert every alien within fifty meters."

She opened her mouth to say something and he jerked up a stern finger. "Zip."

Her lovely lips pressed together. Fury made her breasts rise and fall beneath her silver blouse. Oh, those perfect, pink-nippled breasts. How he'd miss them.

Shaking his head, Decker pulled her behind him. "On the count of three, we open the door and make a run for it. This bay is used mostly for repairs, so we'll probably be okay."

"What's the code for the Andromeda?"

"Fuck, I forgot." He thumped his head with his fist. "It's so old, it uses handprint recognition. Listen, I'll get you that far." He caught her gaze to make sure she paid attention. "Once you're airborne, don't stop, not for anything. If the engine turns off, you won't be able to get her started again, understand?"

She nodded but her eyes were wide with uncertainty. He touched her cheek gently. Her skin felt like silk. He tried not to think about never being able to touch her again. "It'll be okay. Once you're on Earth, you'll be safe and none of this will matter."

"It will always matter." She gripped his fingers.

Why'd she have to make this so difficult? Decker frowned and turned back to the door panel. He prayed she would listen to common sense and ignore whatever this weird bond was between them. He took a deep breath and powered his blaster. "Ready?"

On the count of three, he jabbed the final number and the doors shushed open.

He stumbled mid-stride and spat out a curse. A Tarsian assassin sneered at him, his long blade pressed to Wejar's throat.

✴〰️(☾☼)〰️✴

Fanta felt Decker hesitate and followed his gaze. The big blue lizard stood four meters away, and behind him, a Tarsian. The wicked bronze dagger he held forced Wejar's head up.

"Go!" Wejar barked.

Decker sprang into motion, pulling her forward between parked vehicles. A grunt and a shout burst through the air. The thud of flesh against flesh. Icy dread dragged at her steps. Poor T-Rex. "Decker, we should go back and help him!"

"He can handle himself. Move it!"

The red tarp seemed to glow in the corner. Freedom. But at what price?

The ting of darts ricocheted off metal hulls. She threw her free hand over her head. Decker's long legs stretched into a dead run, and she could barely keep up. They slammed into the side of the Andromeda. He ripped off the tarp. More shouts—security coming to seal off the bay.

"We'll never make it," she said, even as she helped him uncover the gleaming machine.

"Don't worry about them." He spared a quick glance to the security detail running toward them. "Where's the Tarsian?"

"I don't know." Then she caught the shadowy form whipping between vehicles. "There!"

He thrust the blaster into her palm. "Shoot to kill. I gotta get this baby started." He popped the cockpit and hopped in.

Fanta tried to follow the Tarsian's movements. She let off a wild blast. A dart sliced by her cheek, leaving a streak of pain before the side of her face went numb. "Faster, Decker!"

"I'm trying."

The engine coughed and sputtered, then hummed to life. "Give me your hand!"

The Tarsian sprang for her, barbed claws outstretched, obsidian eyes gleaming. Fanta screamed.

The creature exploded. Its sleek, slender torso splatted in chunks at her boots. Wejar, spines bristling, stood with a smoking blaster behind the mess. "The other Tarsian's coming. Better fly."

She spun toward Decker and grabbed his hand. He hauled her into the Andromeda. The cockpit smelled of old leather and Decker's cigarettes.

"You know these controls?" he asked tensely.

Vibrating with adrenaline, she nodded. "Yes, I can fly it."

"Good luck, baby." He put his hand on the cockpit ledge to push out. She seized his arm.

"Wait, that's it? You're just going?"

His brows bunched. "Yeah. I go fight the bad guys, you escape, that's the plan, right? Hurry, there's no time for—"

"Not so fast." She yanked him back inside and kissed him hard on the lips.

He stared at her, winter blue eyes wide and wild. Heat flushed through her, and longing so intense it threatened to burst her apart. "Last chance," she whispered.

He shook his head, once. "Not for me, sweetheart. I used them all up. But I won't forget you, Fanta Rae."

"Damn it, Decker!"

He punched the cockpit controls and rolled out before the fabriglass shield lowered over her. On the ground now, he smacked the Andromeda's side and shouted, "Fly!"

What choice did she have? Stupid, stubborn man. Heart rocking in her chest, Fanta stepped on the controls and the Andromeda growled into motion.

Three security guards darted into her path, blasters drawn. She jammed on the brakes. Over the rumble of the Andromeda's engine, she heard them order her to power down. Where'd Decker go? She twisted to locate him between two sprinters. His laser bursts held off the remaining Tarsian who crouched behind a row of barrels, thin black lips peeled back from yellow teeth.

A Vuilite guard moved toward her vehicle. Fanta revved the engine, hoping to scare him off. Of course, they wanted her alive. They would hand her over to the Tarsian, collect their reward. A sick feeling pooled in her gut. She'd come so far, just to flee like a slave. And a slave she would be, as long as she ran.

As for Decker... He'd be arrested for defying orders, sent to the Krackus mines or given to the Tarsians for their terrible revenge.

The guards edged closer.

Crap! If only this thing had stun lasers on it. But it didn't, and she had nowhere to go unless she wanted to mow down the guards. Fanta gripped the control switch to power down. Something sharp bit into her palm. A small lasergraph had fallen onto the switch. A pretty woman with long brown hair smiled from the image. Two children, a sturdy little boy and a freckle-faced girl, showed off toothy grins. She flipped the photo over. "Alex, come home to us safe, and soon. We love you."

His family. Gone. Her breath stilled in her chest.

Fanta's decision clicked in her mind. Logic played no part. She knew only that Decker—Alex—had given her hope and strength when he had none left for himself. She'd be cold ash in deep space before she'd let it end this way.

Gunning the Andromeda's engine, she wheeled the vehicle toward the interior of the bay. Decker and Wejar saw her coming. Decker waved his arms, gesturing frantically toward the bay doors. The stunned security guards began to fire. Their shots rocked the Andromeda's wings. The old bird was tough. She could take a few hits.

Fanta's pulse sang in her ears as she powered the machine toward the Tarsian.

The barrels exploded on impact. Amber liquid erupted over the fabriglass cockpit. Tires squealed and skidded. Fanta struggled against the g-forces as she worked the controls. The Tarsian bolted, but no way would she let him get away that easy. She hit the brakes and shoved at the cockpit. Decker shouted, "No!" just as the Tarsian sprang of nowhere and knocked her back on the seat.

The thing was everywhere, hissing, grappling. Fanta kicked hard at its slippery torso. One strong, clawed hand closed around her throat. Reptilian eyes narrowed while the other hand raised a glinting silver needle. Heart about to burst, Fanta fixed on it. *Alex.* She prayed he'd be safe.

Then air, light, and an outraged snarl. Fanta sat up as the Tarsian's black boots disappeared over the edge of the cockpit. What the—? She looked over the side. Decker grappled the mercenary to the ground. His flying fists knocked the evil thing's head side to side. The Tarsian roared and ripped at Decker's throat, barely missing.

"Decker!" Oh, great—now her brilliant plan would get him killed. Fanta leapt out of the cockpit. The security detail formed a loose circle around Decker and the Tarsian.

"Do something!" she screamed, but they just stared stupidly.

The Tarsian got its long, lean legs underneath Decker and kicked him off with a violent thrust. Decker rolled, stunned. His blaster clattered across the grid. Fanta dove for it, lifted it. The surprised yellow eyes of the Tarsian filled the sights.

"Die, you bastard." She squeezed the trigger.

Crazy woman! Fanta's shot went wild, almost took off Wejar's head.

But it stopped the Tarsian long enough for Decker to tackle the brute from behind and wrestle him to the floor again. The assassin hissed and lurched beneath him. Wejar, bless him, moved in to help. At least someone hadn't gone into shock. Together they managed to get cuffs around the narrow black wrists, then just for good measure, Decker shackled the mercenary's legs, too.

"Unacceptable!" the Tarsian growled, twisting to glare at Decker. "Your captain promised free capture. I have the right—"

Decker slammed the thing's head into the cold metal floor. "You have the right to remain silent. Her contract is finished. And so are you."

Wejar hauled the creature to its feet. A thin line of blood trickled down the Gana's throat from where the Tarsian's blade had sliced him. Decker pointed to it. "You okay?"

"Never better." Wejar always had loved a fight. Ganas couldn't grin, but he flicked his spines and snorted. He gave the grumbling Tarsian a shake. "You're under arrest for assaulting an officer."

"And maybe some other things, too. Give us time, we have good imaginations." Decker rubbed his hand over his throbbing jaw. His knuckles killed, and the damned mercenary had managed to get in a couple of good knocks before Fanta had distracted him.

Fanta. He turned to see her shaking in her little silver boots, blaster still outstretched.

He reached for the gun. "It's okay, sweetheart. Give it to me now."

Her eyes focused on him as if he stood miles away. Then she cried out and rushed into his arms. He held her hard. Ah, the sweet feel of her body against his. She fit so perfectly. Even one more moment of this was such a gift. He loosened his grip enough to take the blaster from her and tuck it back into the holster. Then he kissed her upturned, urgent mouth.

"Fooking humans," Wejar groused.

"What about her?" another voice said.

Decker glanced up. The security guards goggled at them, clearly at a loss.

He held Fanta at his side and narrowed his eyes. "She makes a miraculous escape."

The Vuilite gestured helplessly. "But the brass says—"

"Fuck the brass. I'll take the fall." He tightened his arm around

Fanta's waist, put his other hand on the butt of his blaster. "Anybody got a problem with that?"

Obviously glad to be relieved of responsibility, they shook their heads or drooped their appendages, and shuffled back from the scene.

"Alex."

Fanta's soft voice jolted him. *Alex...* Chills prickled across his skin. That had been his name once, a long time ago. He stared down at her as if she were a stranger.

She touched his jaw with her gentle fingertips. "Come home with me."

His mouth went dry. The sudden silence in the bay fell between them. Even the Tarsian shut up.

"I need you," she whispered, eyes pleading. "More than they do. More than you need to be alone."

"Can't." Why did his voice sound so rusty?

"This isn't what your family would've wanted."

He latched onto the old, familiar hurt. "They're dead."

"You're not. I'm not. Don't you feel it?" She took his hand and put it over her chest. He felt her pulse flying beneath. "Life, Alex. Earth is right out there, through that bay door, waiting for us."

He wanted to snatch his hand away, but couldn't give up the vibrant warmth of her beneath his palm.

Wejar cleared his throat. "Won't go good with you here, man. Brass'll hang you out to dry."

Decker snapped, "Maybe that's what I want."

"You're a stubborn ass, then," Wejar said. "As if I didn't know."

The Tarsian snarled. "Let me take her and solve all your problems. You'll be well compensated. Is one human female worth this much trouble?"

Was she? Decker let his hand drop away and felt the cold air slide between his fingers. A preview of the chilly emptiness he'd feel once she left. He scowled at her. "You know, my life was going just fine before you showed up."

"I'm not sorry." She smiled to break his heart. Christ. Decker felt as if invisible hands pushed him toward the door. The chills zipped over his spine again. Maybe they were. Maybe his wife, his kids, laughed down at him now from some place like heaven, daring him to take a step.

Maybe Fanta was a gift after all.

"You might regret this some day," he muttered.

She threw her arms around him, pressed her cheek against his. She whispered, "I think I could love you, Decker."

Chapter Five

Fanta lay in bed staring out the window at the brilliant moon. Not just any moon. *The* moon. They'd been back on Earth for two months, and it still didn't seem real. The night sky might be a painted fantasy, and the burbling brook outside their bedroom window a sound effect.

But no. It was all real. Including the gorgeous man who slept beside her now.

Silver light cast dapples in his hair and across his face. His sculpted chest rose with his deep breaths. He slept naked, despite the cool, piney breeze wafting through the screen. She smiled to herself. Just one more thing to be grateful for. Softly, she ran her hand over his chest, followed the light covering of hair down his flat belly to his cock.

Alex had gone to bed early tonight, after a hard day of pounding nails and hauling stone, trying to get their little cabin into livable shape. Even though they knew it would be a rougher start, they'd shunned the cities and staked a claim in the Colorado mountains. Room to grow. Room to have a family.

With this man by her side, anything was possible.

Feeling mischievous, Fanta stroked his sleeping cock lightly. Such a magnificent instrument of pleasure. Her body began to heat as she thought about the carnal delights they'd learned together. They never went a day without sex. Without making love.

His erection swelled beneath her gentle ministrations. His head moved restlessly on the pillow. Fanta grinned. Some dream he must be having. She edged down on the mattress and cupped his shaft, then dragged her tongue slowly over it, taking the rounded head between her lips. Then she moved lower to tease his balls. They'd bathed together earlier, and he tasted soapy and clean. She could suck him all night. Could she make him come without waking him? Worth a try.

Her tongue swirled, her lips suckled. She took his thickening cock deep into her mouth. The loose skin tightened as he responded to slow, hot laps of her tongue. He got hard so fast for her, she loved it. Opening wide, she drew on his heavy sac and warmed it with her mouth. Alex's hips shifted and he moaned in his sleep.

When she tasted pre-cum on the tip of his penis, she almost came herself. Her soaked pussy ached for penetration. While she held his cock inside her mouth, she reached between her legs to rub her swollen clit. Moisture seeped between her fingers. God... Maybe if she... Was there any way she could mount him without waking him up?

"What kind of trouble are you getting into down there, naughty girl?"

The sleepy, masculine voice drew her gaze. Alex sloped a lazy grin at her and pushed his fingers through her hair. She had his cock in her mouth and her hand between her thighs and, judging by the heated interest in his eyes, she had his full attention, too.

In answer, she reached up to slide her damp fingers between his lips. He drew on them hungrily and growled low in his throat. "Only the best kind of trouble," she purred. "Care to join me?"

In one smooth motion, he reached down to her and flipped her onto her back. His big body covered hers, hot and hard.

"You are incredible," he said. His appreciative, dark tone sent a ripple of delight through her. "Like a living wet dream. I almost shot off in your mouth."

"Mm, that would've been fine." She ran her finger across her lower lip, loving how aroused she could make him. "I really didn't want to wake you."

"Yeah?" He kissed her damp lips, then her throat, his mouth slow and sleepy on her skin. "Try again tomorrow, and the night after if you want. I don't mind at all." He reached down between them and slipped his fingers through her soaked curls. He traced her plump cunt lips and skimmed maddeningly over her clit, making her shiver and clench. "But tonight, I wouldn't have wanted to miss this." He slid down her body. "Or this..."

He massaged her breasts in his big hands and kissed the pink tips taking each one in turn into his mouth. His caressing tongue sent shivers of lust down to her cunt. Drifting lower, he kissed her belly, the tuft of her mound, down to lick the crease of her thigh, a fraction from her drenched pussy.

She tried to roll to bring her sex to his mouth, but his hands on her hips held her still. "What have you been doing that's made you so wet?" he murmured. He parted her folds with his fingers, pressing and stroking while her neglected clit throbbed. He nudged the tip of one finger inside and stroked around the rim of her hole ever so slowly, making her hyperaware of each millimeter of needy skin.

She gasped his name and arched her back.

In response, he chuckled low in his throat and let his tongue play along the crease of her thigh. His unhurried fingers continued to tease the moisture from her and trace its passage down to her bottom. She felt a slight, insistent pressure on her anus and gasped. He'd never done that before. Uncertainty flooded her, along with a desperate, dark curiosity.

He pressed again gently, but this time kissed her clit, too, suckling it lightly.

"God, Alex, please…"

"You've been touching yourself." His voice was deep, sleep-roughened and sexy. "Your clit is swollen, sensitive. Ah, there—" He nuzzled the rough stubble of his chin against the swollen nub, proving his point when she writhed beneath his hands. "Do you know how hot that makes me? God, Fanta, you taste like heaven…"

He circled the bud of her anus. A thrill of nerves shot through her. She never knew that area could be so sensitive. Her nipples tightened almost painfully. She reflexively grasped them and pinched.

"Yeah, Fanta. Does that feel good, sweetheart?" He pushed farther into her little hole, withdrew, pushed, just a fingertip but it made her squirm and lift her bottom off the sheets. "I knew you would like this. I've dreamt about it. Your ass is too sweet, and your pussy, and your lips, every inch, I want to make you feel so good…"

She had no words, only soft, needy moans. When he repeated the motion and lapped at her clit, such pleasure rocketed through her that she thought she would come right then. But he backed off, leaving her tingling and unsatisfied. More moisture seeped from her pussy, soaking her thighs and her cleft, making it easier for him to gather up fluid and explore her ass. He tongued her pussy, sucked on her swollen lips while his finger found easier passage into her nether hole.

Fanta rolled her nipples between her fingers, hard. She groaned as fierce, foreign sensations pulsed through her, feelings she wanted to know, to explore...

With his tongue thrusting rhythmically into her cunt and his finger plumbing her virgin hole, Decker growled his approval.

"Someday," he whispered, "I'm going to fuck your ass. Do you want that? Do you want it, Fanta?"

"Yesyes—" *Anything...*

He danced his tongue over her clit, harder, softer, little butterfly flickers, feeding on her moans until she crested and writhed, her pussy clenching like a fist, her mind shattering with his sensual promise, his relentless touch, his love for her...

She'd barely floated back down to reality when he moved over her. He soothed her with long strokes of his hands. His touch was cool on her hot skin and his eyes adored her. Riding the ripples of pleasure that strummed through her body, Fanta smiled up at him.

"Well," she said, sliding her hands across his broad shoulders, "now I am glad you woke up."

He cradled her against his sweat-dampened chest and kissed her lips softly.

"Thank you, angel," he murmured. "I think I must still be dreaming. That was too good to be true."

"Very sweet," drawled a voice from the doorway.

Alex bolted upright and Fanta whipped the sheets over her breasts. Too late to cover them from the intruder's narrowed gaze. As if it would matter.

"Tirrell," she gasped.

Chapter Six

Alex shifted to grab his blaster and a silver disintegrator appeared in Tirrell's hand, glinting in the moonlight. "Don't bother, sir. I'm no Tarsian, but I assure you I can vaporize your hand long before it reaches your weapon."

Alex growled under his breath. Fanta knew what he was thinking: In the two months they'd been here, they'd gotten sloppy and incautious. She'd thought they were safe. She'd thought... Shock and fear made her heart leap into her throat. Tirrell, here—how? She swallowed down her nerves and balled her shaking fists in the sheets. "What do you want, Tirrell? I don't belong to you anymore."

"Ah, exactly what I'm here to discuss." In the moonlight, the tall, gaunt form looked black, but Fanta knew how that slightly pebbled skin could streak with deep bronzes and indigos when the M'gambi moved, as he did now, strolling to the foot of the bed. He was a beautiful creature, but more sinister even than the Tarsians.

He wore dark clothing much like a business suit. While M'gambis thought nothing of taking human lives, they ironically adored human fashion. Seeing him in it now reminded her that Tirrell was first and foremost a business... man... for lack of a better word. He wouldn't be quick to disintegrate his best money-maker. She hoped...

Fanta sat up straighter in bed. Her skin must be flushed with passion, her lips swollen. How long had Tirrell been standing there? He might have seen... everything. Heard everything. She spared a glance out the window but saw no transport. Was he alone? Too many questions. For now, she hardened her heart and focused on her old bond-master. She forced her voice to sound calm. "If you've come to talk me into another contract, it's too late."

"Is it?" He slid the plain cotton comforter through his multi-jointed fingers and hummed to himself. "Does this scratch your fair skin, Fanta Rae? You once slept on finest skilas, woven by a thousand prettle birds." His pale eyes glanced up to Decker. "Did she tell you that? How she lived as royalty, how she dined upon luxuries and spread her white thighs for me on a bed of tappas clouds?"

Decker stiffened beside her. She slid her hand under the cover and touched his sweat-dampened skin. Tension radiated from him. What crazy, dangerous thoughts must be going through his head right now—

Tirrell suggestively pumped the slim barrel of his disintegrator through his circled fingers. "She's very good, don't you think? I was so pleased when she chose to stay with me long after her contract was fulfilled."

"Alex, you know he's lying." One wrong move and he'd be ashes. She had to protect him.

"And while other humans were dying," he went on in his deep velvet voice, "while mothers and children boiled alive in the hell you made of your atmosphere, Fanta Rae sang. For my pleasure. And hers."

She hissed in a sharp breath. "Damn you, Tirrell."

"You cannot deny you enjoyed your celebrity, my dear. Your... privileges." He flicked his cold gaze to Decker again. "Has she sung for you? Lovely, isn't it? As sweet as her cries when she comes. I often compared the sounds in my more leisurely moments."

Decker spoke through clenched teeth. "Get out of my house."

Tirrell arched a brow. "Will you make me? I am armed, you are not. While you look like a healthy specimen, I am infinitely stronger." He grasped Fanta's foot through the sheet. "It was a mistake sending the Tarsians after you, my dear. They only frightened you, drove you to this sorry destination. I was indisposed at the time, but now I've come myself, in person, to plead for you, for our love."

Fanta jerked her foot away. "I never loved you, Tirrell. And you're not capable of it."

He pressed a hand over his chest. "My wounded hearts. After all I went through to find you."

Suddenly, Alex rolled and reached for his blaster—which went up in a buzzing white ball along with half the table it had been sitting on. The table legs clunked to the floor. Alex leaped back.

"The next time I'll aim slightly to the left." Tirrell pointed the silver weapon directly at Alex's chest.

Fanta flung herself in front of him. On her knees, naked on the bed, she cried, "Get out, Tirrell! It's over. I'll never sing again if I have to cut out my vocal chords."

Alex jerked her back and put her behind him. She grasped his arm. If Tirrell disintegrated Alex, he'd destroy her, too. To her horror, indecision rippled across the M'gambi's face. God, he was actually considering it.

"If I go," she said, "will you let Alex live?"

Alex clenched his hand over hers. "No, Fanta."

The M'gambi gave a cold smile though he didn't lower his weapon. "Of course, if he means so much to you. I know how attached you get to your pets."

"Only you would think of love that way, Tirrell. You'll never understand."

A black-suited shoulder lifted in a shrug. "So, we'll have a philosophical discussion about it on our long trip back to Pegasus Nine."

⁂

Taut with rage, Alex refused to be butted out of the negotiations. He moved so his body shielded Fanta completely and brushed her hand from his arm. "You won't get ten steps from here before I kill you."

"No." Fanta touched his back. "If you kill him, others will come for revenge."

"They won't get through the security grid."

"Why not? I did." The alien expression remained serene. "Come with us. I could find employment for you as well. Well-developed human males are much desired in the pleasure malls. Your life would not be... intolerable."

"Thanks, but I've got everything I need right here." Alex had never seen an offworlder like this before. The black face looked ancient

Egyptian, with over-large, up-tilted eyes, high, sharp cheekbones and an aquiline nose. Dark hair hung to one side of an otherwise bald head in a sleek braid bound with shiny thread. The hands were long and thin and handled the disintegrator with familiar ease.

Tirrell dismissed him with a shrug. "A pity, but no matter. She is my primary concern."

"Mine, too."

"Then we must reach an accord." Emotionless eyes assessed him. "If we both want what's best for Fanta Rae, what can you offer her that I cannot?"

"Freedom," Alex snapped.

"Once a slave, always a slave. She seemed to be serving you well enough." The hard mouth curved. "If she won't sing, I can find other uses for her."

"Like hell you will."

Tirrell laughed unpleasantly. "Bold words, sir. Now get out of my way. My lover is ready to leave."

Fanta, who had pulled a sheet around her, touched his arm. "It's better this way, Alex." Her eyes were glossy, her blonde hair, fuchsia now only at the tips, mussed over her forehead. She looked like a waif, a lost soul, and he couldn't believe she gave up this easily. She turned her sad gaze on Tirrell. "Let's get this over with. I know you can't handle Earth's atmosphere for long."

The alien even then breathed in vapors from a slender bar held on a cord around his neck, some substance that probably helped him deal with the air. "Thank you for your consideration. I might have had more time if you two hadn't been fucking so long. Anthropological curiosity kept me riveted, I admit. But truly, this planet gives me a headache. Worst weather in the solar system. I never understood its appeal." He rubbed the back of his neck as if a pain had settled there.

"Just let me get dressed," Fanta said.

Alex reached for her, but she shook her head and stepped away from him. When he tried to follow, the damned alien reminded him with a jerk of the barrel that he still had his heart in his sights.

Fanta couldn't give up like this. She wouldn't. Battling down his rage, Alex made himself think. Was she giving him messages somehow, through her gestures, through her words? Was she buying him time?

He held up his hands and spoke to Tirrell. "I'm just putting on my jeans." He kept his voice neutral. "If I'm going to see you two off, I'd rather not have my bare ass hanging in the breeze."

"Very well. But move slowly." Tirrell's gaze roamed his body with an avaricious gleam. "Hm, you are a big one. Certain patrons might pay a million parnecs or more, depending on your... abilities."

A chill breeze blew though the open window and raised goose bumps on Alex's back. He had a bad feeling he wasn't going to get out of this one without a scrape. Or a hole in his gut.

He pulled on his jeans. "How'd you even get through terran security?"

"Earth for Earthers, is that it? Yes, it was tricky to pass through the patrol grids, but a small enough transport can slip in."

"And slip out again? If you're caught, it'll be life on a prison moon for you. You won't be able to bribe your way out of this one."

"No worries, sir. I'm a fine pilot, especially when I'm motivated." He tilted his head. "Are you sure you won't come along for the ride? My stringer is only large enough for two, but perhaps you could sit on Fanta's lap." He chuckled at his own wit and glanced at her. "I'm feeling inclined to take your lover along after all. I can think of several patrons who would be extremely interested."

Fanta rushed toward Tirrell. "Leave him alone!"

He caught her wrists with one hand. "Please, we don't want any bruises on your lovely skin."

The way she gasped in his easy grip made his strength obvious, though he wheezed with the effort—a hopeful sign. Alex fought every instinct to rush forward and save her. He knew she'd bought him a fraction of time to do... something. He reached under the bed. Where the hell was it?

He groped while Tirrell restrained Fanta. Just before the slanted eyes moved back to him, his fingers found the palm-sized stun bomb he'd hidden away. His only weapon. Not much, but it would have to do. He bent to pull on a boot and tucked the bomb into the top.

The alien clutched Fanta against his left side. She wrapped her arms around herself. He could see she trembled. Tirrell looked at her thoughtfully, but spoke to Alex. "If it's any consolation, your child will be raised in luxury."

A cold stone dropped in his belly. *Child?* Fanta's huge, liquid eyes pleaded with him from across the room.

Tirrell bent to inhale deeply of her hair. "A boy. Congratulations. Well, this is a bonus. I've always wanted a son."

"I wasn't sure, Alex," Fanta whispered. "I'm sorry. I wanted to be certain before I told you."

The alien's spidery hand stroked Fanta's shoulders. "Don't be too hard on her, she's telling the truth. The fetus is only a few weeks along." He wrinkled his aristocratic nose and sniffed. "Smells fresh."

Such a shock of horror razored up Decker's spine that only enormous will kept him from rushing across the room and strangling Tirrell. "It'll be all right, Fanta," he said, his voice sounding foreign to his own ears. "Do what he wants. Keep yourself safe. And the baby." *Baby... Good God...*

Tirrell waved him forward with his disintegrator. "That's more like it. You humans aren't nearly as stupid as you're reputed to be."

His legs wooden, Alex went through the house then outside. Tirrell and Fanta followed. There by the edge of the woods sat the alien's stringer, a small streamlined transport specially constructed to avoid detection. Expensive, illegal and perfect for kidnapping.

Tirrell inhaled his vapors again. His breathing had grown raspier, or so Alex hoped. The atmosphere was taking a toll. He counted on it.

Tirrell stopped them two meters from the stringer. The disintegrator lifted toward Alex's chest. "Now we say goodbye, sir. I thank you for keeping my property well-maintained." He pulled Fanta closer to him. "Any last prayers? That is what you humans do before you die, correct?"

Fanta tried to shove away. "You liar! No—"

Tirrell's grip couldn't be breached. "Take a cue from your lover. He understands his fate."

Alex kept his hands by his sides. "He knows I'll follow him to the ends of the universe to find you. And kill him."

"Exactly," purred Tirrell. "Now we can't have that, can we?" His words trailed off in a rattle. He pulled in another mist-laden breath and rolled his eyes. "All right then, let's get this over with. Ten seconds."

Alex sank to his knees on the damp earth as if to pray. He pressed his hands together, and over them caught Fanta's gaze. She gave the slightest nod and no fear shone in her eyes. God, he loved her. He bent his head before the alien caught on. He didn't pray for his life, but that he and Fanta were on the same page with this unspoken plan.

In a bored voice, Tirrell counted down the remaining seconds of his existence. "Five... four... three..." Fanta gasped as Tirrell gripped her tighter. Alex gritted his teeth. This better work...

"Two..."

In one fluid motion, Alex sprang up and snatched the stun bomb from his boot. He hurled it at the stringer. On impact, it flashed, searing his vision and blinding the alien's large, light-sensitive eyes.

Tirrell barked out in surprise. His gun hand flew up defensively. Fanta grasped the cord holding the inhaler and yanked just as Alex punched Tirrell in the belly. With a twist and a vicious tug, he wrestled the disintegrator out of the black hand and kicked the alien to the ground.

His first shot took out the stringer's tail rudder. His second shot should have blasted Tirrell's skull, but he held off, shaking with rage, while the stunned alien focused on him and the impact of the situation dawned in his widening eyes.

"That's right," Alex drawled. "You're stranded."

"And dead in about an hour." Standing beside Alex, Fanta held up the ruined inhaler. "Unless we call for help."

"Help?" the alien rasped, clutching at his throat. "New Ellis security..." He uttered an asthmatic rasp of dismay. "Your Andromeda. I'll buy it, twenty million transferred into any account you like. Surely here you could use the money." An almost pathetic grin revealed even, pearly teeth. "Was I so bad to you, Fanta Rae?"

She shuddered visibly. "Yes. And I'll never forget it."

Alex began to think it was a good thing he held the disintegrator and not Fanta.

"There's a wire in the Andromeda," he said aside to her.

She nodded. "I'll call for backup."

With one last, nasty glance at her old bond-master, she turned and ran to make the call.

He turned back to Tirrell, who sat up unsteadily. "Hands where I can see them," Alex said.

The alien brushed the dust from his impeccable suit. The only evidence of his discomfort was the strain in his voice as he struggled to breathe. "Earth for the Earthers. Well, sir, it appears my gamble was rash."

"She must have made you a lot of money for you to take the risk," Alex said.

"It wasn't that, ever." Tirrell tipped his head. "She was my most precious possession. A rare jewel." Cool as ice again, he tugged at his sleeves, straightened his collar.

"Are you saying you loved her?" He'd been fighting off visions of Fanta with the alien since Tirrell had first mentioned it. He wasn't sure he really wanted to know the depth of their relationship.

Tirrell laced his long fingers over his bent knees and took a moment to breathe. "As well as an M'gambi could perhaps. We do not recognize this emotion, but we do *value*, deeply, certain objects."

"She's not an object," he snarled.

"You misunderstand. I would give up my fortune for her, gladly."

"If you valued her that much, you would never have kept her as a slave."

He shrugged eloquently. "What good is a possession if you don't have it close at hand to enjoy?"

Alex shook his head in disgust. The alien merely smiled. "Have you ever been to the far reaches, sir?"

Alex shook his head.

"If you do travel that way, be sure to visit the sin markets of Mirana. With enough credit, you can purchase the most fascinating, the most exotic or dangerous creatures to surpass your imagination." His gaze found Fanta where she sat in the Andromeda, making the call that would seal his fate. "Had I not intervened, she would have ended her days there." Something almost poignant gleamed in his eyes when he looked back. "She has found her way home, when so many will not. In a way, I believe I'm glad."

Already yellow streaks shot overhead. Security rushing to the scene. A serene smile bent Tirrell's black lips and made Alex's stomach clench. The damned alien was so calm, too calm. Like he knew he could, in fact, bribe his way out.

Alex took a step toward him, his voice a growl. "If I see you again anywhere near her, I won't waste time talking." Nothing would take his family from him. Not again. He curled his finger around the trigger.

Tirrell heaved a wheezing, disappointed sigh as if Decker was a slightly stupid child. "Stay home, Earther. Love her. The universe is no place for such fragile beauties as you."

Epilogue

"I think he's asleep."

"Is he? Finally?" Alex gazed down at his son's face and Fanta's heart warmed like the spring sunshine gracing the glade around them. She tucked the blanket around Kyle's small shoulders and gently set him aside on the blanket. Her wet, rosy nipple slipped from his perfect, tiny lips.

"Lucky guy," Alex teased softly. She smiled at him and put her hand on his cheek.

"I think I'm ready for you again. At last." She didn't bother to button up her cotton dress. Her full, round breast peeked from the soft fabric.

Alex slid his hand over her belly. "Are you sure?"

"It's been over a month. I miss you." She curved her hand around the back of his head and pulled him down for a kiss. He feathered his fingertips over her sensitive nipples and around her pebbled aureoles and a potent rush of desire flooded her belly. She drew his tongue into her mouth and dug her fingers into his shoulders with a moan. Alex laughed against her eager lips.

"Easy, woman. I guess I've been a little too patient."

He reached across her to pull back the blue-striped blanket from Kyle's face. "He'll be asleep for an hour, at least. Move over a little." They edged away from the baby, not that he would care. The burbling brook was his nursery music and birdsong trilled him to sleep.

Fanta let Alex draw her dress over her head then lay gloriously naked in the fresh air. "Sometimes I feel like we're Adam and Eve, in the garden of Eden all over again."

"Only no fig leaves." He grinned, as naked as she now that he'd shucked his jeans and shirt. "And no sin but love."

He kissed her again while his hands stroked her body. Her pussy responded as always, weeping with need, swelling and aching sweetly beneath his touch. When his fingers parted her cunt lips and his hungry mouth followed, her back arched with almost agonizing pleasure.

"Sweeter than ever," he whispered, his breath warm on her clit. He left her sopping and unsated, ravenous for his cock. He moved over her, supporting his weight on his arms. "If it's painful, I'll stop."

She wrapped her legs around him and whispered, "You could never hurt me. I want you so bad, Alex, come to me, come inside."

He lowered his head to her breast and drew the tightly budded nipple into his mouth. He was almost rough, using his teeth and even the light beard on his cheek to chafe her tender flesh. Little electric shocks of pleasure arced to her womb. Lust stirred in her belly, like embers caught fire.

She wrapped her legs around his lean waist, spreading herself wide. "Love me, Alex."

"I do. Forever." He caught her lips with his and plunged deep with his tongue just as his heavy cock pushed inside her. No matter how often they fucked, that first thrust always wrung a gasp from her. The enormous, full feeling, the sense of invasion. Of completion.

He lowered himself so his chest hairs rubbed her erect nipples. Pleasure spiraled through her. She gave herself up to the force of his passion and the delicious friction of skin against skin. His cock plundered her slick hole, pushed in hard then lazily withdrew to leave her squirming. He knew just how to tease.

Her orgasm rose like a wave inside her, rolling to the crest with each leisurely pump of his hips. He suckled her lips, played with her tongue until the heat spread through her from heart to toes. Her pussy balanced on the edge of a shuddering climax while he caressed and coaxed the rest of her body to join the dance.

She'd never known sex could be like this, so entirely, utterly consuming. More than lust warmed his gaze. More than need worked in his kisses. He stroked her everywhere, her hair, her lips, her breasts and thighs.

"I want to come with you," he said, circling his palm over her breast. "Feel you come when I do."

Oh, sounded good to her. She moved her hips in time with his. She'd never been so wet, so slick. "I'm so close already," she murmured.

"I know." His confident, sloping smile made her even hotter. He knew her body so well, could play it like a master. Giving over to him was a precious joy.

He rolled them onto their sides so they faced each other and drew her leg over his hip.

"Slow now," he whispered. His intense blue eyes held hers. His cock forged her body and her tender flesh stretched around him. Sweet friction built, spiraling rings of exquisite sensation. All the while, she held his gaze, saw the love there. The undeniable love that bound them together.

Her heart opened to him, even as her body reached that exquisite moment of release. She couldn't stop herself any more than she could stop the sun from rising. Fanta gripped him hard. "Alex. I'm coming."

"Yeah, baby, now, now."

His guttural groan of release matched her own cry as pure pleasure rang through her. It went on and on, strumming through her core, pulsing into her fingers and lips. He came into her, deep, to her womb. Fanta gasped as the strong orgasm stunned her, stole her breath away.

A sweet smell of grass and flowers mingled with the scent of their sex. Primal. Delicious.

Even as he curled her into his arms and whispered his love against her throat and cheek, her mind wandered to the pleasures that lay ahead. They could make love again later, in the bath. She had plans, and all the time in the world...

Fanta threaded her fingers through his hair, now that she could, now that it had grown out. Thick, dark hair that slipped through her fingers. So many things had changed. Their bodies, their lives, their love, ever deepening.

Cradling him against her body, she stroked his back and listened to his even breathing. "Are you falling asleep, too?" she whispered.

"No, just relaxing." He rolled part-way off her onto the blanket and lay on his side facing her. His arm still looped around her waist.

"Thinking how everything's worked out. How happy we are."

"Then why do you look sad?"

"I miss cigarettes."

She laughed. "Tough luck, buddy."

"But they were so perfect after sex."

"I'll find ways to make you forget."

"Maybe we can grow tobacco in the field—"

She tsked and shook her finger. "Don't even think about it. We've got a fresh earth and fresh lungs. Let's not screw it up again."

"Eh, you're no fun." He teased, but his smile faded and something serious hovered in his eyes. He traced the shape of her breast with the backs of his knuckles. "Do you ever think about the others? The ones who didn't make it back?"

Fanta let out a long breath. "Mm. Sometimes. Why are you thinking about that now?"

"Something Tirrell said. That we're too fragile for the universe."

She propped her head on her palm. "He was a lousy philosopher."

Alex's brows drew together. "I don't know. We almost destroyed ourselves before. We got a second chance. Us and the human race. Everything could have ended up so differently."

"But it didn't." She took his face in her hands and kissed him. "And there's always hope. You taught me that."

"Did I?"

She nodded and twined his fingers through his. Then the baby sneezed and began to cry, and Alex sloped her a smile. Fanta grinned back.

"Reality beckons," she said, and kissed him. "Time to take us home, Alex."

"My pleasure, my love." He picked up his son and their clothes. Fanta took his hand and together they walked barefoot through the sun-warmed grass toward home.

About the Author:

Linda Gayle is an award-winning author who lives in Connecticut with her husband, two children and many, many pets. This is her first foray into erotica, and she would like to thank her wonderful critique partners who were faithful friends on the journey.

The Wolf's Mate

by Cynthia Eden

To My Reader:

I published my first werewolf story, *Bite of the Wolf*, with Red
Sage in December of 2005, and I was thrilled to be able to follow-up
that tale with an additional story about my French wolves. *The Wolf's
Mate* is Michael Morlet's story. Michael is the pack protector. He is a
strong, fierce hunter, a guardian, and right now, he has set his sights
on guarding his soon-to-be mate, Kat Hardy.

I had a wonderful time writing Michael's story! I hope you enjoy
the tale, and my take on the werewolf legend. Please feel free to
visit my website at cynthiaeden.com or you may email me at info@
cynthiaeden.com.

Prologue

Michael Morlet gazed up at the rising moon. He could feel the beast within him growing, could feel the call of the ancient hunger that filled his blood.

And always, always, he was aware of an... emptiness. A deep, consuming ache... a hunger for his mate.

His pack leader Gareth had recently found his mate, Trinity. After years of searching, Gareth had found her.

And Michael envied him.

Would he ever find his own mate? Find the one woman who would bond with him, forever?

The moon shone down on him, full and wide, and his hunger and need grew.

As the man changed into the beast, the hunger followed him, and he howled, calling out for the woman who waited for him, for the woman who was destined to be his...

If he could just find her.

Chapter One

"No! No! Stop! *Help!*" A woman's terror filled scream filled the air.

Michael jerked at the sound, his blood heating. He bounded down the deserted street, tracked the fading scream down the dark, garbage laden alley, and saw—

Her. A small, delicate woman with a tangled mass of red hair. With a face too pale, with green eyes that were wide and full of fear.

And he knew... knew in that instant, as he stared at her, as he saw her fighting with the two men who held her, that his life was about to change.

The beast within recognized her instantly. And he wanted to howl in triumph. Finally. After years of waiting, of searching... *He'd found her. He'd finally found her. His mate.* He knew it, knew it deep inside with utter certainty.

Elation filled him. He would not be alone any longer. She would be by his side, forever his companion, his lover.

He could smell her, a light, fragrant scent of flowers, a scent that rose over the grime and decay, a scent that called to him, that—

The glint of metal, shining in the moonlight, caught his eye. One man raised the weapon, its blade lowering toward his mate...

And the beast sprang forward.

Bones crunched beneath his fingers when he grabbed the man's wrist, but he didn't care. He shoved the fool back against the brick wall of the alley, watched with pleasure as he fell to the ground in a crumpled heap, then turned in a flash to confront the man who held the woman.

The guy was dirty, his clothes torn and old, but he was young, barely eighteen from the look of him. His eyes were wild, his hands shaking.

"Let her go," Michael ordered, not looking at the woman's face. He couldn't, not right then. Because if he saw her fear again, he would lose control.

The guy's Adam's apple bobbed. "T-this ain't you-your busin—"

Michael's hands clenched into fists. His fangs, burned, lengthened. The beast was very close to the surface. Too close. "Let. Her. Go." The words emerged as a growl, barely human.

The woman struggled, kicking and squirming. "Yeah, let me—"

The assailant's arm tightened around her throat, cutting off her words, cutting off her air.

"Bad mistake." Michael shook his head, aware that his nails had lengthened into claws. "Very bad." The woman wheezed, struggling to draw in her breath.

The punk curled his lip. "Yeah? What you gonna—"

Michael grabbed him, his claws slashing the arm that held his mate. The young guy cried out, his face bleaching of color as blood poured from his wound.

And then he ran, fleeing down the alley, disappearing into the night, and his friend was right behind him. They ran without looking back, ran as if the devil himself were in that alley.

Michael watched them leave, and the urge to track them, to finish them off, rose within him. It would be easy... so easy.

Humans, after all, were weak. And made such tempting prey.

"Th-thank you." The woman's voice, strained and husky, cut through his thoughts. His gaze returned to her. She huddled against the wall, her shirt torn, hanging off her pale shoulder and showing the white strap of her bra. "If you hadn't come into the a-alley..." she broke off, shuddering slightly, and he knew she understood how close she'd come to serious harm. That knife had been all too deadly, and rage filled him as he thought of what it could have done to her delicate skin.

His gaze slipped down her body, down past the torn shirt, over the soft, thrusting roundness of her breasts. He could tell she had nice breasts. Not too big, not too small. But just right... just right for his hands, his mouth.

Her waist was small, and she had slim hips. She was a tiny woman, probably no more than five foot two or three. And built rather... delicately. She wore a simple black skirt, a skirt that showed off the pale expanse of her legs, legs that he couldn't wait to feel wrapped around his hips as he thrust into her, deep and hard, over and over.

His mate. Finally.

She glanced down at her shirt, blushing as she realized that her bra was showing. "I-I didn't think anyone was going to hear me. The area's so deserted—"

Yes, the area was deserted. They were on the far side of Shellsville, Georgia. It was well after midnight. And they were alone. All alone.

His heart began to pound in anticipation.

She stepped forward, into the glowing light of the moon. And he got his first good look at her face. Such a sweet, lovely face. She had big eyes, eyes that swam with emotion, a small, slightly upturned nose, high cheekbones, and full, pouting lips. Lips that would look and feel so good wrapped around—

"Well, I'd better be going." She flashed him a smile, showing perfectly white, even teeth. "Th-thanks again."

He blinked. Surely she didn't think that she was just going to walk away from him now? Oh, no...

He lifted his hand, catching a strand of her red hair. *Little red riding hood had stumbled onto a wolf. A very hungry wolf.*

She stilled at his touch, her eyes widening even more.

"*Mademoiselle*, I'm afraid that I cannot let you leave yet..." No, not yet. *Not ever.*

She licked her lips, a quick, nervous move that caused his cock to swell with arousal. "Wh-why not?"

He stepped toward her, and she scrambled back, hitting the rough wall of the alley. He stared down at her, drinking in the sight of her beautiful form, and his nostrils flared as he inhaled her sweet scent.

A scent that called to him, a scent that marked her... marked her as the woman he'd been searching for his entire life.

A human. His mate was a human, like Gareth's. He would have to use care with her, try not to frighten her too much...

"I saved you," he whispered, bending toward her. His arms were on either side of her body, caging her in place. "Those men... they were planning to hurt you tonight."

Her chin lifted. "And I thanked you for that. Now... now I want to go. I should probably go call the police and—"

He shook his head. "I told you, I cannot let you leave yet. After all... you owe me."

Her lips thinned. "I don't know what you want but—"

"Oh, it's quite simple, really." His gaze dropped to her mouth. Such a sexy mouth. "I want you. And when I see something I want, I take it."

❦

OhmyGod. Talk about jumping from the frying pan into the fryer... Kat Hardy stared up at the stranger before her and felt fear shudder through her body.

What was worse? Being trapped in the alley with two teenage punks who had a knife? Or being trapped with... tall, dark, and sexy?

When the man had first appeared at the mouth of the alley, she'd been thrilled. Someone had heard her, someone had come to help her!

After midnight, Shellsville shut down, becoming almost a ghost town. She'd just finished her shift at Bernie's Bar and she'd been walking home, and then those idiots had grabbed her.

An attempted mugging in Shellsville... that wasn't what she'd expected. Not in this bumpkin town. Maybe back home in Chicago, yeah. Muggings there she understood. But here?

So when her brave savior had walked into the alley, she'd been so relieved.

Then she'd gotten a good look at him.

And she'd been terrified. Because the guy looked tougher, a hell of a lot tougher, than the punks with the knife. For one thing... he was big. Way over six feet. And muscled. The guy looked like he spent the better part of his days lifting weights somewhere.

And he fought... hard. Dirty. He'd taken care of her two assailants in moments and not even broken a sweat. He was dressed like a businessman, in a dark black suit. But he fought like a predator. Hard. Fast. Brutal.

Now that he stood right in front of her, *literally pinning her to the wall*, she had a chance to look at his face, really look at him.

Her heart sank. The guy was gorgeous. Absolutely, freaking, I'm-super-perfect-gorgeous. In the faint light, she could tell he had light blue eyes, bedroom eyes, eyes that made her tingle in places she shouldn't be tingling right then. He had strong, high cheekbones, a nice, strong jaw, and a sexy little cleft in his chin. His hair was midnight black, and thick. Very thick and just a little too long. It brushed against the back of his suit.

Oh, yes, the guy was gorgeous. She *hated* gorgeous guys. They tended to act like they were God's gift to the world. And to top it all off, this guy was foreign. French, by the sound of him. Women probably threw themselves at him all the time when they heard that sexy accent.

Well, she was most definitely *not* one of those women.

She lifted her chin, her eyes narrowing when she realized his gaze was on her breasts. "Look, buddy, I thanked you, now I want to get out of here." The alley smelled to high heaven, she had bruises all over her body, and she desperately wanted to get home, lock her door, and fall into bed. *After* she took one serious shower.

His gaze lifted, locked on hers, and he smiled at her, a faint smile that showed the edge of his teeth.

Wow. He had some really sharp teeth. She blinked. *Way sharp, like—*

"I think a token of your gratitude is called for in this situation."

"What?" Did the guy want some kind of payment or something? What a jerk! "Look, I don't have any money on me." Okay... so she had forty-two dollars and fifty-one cents in her back pocket. She'd

worked for that, slaved in that crappy bar. No way was she parting
with her money!

He shook his head. "I don't want your money... but I do want
you."

She gulped. "I don't think—"

"Relax." He leaned closer, his body surrounding hers. "In return
for saving you, I want a kiss. A simple kiss." His brow lifted. "Is
that so much to ask?"

Yes. Her back teeth clenched. But surely a kiss wouldn't be that
bad. She'd give him a peck, then hightail it out of there. And never
see the sexy Frenchman again. "Just a kiss?" She wanted to be
certain.

His gaze dropped to her lips. "That's where we'll start."

And where they would finish. She didn't know what kind of
woman the stud was used to, but she wasn't the type of girl to have
sex in an alley. "Okay. You can kiss me." She closed her eyes and
lifted her chin. Best to just get it over with, best to just—

His fingers lifted, cupping her chin, stroking her. Then his thumb
was on her lips, brushing them lightly apart. "You have such beautiful lips. Full. Red. I cannot wait to feel them."

Her heart pounded in a double time rhythm. And sweat coated her
palms. She kept her eyes tightly closed, and her lips parted.

"Relax. This isn't going to hurt, I promise."

But she couldn't relax. She was alone, in a dark alley, with a sexy
stranger who was about to kiss her because he felt she owed him.
And the damn thing was, she wanted him to kiss her. Wanted him
to do it so badly that she trembled.

What would those sensuous lips of his feel like? What would—

He pressed his mouth against hers, his tongue sliding past her lips
and sweeping inside. She gasped, her mouth widening. *Oh, my...*

He kissed her like he owned her, like he had a right to taste her,
all of her. His tongue thrust, teased, drove her crazy, and had her
moaning and wrapping her hands around his broad shoulders and
holding on for dear life.

His mouth locked on hers. Hot, wet. And his tongue... *Oh, my...*

His hands slid down her body, moving over the curves of her breasts, cupping her, teasing her nipples, and it felt so good. So unbelievably good. And all the while, he kept kissing her, stroking her with his tongue, seducing her...

The bulge of his arousal pressed against her. Thick, long, and hard. His hips rocked against her, pressed, rocked...

He tore his mouth from hers and began to lick her neck. "You taste so good," he whispered, his breath hot against her skin. "I knew you would, I knew..."

His mouth pressed against her throat. His tongue stroked her, and his hands—

She shuddered. *This couldn't be happening. They were in an alley, for heaven's sake!*

His teeth bit lightly into her flesh. And his fingers slipped under the torn shirt, under the edge of her practical white bra and stroked her breast, plucked her nipple.

"I can smell you." His head lifted. She forced herself to look up at him, to meet that blue stare. "You're wet for me. You want me to take you."

Kat shook her head. No, she didn't want that... did she? Confusion filled her. Her body was heavy, hungry. Hungry, for him. For a man that she didn't know. Her eyes widened. She didn't even know his name!

She pushed against him. "Let me go." Her voice sounded like a frog's croak. Probably from all that moaning she'd just been doing.

Those bedroom eyes narrowed. He pressed his hips against her, his arousal pulsing.

And fear pounded through her, dousing the passion. She didn't know him. They were alone. He was a hell of a lot stronger than she was. If she screamed now, who would save her... from him?

Kat licked her lips and forced herself to hold his stare. "Let me go," she repeated, her voice stronger.

His jaw clenched and his eyes narrowed. And she knew, he didn't want to let her go. He wanted to take her, right there against the wall, hard and fast.

She held her breath, gathered her strength, and prepared to fight him.

Then he stepped back.

Relief swept through her, making her slightly dizzy. She stumbled away from him, heading for the street.

"You don't need to be afraid of me."

His voice stopped her cold. She glanced back over her shoulder, aware that she could still taste him. "I don't even know you," she muttered. And she'd probably never see him again, probably never—

"My name's Michael, Michael Morlet." He bowed slightly to her, his lips twisted into a tight smile, his eyes still burning with lust.

She hesitated. Part of her wanted to run, run as fast as she could. But... She turned to face him. "I'm Katherine. Kat. Kat Hardy." Exchanging names felt... normal. Safe.

His smile widened. "It's been a... pleasure... meeting you, Kat."

She sent him a trembling smile in return. "Well... uh... good-bye, Michael." She inclined her head. "And... uh... thanks for saving me."

Then she all but ran down the alley. Because she had the feeling that if she stayed there much longer... she wouldn't want to leave. And she'd be asking him, no, *begging* him to take her into his arms again, to hold her, to kiss her. *To take her.*

Michael had been right. She did want him. Her body ached for him. And that fact scared her to death.

So she fled, running into the night, running down the street, her sandals snapping against the pavement, her heart beating frantically.

※❀(☙☺❧)❀※

Michael watched her as she left, watched as the moonlight danced over her skin, watched as she darted down the street. And then he began to follow her, tracking her slowly, carefully.

He'd always enjoyed a good hunt. "Run, sweet Kat," he whispered, moving as one with the shadows of the night. "But I'll be right behind you." Now that he'd finally found her, there was no way he'd let her go.

She feared him, he knew that, he'd seen the alarm in her eyes. But he would get past that fear, in time.

After all, she was his. The wolf within had recognized its mate. He had her scent now, and there was no way that he would let her escape.

She was human, so he knew that she wouldn't understand the bond between them, not at first. He would have to be patient with her, would have to teach her about the ways of his kind.

And he'd have to claim her. Mark her. So that she understood there would be no other for her. Or for him. "I'm coming for you, Kat," he told her retreating figure softly, enjoying the feel of her name upon his lips. *Coming to take you, to thrust deep and hard into that silky little body of yours.* "You're going to be mine."

Forever.

She just didn't realize that fact yet. But she would, soon. He'd make damn sure she understood.

After all, wolves mated for life.

Chapter Two

He was there again. The mysterious Frenchman with the bedroom eyes. He was there as he'd been for the last three nights. Sitting in the back booth of Bernie's Bar, hiding in the shadows. Watching her.

Kat stiffened her shoulders and walked slowly across the room. Enough was enough. She didn't like the feeling that the guy gave her. Didn't like the feeling that he was—

"Hey, pretty lady!" A blond man with a black cowboy hat grabbed her by the waist. "I was sure hoping you'd be coming my way." He smiled at her, and she smelled the whiskey on his breath.

Just what she didn't need right then. She forced a smile to her lips and said, very politely, "Uh, I'm not your waitress, so—"

He laughed. "Ah, baby, I don't want you to get me a drink." His brown eyes dropped to her chest. "But I got something else in mind you can do for me…"

Great. One of the lovely perks of working at Bernie's. She got to deal with drunken idiots. "Sorry," she muttered, trying to keep her voice expressionless. Her smile was long gone now. "I'm not on the menu."

His fingers tightened around her. "But you're on *my* menu, baby—"

"Remove your hands from the lady."

Kat closed her eyes. She knew that voice. Knew that musical accent. It looked like her Frenchman had given up watching, and was about to get involved in her life again.

She opened her eyes and craned her head to the side. Yep, sure enough, Michael stood there. Arms crossed over his muscled chest.

Blue eyes narrowed. Face as hard as stone. "I can handle this," she muttered.

One black brow rose.

"The *lady* likes my hands on her," the cowboy snapped. "She— happens to—"

"What?" She slapped at the said hands. "I most certainly don't like them on me. Now take them off!"

He shook his head. "Aw, you're just saying that, you know you like—"

It was as far as he got. Michael moved in a blur, grabbing the fellow's hand and twisting. The cowboy went white and dropped to his knees.

Kat stepped back. And noticed that they were beginning to attract a crowd. Hell, even the small country western band had stopped playing. All eyes were on them.

Just great.

"You don't touch her," Michael told the guy softly. "Ever."

The cowboy nodded. And Kat saw a tear leak from the corner of his left eye.

"Now, apologize to the lady, and then get the hell out of here." Michael's voice was calm, cool. He released the cowboy and moved to Kat's side.

"Uh, sorry." Red color blotched the guy's face. He stumbled back, hit the table, then turned and disappeared into the crowd.

Michael raised his brows and glanced around the bar. As if on cue, the music began to play again, and a soft rumble of voices filled the room.

Kat swallowed. "You didn't have to do that," she said, lips tight.

He blinked. "He had no right to touch you."

"Yeah, well, you had no right to jump in. I was handling things." Her hands were on her hips now. She glared up at him. "I can take care of guys like him." She'd been doing it for years. "I don't need your help."

"It did not look as if you were... handling things to me." He lifted his hand and stroked her cheek. "You looked frightened."

She jerked away from him. "I wasn't. I had things under control."

"Like you had things under control in the alley?" His voice was low, but tense.

"That was different." Jeez. She wasn't some kind of damsel in distress. She didn't need the big, strong stud to keep sweeping in and saving her. "Look, you just can't—"

He reached for her hand. His fingers wrapped around her wrist, warm, strong. Her pulse rate immediately doubled.

"I've been looking for you... searching for you... for so long."

She licked her lips. "I-I think you have me confused with-with someone else."

He shook his head, and his thumb began to stroke the sensitive skin of her wrist. "No, you're the one."

The one? Just what did that mean? The one what?

"We're going to be good together," he whispered, stepping closer to her. His nostrils flared, as if he were inhaling her scent. "So good."

Her heart pounded. "No, we aren't, because there's no us—"

"Don't be afraid of me," he continued in that same soft tone. The tone he'd probably use in bed, when he whispered to a woman, when he thrust deep, deep into her body. "I'll never hurt you, I promise."

Like she hadn't heard that line before. Kat's chin jutted into the air. "There *is* no us." She tugged against his hold. His eyes narrowed, but he let her go. "There will be no us." No matter how damn sexy he was.

"Yes, there will be." His eyes seemed to glow, to shimmer. "Count on it."

A strange chill chased down her spine. He sounded... so damn certain. Kat took a few steps back, wanting to put some space between them. "Look, just stay away from me, okay? Just stay away." Because she wasn't up to handling him right then. And she wasn't sure that she trusted herself around him, because there was something about Michael Morlet... something that tempted her.

She took a deep breath and turned away from him. She could feel his gaze on her as she crossed the room. But when she stopped at the bar and finally glanced back, he was gone.

❧❀⊱✦⊰❀❧

Four hours later, Kat finally closed Bernie's Bar. She stacked the last of the chairs onto the scarred tables and glanced around, wanting to make certain she hadn't forgotten anything before she left.

It was her first time to close, and being in the bar, all alone, well, it made her kind of... nervous.

It was just that the bar was so dark. Even with the faint overhead lighting, shadows filled the room. And the building... it creaked. And groaned. Like an old woman. And every time she heard one of those sounds, she jumped.

She exhaled heavily and crept toward the back room. What had happened to her? When had she become such a scaredy cat?

Was it back in Chicago? When she'd nearly been run down by that black car?

Or had it been before that, when she'd walked into her apartment and found Sean and—

Creak.

She froze. Damn, but she really hated this building. Buildings should *not* make noises on their own. She didn't care how old and decrepit they were. There should be some kind of rule, some kind of—

Creak.

Her heart pounded in her chest. And that noise... it had sounded different... closer.

She reached for her purse. It was past time for her to leave, past time for her to get her butt out of there and—

Creak.

Kat spun around—and came face to face with a man in a black ski mask.

She should have come out of the bar already. Michael stood in the shadows across the street from Bernie's, and stared into the bar's glowing windows.

Kat should have left already. She'd been inside, cleaning, for almost two hours.

He'd been waiting on her, waiting to apologize for his behavior. He'd scared her, again. He hadn't meant to scare her. He wanted to seduce her, not frighten her away. But when he was around her, he just said the wrong things. Did the wrong things.

When that idiot had grabbed her earlier, it had been all he could do not to rip the man apart. No other should touch Kat. Ever.

Kat obviously hadn't appreciated him coming to her aid. What had she said? Oh, yes. That she could have "handled" things. The cowboy had been a foot taller than her, and he'd outweighed her by at least a hundred pounds. But she could have handled him.

Michael snorted. Right.

He'd only wanted to protect his mate. Protecting her was his duty, his right.

He gazed into the bar's windows, feeling tension sweep through him. She'd told him to stay away from her. But he couldn't. He needed her too much.

So he would apologize, he would try to start over with her, try to treat her with the kindness and patience she needed, try to—

A crash sounded from inside the bar.

Kat!

He ran for the building, his heart pounding.

He smashed in the door, yelling her name. His senses were on high alert, the beast within sensing danger. His gaze scanned the bar. Where was she? Where was—

Kat stumbled out of the back room, her face flushed.

"Kat!" He ran to her side.

Her eyes widened. "What are you—"

A slam sounded behind her, followed by the thud of retreating as if someone had run out the back door.

He lunged forward, but Kat grabbed his arm. "No!"

No? Michael stared down at her in disbelief. "What's going on?"

Her lips trembled. "A man... in a mask... I-I think he wanted to rob the bar."

He grabbed her, locking his arms tightly around her. "Did he hurt you?"

She shook her head. "No, but I think I hurt him." Her mouth curved just the faintest bit. "I-I hit him over the head with Bernie's lamp."

His eyes widened.

Her brows lifted. "Why the surprise? I told you, I can handle myself." Her smile disappeared. "All the same, I sure as hell am glad that you showed up when you did."

And so was he. Twice now his mate had been in danger. And that was unacceptable. Steps would have to be taken. He could not allow her life to be at risk.

She was far too important.

"I-I'd better call the cops."

His hold tightened on her. Her scent surrounded him, tempted him. Her body was pressed against his, her soft curves rubbing against his flesh.

His cock stiffened with hunger.

And he knew, by the way her eyes widened, by the way a soft flush coated her cheeks, that she felt his hunger, too.

Her lips parted and he moved forward, lowering his head and plunging his tongue deep inside of her mouth. And, *Mon Dieu*, but she tasted good. Sweet. Hot.

His.

She kissed him back, her mouth widening against his, her tongue stroking him. Her hands curved over his shoulders, and her short nails bit into his skin as her fingers clenched against him. And it felt good. Damn good.

He growled low in his throat and pulled her closer, pressing her against his growing arousal. Oh, but it would feel great to thrust into her. To thrust hard and deep, to feel her slender legs wrapped around him as he moved, to hear her moan, to hear her cry out his name—

His cock thrust against her, and he began to kiss and lick his way down her throat. He inhaled her scent. Light, sweet. Like flowers. Roses. He loved the way she smelled, loved the way she tasted.

His incisors burned. The need to mark her, to brand her, raged through him. *His mate.* Kat was his. He'd found her, finally, by sheer blind luck he'd stumbled onto her. *His mate, his—*

Kat stiffened in his arms. "What? What did you say?"

Michael stilled. Lust pounded through him. And he wanted, so very badly, to lift her up onto the old, scarred bar, to push up her skirt and yank her panties away, and to slide deep into her wet heat.

And she was wet. He could smell her arousal. Smell the lush scent in the air.

"Did you call me your mate?" Her hands weren't clinging to him anymore. They pushed against him.

Now was hardly the time to tell her that, yes, he'd called her his mate, and that, yes, he planned to bond with her in the way of his kind as soon as possible.

His kind. Yeah, he'd probably better not tell her about that little family trait yet, either. If she learned he was literally the kind of guy to howl at the moon, sweet Kat would run screaming from him.

And he couldn't allow that.

He took a deep breath and forced his hands to let her go. Forced himself to step back, to give her space.

Hell, the woman needed space. She'd just been nearly robbed. And then he'd jumped her.

But she was just so damned tempting to him... "I apologize," he told her formally, his voice stiff. "You just... tempt me beyond control."

Kat blinked those gorgeous green eyes of hers. And a soft flush stained her cheeks. "Oh. Um... thanks. I think." She shook her head. "What the hell am I saying? I don't have time for this! I don't have—"

He reached for her hand. He loved the silky smoothness of her skin. "I want to make love to you." Over and over. Until she screamed his name. Until he felt her body clench around him as her orgasm pumped through her. Until she felt the same, shattering link that he felt.

Her cheeks became even redder. "Wow. You're the direct kind, huh?"

He didn't reply.

She swallowed. "Look, I'm... um... not really looking for a relationship right now. Things in my life are... complicated."

Too bad. Because he wasn't going to leave her. She was too important to him, to his kind. Unless he was very wrong, Katherine Hardy was one of the few women capable of a complete mating with his kind. That meant... she could give him a child.

Of course, she would have to be tested by his family's doctors. Her DNA would have to be analyzed... but he was sure, absolutely sure, that she would pass the test. After all, his kind recognized their mates on sight. And he sure as hell had recognized her.

"You're... um... really good-looking," she told him earnestly. "You're not going to have trouble finding another woman who—"

His eyes widened as disbelief filled him. Surely she wasn't telling him to find another? "I do not want any other woman. I only want you."

Her mouth dropped open. "Oh." She shook her head. "Well, that's... um... too bad because—"

He stroked her wrist and felt her pulse pound. "And I'm going to have you. Get used to the idea." The sooner, the better. He wasn't certain how long he'd be able to maintain his control with her. The beast within him was hungry, starving for a taste of its mate.

"I-I'm going to call the cops." She licked her lips. "I want to report that guy."

He nodded. Fine. She could call her policemen. He would stay with her.

"You can go now," she continued, pulling her hand away from him and moving around the bar. "I'm sure I'll be fine here—"

"I'm staying." And once she finished talking to the cops, he would take her home.

She paused, her hand on the black telephone. "I don't get you, Morlet."

He raised a brow.

Kat frowned. "I mean, why are you doing this? Why are you even here? Shellsville, Georgia, can't be your usual kind of place."

No, it wasn't. Shellsville had been a temporary stop on his way to the pack's compound just outside of Atlanta. His gaze swept over her. "Let's just say I found something here that is important to me." *Very important.* "And I'm not leaving town without it."

He could tell by her puzzled expression that she didn't understand him, but that was all right. She would understand. Very soon. Once he'd claimed her, once they'd mated in the way of his kind, everything would be clear to her.

He smiled at Kat, what he hoped was a nice, non-threatening smile.

And he started planning her seduction. Because before the morning sun rose, he intended to have her.

Chapter Three

Oh, God, but she wanted him. Kat took a deep breath and tried to calm her racing heart. She was in Michael's car, a sleek, black BMW with an all leather interior. *Cause didn't it just figure that the guy would be gorgeous and rich?* And all she could think about was... the kiss.

Wow, but what a kiss it had been. A toe-curling, knee-weakening, sex-clenching kiss. The things the man could do with his tongue...

She shivered. She was in trouble. Deep trouble. Because, despite her words, despite all of her tough talk, she knew the truth... And the truth was that she wanted Michael Morlet. Wanted him so badly her body was aching.

It was all she could do not to pounce on the man as they drove to her small cottage. All she could do not to lean over him, unzip those sexy black pants, and reach for that thick cock she'd felt pressing against her earlier.

And, after all, why didn't she do that? She wasn't involved with anyone. Hadn't been for over a year. And she was young, only thirty-one. And healthy... and hungry...

Hungry for Michael.

Hell, how often did a woman have a chance to have sex with a man like him? The guy oozed sex appeal. He was freaking physically perfect, and—

"Are you all right, Kat?"

She jumped, and realized she'd been staring at his crotch for the last five minutes. And that he'd stopped driving at some point. And that his gaze was locked on her.

He'd caught her staring at his groin! Humiliation burned through her. *Damn... so much for playing Ms. Sophisticated.* She took a breath. All right, if she was going to do this, she'd better go ahead and clear the air. A man like Michael, he probably expected his partner to be some sort of sex queen. Which she so wasn't. "There are some... things you need to know about me."

He turned off the car and looked at her. The light from the moon spilled into the car, sliding across the side of his face. "Such as?"

She wet her lips. "I'm not... very good at this kind of thing."

He stared at her.

She cleared her throat. "You know... um... sex." She waved her hand vaguely in the air. "I tend to mess it up." Or at least, she tended to have a really, really hard time enjoying herself. Sean had called her frigid once. Okay, more than once.

He tapped the leather steering wheel with his index finger. "I don't think you'll have to worry about messing anything up."

Easy for him to say. He'd probably been with dozens of women, and given them dozens of orgasms. A sharp pang of jealousy shot through her. "You don't understand, I—"

"I'd planned to seduce you." He inclined his head toward her gleaming porch light. "I was going to walk you to your door, convince you to invite me in for a drink, and then I was going to get you so hot and hungry that you'd let me stay... that you'd let me make love to you."

She blinked.

"I was going to take off your shirt, then take off that prim little white bra I know you're wearing. I was going to stroke your breasts, tease your nipples. Then I was going to taste them. I was going to suck them, to lick them, and I was going to get you out of that black skirt that drives me crazy. I was going to strip it off you, leaving you in just your panties and those sexy as hell shoes that you're wearing."

Her heart pounded. Her nipples were tight. And her panties were getting very wet. "Y-you were?"

He nodded. "I know... you told me you weren't interested."

Yeah, she'd lied right through her teeth.

"But a guy can hope, can't he?"

She looked back up at her cozy cottage, at the sturdy brick frame. "Would you, would you like to come in... for a drink?" Her palms were damp with sweat and she couldn't believe she'd just invited him inside, and that what she'd really meant was... *do you want to come in for sex?*

She was not that kind of girl. Really, she wasn't. But there was something about Michael, something that made her feel hot, achy, needy. Primed and ready. And she couldn't ever remember feeling this ready for a man.

So for once, just once, she was going to do what she wanted. She was going to live in the moment.

And she was going to make love with Michael. She hoped.

Kat held her breath, staring up into his face. He'd wanted her before. Hell, the man had said that he'd planned to seduce her. But now, now he said nothing.

Not. A. Single. Word.

Her stomach clenched. Surely he hadn't changed his mind. Surely he hadn't—

"You had better not be teasing me, Kat." His voice was hard, nearly a growl.

"I-I'm not."

"If I come inside, I'm going to take you."

Oh, that sounded good to her. Very good. "I-I know." Her voice was husky, a thin whisper.

"There will be no going back once I've claimed you."

Her breasts ached. Her nipples tightened. She barely heard what he was saying. She'd never, never wanted anyone like this before.

Maybe it was the adrenaline that was still shooting through her. That idiot in the ski mask had scared her silly.

Yeah, maybe it was the adrenaline.

Or, maybe it was the fact that every time she looked at Michael, her hormones shot into overdrive.

"Will you accept me?" Michael asked her, his fingers clenching around the steering wheel.

"Yes..." *Accept him?* Her body was on fire for him. She was so

hungry, so ready, so—

"Then you had better get your sexy ass out of the car right now, or our first time's going to be right here in the front seat."

She gulped and jumped from the car.

Lust was riding him hard. Michael stood behind Kat, inhaling her sweet scent as she fumbled with the lock on her door, and he prayed that he would be able to maintain his control.

He couldn't believe his luck. Kat wanted him. She'd invited him back to her home. He hadn't had to trick her or to seduce her.

She'd invited him in…

Kat turned the keys and pushed the door open. "I-it's not much, but…" She turned on the light and waved her hand vaguely in the air, "It's all mine."

He didn't bother glancing around the cottage. He couldn't take his eyes off her long enough to spare the room a look.

After following her inside, he kicked the door shut with the heel of his shoe. Kat watched him, her green eyes wide.

Her nipples thrust against the white shirt she wore. He knew the shirt and black skirt were the required uniform for waitresses at Bernie's. And damn if those clothes hadn't been driving him crazy for the last few nights.

He couldn't wait to strip them off her. Couldn't wait to see her sweet, sexy body.

If only he could hold on to his control.

Good thing the moon wasn't full. There would have been no way he would have been able to keep the beast in check then.

"Where is your bedroom?" he asked, keeping his gaze on her nipples. And such lovely nipples they were. How would they taste?

Lifting her hand, she pointed down the dark hallway. Her shirt rose, brushing against her breasts.

"Too far," he muttered, and reached for her. He grabbed her shirt, aware that his hands shook. With one quick yank, he sent buttons flying, and ripped open the shirt. Her breasts, soft white mounds he couldn't wait to lick, spilled from the cups of her virginal white bra.

She lifted her hands, instinctively trying to cover herself.

"No." His teeth burned, sharpened. "I want to see you."

She bit her lip, and dropped her hands.

He growled. *Mon Dieu*, but the woman was lovely. And she was his. *His.*

He kissed her, thrusting his tongue deep into her mouth and drinking her sweetness. And his hands slid around her body, found the clasp of her bra, and slipped it free. He pushed the tattered remains of the shirt aside, and dropped her bra to the floor.

He pulled his mouth from hers, licking her lips, then licking the slender column of her throat. His hands were tight around her hips, holding her against him, letting her feel the hard bulge of his cock.

Her pulse raced beneath his mouth, and his teeth brushed against her flesh, a light, teasing bite that made him hungry for more.

He wanted to mark her…

She moaned, tilting her head back and closing her eyes. Her hands wrapped around his arms. Her breasts brushed against him…

With an effort, he lifted his mouth away from her neck. He breathed deeply, greedily gulping the air. Her scent surrounded him. The light, sweet scent of flowers, the heavier, rich scent of woman that told him she was ready for him, that she was wet. He couldn't wait to feel the wet heat of her cunt wrapping around him. She was going to feel like heaven.

Her nipples were pink, a light, pretty pink. His fingers stroked her, teasing her and plucking her nipples. She arched into his touch, her green eyes flaring with arousal.

Then he took her nipple into his mouth, swirling his tongue over the tight peak and sucking.

"Michael… God, that feels so good."

He kept suckling her, drawing the peak of her breast deeper into his mouth. She tasted so good. So damn good. He licked her nipple, then bit lightly.

She shuddered against him. "Michael…"

He lifted his head. Her breast was tight, flushed, gleaming with moisture from his mouth. He blew lightly over the puckered skin, and she choked out a breath. Then he turned to the other breast, and licked his lips. "You taste delicious." And he took her into his mouth.

Her body trembled against his. Her hands dug into his arms, sweet moans spilled from her lips, and her hips rubbed mindlessly against him.

He swirled his tongue around her nipple and pulled back, a smile on his lips. If she thought that was good, then she was going to love what came next...

The sofa waited behind them. He pushed her back a few steps, and she tumbled, falling onto the soft cushions, her legs sprawling apart.

In the absolute perfect position for that he wanted.

Her skirt had hiked up, revealing the pale skin of her thighs, and higher, the soft white cotton of her underwear.

She tried to sit up, but he pushed her back down. "No, I want to see you." *All of her.*

She licked her lips and watched him, her huge, green eyes shimmering with arousal.

He stoked the skin of her legs, pushing her thighs even wider apart, and lifted the black skirt up several more inches.

She wore a pair of white bikini panties. They rode low on her slender hips, and he could just barely see the shadowy outline of her sex beneath the soft fabric.

And he could smell her. Warm, hot pussy.

He slid his finger under the edge of her panties, and found her, wet, ready.

Her hips lifted against his hand. "Michael..."

"Shhh..." He pulled the panties down and tossed them to the floor. Then he shoved her thighs apart again and stared at the glistening folds of her cunt. "So pink and pretty. I think I'm just going to have to taste you..."

She lifted her hands, but he pushed them back, pinning them to the soft cushions of the sofa. And he lowered his head, licking her folds, sucking the soft button of her sex.

Kat moaned, the sound deep, hungry. Her body tensed against his. And he licked again, sliding his tongue over her clit. "Mmmm... You taste good, Kat. Like warm honey." Her thighs trembled against him. Her hands clenched into fists. And her cunt... her cunt was so warm and ready. He thrust his tongue into her, shoving deep inside.

She screamed as her orgasm ripped through her. Tremors shook her slight body. And his control snapped. He lapped at her, drinking deeply of her sweet juices, loving her taste, loving the feel of her. She moaned his name, lifted her hips mindlessly against him, and shook with pleasure.

He lifted his head, licked his lips, and tasted her. His cock was so stiff and hard it hurt, and he wanted to slam into her, to thrust into her tight little pussy and feel her come around him.

He shoved down his pants, not bothering to undress. Hell, he wouldn't have lasted long enough to undress. His eyes were on the red curls of her sex, glistening, a sweet temptation. He pushed his cock against her, letting her wet heat coat the head of his shaft.

Kat looked up at him, her green eyes stunned. She licked her lips. "That was... amazing."

He smiled down at her. "I'm not finished yet." And then he thrust deep into her tight cunt.

His hands clenched around her hips, and he lifted her, thrusting over and over, harder and deeper. And she met him, wrapping her legs around him, squeezing him, sliding up and down his cock. His jaw clenched. His nails lengthened, and the beast within him began to howl for release.

So close...

So close...

He took her breast into his mouth, sucking hard, drawing the nipple deep. And his cock thrust into her, deeper, ever deeper...

His climax was approaching, he could feel it in the tightening of his spine, the increasing tension in his cock. Kat felt incredible around him. So hot. So freaking tight...

He lifted his head, breathing hard, and gazed down at her. "Come for me again." His hips slammed against her. "Come for me!"

Her body buckled against his, and her muscles clenched, milking the link of his cock.

He jerked his hands away from her hips and buried his claws in the cushions of her sofa. And his climax slammed through him, hard, fast, leaving him shuddering as he pumped his semen deep into her core.

And, unable to stop himself, he bent his head to her neck, inhaled her sweet scent... and gave her a wolf's bite.

~⟨⟨⟨◯⟩⟩⟩~

OhmyGod. OhmyGod. OhmyGod. Kat stared up at her ceiling and tried to determine if she was still alive.

Her body felt so good, so damn satisfied, that she wasn't sure.

But then Michael moved, lifted his dark head and gazed down at her. "Are you all right?"

She tried to talk, but her mouth was so dry she wound up nearly choking. She swallowed, tried again, and managed to croak, "Fine."

Her body still tingled. Still shivered. And she could still feel him, feel his cock, inside of her.

OhmyGod. She'd just had an orgasm. *Two* orgasms. And they'd been so *good*!

So much for being frigid. She should have known better than to listen to a jackass like Sean. All she'd needed was a guy... like Michael.

He gazed down at her, his blue eyes shining. "You are something else, Kat."

"I-I... was going to say... the same thing." The man had to be some kind of sex god. Had to be. She realized then that her toes were curled. She tried to relax them.

His finger trailed over her breast, circled her nipple. And her sex clenched around him.

He smiled at her. "Ah, Kat, ready to go again?"

Oh, yes, most definitely. Kat the nympho was ready, willing and able to go again—

Michael stiffened against her, his eyes narrowing. "Do you hear that?"

She blinked. "Hear what?" All she could hear was her heart pounding. *Two orgasms.*

He pulled away from her, sliding his most impressive cock out of her and jerking up his pants. "Someone's outside."

She blinked again. "What?" She felt cold without him. And her body was starting to ache.

"Stay here." He didn't even bother to look at her as he gave the order.

And some of her happy, post-sex glow began to fade. Yep, she was most definitely alive and still on earth. "Look, Michael, I—"

He looked at her, his blue eyes glacial. "Stay. Here." And then he moved, turning out the lights and plunging the room into darkness.

"Well, damn," she muttered, tugging her skirt down. This was hardly what she'd expected. Where was the cuddle time? The Was-It-Good-For-You time? The—

The crack of a gunshot pierced the night. A man yelled, pain and fear thick in his voice.

Kat's heart stopped. *Michael.*

She jumped to her feet, and ran to the door. *Please, please, let him be all right, let him be—*

She jerked open the door, clad in only her skirt and high heels. "Michael!"

A low growl answered her call, and Kat watched, horror filling her, as a big, black wolf sprang from the bushes and lunged toward her, its sharp, white teeth bared in a snarl...

Chapter Four

She screamed and slammed the door shut. *OhmyGod, Ohmy-God...*

Where the hell had *that* thing come from? And what had happened to Michael? Oh, God, Michael...

Her back was against the wooden door, her body was shaking, and she was so scared she thought she might vomit.

Kat took a deep breath. She needed to find a weapon, fast. And then she needed to go out there, back out there with that rabid wolf-dog, and try to find Michael. Cause there was no way she could just leave him out there, alone with that—that thing!

A soft knock sounded on the door behind her. She yelped and jumped as if she'd been scalded.

"Uh, Kat?" The door knob rattled, and she realized that in her blind rush, she had, blessedly, locked the door behind her. *The better to keep the big, snarling wolf away.*

The knob rattled again. "Kat, open the door."

Relief swept through her. *Michael.* She'd know that sexy accented voice anywhere. The wolf hadn't gotten him. He was all right, he was—

His fist slammed into the wooden frame. "Open the damn door!"

She jerked the lock back and pulled open the door. Michael pushed his way inside, slamming the door shut with his heel.

And she stared at him, stunned... because Michael... Michael was naked. Completely naked. And heavily aroused. Oh, my. She licked her lips. "What, ah... where are your clothes?"

Those intense blue eyes of his blinked once, twice. But he didn't answer her. Didn't say anything.

"Michael?" She crossed her arms over her exposed breasts. He was naked, she was half-naked, and things felt really... weird. "Are you all right?"

His gaze dropped to her chest, heated.

She stumbled back, saw her shirt on the floor and scooped it up. There were only two buttons left on it, so she jerked it on and tied the edges of the shirt into a knot, just below her breasts.

Michael took a step toward her, lifting his hand as if he were going to touch her...

"Where are your clothes?" she asked him again, her voice rising slightly. Okay, she sounded a wee bit hysterical. But she'd just been nearly attacked by some kind of giant black wolf.

He shook his head and a sudden awareness filled his gaze. He glanced down at his body and shrugged. "Don't worry, I have an extra set in the car."

An extra set? Well, that was good, but it still didn't explain how he'd lost his first set of clothes!

"Go call the police," he ordered her softly.

"Wh-what?"

"There was a guy outside, he had a gun." His face tightened. "He was trying to break in, trying to get to you."

A chill slipped over her. "I-I didn't see anyone." She hadn't seen anything, other than... "Except for that dog." *Had to have been a dog. Couldn't have been a wolf.* There were no wolves in Shellsville. Yes, it had just been a very large, very pissed, dog. And it had looked like it wanted to eat her.

Michael stiffened. "A dog?" His lips tightened.

"Uh, huh. Ugly thing. Huge teeth. Thick, matted black fur." She shuddered. "The thing came at me, tried to attack me."

His cheeks flushed.

"But I didn't see a man with a gun. Just that dog." And she really hoped she never saw that beast again. It had scared a good ten years off her life.

"Go call the police," he ordered again, his teeth clenched. "The...

dog… was not after you, but the man sure as hell was. And if I hadn't been here, he would have gotten you."

A dog. The woman had called him a dog. An ugly dog. Michael glared at Kat as she talked to the two policemen who'd answered her call.

Could the woman not tell the difference between a wolf and a dog? Was she blind? Didn't she know—

"We'll have a patrol car cruise the neighborhood tonight, ma'am, but it's not likely the guy will come back." The older officer, a short, bald man, offered Kat a weak smile. "Probably was just some guy looking for a TV to steal."

Michael stiffened. "I do not think he was after her television set, officer." No, his gut told him the guy had been after Kat. "This is the third time this week that Kat has been attacked. Someone is obviously after her."

Kat's green eyes widened and she blanched, all of the color fading from her cheeks.

The officer glanced back at Kat, his gaze narrowing, his smile fading. "Is that true?"

"Well… um… some guys tried to mug me in an alley a few nights ago. But, Michael," she pointed vaguely to him, "he stopped them."

"Probably not related." It was the younger cop who spoke. Officer Frank Daniels, according to the gold name badge on his chest. He had light brown hair, and gray eyes that tended to stray far too much to Kat's chest and legs.

Michael stepped forward, moving to position himself at her side. Because if that guy's gaze dropped one more time… "Someone tried to break into the bar where she works earlier tonight. We called the authorities then, too. Check at your station, and they'll tell you what happened."

Frank whistled. "Two near hits in one night." His gaze appeared sympathetic as he stared at Kat. "You poor thing."

She frowned at him.

"Someone's after her," Michael said, his voice hard. "She needs protection."

The cops looked at each other. "Well, we can send the patrol out," Frank said, echoing his partner's earlier comment.

Michael glared at the men. *Idiots.* They weren't going to be any help. They didn't understand the peril that his mate faced. But he did.

Kat walked the officers to her door, thanking them for their time. She sounded grateful. He snorted. The men hadn't done anything. She didn't need to be grateful to them.

She locked the door behind them and turned to face him, her lips turned down in a frown. "Well, that was a huge waste of time." No trace of gratitude filled her voice.

He blinked.

"A patrol car. Big whoop. Like that's going to do any good." She rubbed her arms and stared up at him. "You think... you really think someone's after me, don't you?"

He nodded. Yeah, he *knew* someone was after her. And he was going to make absolutely certain that person didn't so much as touch her.

Her lashes fell closed and she shuddered. And he thought he heard her whisper, "Not again."

His heart pounded. A normal man wouldn't have heard that whisper. But he wasn't normal. Far from it. "Kat—"

Her lashes lifted. Her green eyes stared blankly back at him. "You should leave now. It's... really late."

Leave? Now? Not likely. He shook his head.

She nodded right back at him. "It was... interesting. Thanks for your... um... help tonight. Sorry your clothes got ruined or whatever happened to them." A red flush stained her cheeks. "I know this probably isn't how most of your nights end, and I'm... sorry."

She was trying to throw him out. Unbelievable.

Kat opened the door and stood there, not quite meeting his gaze. "Good night, Michael."

A slow, hot anger began to burn in his gut. After the best sex of his life, his mate wanted to kick him out. Didn't she understand? Didn't she realize what was happening between them? There would be no more separations. The bonding had started. They would stay together now, stay with each other until—

Her foot began to tap against the wooden floor. "Please, don't make this anymore awkward than it has to be."

Awkward. He would show her awkward. He stalked forward, reached for the wooden door, and slammed it closed.

Kat gasped, her eyes widening and finally lifting to meet his stare.

"You are not kicking me out." He grabbed her, locking his hands around her arms and pulling her against his body, letting her feel the arousal that still burned for her, hot and hard. "We're not finished yet." If he had his way, they'd never be done.

"Michael..."

He kissed her. His lips pressed against hers, his tongue thrusting deep into her mouth. Her breasts pushed against him. He could feel her nipples through the thin fabric of her shirt. *Mon Dieu,* but she felt good, tasted good...

He lifted his mouth a fraction from hers. "I want you," he whispered. "I want to feel you beneath me, your cunt squeezing me, your legs wrapping around me..."

Her lips trembled. Desire blazed in her eyes... desire and fear. "Y-you should leave."

His hold tightened on her. "Is that what you want? What you really want?" Every instinct he possessed screamed that he take her, hard and fast, that he brand her, that he thrust deep, deep into her core until her climax ripped through her, through him.

But she was his mate. And above all, he had to protect her, even from himself. So, if she wanted him to leave...

His hands lifted, released her, and he stepped back. His cock pulsed, hard and thick with desire. And he could still taste her in his mouth.

But he wouldn't force her to accept him—that wasn't the way of his kind...

Kat grabbed him, her nails digging into the fabric of his shirt. "Don't."

He stilled.

She licked her lips, her pink tongue sliding out, tempting him. "Don't leave."

"You know what will happen if I stay." He'd have her naked and spread beneath him within two minutes. He'd had a taste of her earlier, and he wanted more, a hell of a lot more.

Her breath caught, and hunger flashed in her eyes. "I-I know." Her chin lifted. "I-I want you. Don't leave tonight."

Desire coated her words, but fear lingered in her voice. Why? Why was she afraid? Didn't she understand he would never hurt her? Could never hurt her?

"The way... I felt with you." A quick swallow. "I've never felt that way before."

And she'd damn well better not ever feel that way with anyone else.

"And I-I want to feel that way again... just one more time." A plea.

His hands locked on hers, and he drew her arms down to her sides. He held her gaze, letting her see all of the hunger, all of the lust that swirled within him. "*Ma petite*, you're going to feel that way a hell of lot more than one time." One time wouldn't even begin to quench his need. And if she thought she'd just screw him once more and then kick him out, well, she would be in for quite the surprise.

There was no way he would give her up. No. Way.

Her breath whispered out on a sigh.

He glanced down her body, saw that her nipples were pebbled, tight. Perfect. "I want you in a bed this time. Naked, stretched out, and so ready for me that you think you'll go mad if you don't feel me inside."

"I... feel that way... now."

A growl rumbled in his throat. "Go get in bed," he ordered. Before he gave into his hunger and took her there, up against the door. It would be so easy. She still wore her skirt, but no underwear. And she was aroused. He could smell her sweet cream, the scent filled his nostrils, driving his hunger. All he had to do was lift her up, spread those legs, stroke her soft cunt and thrust inside.

She stepped around him, walking slowly. Her right hand stayed on the wall, it trembled faintly. He watched her, watched the sway of her hips, the soft glide of her legs...

Kat paused at her bedroom door, glanced back at him over her shoulder. "I want you naked this time," she whispered. "I want to feel you, skin against skin."

He jerked his shirt off in one quick move and tossed it to the floor. Oh, *oui*, he wanted to feel her. *Skin to skin.*

"Come on," she told him, a faint smile curving her full lips. "Come and take me." And she disappeared into the darkened bedroom.

He smiled, the wolf within growling in anticipation. Oh, yes, he loved a good hunt.

✥✥❨❩❨❩✥✥

What was she doing? Kat lay on her bed, completely naked, and stared up into the darkness. Why had she asked him to stay? Hell, forget asked. She'd all but *begged* him to stay. Talk about being desperate and needy.

But when she'd stood there, gazing up into his eyes, she hadn't been able to tell him to leave. Because if she'd done it, if she'd told him that she didn't want him, well... it would have been over. She never would have seen him again.

Her time in Shellsville was over. She knew that. Tomorrow, she would have to pack up and get out of the country town as fast she could. And when she did, she would leave Michael behind. Forever.

Her heart lurched at the thought.

So, she'd been greedy. Been desperate. Desperate to stay with him, for just a little longer. Desperate to feel the passion that only he could arouse in her. *One more time...*

Yes, tomorrow she would leave. But tonight... tonight she would stay with him. Maybe it was crazy, maybe *she* was crazy, but she wanted him. And she was damn well going to take him.

"Good. You're naked."

She jumped at the sound of his voice. She hadn't heard him come into the room, but he was there, right next to the bed. The light from the moon spilled through the window, fell over his muscled body.

He was naked, too. She gazed at him, her mouth dry. His chest rippled with muscles. A light thatch of dark hair covered his chest and arrowed down his tight abdomen. And his cock... *Oh, my,* but the man was impressive. His cock was long, hard, and easily bigger than her wrist. The head appeared full, stretched taunt, and she vividly remembered how it had felt when he'd thrust into her, so hard and deep...

A soft moan slipped from her lips.

"I can smell your cream, Kat. Your sweet little cunt's ready for me now, but you're going to have to wait. I want to play with you first."

A heady excitement filled her. "No, it's my turn to play." She sat up, tossing back her hair and gazing at his erection. "And I want to play with you." She caught her breath, waiting for his response. She'd never wanted to do this before, never thought of—

He growled. His hands lifted, locked on her shoulders, and he drew her closer, closer to him, closer to the edge of the bed. "What are you saying?"

Oh, God. Her heart was pounding so hard that her chest hurt. Her nipples tightened. Desire filled her. Hungry, heady desire. She wanted him to touch her, to taste her. And she wanted to taste him, was desperate to taste him. To feel his thick arousal in her mouth, against her tongue. She slid forward, and her fingers wrapped around him.

Michael inhaled sharply, his hands tightening.

"Get in the bed, Michael," she ordered him, looking up through the veil of her lashes. "Lie down."

At first, he didn't move, not a single inch—her breath caught. Michael was so dominant, maybe he wouldn't—

His hands dropped. His eyes heated, seemed to smolder. Kat

scooted back. Michael slid into the bed and, as she'd ordered, he got on his back, flat on his back. And his cock pointed straight up. "Is this what you want?" He put his hands behind his head, staring up at her.

Oh, my... so much strong, sexy man... "Yes," she whispered. *It's exactly what I want.*

"Then have your fun, but just remember, I get to play, too."

Her sex clenched in anticipation. And her hands reached for him.

She started at his chest. His strong, muscled chest. She stroked him, her nails lightly scoring his flat nipples. When he groaned, satisfaction filled her, and she bent down, licking him lightly, sucking his nipples.

"Oh, that's good. Very good."

She bit him, a soft, teasing bite. He shuddered.

And while her tongue licked him, while her lips stroked, her hands slid down his abdomen, down to the thick, hot length of his cock.

Her fingers locked around him. Stroked up and down. Once. Twice. God, he was thick. So thick and hard. And hot. She couldn't wait to feel his cock in her, plunging deep and hard into her sex.

She licked her way down his stomach, her breath blowing against his skin. And her hands kept moving on his cock. Up. Down. His breath panted out, and his body felt like corded steel beneath her.

His cock was so close to her mouth now, just inches away. She stared at the thick head, hunger burning through her.

His hands flashed out, locked around her, pushed her down. "Do not tease me, Kat."

She looked up at him, a smile lifting her lips. "Didn't I tell you? You don't get to touch me, not while I'm playing."

His jaw clenched. But his hands released her.

"That's better." And to reward him, she lowered her head and licked the base of his cock. Then she moved up, licking the full length, and finally taking the head of his arousal into her mouth.

She sucked him, her tongue sliding over his cock. And he tasted good. Salty, strangely sweet. She licked him, tried to draw his cock in her mouth deeper, loving the way he groaned, the way his body tightened, the way—

"Playtime's over," he snarled, grabbing her and pulling her up his body. His mouth crashed down on hers, his tongue plunging into her mouth.

The world spun, and she found herself on her back, her legs spread, with Michael over her. His legs were between hers, his cock pushing at the mouth of her sex. She lifted her hips, tried to force him inside, to force him to move those few precious inches...

His hands locked on her hips. His gaze, bright, burning blue, filled with hunger, met hers. She pressed down, rubbing her clit against him, moaning softly at the feel of him. So close... so close...

His dark head lowered and his mouth locked onto her breast. And his tongue... his tongue...

Her climax bore down on her, her orgasm just seconds away. She could feel it. Her muscles tightened, her sex clenched. He hadn't entered her yet, hadn't thrust that thick cock inside of her, but she her body was so ready, so eager that—

His fingers slid over her, slid *into her*, those thick, hard fingers parted her creamy folds, stroked her clit, pressed, teased...

"Come for me," he growled, the words rumbled against her breast as he licked her, kissed, suckled. "Come for me."

His fingers plunged inside, his thumb pressed against her clit, and his tongue laved her breast...

"*Oh, God, oh, God, oh, God...*" She was so close, so close to coming... but she wanted him... wanted him inside... wanted to feel *him*. Her nails dug into his hips. She strained, trying to pull him forward, just a little closer...

And then his fingers slid out of her. A ragged cry choked past her lips. Her body was too tense, too tight, she needed—

His cock slid inside of her, just an inch... not enough...

"Do you accept me?" Another inch. So thick. So full.

She nodded, wrapping her legs around him, licking her lips. She needed him to thrust. Hard. Deep—

"Say the words. Say that you accept me, my claim."

His what? She didn't know what he was talking about, but if he didn't move soon, she was going to—

His fingers stroked her clit. She shuddered, hissing with pleasure. *Oh, that was good. So good.*

"Do you accept me?" he repeated, his body tense.

"Yes! Yes!" She gasped. "Now, move—"

He slammed into her, his cock sliding deep. Her orgasm ripped through her, and she could only lie there, moaning, as he moved, in and out, harder, deeper—

"You're so tight. So hot..." He brought his fingers to his lips, and licked them. "And you taste so good, *ma petite,* so good."

And he kept thrusting. Kept burying that strong cock in her, and the pleasure roared through her, consumed her.

She didn't even feel it when he bent toward her neck, opened his mouth... and bit her.

Chapter Five

It was the sunlight that woke him. The bright rays shone through the window, falling directly on his face. He stretched slowly, enjoying the feel of the sheets against his skin. He reached out, knowing Kat was beside him, that her soft body was just inches away—

But he couldn't find her. Couldn't touch her.

His eyes snapped open. Kat's side of the bed was empty. And cold.

"Katherine!"

He jumped out of the bed. She wasn't in the bedroom. He reached for the door, jerking the handle. "Katherine!"

He heard a yelp, then a thud. He turned down the hallway and saw her... dragging a big, black suitcase and wearing a hunted expression.

What in the hell was the woman doing? He crossed his arms over his chest and glared at her. She should have still been in bed, with him. They should have been getting ready to make love again. She shouldn't be running around, dragging some battered case—

His eyes narrowed. Why did she have the suitcase? Just what was his Kat up to?

"Uh... hi... Michael." She dropped the case and tried to scoot it behind her with her left foot. "I... uh... didn't mean to wake you."

Yes, that fact was obvious. And it brought up a damn good point. Just how had she gotten out of the bed without waking him? His hearing was five times stronger than a human's. There was no way she should have been able to sneak away from him.

Of course, the woman *had* wiped him out with some incredibly good sex.

But it looked like instead of offering him another delicious taste of her body, she was trying to run away.

He motioned toward her bag. "What are you doing?"

She looked just over his shoulder. "Cleaning."

Right. He cocked a brow. "Well, why don't you leave the *cleaning* for now, and come back to bed with me?" His gaze dropped over her body. "If I remember, it should be my turn to play."

She swallowed and stepped back, ramming her heel into the suitcase. "Um... no. It's... ah... time for you to leave."

"Trying to throw me out again?" he asked, taking a step forward.

Her pointed little chin shot up into the air. "No, I'm not throwing you out—"

"Good, because I'm not leaving." He was just a few steps away from her now. Her scent filled his nostrils. Roses. Sweet roses.

Her sexy, kiss-me lips thinned. "I have things that I need to do this morning, all right? Last night was great. Really. It was—"

"The best sex I've ever had," he murmured, sliding another step closer.

Her lips parted. "Oh."

He smiled.

She shook her head. "But I-I'm not looking for a relationship, okay? It was great, but now I—"

Anger started to simmer within him. She wasn't looking for a relationship? Well, that was too bad. What did she think? That he'd be satisfied with a few quick tumbles in bed? No, not likely. He took another gliding step toward her. He was close enough now that he could see the faint mark on her neck. *His mark.* His bite.

"I'm not walking away from you," he told her clearly, unable to take his eyes off that mark. No, he'd spent too many years searching for her. There was no way he'd turn away now, not when he was so close to claiming his mate.

She took a breath. "You don't have to." Her shoulders stiffened, and she glanced over his shoulder again. "My mother called me this morning—she needs me to come back to Chicago. I'll be leaving within the hour."

So, her story had changed. She wasn't doing a bit of frantic morning cleaning anymore. Now, she was going to visit her mother. *Right.*

"So," she continued. "I guess I'll be the one leaving you." She held out her hand. "Thanks, Michael, for all that—"

He grabbed her hand and tugged her forward, right into his arms. And he kissed her. Hard. Deep. Oh, yeah, she tasted good. His tongue slid against hers, her breasts pressed against him, and he wondered how long it would take to get her naked...

Kat jerked back, her eyes wide. "What are you—"

"You cannot lie worth a damn."

She gasped. "How dare you—"

"You're not going to visit your mother," he told her, keeping his voice soft. "So, why don't you try telling me just what the hell is going on with you today?" *And why you're trying to run from me.* He'd tried to be patient with her, tried to rein in the beast. But she was pushing him, and there was no way he could let her walk away.

Kat's features tightened. She strained against him, struggling against his hold, but he just tightened his arms around her.

She huffed out a breath. "Look, it's not your problem, okay?"

If it involved her, it most *definitely* was his problem. He stared down at her, waiting, tense.

Her lips trembled. "You were supposed to just let me go. You got what you wanted last night, you were—"

"I didn't get what I wanted," he told her, hearing the rough edge to his own voice. Yes, they'd made love. But he wanted more, needed more. He wanted all of her, every bit. And he wouldn't be satisfied until he'd claimed her completely, in the way of his kind.

Her red curls trembled as she shook her head. "I don't understand. What do you want from me?"

Everything. "Let's just start with the truth."

"The truth?" Her lips curled, but her smile was sad, so sad. "The truth is that someone's trying to kill me, and unless I get out of town, fast, I'm a dead woman."

All in all, Kat thought Michael took the news of her impending demise rather well. He just stared at her, those sexy eyes of his intense, and shook his head. Finally, after a good three minutes, he muttered, "That's not going to happen."

Kat blinked. "Excuse me?"

"No one's going to hurt you, not while I'm here."

And damn if her eyes didn't start to tear up. After months of running on her own, months of looking over her shoulder, to have Michael say that—she blinked quickly. "That's really sweet, but—"

"Screw sweet, it's a fact." His hands tightened around her arms. "I won't ever let anyone hurt you, I promise."

Like he would be able to stop the man who was after her? Michael was a gentleman, refined, elegant. He wasn't a fighter, a killer. "You don't understand," she told him, "the man who's after me, he's dangerous. *Very* dangerous." And there was no way she'd put Michael in that bastard's sights.

"There is something you should understand about me," he said, his voice harder, rougher, than she'd ever heard before. "I can be dangerous, too."

And his blue eyes were suddenly flat and hard. And his face... his cheeks were hollow, his lips thinned, his teeth—they looked somehow longer and sharper. Kat shook her head, feeling like she was staring into the face of a man she'd never seen before, of a—

He dropped his hands and stepped back. "Give me his name, Kat. All I need is his name."

Her hands shook. "What?"

"Give me his name. Just his name, and I'll make it so that you never have to worry about him again."

Now he was starting to scare her. Really scare her. The gentleman was gone. The man who stared back at her, the man with the icy stare and lethal voice... he reminded her... reminded her so much of Lou.

And Lou was trying to kill her.

She took a slow step away from him, and began to edge her way down the hall. What did she really know about Michael? They'd only met a few days ago. There was so much about him that was a mystery.

She kept moving slowly, acutely aware that he followed her, keeping perfect pace with her movements. The den was only a few feet away. If she could get there, it would be just a quick sprint to the front door.

"I've frightened you," he said, his voice softer now. "I did not mean to do that. I don't want you to ever be scared of me."

Her brows lifted. *Well, then don't go around offering to kill people for me!* Killing people, that was Lou's specialty, and to hear Michael speak so casually of—

She forced herself to take a deep breath. "I-I'm not scared." She was terrified. Oh, him, of Lou. Of herself. She slipped into the den. The door was close, it was—

"What the hell happened here?" The words burst from her lips. She stared at her torn and shredded sofa cushions, her mouth hanging open. When had that happened?

"I think I may have... gotten a little carried away last night." Michael spoke from directly behind her.

She whirled around. "You did that? How?" It looked like someone had taken a very sharp knife to the cushions and cut them in long, hard swipes.

He pursed his lips. "Don't worry, I will replace them."

"Right." Okay, now she was really, really nervous. One nut job on her trail was bad enough, but two—

A frown pulled his dark brows down. "You have the wrong idea about me." He reached into his back pocket and pulled out his wallet. He flipped it open, showing her an official looking ID badge. "I'm a private detective, Kat. I'm not some sort of deranged killer."

Her knees went weak. And she thought she might fall into a puddle on the floor. "Oh, thank God!" And she threw her arms around him, hugging him tightly. "Oh, thank God!" His body was hard, tense against hers, but she didn't care. She was just so damn relieved. "For a minute there, you had me worried... I thought you might be—" She broke off, shaking her head.

"That I might be what?" He murmured, his hands wrapping around her waist.

She swallowed. "That you might be the guy Lou had hired... to kill me."

"What, you think I came to screw you, then murder you?"

"The thought did cross my mind." She wouldn't lie. For a moment there, one horrifying moment, she'd been afraid that she'd made a terrible mistake in letting Michael into her home, into her bed.

He picked her up, spun around, and pressed her against the wall. She stared at him, her pulse racing. His hands were still on her hips, her legs were spread, open to him, and he was glaring down at her, rage in every line of his face. "You're a real trusting one, aren't you?"

His cock pushed against her, hard, thick. His hips pressed down on her, forcing his cock tighter against her.

"You're right about the screwing... I plan to take you, over and over, until you cannot remember what it's like to be without me." His cheeks were flushed, his eyes dilated. She felt a faint pinch on her hips where he held her. "But as for killing you..."

She held her breath, aware that she'd pushed him too far... aware that they were alone... aware that he was pissed... and way, way bigger than she was...

And aware that, despite everything, a hot, hungry need for him was starting to burn within her.

"As for killing you," he muttered. "It isn't going to happen. *No one's* going to kill you, because I'm going to protect you. Do you hear me? I'm your new twenty-four hour a day bodyguard. No one will get to you, no one will touch you, but me."

Chapter Six

Michael took a deep breath and forced himself to step back, forced himself to let her go, when what he really wanted was to strip her and thrust deep into her tight, little pussy.

Later. He had to make certain she was safe first. He locked his jaw. "Do you have everything you need in that suitcase of yours?"

She nodded.

"Good." He walked down the hall, grabbed the case, and headed for the front door. "We're getting out of here, now."

"What?" She grabbed his arm. "No, we can't—"

He closed his eyes, and counted to ten. The woman had no idea how close she was to pushing him past his control. "You were planning to leave on your own less than ten minutes ago."

"Yes, but—"

"Well, now, you are going to be leaving with me." And he'd take her someplace safe, someplace where she'd be protected, until he figured out what in the hell was going on.

"I can't go with you." That stubborn chin shot into the air again. "I appreciate you offering to help, but this is my problem, okay? You don't know how serious it is, how deadly—"

"I have a pretty good idea," he muttered and headed outside.

Kat followed at his heels. "I'm not going with you!"

He tossed her bag into the back seat. "Yes, you are." And she could go easily or—

He turned to face her. Kat's face was flushed, her hands fisted at her hips. "You can just take that bag right back out," she snapped. "You might be the big, strong detective, but you can't make me go with you! This is my life, my—"

"Oh, but I can make you go with me," he told her softly.

She shook her head. "No, no, you can't! I'm a grown woman, okay? I've been on my own a long time. I can take care of—"

He glanced down the street. A few of her neighbors were outside, and since Kat was screeching, they were starting to look rather nervous. He sighed. He hadn't wanted to do this, but the woman had given him no choice.

Her safety had to come first. And they couldn't stay at her cottage. There had been too many attempts on her. "I'm really sorry about this, Kat, and if there was another choice…" He shrugged. "But there isn't." He reached for her.

She knocked his hands aside. "What are you talking about? What are you—"

"Close your eyes, *ma petite*. Close your eyes." He pitched his voice low, calling on the special power of kind. He didn't like controlling her, didn't like using his gift against his mate, but, as he'd told her, there was no choice.

Kat would come with him, whether she wanted to or not.

She blinked, her gaze becoming hazy. "Wh-what?" Her body swayed.

He wrapped his arms around her. "Sleep. Just close your eyes and sleep." *And when you wake up, we'll be far away from here, and you'll be safe.* And probably royally pissed off at him.

"Michael?" Her voice was slurred, tinged with a hint of fear. "Wh-what's wrong… with me?"

Nothing. Absolutely nothing. She was just responding to his compulsion. His kind had certain psychic powers. He could use those powers to influence others when the need arose, just as he was influencing her now.

"Y-your eyes…" Her knees buckled and he caught her as she fell.

And he knew that she'd seen his eyes glow. Seen the blue shimmer with force of his psychic push. But, hopefully, she wouldn't remember that.

"Sleep, my love. Sleep." And her body slumped against him, her lashes fell closed. He carried her to the car, tucked her safely inside, and then drove away.

A dark blue sedan pulled out from a nearby house and followed closely behind them.

My love. The words rang in her head. "Did you call me your love?" Kat asked, her eyes snapping open. "Michael?"

But Michael wasn't there. No one was there. She was in a huge, white room, lying in the middle of a brass four-poster bed, and she was alone.

What in the hell... She sat up, shoving the covers aside. Where was she? What was happening?

The last thing she remembered, Michael had been apologizing to her, rambling on about how he didn't have a choice... Then, *bam*, she'd woken here... wherever here was.

And, quite obviously, *here* was someplace fancy. Huge bed. Silk covers. Heavy cherry dresser and chest that looked like they were about three hundred years old. Oh, yeah, she knew money when she saw it. And this place reeked of money. Old money.

Was this Michael's house? It had better not be. He'd better not have taken her to—

The door swung open. A tall, blond man sauntered inside. "You were right, Michael. As usual. The test showed that she's a perfect—" He broke off, golden eyes widening "Well, *bon soir, ma cherie.* I... didn't expect you to be awake." He flashed her a winsome smile.

Her eyes narrowed. Damn. Another too-attractive man with a French accent. "Who are you?" she snapped, climbing out of bed. She still wore her jeans and tee shirt. Her shoes were gone, socks stolen. But at least she wasn't talking to this guy in her nighties or, even worse, stark naked.

He bowed slightly, his smile stretching another notch. "I am Alerac La Mort."

She crossed her arms over her chest. "Is that supposed to mean something to me?"

For a moment, his lips drew down in the faintest of pouts. "Michael didn't mention me?"

A quick shake of her head.

"Of course." The smile flashed again. "He probably was afraid if you found out about me, you would leave him. After all, I am, obviously, the better choice for mate. I'm—"

The better choice for mate. She choked. "Excuse me?" Was the gorgeous guy crazy? What a pity.

He walked fully into the room, leaving the door slightly ajar behind him. "You certainly are a tempting little morsel. All that red hair and those big, shining green eyes. Kind of like a sexy red riding hood." He stood just a few feet away from her now, his gaze intent. "And you know the wolf was always wanting to… gobble her up."

Oh, my. Up close, the guy was even better looking than she'd first thought. Perfect bone structure. Sculpted cheekbones. Strong jaw. Full, sensual lips. A thick head of golden hair to match his eyes. And a body that was… she swallowed. Very nice. As tall as Michael, and he seemed to be Michael's match in muscle, too. His body was strong, his shoulders broad, his—

He reached out and touched her hair, his nostrils flaring as he inhaled her scent.

She knocked his hand away. The guy was some kind of eye-candy, *but he wasn't Michael.* "I don't remember saying you could touch me, bud."

One golden brow arched. His hand dropped.

"Where's Michael?" And why had he left her alone with—with— what was his name? Alan? Alex?

A tiny shrug stretched his muscles. "I thought he was with you. He has been in here all day, mooning over you. Worrying." He shook his head and sent her a censuring frown. "You're too responsive to his compulsions. You didn't wake like we thought. When I was here last, poor Michael was starting to pull out his hair."

She blinked. "What? Look, Al—" That seemed like a safe enough version of his name, whatever it had been. "I don't know what you're talking about—" And that was starting to seriously piss her off. When she saw Michael…

"When the bonding is complete, it won't be a problem anymore," he continued, as if she hadn't spoken. "So it would probably be best if you went ahead with the ceremony. He's already bitten you, so he's had a taste." His gaze darted to her throat. "He won't be able to hold out much longer anyway, not with the scent of your need burning through the house like it is."

Her mouth dropped open. Her hand lifted, touched her neck, touched strangely tender skin. "Michael… gave me a hickey?"

His lips thinned. "Hardly. It's a bite, the bite of the—"

"*Alerac!*" Michael stood in the doorway, his hands clenched. "What in the hell are you doing?"

Kat jumped at his voice, but Alerac just shrugged. "Talking to your mate."

His mate. There was that word again. Maybe it was some kind of French thing, some translation bug. But just to be sure… "I'm not his mate," she told him clearly. Yeah, they'd had sex that left her trembling and thinking that she'd touched heaven, but they weren't married or anything. Or—

"You are his mate," Alerac told her, his voice hardening. "His scent is on you. You carry his mark on your skin. The tests showed that—"

"*Alerac.*"

Wow. She'd never heard that particular tone of menace in Michael's voice before.

Alerac turned his head slowly toward the door. "Yes, cuz?"

Cuz? As in cousin?

"Outside. Now." A muscle flexed along Michael's jaw. And damn if he didn't sound like he was having to restrain himself from jumping across the room and *jumping on* Alerac.

But Alerac didn't seem particularly concerned. He winked at her, then turned on his heel and headed toward Michael. "Relax. I wasn't trying to steal your mate."

Michael grabbed him, his hands fisting in Alerac's shirt. "You damn well better not."

Kat leapt forward, horrified. "Michael, what are you doing?"

He bared his teeth at the other man, a low growl rumbling in the back of his throat.

Alerac tilted his head back, meeting Michael's fierce stare without flinching.

"You don't touch her," Michael rumbled. "*Ever.*" He leaned in toward Alerac. "She's *mine, mine—*"

She pushed between the two men. "What are you doing?" She could barely understand him, his voice was so thick, so guttural, almost like an animal's.

Alerac didn't move. "You should step back now, Little Red."

But she didn't move. She looked up at Michael, and realized that he looked... different. Kind of like the way he'd looked for a moment back at her cottage. His cheeks were hollow, his eyes seemed to shine, and there was something about his teeth...

He grabbed her wrist, pulling her against him. "You defend him?"

She blinked. "Look, I don't know what's going on here, but I think we all need to take a few deep breaths." His teeth really did look different. Sharper.

Michael stared down at her. His hand was like steel around her wrist, so tight that—

"Ouch!" She stared down at her hand, at the thin trickle of blood that oozed from her skin.

Michael stepped back, releasing her as if he'd been scalded. "I-I did not mean—"

There was a long, thin scratch on the back of her wrist.

"You don't have control," Alerac muttered. "You need to bond with her, before the beast—"

Michael shook his head and took another step back. "Kat, I'm sorry—"

He was pale, his golden skin bleached of color. *Something was wrong with him.* Her heart lurched and she reached out to him. "Michael?"

He flinched away from her. His jaw was locked, his body shaking faintly. "I-I have to—" He broke off, his gaze meeting hers, and there was pain there, in his blue eyes. Pain, and hunger.

"Give the beast reign," Alerac told him softly. "Go into the night, run, and—"

"*Dammit, she doesn't know!*"

Alerac swore.

And Kat felt like she was missing something, something very, very important. "What don't I know?" Other than where she was, why Alerac kept calling her Michael's mate, why Michael looked so pale and—

"Lock her in the room," Michael ordered, moving toward the door. "Lock her in so that she'll be safe."

Oh, no. She didn't like that idea. "No one's locking me anywhere!" Wasn't it bad enough Michael had dragged her to wherever the hell she was? She wasn't going to be locked up like some kind of—

"Michael, I don't think that's a good plan." Alerac looked sympathetically at Kat. "She should not—"

Michael's skin rippled. The skin on his face and arms actually rippled, as if something moved under it, something alive—

A hoarse cry sprang to Kat's lips. She stepped toward him, reaching out—

Alerac grabbed her, pulling her back against the hard wall of his chest. "Trust me, Little Red. Now is not a good time for that."

Michael looked at her, his teeth bared, his shoulders hunched. "Kat—" His body shuddered. "Lock. Her. In." Then he was gone.

Her heart raced, the beating filling her ears. Michael had looked… looked like some kind of monster there for a moment. His face had been twisted, his eyes glowing, and his voice. She shivered. That hadn't been the voice of a man, more like a—

Alerac released her and headed for the door. He pulled a small, black key from his pocket. He was going to lock her in. *Freaking unbelievable.* This couldn't be happening to her. On top of all the other crazy shit in her life, she was being held captive in some kind of fancy ass mansion.

"Sorry, but it is for your own safety." His gaze was hooded. "Can't have you wandering the Compound tonight, it would not be safe."

She inched closer to him. "The... Compound?" Oh, that didn't sound good. Was he talking military compound, crazy-people compound, or what?

He huffed out a hard breath. "Michael didn't even tell you about this place, did he?"

She shook her head. Dear Michael hadn't told her a hell of a lot.

"Give him time." His mouth hitched into a half-smile. "He'll come to you tomorrow, tell you everything you need to know."

"I want to know *now*." Screw tomorrow. She didn't have time for this junk. Not only did she have to deal with whatever was happening here, but she still had a killer on her trail, still had—

"The Compound's one of the most secure places on earth." Alerac told her, his hand tightening around the door knob. "No one gets in or out without us knowing. Michael brought you here to protect you from the guy who's after you."

Her heart seemed to stop. "You know about that?"

A slow nod. "I know everything."

Oh, damn. She really, really hoped he didn't.

"But like I said, Michael brought you here to keep you safe. You don't have to worry about anything."

She grabbed the door before he could shut it. "If I don't have to worry, then why am I being locked in?"

His golden eyes narrowed.

And she knew he wasn't going to tell her anymore, knew he was going to shut that thick wooden door, going to lock her in, and leave her there until tomorrow. "This could be considered kidnapping, you know. I mean, I didn't choose to come here." *Don't even know how the hell I came to be here.*

He nodded. "*Oui*, it could. But I like to think of it as more protection." His hand tightened on the key. "And from what I've read about Louis Turello, you need protection."

Louis Turello. Lou Turello. She bit her lip. He really did know what was happening, he knew who she was running from.

"Try to get some sleep. In the morning, Michael will come and—"

She lunged forward, shoving the full weight of her body against him. *No way.* No way was she going to stay in that room, like a sitting duck, when Lou could be out there, when he could have followed her, could be waiting to kill her—

Alerac grunted when she hit him, and he stumbled back a step. That one step was all she needed. She'd been on her high school track team, once upon a time. Yeah, she was small, but she was fast. Damn fast.

She shot past him, her bare feet pounding against the lush carpet. She needed to get away from him, away from the Compound, away from Lou—

Alerac yelled behind her, she heard him racing after her, heard the harsh grunts of his breath. Damn, he was close, almost on her—

The stair banister was in front of her. She grabbed the wooden frame, shooting down the stairs. If she could get to the ground floor, and if she could find a door, then she could get out of there.

She jumped down the last few steps. Stumbled forward, and—

Came face to face with the same big, black wolf she'd seen at her house.

The wolf's teeth were bared, its blue eyes flashing. And its hot breath blasted against her skin. So close—

Oh, God, it was close enough to rip her apart.

She froze, her breath panting.

Alerac grabbed her, jerking her behind his body.

The wolf snarled, pacing forward, its massive body looked ready to pounce, ready to attack—

"You couldn't just stay put, could you?" Alerac whispered, placing his body, shield-like, between her and the wolf. "Oh, no, you had to run."

She couldn't speak. *Jesus.* There was a wolf there. *In the house.* How had a wolf gotten into the house?

"Easy. *Easy.*"

She didn't know if Alerac spoke to her or the beast.

The wolf's jaw dropped, its white teeth glistened. Its eyes, those bright blue eyes, were locked on her and Alerac. Locked on the hand that Alerac had wrapped around her wrist. The creature snarled.

"Damn." Alerac sounded resigned. "This is not going to be pretty."

Kat's right hand lifted, touched his shoulder. She didn't know what was happening, but Alerac seemed to be trying to protect her, trying to—

The wolf growled, its hackles rising.

Alerac dropped her hand. "I don't think you should touch me," he told her, his voice whisper soft.

"What?" She inched closer to him. What was he talking about? Why would it matter if she touched him—

The wolf lunged forward, stopping less than a foot away from Alerac.

"He... does not like it when you touch me."

Her hand clenched around his shoulder. *Too damn bad for wolfie.* "Yeah, well, I don't particularly care—"

The wolf's powerful jaws snapped closed. Its muscles bunched.

"Wrong answer," Alerac said, his voice thick.

The wolf leapt at them, claws flashing.

Chapter Seven

Kat screamed and closed her eyes. When she opened them a second later, Alerac lay on the floor. The wolf crouched on top of him, its teeth bared, its mouth hovering bare inches from his throat.

Oh, Jesus, oh, Jesus... That thing was going to kill Alerac! She leapt forward, grabbed the wolf's long black tail, and yanked as hard as she could.

The wolf jerked in surprise... and turned on her.

What the hell am I doing? She dropped the creature's tail with a yelp, stumbling back. *That thing is big enough to eat me.* And it sure looked hungry.

The wolf began to stalk toward her, its bright eyes locked on her. Alerac kneeled on the floor behind it, not moving.

Great. She'd saved his ass. Now he was just going to stay there and let the big, bad wolfie eat her. *Jerk.*

Her back slammed into the wall, and she realized there was nowhere else for her to go, nowhere else to run. The wolf was in front of her, its mouth open, its sharp teeth glistening. And its eyes... those shining eyes... they seemed to burn her, to pierce right through her—

"Don't be afraid of him, Little Red. He won't hurt you. He's still... in control. Otherwise, I would be a dead man right now."

Kat tore her gaze away from the wolf and stared at Alerac, thinking he'd surely lost his mind. The wolf had been seconds away from ripping his throat out, and he expected her to believe the—the thing wouldn't hurt her? *Yeah, right.*

A low growl rumbled in the wolf's throat.

Her knees started wobbling. And she found herself gazing into the creature's eyes again. Strange... the eyes, they were like Michael's. That same, intense blue.

Just like Michael's.

She blinked, shaking her head. That couldn't be, that couldn't—

The wolf slipped forward, opened its mouth... and licked her hand. A soft, light lick.

"See, I told you," Alerac all but crowed, climbing to his feet. "He will not hurt you because you're his—"

The wolf's head turned, and he growled at Alerac.

Alerac smiled. "Sorry, cuz."

Cuz. The lights in the room seemed to flicker. Kat's face felt hot, then cold. Alerac had just called the wolf *cuz*. He'd called Michael that earlier, back in the bedroom. *And the wolf's eyes were just like Michael's.*

She'd seen the wolf before, at her house. When she'd gone out to look for Michael, she'd found the wolf, crouched and waiting on her doorstep. And then Michael had reappeared, naked. Why had he been naked? He'd never explained that to her...

Her knees gave way and she slid to the floor. The wolf made a soft rumbling noise and inched closer to her.

Oh, God, oh, God. Could it be possible? No, no, the wolf couldn't be... Michael. Could it?

She lifted her hand, her fingers trembling. She took a quick breath, and touched the beast. Her fingers sank into its fur, into its thick, lustrous black fur. The wolf stretched beneath her touch, arching its back. Its blue eyes flickered closed for a second, then opened.

She saw movement behind the wolf.

Alerac inched closer to them. "Are you all right?" he asked.

The wolf's stare never wavered.

"I don't know," she whispered, feeling a little hysterical. *Is my lover a wolf? Or have I just gone completely insane?*

She was being ridiculous, of course. There was no way Michael could possibly be the wolf in front of her. People did not turn into wolves. They. Did. Not.

But her sofa cushions had been shredded. Like something with...

claws had gotten a hold of them.

And Michael's teeth... before he'd left her room... his teeth had been long, sharp. Too long, too sharp... for a human.

She stared at the wolf. "Michael?" Surely, he wasn't, there was no way the beast could be—

The wolf nodded.

And then, before her eyes, the wolf began to change. Its body shifted, contorted. The fur melted from its body.

She heard the sound, the horrible, wrenching sound, of bones popping, stretching, growing.

She watched, unable to look away, strangely drawn, as the wolf disappeared, and Michael, strong, naked, *Michael*, took its place.

It was a good thing she was on the floor. Otherwise, she would have fallen.

OhmyGod...

In mere moments, it was over. Michael gazed down at her, his handsome face tense, his lips thinned. "I should have told you sooner," he muttered, his voice thick.

OhmyGod... her lover was a wolf! A freaking wolf!

"But I was afraid that you'd be afraid, that you'd run from me." He shook his head. "And I could not let you do that. I could not let you leave me. Not when I'd just found you."

She rose on legs that shook. And she touched him, touched his chest, her fingers light. She didn't know what she expected. Maybe to feel fur, and not warm, hard male skin.

But when she touched his flesh, she touched *him*. Touched his warm, naked skin. Felt his strength, his power. Felt him. *Michael*. She drew her hand back almost instantly. "I don't understand," she managed, her throat so dry she felt like she was choking. "What the hell is happening here?"

Michael's hand rose, and he reached for her.

She flinched, jerking back.

His blue eyes flashed. "It is simple, Kat. I'm a werewolf. And you, you're my mate."

He hoped she didn't start screaming. Michael gazed down at Kat. *Mon Dieu*, but she looked pale, and her green eyes had doubled in size.

"You're a what?"

He was aware of Alerac slipping away behind them. He knew his cousin was trying to give him alone time with Kat. Time to bring her to terms with her new situation.

He'd hoped she might be more accepting of his true nature. Of course, he hadn't intended for her to find out about him in quite this way, but… well, there was no going back now.

He reached for her again, but she flinched away, looking at him like he was evil incarnate. He took a deep breath. "I'm a werewolf." And so was Alerac, but he decided not to point that fact out to her, not yet.

She scrambled to her feet. "Werewolves aren't real."

He lifted a brow. After what she'd just seen, how could she say that? "I assure you, I'm quite real."

Kat sidled around him. He turned, following her closely. She looked like she might bolt at any moment.

"I-I think I'd like to go back home now." She sounded like a polite little girl.

He shook his head. "It is not safe for you there." The man who was after her was still on the loose, and until he was caught—There was no way he would let Kat out of his sight.

He'd had Alerac do a full background check on her. And he'd discovered Katherine Hardy didn't exist. Or at least, she hadn't existed, until a year ago.

Until then, she'd been Katherine Barlow, an artist working in Chicago. But then, one night, she had stumbled onto a murder. Her ex-boyfriend, a guy by the name of Sean Reynolds, had been killed by Lou Turello. According to the information he'd gotten, Lou was a big player in the Chicago mob scene. The police had been thrilled when Kat had come to them with her testimony.

But on the last day of Lou's trial, he'd just vanished. And Kat Barlow had disappeared, too. He figured she'd been put in the Witness Protection Program. Unfortunately for Kat, the program did not seem to be providing that much protection. Lou had found her, and it looked like he was trying to settle a score with her.

And Michael was not going to let that happen. Lou wouldn't get to Kat. Not while he was alive.

"But I really, really want to go home," she whispered, sounding so lost that it was all he could do not to step forward, to draw her into his arms and hold her.

"Until Lou's caught, you cannot leave." The Compound was the safest place for her. Built to protect his pack from the outside world, no one would be allowed to get in without his knowledge.

She blinked. "You—you found out about Lou?"

He nodded.

"He wants to kill me," she whispered. "I saw… what he did to Sean. And I told the cops. And now, now he's after me."

Michael stepped forward. "I won't let him get to you, I promise."

A strangled laugh slipped from her throat. "Oh, God, I don't know what's worse. Having a killer on my trail, or finding out that you, that you're a—"

His eyes narrowed, and a dark anger began to boil within him. "Don't compare me to him."

Her gaze flew to the door. "I've got to get out of here. I can't handle this—*you,* now."

Too damn bad. She was going to have to handle him. "I'm the same man, Kat. The same man you made love with. The same man you took into your body."

"*You're a freaking werewolf!* You have fur, huge teeth! Four legs!"

His jaw clenched. "I'm a man." His hand stroked down his body, slipped over the erection that was growing, stretching, for her.

Her gaze dropped. She swallowed, staring at his cock.

"And you're my mate," he grated, licking his lips. It was time. Time to take her, to bond with her, forever. Once he did, she wouldn't be afraid anymore, wouldn't want to leave him—

"No," she breathed, lunging for the door. Her fingers fumbled with the lock. "I-I'm not!"

"Yes, you are." He breathed deeply, inhaling her scent. "You're the woman chosen for me, chosen from the moment of your birth." The tests had proven it, proven she could bear his children. They'd taken a sample of her blood, a strand of her hair, and their scientists, the same scientists who'd found Gareth's mate months before, had preformed the analysis. Only a very select group of human women could mate with werewolves. And Kat... she was one of those women. She had the perfect DNA to merge with his.

And he'd known, from the moment he'd seen her. He'd sensed the connection. Known she was meant to be his.

It was time to take his mate.

She jerked open the door. The darkness of the night slipped inside.

"Where are you going?" he asked softly, deliberately pitching his voice low, soothing her as he would any frightened creature.

She blinked.

"There's nothing out there. Once you leave the main house, you won't be able to get past the gates." *Or the guards.*

"You—you can't keep me here," she whispered, a light patch of pink appearing in her cheeks. Her eyes narrowed. "I didn't ask to come here. You used some kind of—of hypnosis crap on me and you forced me to come here!"

He'd actually used a compulsion on her. But he just shrugged. "I did what I had to do." And he would do it again. Her safety would always come first with him. "Now, why don't you come back upstairs with me..."

Her pointed chin shot up into the air. "You think I'm just going to jump back into bed with you? *You're a werewolf!*" she reminded him, her voice close to a screech.

He flinched. "I am the same man I was before." And he'd prove it to her. Michael reached for her—

And she ran. She lunged through the door and ran into the night.

He stared after her a moment, feeling the blood pound in his veins. She shouldn't have run. He understood her fear, but... she shouldn't have run. The wolf within him stirred, aroused by the idea of a hunt.

The man smiled, inhaled his mate's sweet scent, and stepped into the night.

No, she shouldn't have run, because now, now he was going to have to hunt her.

And the wolf loved to hunt.

He would hunt her. Then, when he caught her, and he *would* catch her, he would strip her. He would spread her beneath him, plunge deep, deep into her creamy core, and claim her.

And she'd learn what it truly meant to mate with a wolf.

Chapter Eight

She ran until her side ached, ran until her breath panted out, ran until she hit a huge, stone wall.

"Dammit!" Kat looked up. Floodlights were on the top of the wall, glaring down at her, and the wall had to be at least fifteen feet high. How the hell was she supposed to get over that thing?

She took a deep breath. *Think*. She had to think.

Okay, she was trapped in the middle of God-knew-where, and she'd just found out that her lover was, in fact, a werewolf.

Jeez... a werewolf. Hadn't her life been nightmarish enough before? Running from the mob was one thing, watching your lover shift from a wolf to a man... that was a whole new ball game.

And it was so not supposed to happen! Men weren't supposed to turn into wolves! It was the twenty-first century, werewolves weren't supposed to be real...

But, she guessed no one had ever bothered to tell Michael that important fact.

"Oh, Katherine..." His voice slipped out of the darkness, called softly to her.

She froze. The hair on her arms, on the nape of her neck, tingled. And, quite suddenly, she knew... this is what it feels like to be hunted.

Pressing back against the wall, she strained to see beyond the pool of light created by the flood lights. But beyond the small glowing area, she saw only the darkness of the waiting night.

"Freeze, lady!" A voice barked to her left.

She screamed, spinning around, and most definitely not freezing... or at least, she didn't freeze, not until she saw the gun.

A uniformed man crouched, gun drawn, glaring at her.

Sonofa—

The gun was pointed straight at her chest.

"You shouldn't be out here," he snapped.

Yeah, well, she was knew that. She just hadn't counted on running into an armed guard when she'd made her escape attempt. She motioned to the gun. "Um… could you put that down?" Call her crazy, but she hated it when a gun was pointed at her heart.

He blinked. "You're Ms. Hardy, aren't you?"

She nodded.

He swore and immediately lowered the gun. "Oh, no, when Morlet finds out, I'm gonna be screwed—"

"It's all right, Marcus." Michael's silken voice drifted through the night. "I'll take care of Kat."

Marcus gulped and stumbled back. "I didn't mean to draw my weapon on her. I-I was just patrolling the grounds, making sure Turello hadn't gotten inside—"

"And that is exactly what you should be doing." Same silken tone.

Kat squinted. Where was he? He sounded so close, but she couldn't see him, not in the darkness.

"I'll take care of Kat," he repeated. "Go back to your patrol."

Marcus frantically bobbed his head. "Right, sir. Sorry. Sorry for the gun—" He hurried off, disappearing around a large bush.

And leaving her alone… with Michael.

"I told you not to run…"

Her shoulders stiffened. "Where are you?" He sounded so close, *too close.*

He stepped forward, out of the darkness, and she inhaled sharply. He was still naked. And his body, his strong, muscled body, was a ripple of menace.

Her gaze swept over him. Over his broad chest, his tight stomach, his aroused cock.

She swallowed.

He smiled at her, the hint of a fang glimmering. Michael stalked toward her, moving slowly, easily, and his hand lifted, rubbing his cock as he walked, acknowledging the arousal, and his gaze, that bright, blue gaze, stayed locked on her.

Then he was in front of her. She could smell him, the rich, wild scent of man, of beast. She stared up at him, her mouth dry. *Now that he'd caught her, what was he going to do?*

His hand lifted, stroked her cheek. "Beautiful little Kat. So lovely, so... delicate." He smiled, barring his fangs. "So tempting."

She flinched, and his gaze hardened. "What? Don't you want me anymore? Now that you know the truth about me, you cannot stand my touch, is that it?"

She didn't answer.

His hand slipped down her throat, his fingers pressing lightly against her pulse, against the faint mark on her neck. "You wanted me before. You begged me to take you, screamed when I thrust into you, cried when you came."

His fingers trailed down her chest. He cupped her breast, rubbing her nipple through the thin fabric of her shirt. She bit her lip, trying to hold back the moan that sprang to her lips.

"But now, you think you are too good to lie with me. To lie with a beast."

Her heart ached at the sudden torment on his face. "No, it's not—"

A warning growl stopped her words. "You're my mate. *Mine.* I've waited for you my whole life. *I won't give you up.*" Then his mouth crashed down on hers. Hard, angry, dominating.

His tongue pushed into her mouth, and she tasted his rage. And his hunger. His mouth fed on hers, lips tasting, taking. His tongue thrust, sliding over hers, teasing, tempting.

Her hands lifted, grasped his shoulders, and her mouth opened wider. *The better to taste him...*

He tore his mouth from hers, gazing down at her with shining eyes. "I'm the same man, Kat. The same man you took into your body yesterday. The same man who saved you in that alley." He drew a deep breath.

"I-I know."

A muscle flexed along his jaw. "I want you. Naked. Spread. But I won't force you. I cannot. Go back to the house, go now before—" He turned away from her, his shoulders tense.

She stared at his back, at his broad shoulders, at the taunt line of his body.

"Go, Kat." His words were a growl. "If you stay, I'll—"

Take her, in the way of his kind. He didn't have to say the words. She knew. She knew what would happen.

And she also knew that it took all of his control to let her go now. To offer her the chance to walk away.

But did she really want to walk away from him? From the man who'd made her feel alive for the first time in over a year? Did she?

I'm the same man. His words echoed in her mind. *The same man.*

The man who'd saved her in the alley, in the bar. The man who made her feel beautiful, desirable, *alive.*

Michael. Her Michael.

She wasn't aware that she'd moved, not until she saw her hand lift, saw herself touch Michael, and watched as he spun toward her, eyes wide with shock.

"Your bonding…" she whispered, "will it hurt?"

He shook his head.

"Will—will I change?" She knew the old vampire legend, knew that if you got bit, a person could become undead, or so the movies said. But what happened when you bonded with a werewolf? Would she become—

"You won't change." His lips curved in the faintest of smiles. "You will stay just as you are, I promise."

A quick sigh of relief slipped past her lips. *That was good to know.* The hairy look wouldn't be good for her.

She reached for the hem of her shirt, and in one quick toss, she'd thrown the shirt aside. Her fingers fumbled with the clasp of her bra, and she gasped slightly when the cool night air touched her nipples.

Michael watched her, not saying a word. But his cock grew, and his eyes burned with hunger. She was still barefoot, so it was easy to just slide out of her jeans. To kick them aside. Then, clad only in her white panties, she stood before him, the floodlights shining down on her, her nipples tight and hard, her sex moist.

"Then take me," she whispered, tossing back her hair.

He was on her in an instant, his mouth on hers, his hands locked around her, touching, taking. He pushed her back against the wall, and she could feel his cock. Hard, thick, pushing against the thin barrier of her panties. She rubbed against him, loving the feel of—

His head lifted, his fingers squeezed her nipple, and a bolt of pleasure shot through her. Then his hand was gone and his mouth, his hot, wet mouth, was on her breast. Sucking. Licking. Biting.

And she moaned, thrashing against him. The wall behind her was cold, hard. And Michael... oh, Michael was...

His fingers slid under the edge of her panties, and he stroked her clit.

"You're so wet," he grated. "I love the way your cunt feels around me. So tight. Hot." And he pushed his finger inside her.

Her legs gave way, and she would have fallen to the ground, fallen in a heap of trembling limbs, but he caught her, holding her up with one arm, and jerking her panties aside with the other.

She was pinned to the wall, held by his weight, his arm, her legs spread, the scent of her sex heavy in the air. Michael lifted her, then slid down, muttering, "I've got to have a taste..."

Then she felt his tongue, felt the rough rasp of tongue on her clit. He licked, licked, licked...

She was almost screaming now, the pleasure was so intense. Her clit was throbbing. Her sex was so hungry... and that finger was still inside of her, thrusting in and out while he licked, sucked...

Her orgasm was coming. She could feel it building, feel her body tightening, feel—

He pulled away from her, and she shuddered. "Michael, no—"

"Shh..." He lifted her legs, wrapped them around his waist. "The guards can hear you, and I don't want them to hear you come. That's for me... just for me."

His cock pushed against her, pushed just inside her sex. "Such a sweet little pussy... so warm and wet." The head of his erection pressed against her, sliding just inside.

She squirmed against him, wanting to impale her sex on him, wanting to take him all the way inside. She was *so close...*

But he held her in an unbreakable hold. And he teased her, tormented—

"Tell me, Kat..." His growling voice had her lashes lifting. "Am I the same man who you took into your body before?" A light thrust.

She gasped and her muscles clamped down around him.

"Am I?" Another thrust, deeper this time.

But still... not deep enough.

"Do you really want me,knowing what I am?"

OhGod, ohGod... she was about to come... she was about to—

"*Do you?*"

"*Yes!*" she screamed, not caring who heard her, not caring about anything but—

He thrust deep. Again and again. His cock buried itself in her body, stretching her, filling her, sliding against her clit—

Her teeth clenched. It felt so good. His body was flush against hers, so strong, so warm. And he thrust deep, his body slamming into hers, over and over—

"Come for me," he whispered, his cock sliding so far into her body it felt like he had to touch her womb. "Let me feel you come..."

And with a choked cry, she came, her orgasm ripping through her.

Still, he pumped into her. Thrust. Hard, deep thrusts that shook her body, and then she felt him... felt the hot tide of his semen in her core, felt him shudder against her.

When she could breathe again, when she could open her eyes, she looked at him. Her breath panted, hard and fast, and her body hummed with aftershocks of pleasure. "S-so..." She licked her lips, tried to speak again and managed to say, "that... was... bonding?" *Cause if so, it had been pretty damn amazing.*

He shook his head and slid his cock out of her. Her eyes widened.

He was still erect, still just as hard and strong as he'd been before his climax.

"No, Kat. That… that was the beginning." He picked her up, cradling her against his chest. "Now… now I take you in the way of my kind."

He carried her easily through the night. She couldn't see a damn thing, but she knew he could. His blue eyes shone, and he walked unerringly over the ground.

Then she saw a light, a small, faintly glowing light, over the door of what looked like a large barn. Michael took her inside, kicking the door closed behind them.

The fresh scent of straw filled her nostrils. The rich scent of pine surrounded her.

Michael set her down, and stepped back, gazing at her body in the soft light. Desperate hunger was etched onto his face, and need blazed in his eyes… those shining eyes…

"The guards heard you," he muttered, and his face tightened.

She winced. She knew she'd been loud, especially there at the end, but she hadn't been able to stop herself. It'd been too—

"They knew I was taking you," he continued in that same hard voice.

"I-I—" Hell, she didn't know what to say. Part of her was absolutely horrified that others had heard her, but another part, another part was—

"I'm glad they heard." A thin smile curved his lips. "I want them to know you're mine." He stepped toward her, and his smile disappeared. "But for our bonding, I do not want anyone to see you, or hear you, but me."

She swallowed. So that's why they were in the barn. Whatever happened during the *bonding,* it would happen here. Kat glanced around. There were no animals in the barn. Straw was sprinkled on the floor, the stalls were clean and—

"Get on your hands and knees."

Her mouth dropped open. "Wh-what?"

His cock strained toward her. "Get on your hands and knees."

A dark excitement curled through her. She licked her lips, her tongue snaking out, and his cock twitched at the slight move.

She was still wet from their lovemaking, but her sex clenched watching him. She crouched on the floor, putting her hands down in front of her, on the soft straw, and she drew her knees up, tilting her ass into the air. "L-like this?"

He walked toward her, crunching the straw beneath his feet. The sharp hiss of his indrawn breath sounded behind her. "Yeah, *ma petite*, just like that." Then his hand touched her, slid down the curve of her ass, between her cheeks...

"Michael..." Her body tensed.

"Shh, relax... let me touch you." His fingers slipped between her legs. "Ummm, your pussy feels so soft." A thick finger slid into her. "And wet."

Every muscle in her body tensed. Her sex felt ultra-sensitive and the touch of his finger... She shuddered.

His thumb rubbed over her clit, pushing, pressing. Her hands curled into fists and a keening cry sprang from her throat.

"Ah, that's what I want to hear. Good, Kat. Very, very good." Another large finger pushed into her.

She was stretched so tightly that he had to push, *push* up into her. Her recent climax had made her sex slick, but plump, her folds were ripe, making it hard for him to slide his long fingers into her.

But, oh, it felt so good...

He pulled his fingers out, then pushed them deep. "Come on, take me... open for me."

Her legs trembled. Her heart raced. When he pushed her thighs farther apart with his left hand, she moaned softly, and opened for him.

He growled in approval.

And his fingers kept stroking. Deep. Hard. He worked her sex, opening her, readying her again for him.

Then he moved, sliding his hand away from her, and crouching over her. She could feel him, feel the heat of his body surrounding her. Kat looked back at him, glancing over her shoulder.

His eyes were fixed on her, blazing with hunger, shimmering with a strange, bright glow...

And his teeth, his sharp teeth, glinted at her.

His cock brushed against her, pushing at her wet sex. His hands lifted, his fingers sliding over her back, around her side, and moving to cover her nipples. Stoking. Squeezing, plucking the tight peaks and sending heated arousal pulsing through her.

She pushed back against him, moving on instinct. She could feel his cock, feel it pushing into her. And she wanted more. She pushed again, rubbing her hips against him, against his heavy cock. And then he thrust, slamming deep into her.

"Oh, God, Michael!" Every muscle in her body froze. He'd never gone so deep before, never gone so—

He pulled out of her, drove deep. Again. Again. Hard. Fast. The slap and thud of their pounding flesh echoed around them.

He held her tightly, completely surrounding her, and all she could do was take him, take the pleasure that he gave her, take the thick length of his cock—

He growled, his breath panting against her. And still he thrust. Deeper. Harder.

She closed her eyes, shuddering. His hands stroked her, moving all over her body. One hand slipped down her stomach, slipped into the thatch of curls at her thighs. And his fingers... they stroked her clit, rubbed...

And he thrust, his cock burying itself in her body, over and over...

Her teeth clenched. Red spots danced before her eyes. Her orgasm was coming, coming—

"Give me your throat." Barely human. More the growl of a beast than the words of a man.

A deep, hard thrust.

Her sex clenched.

"Give. Me. Your. Throat."

She tossed back her head. Tears streaked from the corners of her eyes.

His cock slammed into her. *Oh, God—*

Her climax erupted, bringing a scream to her throat, clenching her sex, leaving her shuddering, moaning, lost—

His teeth sank into her throat. He bit her, marking her...

And she could feel him. *Michael.* Feel his body around her, feel his heat... and more. For an instant, for one amazing, terrifying instant... she felt him. Felt his hunger. His need. Felt the orgasm that ripped through him.

His emotions spilled over her. Blasted her. Every feeling that he had, his hopes, his fears... everything poured into her.

His love.

Then the world seemed to splinter away from her. A dark spiral swept over her, and with a startled cry, Kat fainted.

Chapter Nine

Michael carried Kat back to the house and put her in bed. Then he watched her, watched her as she slept.

His mate. He'd finally claimed his mate.

He brushed back a red curl from her face. She murmured softly at his touch, and her eyes opened.

She blinked up at him. "Michael? What—" Horrified comprehension filled her green stare. "Tell me I didn't faint."

A smile tugged at the corners of his mouth. "It's all right. That happens sometimes during the bonding." Or so he'd been told. Bonding emotions between mates were strong, damn strong. It would be easy for them to overwhelm—

Kat licked her lips. "That was… pretty intense."

Yes, that was the way of his kind.

He stared down at her, an overwhelming joy coursing through him. Finally, *finally*, he'd found the one woman he could bond with, share his life with. He wanted to howl his pleasure for all to hear. *His mate.*

He wouldn't be condemned to the half-life that the lone wolves of his pack faced, wouldn't be forced to spend his days alone, empty, without—

"Michael… Oh, God, last night—it was incredible. Being with you, feeling the way—" She took a quick breath, swallowed. Tears seemed to glisten for a moment in her eyes. "But I-I can't stay. *I can't.* I'm sorry. I-I have to leave now." Kat sat up slowly, her beautiful face solemn. Sadness lurked in her eyes. So much sadness.

He blinked. That wasn't exactly what he'd been expecting. "What?"

"I have to leave," she said softly.

No. No damn way. They had bonded. Bonding was forever. Their emotions were locked, their hearts joined.

I have to leave. Her words echoed in his head, seemed to burn his very soul. Hadn't they already been over this? She wasn't leaving him. Didn't she understand? There was no going back for either of them now. The bond had been set. Separation... it wasn't an option.

Wolves mated for life.

The loss of a mate... it would be hell. Like losing half of your soul. Because that's what Kat was to him. The other half of his soul. And he'd be damned if he lost her. He grabbed her arms, holding her tightly when she tried to break free. "You're not going anywhere."

Her lips trembled, but she lifted her chin, that stubborn chin, and met his stare. "I-I have to leave. I can't stay here, not with Turello out there. I can't, I *won't* risk you."

She wouldn't risk him? Michael shook his head. "There's no risk to me, I'm—"

"You don't know Turello!" She jerked free of him, grabbed the sheet, and wrapped it around her body. Her hands shook. "You don't know what he's capable of!" She climbed from the bed, and gazed down at him with desperate eyes.

He stared up at her, struggling to control the anger that rushed through him. He knew what Turello was like. He knew exactly what the bastard was like. That's why he was going to stop him, before he had a chance to hurt Kat.

She paced next to the bed, the sheet trailing behind her, her cheeks stained a faint pink. "He's a killer, Michael. A cold, hard killer." She swallowed. "I know. I-I saw what he did. What he did to Sean." Kat drew a deep, shuddering breath. "*I saw.*"

And she'd been running ever since that night, Michael knew. Running, living in the shadows, hiding from Turello. But it was time to stop running. "I'm not afraid of him," he told her softly. "I'm going to stop him. I'm going to make damn sure you never have to worry about him again." No, she would never know fear again. He would keep her safe, keep her protected and-

"You don't understand!" The hands that held the sheet were clenched into tight fists. "The cops can't even catch this guy! *He's too good!* And he's not going to stop until I'm dead. He wants to punish me for testifying, and he's not going to stop. He's not ever going to stop!" There was a shrill edge to her words. "He'll do whatever he has to do, hurt whoever he has to, in order to get to me."

Fear, anger, a torrent of emotions chased across her face. He wanted to hold her, to pull her back into his arms and his bed. To make her forget the killer on her trail. To make her forget everything, but the two of them.

"I can't let him hurt you," she whispered, and the words sounded as if they'd been ripped from her. "I can't."

Her eyes closed and she drew a deep, shuddering breath. "I-I just wanted to be with you. From the first moment I saw you, I-I wanted to be with you." Her jaw clenched and eyes opened. Her emerald stare was hard, determined. "But I shouldn't have given in. I shouldn't have—"

He sprang from the bed. Now he was really starting to get pissed. "Do not say that you regret being with me." No, she'd damn well better not say she regretted opening herself to him, offering her beautiful body to him. *Bonding with him.*

Her gaze met his. "When I'm with you... I feel alive. You do that... you make me feel that way. And when you touch me..." A shiver slid over her. "I can't think."

A pleased growl rumbled in his throat.

She took a deep breath. "But it's too dangerous, don't you see that? Lou is going to find me. He tracked me to Shellsville, he'll track me here. And I can't risk him coming here, hurting *you*—I just can't risk it. Not with the way I—" Kat broke off, her shoulders tensing. "I won't risk it."

She wanted to protect him. When was the last time someone had actually tried to protect him? *He* was the protector. He guarded the pack, saw to their care, their needs. But Kat, Kat was trying to protect him.

She was human. Weak. She didn't have his physical strength, his psychic gifts. But she wanted to protect him.

His mate was really something else.

And she thinks I'm just going to let her walk away from me? No damn way.

He reached for her. "Kat—"

"No! Dammit! What did I just tell you? *You can't touch me*! I stop thinking when you touch me and turn all nympho! I can't do that again! I've got to get out of here, while there is still time, before Lou finds me—"

"He's already found you." Alerac's voice cut easily across her words.

Kat gasped and spun around, clutching the sheet, if possible, even tighter.

Alerac stood in the open doorway, his face tense. He didn't look at Kat, instead, he kept his gaze locked on Michael. "A guard on the back quadrant was just found. He's been beaten pretty badly."

"So Turello's on the grounds."

A slow nod.

Michael's lips twisted into a smile. "Perfect."

⁂

Perfect. Kat shook her head. Was he crazy? It was definitely not perfect to have a maniacal killer running around somewhere outside.

Had he not been listening to her? Didn't he understand the danger? *Lou could kill him!*

But Michael, he didn't seem afraid. Didn't seem afraid that a professional killer was nearby, stalking them.

And the way Michael smiled... she shivered. The wolf stood before her, barely cloaked in the shield of the man. His fangs, his long, wickedly sharp fangs were bared. He looked hungry, wild, *damn dangerous.*

He pushed by her, and she grabbed his arm, struggling to preserve her modesty and stop him from leaving. "Michael, what are you doing?"

He glanced down at her, his eyes starting to sparkle, starting to shimmer in that way she'd quickly learned meant the wolf was close to the surface. *Too close.*

"I'm going to eliminate your problem," he told her softly.

She gulped. "You—you—"

He stroked her cheek. "Don't worry, sweet Kat. Lou won't be bothering you again."

Real terror pounded through her. Michael didn't understand. He didn't know what Lou was capable of! But she did. She'd seen the blood... "If you go out there, he'll kill you!" She couldn't bear the thought. Couldn't bear the idea that—

"No," he told her, sounding so utterly confident she wanted to slap him. "He won't."

Michael kissed her. A hard, quick kiss. And then he headed for the door, leaving her staring after him, her mouth ajar.

"Sorry about this," he told her, his eyes still shining. "But it is really for your own good."

She realized what he meant two seconds too late. She lunged forward, but Michael had already closed the door and turned the outside lock. A faint, telling squeak sounded even as she wrenched the doorknob.

"No! Dammit, Michael! Don't do this!" The thud of his retreating footsteps echoed back to her. He was leaving. "No!" Her fist pounded against the door.

He was going after Lou. He'd locked her up, no doubt he thought he was keeping her safe. *The sweet, arrogant jerk.* And he was going after Lou...

She dropped her sheet and ran for the closet. Please, please let her clothes be there, let—

Her suitcase sat on the floor. She jerked it open, and threw on her jeans and shirt in record time. She didn't bother with underwear or socks. She jammed her feet into a pair of tennis shoes, then raced for the window. She jerked it open, and peered down at the ground. She was at least fifteen feet up. Maybe twenty.

Sonofabitch!

How was she supposed to get down? How was she supposed to help Michael? And she had to help him. There was no way she could let him face Lou alone.

There was an old, gnarled oak tree near her window. Well, about five feet from her window. But she'd have to jump for it.

She looked down, down at the hard ground, and gulped. She'd never been a fan of heights. A step ladder was too high for her.

Kat glanced behind her at the wooden door. Maybe she could break it down. Maybe she could—

A wolf's howl split the night.

A man screamed.

Kat took a few steps back, prayed, then ran forward and jumped through the window.

The wolf had taken over. The beast controlled him, consumed him. He snarled, advancing slowly upon the man who stood in the shadows of the barn. He could still smell the sweet scent of his mate, and the idea that this man, this *killer* would be so near to her filled him with rage.

Fureur de la mort. The death rage.

Lou had dropped his gun, and he was scrambling back over the straw, his thin face tight with terror.

The wolf leaned forward, already tasting his blood, already tasting—

"Michael!"

The wolf's head jerked toward the scream. Kat ran through the open door, her clothes torn, her hair flying wildly behind her. "Michael!"

He padded toward her.

And Lou snapped forward, pulling out a hidden knife, and plunging it deep into Michael's back.

He howled.

Kat's eyes widened, her face tight with dawning horror. "No!" She jumped on Lou, punching and kicking him. "No, you bastard!"

But Lou just laughed and shook her off, throwing her against the wall of the barn.

The pain coursing through his body was immense. The knife had been thrust deep, and he was bleeding, bleeding out onto the pale straw...

"First I'm gonna kill your dog..." Lou snarled at Kat, his hands clenching around the bloody knife. "Then I'm going to start on you, bitch. I'm gonna cut you apart, one slice at a time..."

He lifted the knife again.

Michael's muscles tightened.

And when the blade flashed down, he was ready. He jumped, springing forward with his powerful legs. His mouth locked around Lou's arm, his teeth digging into muscle, bone. Rich blood flowed into his mouth, over his tongue.

The knife clattered to the floor. Lou shrieked, pain and fear rich in his voice.

Michael slashed out with his claws, raking open the skin of Lou's legs, sending him crashing to the ground in a writhing heap. He drew back, ready to attack again—

Kat slammed a shovel into Lou's back. "He's not a dog, you bastard! He's a wolf! *My wolf*!"

Lou whimpered.

Michael moved in for the kill. It would be so easy now. He eyed Lou's throat. Pale. Wide. Just one bite, that's all it would take. And Kat would be safe. Forever.

She dropped the shovel and ran to him, burying her face in his fur. "Oh, God, Michael!" Her body trembled against him.

His muscles quivered. The beast wanted to lunge forward, wanted to savage, to kill—

"You're hurt." Her hands touched his wound, light and delicate. "I've got to get help for you!"

Yes, and when she went to get help, he'd finish Lou. A snarl slipped past his lips.

Kat stiffened, pulling back lightly. She gazed into his eyes. "Michael?"

He could taste the blood in his mouth. His fangs throbbed… His claws were fully extended, ready to attack. *Ready to attack.*

"Get away from him."

Kat jerked at Alerac's voice.

"Do what I say, Little Red. Get. Away. From. Him. *Now.*"

But she didn't move. She stayed crouched before him, her eyes on his. Behind her, Lou twitched and moaned in agony.

The tempting scent of blood filled the air.

He pushed closer to Lou, muscles bunching in preparation for the kill.

"Kat, you have to get away from him."

She shook her head. A tear slipped down her cheek. "He's hurt. Go get help."

"Help's on the way, don't worry. Michael's going to be fine." Alerac edged closer to them, to her. "But right now… right now, I need you to get up and come to me."

Another quick shake of her head. "No, Michael—"

"Dammit, Kat! He's in a death rage. If you don't move, *now*, he might attack you!"

She flinched, her eyes widening.

Michael turned his head, snarling at Alerac, his jaw snapping.

Alerac stepped back, raising his hands. "Easy…"

"He's in a what?" Kat whispered, her hands still buried in his thick fur.

"A death rage. *Fureur de la mort.* He's been pushed too far." Alerac was grim. "The wolf's taken over. And the wolf… it cannot be controlled."

She swallowed. Her hands tightened around him. "He won't hurt me. He didn't hurt me before. He won't hurt me now."

"*Kat…*"

"He won't!" She took a deep breath. "But if I move… if I leave him…" Her body trembled. "I-I think he'll kill Lou."

Alerac looked at the whimpering man. He shrugged.

"*Michael's not going to kill him!*"

"He was going to kill you," Alerac reminded her. "He was hunting you. He came here tonight with the sole purpose of getting to you. Torturing you, then killing you. That's what he does, remember?"

"I-I can't let Michael kill him." Her hand stroked his fur. "Michael's better—*Michael's not like him.* I won't have him kill for me."

Alerac opened his mouth to reply—

And the wail of a siren echoed in the distance.

"Dammit! The guards must have called the cops." His golden eyes glowed for just a moment. "Knew we shouldn't have brought in those humans." He clenched his hands, drew a deep breath, and his eyes slipped back to an easy shade of amber. "Looks like Lou will get to live, after all. Lucky bastard."

A sigh of relief slipped past Kat's lips. Her hold on Michael loosened—

The wolf lunged forward, wrenching completely free of Kat's grasp, charging for his prey.

His jaws locked on Lou's throat. He felt the beat of his pulse, heard the tempting flow of his blood—

"No!" Kat grabbed him, struggling to pull him back. "Michael, no!"

Chapter Ten

His thick muscles coiled beneath her arms, and then he whirled around, teeth snapping. Kat jerked back, a scream on her lips.

The sirens wailed in the distance, sounding closer now, closer…

The wolf crouched over her, blue eyes shimmering, mouth open, breath heaving.

"Michael?" She didn't dare move. What had Alerac said? Something about Michael being in some kind of rage? *A death rage.*

Just great.

The wolf's taken over, and it cannot be controlled.

She prayed Alerac was wrong. Because if he wasn't—

The wolf snarled, inching closer to her.

She lifted her hand, palm out, entreating. The wolf stared at her, eyes locked on her face.

Her fingers moved toward him. Slowly. So slowly. Then she touched him, stroked the soft fur on his side.

"Damn. Lady, you've got balls." Alerac was right behind her. His hands locked on her shoulders. "But you can't play with a wolf. I've got to get you out of here before—"

Michael pressed forward and rubbed his muzzle against her cheek. A soft, quick rub. Then he turned to Alerac, and growled.

"Well, I'll be damned." Alerac stepped back, holding up his hands. "Sorry, cuz. Didn't mean to touch."

The wolf nodded, as if he understood. Then he licked Kat, a quick, warm lick on her neck.

The sirens still wailed, sounding now as if they were right outside.

Lou moaned and rocked his body back and forth on the straw covered floor.

"The police will be in here any minute." Alerac frowned at Michael. "You need to turn back, do you hear me? *Turn back... or get the hell out of here before they see you.*"

The wolf padded away from them, moving to a darkened corner of the barn. His blue eyes touched on Kat. For a moment, she could have sworn that fear flickered in his gaze, then he shut his eyes, howled...

And transformed before her.

The sickening crunch of bones filled the air. The fur seemed to melt from his body. His limbs stretched, contorted. His claws vanished. His jaw slid back, became that of a man.

She couldn't look away as he changed, didn't want to look away. *That was Michael.* Whether man or beast, it was Michael. Her Michael.

"*Oh, my God!*" The terror-filled scream came from Lou. His eyes were glued to Michael. His face was stark white. He began crawling frantically toward the barn door, scratching, clawing against the ground as he pulled his body—

"Going somewhere?" Alerac asked softly, claws extended toward Lou's throat.

Lou stared up at him, a horrified knowledge in his eyes. And he froze. Every muscle in his body seemed to freeze, and he laid there, eyes locked on Alerac.

"Kat..." Michael's voice. His wonderful, sexy voice. He stretched slowly, then walked toward her, naked and strong.

She ran to him, wrapping her arms around him. "Michael!" Her hands slid down his back, over the knife wound—

A wound that wasn't there anymore. Her hands touched perfectly smooth, strong skin. Kat drew back, staring up at him, stunned. "But how?"

"The change." He brushed back a lock of her hair. "Healing comes with the change."

A clatter of voices sounded outside. Men's voices, a woman's soft drawl.

Alerac reached behind a pile of hay and tossed a pair of jeans toward Michael. "Here. Put these on before they come inside."

Michael arched a brow.

Alerac smiled. "I figured it wouldn't be a bad idea to start stashing some extra clothes around the grounds. For emergencies, you know. I was right, too, wasn't I?"

But Michael didn't have time to answer. He'd barely pulled on the jeans when a group of uniformed officers swept into the barn, guns drawn.

❧⟨✿⟩❧

It took a while to explain the situation to the police. But once they figured out just exactly who Lou Turello was, they wasted no time in handcuffing him and stationing two officers to guard him.

The police chief, who seemed very friendly with both Michael and Alerac, assured Kat that extra guards would stay with Lou until he was safely back in Chicago.

"He's not gettin' away," he told her in his gruff drawl. "That man's goin' to spend the rest of his life in jail."

She hoped so.

"But they're animals!" Lou yelled, his face still paper white. "They're *wolves*!"

The female officer next to Lou, a young blond woman with pale blue eyes, jerked, and her gaze flashed to Michael and Alerac.

"I saw them!" Lou continued, spittle flying from his lips. "That one—he was a black wolf. He tried to eat me!"

Michael laughed.

The female officer paled.

Alerac tilted his head to the side, his eyes narrowing as he sniffed the air. "That woman—"

"*They're animals!*" Lou's shout cut him off. "*They're all animals! Freaking wolves!*"

The police chief sighed. "Should have known a guy like him had a few screws loose."

Alerac nodded. His gaze was locked on the blond officer.

"Mind if I talk to him for a moment?" Michael asked. "Alone?"

The chief hesitated.

"It will only take a moment," he said, blue eyes taking on a faint shimmer. "Just ask your officers to step aside so that I can have a... private word with him."

The police chief nodded at once. "Langley, Hill—take a walk! Morlet needs to talk to Turello."

The woman's eyes widened. "But, Chief—"

"You heard me!" He snapped. "Take a few steps away. Keep the perp in visual contact, but give 'em some privacy."

She still hesitated.

"Now!"

Both officers moved. Michael paced toward Lou, a congenial smile on his face. With every step that he took, Lou seemed to tense.

Then Michael was at his side. He leaned forward, and whispered to him. A quick, soft whisper that only Lou heard.

Kat watched them, wondering what was happening. Why would Michael want to talk to Lou? Why would—

Lou nodded quickly. "I-I promise." His beady eyes flashed to the female cop. "I-I'm ready. I-I'll confess. Let's just... get the hell out of here." He gulped. "*Now.*"

The chief whistled. "Well, I'll be..."

And within moments, they were gone. The cops. Lou. They vanished in a whirl of red and blue lights.

Kat looked up at Michael, curious. "What did you say to him?"

Michael stared into the darkness. "I told him that he was right. That I was an animal. And if he ever came near you again, I'd rip him apart."

Staring up at his implacable face, seeing the hint of the beast's hunger flashing in his eyes, Kat believed him. And she knew that Lou had, too.

✦✧(❈)✧✦

She awoke to the feel of a warm, wet tongue stroking her clit. Strong, masculine hands were locked on her thighs, holding them spread wide.

Her lashes lifted and a moan slipped past her lips. Michael's dark head was bent over her, his mouth between her legs. "Michael..."

His tongue drove deep into her pussy.

OhmyGod! Her body shuddered.

He lifted his head, licking his lips. "I love the taste of you. So sweet and warm." His fingers slipped into her sex. Pushed. Then he crawled up her body, lowered his head, and took her breast into his mouth.

He sucked her, strong, hard sucks that had her nipple tightening, her sex clenching. And his fingers... they thrust deep into her pussy. Deep. They stretched her, opened her, readied her.

Then he kissed her, and she could taste herself on his lips. And his fingers were gone. His cock, his strong, thick cock, pressed against her.

"I was watching you sleep," he murmured, moving to lick her throat. "And I thought about how much I wanted to taste you, so I did."

She squirmed against him. Her body was tight, hot. And so ready for the thrust of his cock that she thought she'd scream. Oh, yeah, he'd just given her one hell of a wake up call.

"I had to feel your sweet pussy against my mouth. Had to lick your cream." The head of his cock pushed lightly against her. "And now... I've got to fuck you."

Her fingers locked around his bare shoulders, her nails digging deep.

His cock slammed into her. Kat climaxed instantly. Her body seemed to explode, pleasure snapped through her, her sex clenched, tightened, clenched—

"*Oui, ma petite.* Let me feel you come." Michael's blue eyes shimmered as he gazed down at her. His jaw was locked tight. His muscled legs were between hers, his cock driving into her, over and over. "Let me feel your hot little pussy squeeze me... ah... just... like... that."

Michael shuddered, his hands clenching around her hips as he rammed into her, sending his semen pumping into her depths.

When his orgasm was over, Michael stayed lodged within her, his cock still hard, his body slick with sweat.

Kat swallowed, tried to ease her dry throat, and managed to say, "That wasn't exactly fair, you know." Getting her so turned on when she'd been asleep, waking her up, wet and hungry—

He smiled. "I like the way you taste." He bent and licked her nipple.

Oh, yes... that felt good. She licked her lips. "And, how do I taste?"

His blue stare met hers. "Like you're mine."

A pang shot through her heart. "Michael—"

"You are, you know. You're mine." His hands crept up her body, cupped her breasts. "And I'm yours."

She stared up into his blue gaze, not sure what to say. Her body was still tingling, his cock was still inside her, and she was afraid.

"We were meant to be together, Kat. That's the way of mates. Mates are meant to be." He smiled down at her. "For me, there will never be another. Only you."

Her heart seemed to stop.

And his smile slowly disappeared. "You saw me at my worst tonight. You saw the beast take control." He swallowed. "Tell me... tell me that you aren't afraid of me now."

"I'm not afraid of you," she whispered, and it was true. She knew what Michael was, *who* he was, and she didn't fear him. No, it wasn't him that she feared...

"Stay with me, Kat," he entreated, his voice thick. "Give me a chance to show you how good we can be together."

She hesitated.

"Kat..." There was torment in his eyes. "I know I-I'm not what you want. Hell, I'm not exactly a normal guy."

"No. You're not." But did she want a normal guy? Would a normal guy have saved her in that alley the first night? Would a normal guy have fought a maniac like Lou?

"But I love you. I do. And I would do anything for you, you have to know that. If you give me a chance..."

"No." She pushed against his shoulders.

His mouth dropped open. And he fell back, sliding away from her, out of her. "No?"

Kat shook her head.

He swallowed, his hands clenching into fists. "I won't make you stay with me. At first, I thought that—but I can't. I can't do that to you, I—"

"Hmmm. Really?" She pushed him onto his back and began to run her fingertip down his chest. "Will you make me leave then? Cause you'd have to, you know. Because I won't leave me on my own." Her finger stilled, right over his heart. "I don't think I could ever leave you." Not and remain sane. Last night, she'd thought she could, she'd thought that she could leave him, in order to keep him safe.

But living without Michael, without his warm smile, his eyes, his strength... no, that wasn't an option for her. Not anymore. Perhaps it never had been.

She took a deep breath, tried to smother the fear that snaked through her. She hadn't done this before, hadn't opened herself to someone so completely—

But it was Michael. Her Michael. Her wolf.

"What? What did you say?"

A slow smile spread across her lips, and her fear... it seemed to fade away. "I realized something last night. Something very important."

Michael stared up at her, waiting.

Her finger inched downward. "When Lou attacked you, when I saw the blood—" Her eyes closed for a moment. "I think, I think I went a little crazy."

"Kat—"

"I realized then... that I loved you. That I probably had since the beginning. That I do, I mean... I love you." There, she'd said it. The words were out, the words she'd been wanting to say, but been *terrified* to say, to him from the moment she opened her eyes. She'd never said the words before but...

She loved Michael. Loved the man who stared at her with patience and care. Loved the wolf who protected her, and licked her neck with soft affection.

His hands locked on her arms. "Do you mean it? Do you really... love me?"

Staring into his eyes, his beautiful, sexy bedroom eyes, she said simply, "Yes." She'd finally found the man she wanted to be with, to spend her life with. She'd found her mate.

Her perfect mate.

He just happened to be a werewolf.

But, hey, no one was perfect.

"*Mon Dieu*, I was afraid you didn't want me, that you—"

She laughed. "Not want you? Maybe you missed out on all the screaming and moaning that I was doing earlier." Kat leaned forward and kissed him lightly on the lips. "Trust me, wolfie, I love you, and I most definitely want you." In fact, she had some serious immediate plans for him...

His blue stare shimmered. "I love you, mate."

"I know." And she did. A warm golden glow spread through her. She'd felt the depth of his love during the bonding, seen it when he fought for her, putting his very life on the line. She stroked him lightly, and a faint smile teased her lips. "But I think I'm going to make you prove it again."

One dark brow lifted. "And how am I going to do that?"

Her finger inched down a little more, rubbing lightly against the base of his cock. "You're going to give me my turn to play."

He sucked in a sharp breath.

Her fingers wrapped around him. "Then you're going to marry me."

He laughed. "Woman, just try to stop me."

She smiled at him, love filling her. Then she lowered her head, and began to play.

And playing with a wolf... she knew it could be dangerous, but it could also sure as hell be a lot of fun.

About the Author:

I have long been a fan of the paranormal genre. I just can't ever seem to get my fill of ghosts, werewolves, or vampires!

The Wolf's Mate *is the second werewolf tale that I've written for* Red Sage. *After the publication of* Bite of the Wolf (**Secrets, Volume 15**)*, I couldn't wait to write another story about my French wolves!*

I would love to hear from my readers. Please visit my website at cynthiaeden.com *or send an email to* info@cynthiaeden.com.

Men you've been dreaming about!

Secrets

Satisfy your desire for more.

eel the wild adventure, fierce passion and the power of love in every *Secrets* Collection story. Red Sage Publishing's romance authors create richly crafted, sexy, sensual, novella-length stories. Each one is just the right length for reading after a long and hectic day.

Each volume in the *Secrets* Collection has four diverse, ultra-sexy, romantic novellas brimming with adventure, passion and love. More adventurous tales for the adventurous reader. The *Secrets* Collection are a glorious mix of romance genre; numerous historical settings, contemporary, paranormal, science fiction and suspense. We are always looking for new adventures.

Reader response to the *Secrets* volumes has been great! Here's just a small sample:

"I loved the variety of settings. Four completely wonderful time periods, give you four completely wonderful reads."

"Each story was a page-turning tale I hated to put down."

*"I love **Secrets**! When is the next volume coming out? This one was Hot! Loved the heroes!"*

Secrets have won raves and awards. We could go on, but why don't you find out for yourself—order your set of **Secrets** today! See the back for details.

Secrets, Volume 1

Listen to what reviewers say:

"These stories take you beyond romance into the realm of erotica. I found *Secrets* absolutely delicious."

—Virginia Henley,
New York Times Best Selling Author

"*Secrets* is a collection of novellas for the daring, adventurous woman who's not afraid to give her fantasies free reign."

—Kathe Robin, *Romantic Times* Magazine

"...In fact, the men featured in all the stories are terrific, they all want to please and pleasure their women. If you like erotic romance you will love *Secrets*."

—*Romantic Readers* Review

In *Secrets, Volume 1* you'll find:

A Lady's Quest by Bonnie Hamre

Widowed Lady Antonia Blair-Sutworth searches for a lover to save her from the handsome Duke of Sutherland. The "auditions" may be shocking but utterly tantalizing.

The Spinner's Dream by Alice Gaines

A seductive fantasy that leaves every woman wishing for her own private love slave, desperate and running for his life.

The Proposal by Ivy Landon

This tale is a walk on the wild side of love. *The Proposal* will taunt you, tease you, and shock you. A contemporary erotica for the adventurous woman.

The Gift by Jeanie LeGendre

Immerse yourself in this historic tale of exotic seduction, bondage and a concubine's surrender to the Sultan's desire. Can Alessandra live the life and give the gift the Sultan demands of her?

Secrets, Volume 2

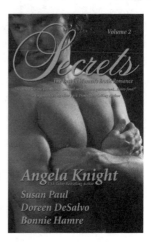

Listen to what reviewers say:

"*Secrets* offers four novellas of sensual delight; each beautifully written with intense feeling and dedication to character development. For those seeking stories with heightened intimacy, look no further."

—Kathee Card, *Romancing the Web*

"Such a welcome diversity in styles and genres. Rich characterization in sensual tales. An exciting read that's sure to titillate the senses."

—Cheryl Ann Porter

"*Secrets 2* left me breathless. Sensual satisfaction guaranteed… times four!"

—Virginia Henley, *New York Times* Best Selling Author

In *Secrets, Volume 2* you'll find:

Surrogate Lover by Doreen DeSalvo

Adrian Ross is a surrogate sex therapist who has all the answers and control. He thought he'd seen and done it all, but he'd never met Sarah.

Snowbound by Bonnie Hamre

A delicious, sensuous regency tale. The marriage-shy Earl of Howden is teased and tortured by his own desires and finds there is a woman who can equal his overpowering sensuality.

Roarke's Prisoner by Angela Knight

Elise, a starship captain, remembers the eager animal submission she'd known before at her captor's hands and refuses to become his toy again. However, she has no idea of the delights he's planned for her this time.

Savage Garden by Susan Paul

Raine's been captured by a mysterious and dangerous revolutionary leader in Mexico. At first her only concern is survival, but she quickly finds lush erotic nights in her captor's arms.

Winner of the Fallot Literary Award for Fiction!

Secrets, Volume 3

Listen to what reviewers say:

"*Secrets, Volume 3*, leaves the reader breathless. A delicious confection of sensuous treats awaits the reader on each turn of the page!"
— Kathee Card, *Romancing the Web*

"From the FBI to Police Detective to Vampires to a Medieval Warlord home from the Crusade—*Secrets 3* is simply the best!"
— Susan Paul, award winning author

"An unabashed celebration of sex. Highly arousing! Highly recommended!"
— Virginia Henley, *New York Times* Best Selling Author

In *Secrets, Volume 3* you'll find:

The Spy Who Loved Me by Jeanie Cesarini

Undercover FBI agent Paige Ellison's sexual appetites rise to new levels when she works with leading man Christopher Sharp, the cunning agent who uses all his training to capture her body and heart.

The Barbarian by Ann Jacobs

Lady Brianna vows not to surrender to the barbaric Giles, Earl of Harrow. He must use sexual arts learned in the infidels' harem to conquer his bride. A word of caution—this is not for the faint of heart.

Blood and Kisses by Angela Knight

A vampire assassin is after Beryl St. Cloud. Her only hope lies with Decker, another vampire and ex-mercenary. Broke, she offers herself as payment for his services. Will his seductive powers take her very soul?

Love Undercover by B.J. McCall

Amanda Forbes is the bait in a strip joint sting operation. While she performs, fellow detective "Cowboy" Cooper gets to watch. Though he excites her, she must fight the temptation to surrender to the passion.

Winner of the 1997 Under the Covers Readers Favorite Award

Secrets, Volume 4

Listen to what reviewers say:

"Provocative… seductive… a must read!"
—Romantic Times Magazine

"These are the kind of stories that romance readers that 'want a little more' have been looking for all their lives…."
—Affaire de Coeur Magazine

"*Secrets, Volume 4*, has something to satisfy every erotic fantasy… simply sexational!"
—Virginia Henley, *New York Times* Best Selling Author

In *Secrets, Volume 4* you'll find:

An Act of Love by Jeanie Cesarini

Shelby Moran's past left her terrified of sex. International film star Jason Gage must gently coach the young starlet in the ways of love. He wants more than an act—he wants Shelby to feel true passion in his arms.

Enslaved by Desirée Lindsey

Lord Nicholas Summer's air of danger, dark passions, and irresistible charm have brought Lady Crystal's long-hidden desires to the surface. Will he be able to give her the one thing she desires before it's too late?

The Bodyguard by Betsy Morgan and Susan Paul

Kaki York is a bodyguard, but watching the wild, erotic romps of her client's sexual conquests on the security cameras is getting to her—and her partner, the ruggedly handsome James Kulick. Can she resist his insistent desire to have her?

The Love Slave by Emma Holly

A woman's ultimate fantasy. For one year, Princess Lily will be attended to by three delicious men of her choice. While she delights in playing with the first two, it's the reluctant Grae, with his powerful chest, black eyes and hair, that stirs her desires.

Secrets, Volume 5

Listen to what reviewers say:

"Hot, hot, hot! Not for the faint-hearted!"
—*Romantic Times* Magazine

"As you make your way through the stories, you will find yourself becoming hotter and hotter. *Secrets* just keeps getting better and better."
—*Affaire de Coeur* Magazine

"*Secrets 5* is a collage of luscious sensuality. Any woman who reads *Secrets* is in for an awakening!"

—Virginia Henley, *New York Times* Best Selling Author

In *Secrets, Volume 5* you'll find:

Beneath Two Moons by Sandy Fraser

Ready for a very wild romp? Step into the future and find Conor, rough and masculine like frontiermen of old, on the prowl for a new conquest. In his sights, Dr. Eva Kelsey. She got away once before, but this time Conor makes sure she begs for more.

Insatiable by Chevon Gael

Marcus Remington photographs beautiful models for a living, but it's Ashlyn Fraser, a young corporate exec having some glamour shots done, who has stolen his heart. It's up to Marcus to help her discover her inner sexual self.

Strictly Business by Shannon Hollis

Elizabeth Forrester knows it's tough enough for a woman to make it to the top in the corporate world. Garrett Hill, the most beautiful man in Silicon Valley, has to come along to stir up her wildest fantasies. Dare she give in to both their desires?

Alias Smith and Jones by B.J. McCall

Meredith Collins finds herself stranded overnight at the airport. A handsome stranger by the name of Smith offers her sanctuary for the evening and she finds those mesmerizing, green-flecked eyes hard to resist. Are they to be just two ships passing in the night?

Secrets, Volume 6

Listen to what reviewers say:

"Red Sage was the first and remains the leader of Women's Erotic Romance Fiction Collections!"
—*Romantic Times* Magazine

"*Secrets, Volume 6*, is the best of *Secrets* yet. ...four of the most erotic stories in one volume than this reader has yet to see anywhere else. ...These stories are full of erotica at its best and you'll definitely want to keep it handy for lots of re-reading!"

—*Affaire de Coeur* Magazine

"*Secrets 6* satisfies every female fantasy: the Bodyguard, the Tutor, the Werewolf, and the Vampire. I give it Six Stars!"
—Virginia Henley, *New York Times* Best Selling Author

In *Secrets, Volume 6* you'll find:

Flint's Fuse by Sandy Fraser
Dana Madison's father has her "kidnapped" for her own safety. Flint, the tall, dark and dangerous mercenary, is hired for the job. But just which one is the prisoner—Dana will try *anything* to get away.

Love's Prisoner by MaryJanice Davidson
Trapped in an elevator, Jeannie Lawrence experienced unwilling rapture at Michael Windham's hands. She never expected the devilishly handsome man to show back up in her life—or turn out to be a werewolf!

The Education of Miss Felicity Wells by Alice Gaines
Felicity Wells wants to be sure she'll satisfy her soon-to-be husband but she needs a teacher. Dr. Marcus Slade, an experienced lover, agrees to take her on as a student, but can he stop short of taking her completely?

A Candidate for the Kiss by Angela Knight
Working on a story, reporter Dana Ivory stumbles onto a more amazing one—a sexy, secret agent who happens to be a vampire. She wants her story but Gabriel Archer wants more from her than just sex and blood.

Secrets, Volume 7

Listen to what reviewers say:

"Get out your asbestos gloves — *Secrets Volume 7* is… extremely hot, true erotic romance… passionate and titillating. There's nothing quite like baring your secrets!"

—*Romantic Times* Magazine

"…sensual, sexy, steamy fun. A perfect read!"

—Virginia Henley,
New York Times Best Selling Author

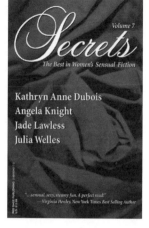

"Intensely provocative and disarmingly romantic, *Secrets, Volume 7*, is a romance reader's paradise that will take you beyond your wildest dreams!"

—Ballston Book House Review

In *Secrets, Volume 7* you'll find:

Amelia's Innocence by Julia Welles

Amelia didn't know her father bet her in a card game with Captain Quentin Hawke, so honor demands a compromise—three days of erotic foreplay, leaving her virginity and future intact.

The Woman of His Dreams by Jade Lawless

From the day artist Gray Avonaco moves in next door, Joanna Morgan is plagued by provocative dreams. But what she believes is unrequited lust, Gray sees as another chance to be with the woman he loves. He must persuade her that even death can't stop true love.

Surrender by Kathryn Anne Dubois

Free-spirited Lady Johanna wants no part of the binding strictures society imposes with her marriage to the powerful Duke. She doesn't know the dark Duke wants sensual adventure, and sexual satisfaction.

Kissing the Hunter by Angela Knight

Navy Seal Logan McLean hunts the vampires who murdered his wife. Virginia Hart is a sexy vampire searching for her lost soul-mate only to find him in a man determined to kill her. She must convince him all vampires aren't created equally.

**Winner of the Venus Book Club
Best Book of the Year**

Secrets, Volume 8

Listen to what reviewers say:

"*Secrets, Volume 8*, is an amazing compilation of sexy stories covering a wide range of subjects, all designed to titillate the senses. …you'll find something for everybody in this latest version of *Secrets*."

—*Affaire de Coeur* Magazine

"*Secrets Volume 8*, is simply sensational!"

—Virginia Henley, *New York Times* Best Selling Author

"These delectable stories will have you turning the pages long into the night. Passionate, provocative and perfect for setting the mood…."

—*Escape to Romance* Reviews

In *Secrets, Volume 8* you'll find:

Taming Kate by Jeanie Cesarini

Kathryn Roman inherits a legal brothel. Little does this city girl know the town of Love, Nevada wants her to be their new madam so they've charged Trey Holliday, one very dominant cowboy, with taming her.

Jared's Wolf by MaryJanice Davidson

Jared Rocke will do anything to avenge his sister's death, but ends up attracted to Moira Wolfbauer, the she-wolf sworn to protect her pack. Joining forces to stop a killer, they learn love defies all boundaries.

My Champion, My Lover by Alice Gaines

Celeste Broder is a woman committed for having a sexy appetite. Mayor Robert Albright may be her champion—if she can convince him her freedom will mean a chance to indulge their appetites together.

Kiss or Kill by Liz Maverick

In this post-apocalyptic world, Camille Kazinsky's military career rides on her ability to make a choice—whether the robo called Meat should live or die. Meat's future depends on proving he's human enough to live, man enough… to makes her feel like a woman.

Winner of the Venus Book Club
Best Book of the Year

Secrets, Volume 9

Listen to what reviewers say:

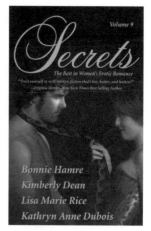

"Everyone should expect only the most erotic stories in a *Secrets* book. ...if you like your stories full of hot sexual scenes, then this is for you!"

—Donna Doyle Romance Reviews

"*SECRETS 9*... is sinfully delicious, highly arousing, and hotter than hot as the pages practically burn up as you turn them."

—Suzanne Coleburn, Reader To Reader Reviews/Belles & Beaux of Romance

"Treat yourself to well-written fiction that's hot, hotter, and hottest!"

—Virginia Henley, *New York Times* Best Selling Author

In *Secrets, Volume 9* you'll find:

Wild For You by Kathryn Anne Dubois

When college intern, Georgie, gets captured by a Congo wildman, she discovers this specimen of male virility has never seen a woman. The research possibilities are endless!

Wanted by Kimberly Dean

FBI Special Agent Jeff Reno wants Danielle Carver. There's her body, brains—and that charge of treason on her head. Dani goes on the run, but the sexy Fed is hot on her trail.

Secluded by Lisa Marie Rice

Nicholas Lee's wealth and power came with a price—his enemies will kill anyone he loves. When Isabelle steals his heart, Nicholas secludes her in his palace for a lifetime of desire in only a few days.

Flights of Fantasy by Bonnie Hamre

Chloe taught others to see the realities of life but she's never shared the intimate world of her sensual yearnings. Given the chance, will she be woman enough to fulfill her most secret erotic fantasy?

Secrets, Volume 10

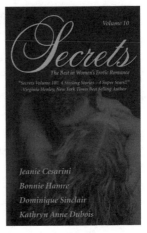

Listen to what reviewers say:

"*Secrets Volume 10*, an erotic dance through medieval castles, sultan's palaces, the English countryside and expensive hotel suites, explodes with passion-filled pages."

—*Romantic Times BOOKclub*

"Having read the previous nine volumes, this one fulfills the expectations of what is expected in a *Secrets* book: romance and eroticism at its best!!"

—*Fallen Angel Reviews*

"All are hot steamy romances so if you enjoy erotica romance, you are sure to enjoy *Secrets, Volume 10*. All this reviewer can say is WOW!!"

—*The Best Reviews*

In *Secrets, Volume 10* you'll find:

Private Eyes by Dominique Sinclair

When a mystery man captivates P.I. Nicolla Black during a stakeout, she discovers her no-seduction rule bending under the pressure of long denied passion. She agrees to the seduction, but he demands her total surrender.

The Ruination of Lady Jane by Bonnie Hamre

To avoid her upcoming marriage, Lady Jane Ponsonby-Maitland flees into the arms of Havyn Attercliffe. She begs him to ruin her rather than turn her over to her odious fiancé.

Code Name: Kiss by Jeanie Cesarini

Agent Lily Justiss is on a mission to defend her country against terrorists that requires giving up her virginity as a sex slave. As her master takes her body, desire for her commanding officer Seth Blackthorn fuels her mind.

The Sacrifice by Kathryn Anne Dubois

Lady Anastasia Bedovier is days from taking her vows as a Nun. Before she denies her sensuality forever, she wants to experience pleasure. Count Maxwell is the perfect man to initiate her into erotic delight.

Secrets, Volume 11

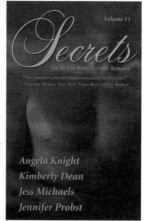

Listen to what reviewers say:

"*Secrets Volume 11* delivers once again with storylines that include erotic masquerades, ancient curses, modern-day betrayal and a prince charming looking for a kiss." **4 Stars**
— *Romantic Times BOOKclub*

"Indulge yourself with this erotic treat and join the thousands of readers who just can't get enough. Be forewarned that *Secrets 11* will whet your appetite for more, but will offer you the ultimate in pleasurable erotic literature."
— *Ballston Book House Review*

"*Secrets 11* quite honestly is my favorite anthology from Red Sage so far."
— *The Best Reviews*

In *Secrets, Volume 11* you'll find:

Masquerade by Jennifer Probst

Hailey Ashton is determined to free herself from her sexual restrictions. Four nights of erotic pleasures without revealing her identity. A chance to explore her secret desires without the fear of unmasking.

Ancient Pleasures by Jess Michaels

Isabella Winslow is obsessed with finding out what caused her late husband's death, but trapped in an Egyptian concubine's tomb with a sexy American raider, succumbing to the mummy's sensual curse takes over.

Manhunt by Kimberly Dean

Framed for murder, Michael Tucker takes Taryn Swanson hostage—the one woman who can clear him. Despite the evidence against him, the attraction between them is strong. Tucker resorts to unconventional, yet effective methods of persuasion to change the sexy ADA's mind.

Wake Me by Angela Knight

Chloe Hart received a sexy painting of a sleeping knight. Radolf of Varik has been trapped for centuries in the painting since, cursed by a witch. His only hope is to visit the dreams of women and make one of them fall in love with him so she can free him with a kiss.

Secrets, Volume 12

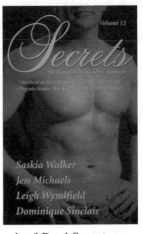

Listen to what reviewers say:

"*Secrets Volume 12*, turns on the heat with a seductive encounter inside a bookstore, a temple of naughty and sensual delight, a galactic inferno that thaws ice, and a lightening storm that lights up the English shoreline. Tales of looking for love in all the right places with a heat rating out the charts." **4½ Stars**

—*Romantic Times BOOKclub*

"I really liked these stories. You want great escapism? Read **Secrets, Volume 12**."

—*Romance Reviews*

In **Secrets, Volume 12** you'll find:

Good Girl Gone Bad by Dominique Sinclair

Reagan's dreams are finally within reach. Setting out to do research for an article, nothing could have prepared her for Luke, or his offer to teach her everything she needs to know about sex. Licentious pleasures, forbidden desires… inspiring the best writing she's ever done.

Aphrodite's Passion by Jess Michaels

When Selena flees Victorian London before her evil stepchildren can institutionalize her for hysteria, Gavin is asked to bring her back home. But when he finds her living on the island of Cyprus, his need to have her begins to block out every other impulse.

White Heat by Leigh Wyndfield

Raine is hiding in an icehouse in the middle of nowhere from one of the scariest men in the universes. Walker escaped from a burning prison. Imagine their surprise when they find out they have the same man to blame for their miseries. Passion, revenge and love are in their future.

Summer Lightning by Saskia Walker

Sculptress Sally is enjoying an idyllic getaway on a secluded cove when she spots a gorgeous man walking naked on the beach. When Julian finds an attractive woman shacked up in his cove, he has to check her out. But what will he do when he finds she's secretly been using him as a model?

Secrets, Volume 13

Listen to what reviewers say:

"In *Secrets Volume 13*, the temperature gets turned up a few notches with a mistaken personal ad, shape-shifters destined to love, a hot Regency lord and his lady, as well as a bodyguard protecting his woman. Emotions and flames blaze high in Red Sage's latest foray into the sensual and delightful art of love." **4½ Stars**

—*Romantic Times BOOKclub*

"The sex is still so hot the pages nearly ignite! Read *Secrets, Volume 13!*"

—*Romance Reviews*

In *Secrets, Volume 13* you'll find:

Out of Control by Rachelle Chase

Astrid's world revolves around her business and she's hoping to pick up wealthy Erik Santos as a client. Only he's hoping to pick up something entirely different. Will she give in to the seductive pull of his proposition?

Hawkmoor by Amber Green

Shape-shifters answer to Darien as he acts in the name of the long-missing Lady Hawkmoor, their hereditary ruler. When she unexpectedly surfaces, Darien must deal with a scrappy individual whose wary eyes hold the other half of his soul, but who has the power to destroy his world.

Lessons in Pleasure by Charlotte Featherstone

A wicked bargain has Lily vowing never to yield to the demands of the rake she once loved and lost. Unfortunately, Damian, the Earl of St. Croix, or Saint as he is infamously known, will not take 'no' for an answer.

In the Heat of the Night by Calista Fox

Haunted by a century-old curse, Molina fears she won't live to see her thirtieth birthday. Nick, her former bodyguard, is hired back into service to protect her from the fatal accidents that plague her family. But *In the Heat of the Night*, will his passion and love for her be enough to convince Molina they have a future together?

Secrets, Volume 14

Listen to what reviewers say:

"*Secrets Volume 14* will excite readers with its diverse selection of delectable sexy tales ranging from a fourteenth century love story to a sci-fi rebel who falls for a irresistible research scientist to a trio of determined vampires who battle for the same woman to a virgin sacrifice who falls in love with a beast. A cornucopia of pure delight!" **4½ Stars**
—*Romantic Times BOOKclub*

"This book contains four erotic tales sure to keep readers up long into the night."

—*Romance Junkies*

In *Secrets, Volume 14* you'll find:

Soul Kisses by Angela Knight

Beth's been kidnapped by Joaquin Ramirez, a sadistic vampire. Handsome vampire cousins, Morgan and Garret Axton, come to her rescue. Can she find happiness with two vampires?

Temptation in Time by Alexa Aames

Ariana escaped the Middle Ages after stealing a kiss of magic from sexy sorcerer, Marcus de Grey. When he brings her back, they begin a battle of wills and a sexual odyssey that could spell disaster for them both.

Ailis and the Beast by Jennifer Barlowe

When Ailis agreed to be her village's sacrifice to the mysterious Beast she was prepared to sacrifice her virtue, and possibly her life. But some things aren't what they seem. Ailis and the Beast are about to discover the greatest sacrifice may be the human heart.

Night Heat by Leigh Wynfield

When Rip Bowhite leads a revolt on the prison planet, he ends up struggling to survive against monsters that rule the night. Jemma, the prison's Healer, won't allow herself to be distracted by the instant attraction she feels for Rip. As the stakes are raised and death draws near, love seems doomed in the heat of the night.

Secrets, Volume 15

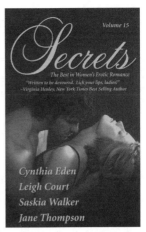

Listen to what reviewers say:

"*Secrets Volume 15* blends humor, tension and steamy romance in its newest collection that sizzles with passion between unlikely pairs—a male chauvinist columnist and a librarian turned erotica author; a handsome werewolf and his resisting mate; an unfulfilled woman and a sexy police officer and a Victorian wife who learns discipline can be fun. Readers will revel in this delicious assortment of thrilling tales." **4 Stars**
—*Romantic Times BOOKclub*

"This book contains four tales by some of today's hottest authors that will tease your senses and intrigue your mind."
—*Romance Junkies*

In *Secrets, Volume 15* you'll find:

Simon Says by Jane Thompson

Simon Campbell is a newspaper columnist who panders to male fantasies. Georgina Kennedy is a respectable librarian. On the surface, these two have nothing in common... but don't judge a book by its cover.

Bite of the Wolf by Cynthia Eden

Gareth Morlet, alpha werewolf, has finally found his mate. All he has to do is convince Trinity to join with him, to give in to the pleasure of a werewolf's mating, and then she will be his... forever.

Falling for Trouble by Saskia Walker

With 48 hours to clear her brother's name, Sonia Harmond finds help from irresistible bad boy, Oliver Eaglestone. When the erotic tension between them hits fever pitch, securing evidence to thwart an international arms dealer isn't the only danger they face.

The Disciplinarian by Leigh Court

Headstrong Clarissa Babcock is sent to the shadowy legend known as The Disciplinarian for instruction in proper wifely obedience. Jared Ashworth uses the tools of seduction to show her how to control a demanding husband, but her beauty, spirit, and uninhibited passion make Jared hunger to keep her—and their darkly erotic nights—all for himself!

Secrets, Volume 16

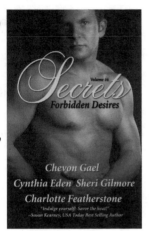

Listen to what reviewers say:

"Blackmail, games of chance, nude beaches and masquerades pave a path to heart-tugging emotions and fiery love scenes in Red Sage's latest collection." **4.5 Stars**
—*Romantic Times BOOKclub*

"Red Sage Publishing has brought to the readers an erotic profusion of highly skilled storytellers in their Secrets Vol. 16. … This is the best Secrets novel to date and this reviewer's favorite."
—*LoveRomances.com*

In *Secrets, Volume 16* you'll find:

Never Enough by Cynthia Eden

For the last three weeks, Abby McGill has been playing with fire. Bad-boy Jake has taught her the true meaning of desire, but she knows she has to end her relationship with him. But Jake isn't about to let the woman he wants walk away from him.

Bunko by Sheri Gilmoore

Tu Tran is forced to decide between Jack, a man, who promises to share every aspect of his life with her, or Dev, the man, who hides behind a mask and only offers night after night of erotic sex. Will she take the gamble of the dice and choose the man, who can see behind her own mask and expose her true desires?

Hide and Seek by Chevon Gael

Kyle DeLaurier ditches his trophy-fiance in favor of a tropical paradise full of tall, tanned, topless females. Private eye, Darcy McLeod, is on the trail of this runaway groom. Together they sizzle while playing Hide and Seek with their true identities.

Seduction of the Muse by Charlotte Featherstone

He's the Dark Lord, the mysterious author who pens the erotic tales of an innocent woman's seduction. She is his muse, the woman he watches from the dark shadows, the woman whose dreams he invades at night.

Secrets, Volume 17

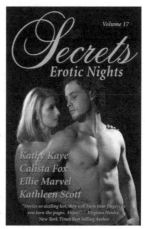

Listen to what reviewers say:

"Readers who have clamored for more *Secrets* will love the mix of alpha and beta males as well as kick-butt heroines who always get their men." **4 Stars**
—*Romantic Times BOOKclub*

"Stories so sizzling hot, they will burn your fingers as you turn the pages. Enjoy!"
—Virginia Henley, *New York Times* Best Selling Author

"Red Sage is bringing us another thrilling anthology of passion and desire that will keep you up long into the night." —*Romance Junkies*

In *Secrets, Volume 17* you'll find:

Rock Hard Candy by Kathy Kaye

Jessica Hennessy, the great, great granddaughter of a Voodoo priestess, decides she's waited long enough for the man of her dreams. A dose of her ancestor's aphrodisiac slipped into the gooey center of her homemade bon bons ought to do the trick.

Fatal Error by Kathleen Scott

Jesse Storm must make amends to humanity by destroying the computer program he helped design that has taken the government hostage. But he must also protect the woman he's loved in secret for nearly a decade.

Birthday by Ellie Marvel

Jasmine Templeton decides she's been celibate long enough. Will a wild night at a hot new club with her two best friends ease the ache inside her or just make it worse? Well, considering one of those best friends is Charlie and she's been having strange notions about their relationship of late… It's definitely a birthday neither she nor Charlie will ever forget.

Intimate Rendezvous by Calista Fox

A thief causes trouble at Cassandra Kensington's nightclub, Rendezvous, and sexy P.I. Dean Hewitt arrives on the scene to help. One look at the siren who owns the club has his blood boiling, despite the fact that his keen instincts have him questioning the legitimacy of her business.

Secrets, Volume 18

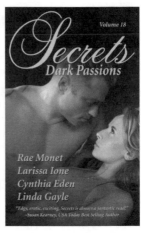

Listen to what reviewers say:

"Fantastic love scenes make this a book to be enjoyed more than once." **4.5 Stars**
—*Romantic Times BOOKclub*

"*Secrets Volume 18* continues [its] tradition of high quality sensual stories that both excite the senses while stimulating the mind."
—CK²S Kwips and Kritiques

"Edgy, erotic, exciting, *Secrets* is always a fantastic read!"

—Susan Kearney, *USA Today* Best Selling Author

In *Secrets, Volume 18* you'll find:

Lone Wolf Three by Rae Monet

Planetary politics and squabbling over wolf occupied territory drain former rebel leader Taban Zias. But his anger quickly turns to desire when he meets, Lakota Blackson. Focused, calm and honorable, the female Wolf Warrior is Taban's perfect mate—now if he can just convince her.

Flesh to Fantasy by Larissa Ione

Kelsa Bradshaw is an intense loner whose job keeps her happily immersed in a fanciful world of virtual reality. Trent Jordan is a laid-back paramedic who experiences the harsh realities of life up close and personal. But when their worlds collide in an erotic eruption can Trent convince Kelsa to turn the fantasy into something real?

Heart Full of Stars by Linda Gayle

Singer Fanta Rae finds herself stranded on a lonely Mars outpost with the first human male she's seen in years. Ex-Marine Alex Decker lost his family and guilt drove him into isolation, but when alien assassins come to enslave Fanta, she and Decker come together to fight for their lives.

The Wolf's Mate by Cynthia Eden

When Michael Morlet finds Katherine "Kat" Hardy fighting for her life in a dark alley, he instantly recognizes her as the mate he's been seeking all of his life, but someone's trying to kill her. With danger stalking them at every turn, will Kat trust him enough to become The Wolf's Mate?

The Forever Kiss
by Angela Knight

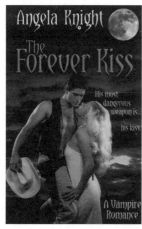

Listen to what reviewers say:

"*The Forever Kiss* flows well with good characters and an interesting plot. ... If you enjoy vampires and a lot of hot sex, you are sure to enjoy *The Forever Kiss*."

—The Best Reviews

"Battling vampires, a protective ghost and the ever present battle of good and evil keep excellent pace with the erotic delights in Angela Knight's *The Forever Kiss*—a book that absolutely bites with refreshing paranormal humor." **4½ Stars, Top Pick**

—Romantic Times BOOKclub

"I found *The Forever Kiss* to be an exceptionally written, refreshing book. ... I really enjoyed this book by Angela Knight. ... 5 angels!"

—Fallen Angel Reviews

"*The Forever Kiss* is the first single title released from Red Sage and if this is any indication of what we can expect, it won't be the last. ... The love scenes are hot enough to give a vampire a sunburn and the fight scenes will have you cheering for the good guys."

—Really Bad Barb Reviews

In *The Forever Kiss*:

For years, Valerie Chase has been haunted by dreams of a Texas Ranger she knows only as "Cowboy." As a child, he rescued her from the nightmare vampires who murdered her parents. As an adult, she still dreams of him—but now he's her seductive lover in nights of erotic pleasure.

Yet "Cowboy" is more than a dream—he's the real Cade McKinnon—and a vampire! For years, he's protected Valerie from Edward Ridgemont, the sadistic vampire who turned him. Now, Ridgmont wants Valerie for his own and Cade is the only one who can protect her.

When Val finds herself abducted by her handsome dream man, she's appalled to discover he's one of the vampires she fears. Now, caught in a web of fear and passion, she and Cade must learn to trust each other, even as an immortal monster stalks their every move.

Their only hope of survival is... *The Forever Kiss*.

Romantic Times Best Erotic Novel of the Year

It's not just reviewers raving about *Secrets*. See what readers have to say:

"When are you coming out with a new Volume? I want a new one next month!" via email from a reader.

"I loved the hot, wet sex without vulgar words being used to make it exciting." after *Volume 1*

"I loved the blend of sensuality and sexual intensity—HOT!" after *Volume 2*

"The best thing about *Secrets* is they're hot and brief! The least thing is you do not have enough of them!" after *Volume 3*

"I have been extremely satisfied with *Secrets*, keep up the good writing." after *Volume 4*

"Stories have plot and characters to support the erotica. They would be good strong stories without the heat." after *Volume 5*

"*Secrets* really knows how to push the envelop better than anyone else." after *Volume 6*

"These are the best sensual stories I have ever read!" after *Volume 7*

"I love, love, love the *Secrets* stories. I now have all of them, please have more books come out each year." after *Volume 8*

"These are the perfect sensual romance stories!" after *Volume 9*

"What I love about *Secrets Volume 10* is how I couldn't put it down!" after *Volume 10*

"All of the *Secrets* volumes are terrific! I have read all of them up to *Secrets Volume 11*. Please keep them coming! I will read every one you make!" after *Volume 11*

Finally, the men you've been dreaming about!

Give the Gift of Spicy Romantic Fiction

Don't want to wait? You can place a retail price ($12.99) order for any of the *Secrets* volumes from the following:

① **Waldenbooks and Borders Stores**

② **Amazon.com or BarnesandNoble.com**

③ **Book Clearinghouse (800-431-1579)**

④ **Romantic Times Magazine** Books by Mail (718-237-1097)

⑤ Special order at other bookstores.
Bookstores: Please contact Baker & Taylor Distributors, Ingram Book Distributor, or Red Sage Publishing for bookstore sales.

Order by title or ISBN #:

Vol. 1: 0-9648942-0-3	**Vol. 7:** 0-9648942-7-0	**Vol. 13:** 0-9754516-3-4
ISBN #13 978-0-9648942-0-4	ISBN #13 978-0-9648942-7-3	ISBN #13 978-0-9754516-3-2
Vol. 2: 0-9648942-1-1	**Vol. 8:** 0-9648942-8-9	**Vol. 14:** 0-9754516-4-2
ISBN #13 978-0-9648942-1-1	ISBN #13 978-0-9648942-9-7	ISBN #13 978-0-9754516-4-9
Vol. 3: 0-9648942-2-X	**Vol. 9:** 0-9648942-9-7	**Vol. 15:** 0-9754516-5-0
ISBN #13 978-0-9648942-2-8	ISBN #13 978-0-9648942-9-7	ISBN #13 978-0-9754516-5-6
Vol. 4: 0-9648942-4-6	**Vol. 10:** 0-9754516-0-X	**Vol. 16:** 0-9754516-6-9
ISBN #13 978-0-9648942-4-2	ISBN #13 978-0-9754516-0-1	ISBN #13 978-0-9754516-6-3
Vol. 5: 0-9648942-5-4	**Vol. 11:** 0-9754516-1-8	**Vol. 17:** 0-9754516-7-7
ISBN #13 978-0-9648942-5-9	ISBN #13 978-0-9754516-1-8	ISBN #13 978-0-9754516-7-0
Vol. 6: 0-9648942-6-2	**Vol. 12:** 0-9754516-2-6	**Vol. 18:** 0-9754516-8-5
ISBN #13 978-0-9648942-6-6	ISBN #13 978-0-9754516-2-5	ISBN #13 978-0-9754516-8-7

The Forever Kiss: 0-9648942-3-8 • ISBN #13 978-0-9648942-3-5 ($14.00)

Red Sage Publishing Mail Order Form:

(Orders shipped in two to three days of receipt.)

Each volume of *Secrets* retails for $12.99, but you can get it direct via mail order for only $9.99 each. The novel *The Forever Kiss* retails for $14.00, but by direct mail order, you only pay $11.00. Use the order form below to place your direct mail order. Fill in the quantity you want for each book on the blanks beside the title.

_____ *Secrets* **Volume 1**	_____ *Secrets* **Volume 8**	_____ *Secrets* **Volume 15**
_____ *Secrets* **Volume 2**	_____ *Secrets* **Volume 9**	_____ *Secrets* **Volume 16**
_____ *Secrets* **Volume 3**	_____ *Secrets* **Volume 10**	_____ *Secrets* **Volume 17**
_____ *Secrets* **Volume 4**	_____ *Secrets* **Volume 11**	_____ *Secrets* **Volume 18**
_____ *Secrets* **Volume 5**	_____ *Secrets* **Volume 12**	_____ *The Forever Kiss*
_____ *Secrets* **Volume 6**	_____ *Secrets* **Volume 13**	
_____ *Secrets* **Volume 7**	_____ *Secrets* **Volume 14**	

Total _____ *Secrets* Volumes @ **$9.99 each = $**_____

Total _____ *The Forever Kiss* @ **$11.00 each = $**_____

Shipping & handling (in the U.S.) $_____

US Priority Mail:
- 1–2 books .... $ 5.50
- 3–5 books $11.50
- 6–9 books $14.50
- 10–19 books $19.00

UPS insured:
- 1–4 books $16.00
- 5–9 books $25.00
- 10–19 books $29.00

SUBTOTAL $_____

Florida 6% sales tax (if delivered in FL) $_____

TOTAL AMOUNT ENCLOSED $_____

Your personal information is kept private and not shared with anyone.

Name: (please print) _____

Address: (no P.O. Boxes) _____

City/State/Zip: _____

Phone or email: (only regarding order if necessary) _____

Please make check payable to **Red Sage Publishing**. Check must be drawn on a U.S. bank in U.S. dollars. Mail your check and order form to:

Red Sage Publishing, Inc.   Department S18   P.O. Box 4844   Seminole, FL 33775

Or use the order form on our website: **www.redsagepub.com**

Red Sage Publishing **Mail Order Form:**
(Orders shipped in two to three days of receipt.)

Each volume of *Secrets* retails for $12.99, but you can get it direct via mail order for only $9.99 each. The novel *The Forever Kiss* retails for $14.00, but by direct mail order, you only pay $11.00. Use the order form below to place your direct mail order. Fill in the quantity you want for each book on the blanks beside the title.

_____ *Secrets* **Volume 1**	_____ *Secrets* **Volume 8**	_____ *Secrets* **Volume 15**
_____ *Secrets* **Volume 2**	_____ *Secrets* **Volume 9**	_____ *Secrets* **Volume 16**
_____ *Secrets* **Volume 3**	_____ *Secrets* **Volume 10**	_____ *Secrets* **Volume 17**
_____ *Secrets* **Volume 4**	_____ *Secrets* **Volume 11**	_____ *Secrets* **Volume 18**
_____ *Secrets* **Volume 5**	_____ *Secrets* **Volume 12**	_____ *The Forever Kiss*
_____ *Secrets* **Volume 6**	_____ *Secrets* **Volume 13**	
_____ *Secrets* **Volume 7**	_____ *Secrets* **Volume 14**	

Total _____ *Secrets* **Volumes @ $9.99 each = $**_____

Total _____ *The Forever Kiss* **@ $11.00 each = $**_____

Shipping & handling (in the U.S.) $_____

US Priority Mail: UPS insured:
  1–2 books .... $ 5.50   1–4 books $16.00
  3–5 books ....$11.50   5–9 books $25.00
  6–9 books ....$14.50   10–19 books $29.00
  10–19 books $19.00

Subtotal $_____

Florida 6% sales tax (if delivered in FL) $_____

TOTAL AMOUNT ENCLOSED $_____

Your personal information is kept private and not shared with anyone.

Name: (please print) _____

Address: (no P.O. Boxes) _____

City/State/Zip: _____

Phone or email: (only regarding order if necessary) _____

Please make check payable to **Red Sage Publishing**. Check must be drawn on a U.S. bank in U.S. dollars. Mail your check and order form to:

Red Sage Publishing, Inc.   Department S18   P.O. Box 4844   Seminole, FL 33775

Or use the order form on our website: **www.redsagepub.com**